No Escaping the Past

Marion Myles

***

Edited by Kathy Case

Cover by Robin Johnson / Florida Girl Design Inc.

***

Join the Marin Myles VIP Reader List at marionmyles.com and you'll be the first to hear about new releases and special offers. Plus, I'll send you a free novella - Valentine's Heart

***

Copyright © 2023 Marion Myles

All rights reserved.

This is a work of fiction. Any resemblance to actual events or any persons, living or dead, is entirely coincidental.

Dedication

To RDM: Still with me every step of the way.

Prologue

Nikolai Davidov had looked forward to this day for a long time.

He'd kept his head down. Done his time. Put in the hard work. And now it was finally coming to fruition.

No more mindless assignments of guarding the higher ups as they went about their daily business. Going on collection routes had been slightly better because at least then he could bring out his full menacing personality and keep the fear alive and well in those they extorted. No way was one of those weak little sissies going rogue while he was on the job. They'd pay their money and be glad he wasn't coming back for another week.

He hadn't minded doing any of the low-level killing either. In fact, he considered it one of the few perks of working his way up the food chain of the Russian Mafia. It was a well-known fact those in charge wanted to be certain a man could be trusted to do whatever was necessary. There was no room for delicate sensibilities when it came to killing man, woman or child. You did what you were told, and you didn't ask any stupid questions.

But he had been a good soldier for what seemed like his whole damn life. Moved away from his family when he was ten. Followed orders to be relocated to the United States for his high school and college years. He'd lived with the Americans and assimilated into their lifestyle while also studying his way into a solid education in finance—from Princeton, no less.

And now, just a few weeks after his twenty-sixth birthday, he was running what he considered his first real job. Today was the final stage of smuggling almost a hundred million dollars' worth of diamonds into this greedy, capitalistic country. When this was a success—and it would be because he'd planned the operation with meticulous attention to detail—he'd no doubt be promoted to Brigadier. Only then would he be living the life for which he was destined.

He stepped out of the car and onto the steaming shipyard pavement. The sun beat down mercilessly and even though he wore sunglasses, he couldn't help squinting against the glare. He hated the heat and humidity and more days than not cursed being sent to Savannah. There he felt as though he was slowly being boiled alive like a lobster in a pot. It wasn't supposed to be in the nineties in April for fuck's sake. He told himself he was tougher than the stupid weather and besides, a man shouldn't show any weakness.

As he crossed toward the shipping container, Alex and Mik fell into step on either side of him. He'd picked them out of the Shestyorka a few years ago and had been grooming them to be his lieutenants ever since. One of the men was exceptionally good and well suited for this life. The other, while there were still some problems to work out, Niko hoped the investment of time and energy would pay off. He knew he'd need to form a core group of soldiers when he took the next big step up in his career and had wanted some of the key players in place well before that time came.

"Whoa. That ain't good," Alex said.

Niko's eyes darted to where Alex pointed, and his heart stuttered for several beats. The door to the shipping container was closed, but where the lock should have been…a piece of paper was wedged into the latch mechanism. He strode forward and grabbed what turned out to be a small section of cardboard ripped from a container of a box of Hammer + Sickle.

The legitimate vodka exporting business run by the Bratva was the perfect cover for smuggling in all kinds of useful things.

He turned the cardboard over in his hands, and his vision went red when he saw someone had written on the back...You snooze you lose

At the end of the hand-printed message a smiley face grinned up at him. After shoving the cardboard at Alex, he wrenched open the container door and stepped inside.

"Mik. Light. Now," he said, snapping out each word.

In the next second, the interior was illuminated. Niko pushed in between the narrow row of boxes in the center and made his way along them keeping his eyes cast upward until he stood directly under a small yellow heart painted on the ceiling.

"Come. Bring it," he commanded, gesturing to Mik who hurried through to meet him in the middle of the container with the flashlight.

"Are they there?" Alex called out.

Niko merely grunted while he lifted the flaps of an already opened box of Hammer + Sickle. "There should be ten bottles in here, right? I only count eight."

Alex pulled out each of the remaining bottles and instructed Mik to shine the light through the liquid. None of them contained the diamonds.

"There's no way some random person would know how to find the right box. There's hundreds of them in here," Alex said.

"Stop talking and help me," Niko said.

During the next twenty minutes, the three men opened every box in the middle section of the container. Niko knew in his heart it was a wasted effort, but he went through the process anyway. And all the while he fought against the incandescent rage flowing like lava through his veins. This shouldn't be happening to him. Not after everything he'd done to make sure this operation was a success.

But it *was* happening. The diamonds were gone. Everything he'd worked for was being ripped out of his grasp, and he felt powerless to stop it.

He pushed his way back outside, and after leaning an arm against the back of the container, rested his forehead and closed his eyes.

"Now what?" Mik asked, his voice high and squeaky. "They're gonna kill us for messing this up."

"We should disappear," Alex said.

"Shut up, both of you, and let me think," Niko said. He lifted his head and did a slow turn while studying the shipyard. "There. A camera right where we need it."

"Hey, I think I've seen that guy before," Mik said. They were huddled together around Niko's phone watching security footage sent to them by the clerk in the shipyard office. On the screen four men got out of a sedan and approached the very container they were sheltering in to avoid the glare of the sun on the screen.

"Which one?" Alex asked.

"The guy on the left. Short. Skinny. Light-colored hair. I think I know him somehow."

"You'd better figure out how right now," Niko said.

Mik tilted his face up and rubbed at the stubble on his chin. "He's been around somewhere...um...I don't know if it was...wait, I've got it. He was in—" He broke off abruptly and stepped back until he bumped against the edge of the door.

"Talk," Niko said through clenched teeth.

"Okay. Don't get mad, but I saw him in Slow Pour last week."

"I thought you weren't drinking no more," Alex said.

Mik's eyes flicked between the two men then quickly away. "I'm not. Not really. It was just a couple of times last week to let off some steam. I only had beer anyway. It's no big deal."

Niko pinned him with a stare. "Mik. I warned you if you wanted in on my unit you had to cut the booze. You're a lousy drunk, and you know it. Because of you we've just let millions of dollars slip through our fingers so you'd better fucking figure out who this guy is."

Mik's breath came out in short gasps and both his cheeks stained with red. "I don't know his name. He was just some guy in the bar drowning his sorrows and talking a bunch of crap."

"And you had to go and shoot off your stupid mouth. Right?" Niko shifted over until he crowded into Mik. "What's the guy's name?"

"It's...shoot...I swear it's on the tip of my tongue. Give me a sec, okay?" Suddenly Mik's face cleared, and his eyes shone in triumph. "Danny Dawson. I knew I'd remember it. He's a low level grifter. Thinks he's all connected because he runs with some local thugs. No big deal to us, right?"

"On the contrary," Niko said softly. "Until we get those diamonds back and kill the bastard, he's the biggest deal we've ever met."

Out of the corner of Niko's eyes, he noted Alex take a step back. He silently commended the man's instincts. Meanwhile Mik continued babbling away in an attempt to make his case. With his left hand, Niko slid his phone into his front pocket. With his right hand he pulled the gun from the waistband of his jeans and shot Mik right between the eyes.

Niko turned to Alex. "Get rid of him. And do whatever it takes to find this Danny Dawson."

Chapter One

Home is where the heart is. At least that's what Mia Reeves had always heard. But until now, she'd never fully understood the sentiment.

She paused partway along her driveway and took in the log house bathed in hues of pink and gold from the brilliant backdrop of the sky. The lawns were manicured and the flowerbeds abundant, overflowing with blooms of every size and color. The place looked like something from the cover of *Home and Garden* magazine.

From the first moment she'd seen the property, she'd felt a piece of herself slot into place…the answer to a question she hadn't known she'd been asking. After wandering and roaming her entire life, she'd finally found home.

And it was hers. All hers. She'd made this sanctuary. Fixing up the sadly neglected house and planting the grounds until it reminded her of a fairytale dream of texture and color and scent.

This, just this, would have been more than enough for her, but as she parked in front of the screened porch, Roman stepped out, surrounded by the dogs. Her heart did a slow stutter and tumble in her chest, a feeling she was slowly getting used to. He was the jewel in her crown, the final piece to her life's happiness and, like the house, something she hadn't even known was missing.

Roman Mancini, with his stunning dark looks and beautiful heart, had touched some part of her. A part she thought she'd long since crushed and thrown away. Somehow though, he'd teased it out with patience and perseverance until she finally understood she could have the impossible—love. Somedays she could hardly believe this was her life. Her man. But it was, and oh, wasn't she the luckiest girl in the whole world?

But then she'd earned it, hadn't she?

When she opened the door and slid out of the car, the dogs launched themselves at her as if they'd been parted for centuries. Mac, the big Doberman, reached her first and rubbed his body against her thigh while his head burrowed in at her side. Fifi, the Pomeranian, twirled around her ankles like a prima ballerina, letting out yips of joy. Tucker, the dachshund, and Layla, the golden lab, ran at warp speed in ever widening circles, dashing in to leap against her and jostle the other two dogs at her feet before racing away again.

Finally, Mac had had enough and growled at the rest of the pack until bit-by-bit order was restored. He remained at Mia's side in the rightful place of honor. The others, still quivering and bumping bodies, calmed.

Mia dropped to her knees and hugged Mac, rubbing her hands along his back. "It's so good to see you, big guy," she crooned, then reached out to stroke each of the other dogs in turn. "And you, and you, and you. Were you good for daddy? Did everyone behave? Now tell me about daddy. Was he a good boy too?"

She lifted her face to gaze up at Roman. Tall and muscled, his thumbs hooked in the front pockets of his jeans, he watched the scene with eyes intent only on her. She stood again, hand resting on Mac's head, and smiled at him.

"You're a sight for sore eyes," she said. "You have no idea how good it is to be home."

In the next instant, Roman had stepped up close to her and lifted her straight into his arms until she was pressed against his chest. His mouth crushed down on hers, hungry, demanding, and leaving no doubt he'd missed her as much as she'd missed him.

"Welcome home, baby," he breathed against her neck. "That was the longest five days of my life."

Slowly, he slid her body down his until her feet touched the ground again. His fingers stroked her back, up her arm, then his knuckles swept across her cheek with a featherlight touch. This time when he kissed her, his lips were soft and sweet, and she melted against him.

"This is the best homecoming ever," she breathed.

He shifted back and grinned down at her. "If you think this is good, wait until we get to the next part. I took the liberty of organizing dinner. I figured you'd be road weary and starving."

"Aw, you cooked for me," she said.

"Organized," he corrected. "Take-out from Gabe's Diner. I got the butternut squash gnocchi you love so much."

"Sounds perfect. Do I need to walk the dogs first? It's a beautiful sunset."

Casually, he linked his fingers with hers and pulled her toward the house. "Nah. They're good. I took them out about an hour ago. Maybe we can go for a stroll after dinner when the moon's up. That'll be beautiful too."

"Okay then. I guess I'll unpack."

She turned back to the Escape but once again he pulled her toward the front door.

"Let me unpack. Why don't you go on up and have a shower?"

"Man, you're really pulling out all the stops tonight. Thanks. This is turning out to be the best night ever."

"Let's hope so," he mumbled before playfully pushing her ahead. "Go on up. I'll have the boxes in your workroom by the time you're done. Then we'll feast."

When she came down the stairs, refreshed after a cool shower, Roman met her with a glass of wine. The aroma from the kitchen had her mouth watering and her stomach rumbling.

"I heard that," Roman said, pointing at her belly. "I'll bet you haven't eaten all day. Didn't you promise you'd take good care of yourself, especially the part about eating at regular intervals?"

"I did, I swear," she said, grabbing for the glass of wine.

Roman raised his arm up and expertly blocked her. "Tell me what you had for lunch."

She sighed and stepped back. "Okay, not a lot but it was only because I couldn't find anything but junk food at the dinky little gas station. I had a Perrier and a bag of sunflower seeds. But I did eat a big breakfast before I left the hotel. Oatmeal, fruit, the works."

He narrowed his eyes and looked her up and down before finally nodding and handing over the wine. "Okay. I'll let it pass—for now. Next time you'll bring provisions with you, right?"

"Absolutely," she agreed before taking a long sip. "Oh, mama, this is so good."

In the kitchen, Mia noted he'd laid the little table in the breakfast nook and even fancied it up with candles and her special occasion napkins. He led her straight over and pulled out a chair, bowing extravagantly.

"You know," she said, gazing around while he retrieved the food from the warming oven. "Maybe I should go away more often because I have to say, I'm loving this homecoming."

"The trade fair was worth the trip?" he asked.

"And then some. I'm completely stocked up for the next few months. Plus, I got some cool ideas for new designs."

He brought the plates to the table and slid in opposite her. She closed her eyes and inhaled while leaning over the food. When she looked up and smiled at him, he thought his heart might burst right there in his chest.

She was so beautiful. Her skin was luminous, and her face fine-boned with high slashing cheekbones. He never tired of gazing into those intelligent hazel eyes or running his fingers through her silky strands of fiery hair.

"What?" she said when he continued staring.

He shook his head. "I guess I missed your face."

Her hand reached across the table and closed over his. "I missed yours too. And the rest of you. Maybe...after dinner...we should get reacquainted?"

"Sounds like a brilliant plan. First, though, we eat."

They dug into the food, sitting quietly for several minutes. Finally pausing, Mia put her fork down and patted her stomach.

"I think I need to slow down, or I'll burst." She took a sip of wine. "So, any news or gossip around here?"

Roman, following suit, leaned back in his chair. "Well, now that you mention it, I might have a little something to tell you."

She studied him for a moment then reached across the table and felt for his hand. Before she could make contact, he pulled it back and placed it in his lap. "Oh, no. I don't want you figuring it out. Let me tell you."

"It's something big, isn't it?"

He nodded. "Yeah. At least I think so."

When he took another sip of wine, she huffed out a breath. "Hurry up. The suspense is killing me."

"Okay. Here goes. The paperwork just came through on my private investigator's license. And yesterday, I signed a six-month lease on the room above Gino's Bakery, so I'll have an office right there on Main Street."

"That's…wow…private investigator? I thought there was an exam to become a PI."

"There is." He paused and winked at her. "I aced it."

"You're really not going back on the force?"

He exhaled. "Believe me, I've thought about it, but after everything that happened with Anita and Tony and…everything…it doesn't feel right. I think being a PI will be a good fit for me. At least I hope so. I figure I'll try it out for a while and see how things go. I've got enough saved to float me for at least a year if need be. You're not disappointed?"

"Disappointed? God, no. I don't care what you do as long as you're happy. It's just…I guess I still think of you as a police detective. Like it's your identity or something. You know what? I bet you're gonna be a kick-ass private eye, like Magnum PI. Or Spenser. Did you ever read those Robert Parker books? Spenser was the best."

"Tell me the truth. Did you even have an inkling about the PI thing?"

She shook her head slowly then narrowed her eyes at him. "I honestly had no idea. How is that possible?"

"Because I'm really sneaky, and I've learned how to work around your superpowers."

"I don't have superpowers."

He chuckled. "Okay. You get psychic visions from touching people and objects and sometimes just from a place itself, but you don't have superpowers?"

"I'm sure you could do the same thing if you really tried." She slid her foot slowly up and down the outside of his calf. Squaring her shoulders and pressing her arms against the sides of her breasts, she pushed her chest out and smiled at him. "What am I thinking about right now?"

"Um...you're wondering if you're going to get a tax refund this year?"

She grinned at him. "So close."

"Okay, before we get to your tax dilemma," he said, pushing back from the table. "I'll *adios* these dishes. Then there's something I want to show you."

"I think the dogs need to go out." She swiveled in her chair, sitting sideways, and ran a hand along Mac's back.

"Perfect. Because the thing I want to show you is outside."

There was something in the tone of his voice that made her turn to study him. He was still smiling but she sensed something else. Anxiety maybe? Yes, definitely. He was wound tight as a drum inside. She pushed in with her mind. Dammit. He was getting really good at blocking because the only things she could sense from him was the anxiety.

"Okay. Fine. After, we'll walk the dogs."

He pointed to the side door of the kitchen. "Let's go this way. And I want you to wear this."

From the counter he picked up a piece of cloth and folded it over several times until she realized he meant to blindfold her.

"What's going on?"

"Trust me. Okay?"

Once he'd tied the cloth in place, she heard the door open. His hand closed over hers and gently, he pulled her forward, telling her when to step down onto the deck. Even still she stumbled.

"I don't like this," she said.

She gasped when he swept her up in his arms. "I think it'll be better this way," he said.

He paused, opening the gate, and she heard the dogs scrabbling down the steps and onto the lawn. The air was warm against her cheek and perfumed with the smell of freshly cut grass.

"Was the garden service here today?"

"Nope. I did a little tidy up. Well, me and the dogs. They were a big help."

"I'll bet. You can put me down now. I'm sure I can walk across the grass."

"We're almost there, Miss Impatient, so just hang on a sec."

She was amazed at how difficult it was to tell which direction they were going. If she had to guess, she'd have said he was taking her toward the outbuilding she used as a garage.

"Did you buy a new car?"

"What? No." He exhaled and carefully lowered her to the ground. "Don't look yet, I need to do something first."

Dogs brushed against her legs, and she felt a paw on her foot. Still on the grass she noted. Minutes ticked by and her heart beat faster. This was actually kind of fun.

"Okay." Roman's soft voice was right by her ear. "Are you ready?"

When she nodded, he unknotted the back of the blindfold. The sky was almost fully dark now, and she blinked against the lights in confusion.

"But...how?...oh my God, it's all fixed." She whirled to face him. "How did you do this without me knowing?" She whirled back again and stared in wonder. "It's amazing. I can't believe it."

She rushed toward the greenhouse and opened the door. Last summer, the place had been vandalized. Since then the building had stood as little more than a skeleton. Recently, Mia had been on a mission to repair it and once again start her hydroponic gardening but had run into nothing but delays at the local glass supplier.

The structure glowed now with every pane of glass in place. Roman had arranged fairy lights around the frame of the door and along the front panels of glass. Inside, pillar candles stood in an enormous semi-circle, the flames flickering against the breeze when they stepped in through the open door. Rose petals strewn on the ground had been shaped into a heart.

Her own heart was in her throat, and when she turned to Roman, it all but stopped. He was down on one knee and reaching for her hand. Numbly, she let him take it.

"You're not...what are you doing?" she stammered.

"Mia, we've been through so much together. This past year has tested us beyond anything most people have to go through in three lifetimes, and we've come out stronger than ever. I love you. The day you walked into the police station, seeing you in the interview room, something hit me straight in the gut. I wasn't looking for this. Or anyone really. But then you went and made me fall for you so hard and deep, and I've never come back from it. I love what we have together. How we fit. You're everything to me. You're my life. My only love. Please will you marry me?"

She trembled uncontrollably as she blinked down at him. This was real. And it was happening to her. A life she'd never dared imagine for herself was literally waiting at her feet. All she had to do was believe and say yes.

She sank to her knees until their faces were level. His liquid brown eyes seemed bottomless.

"Yes." She nodded and pumped his hand. "Absolutely yes. I could never love anyone as much as I love you."

He exhaled in an unsteady stream then leaned into her until their foreheads pressed together. His hand came up and caressed her cheek. "Happiest day ever," he breathed.

"Thanks for making this so perfect."

Tilting her head, she brought her lips to his. His mouth was soft and warm, and the kiss sweet. Almost reverent.

"Our first kiss as an engaged couple." Sitting back on his heels, he smacked his hand against his forehead. "Wait. I forgot. So stupid."

His hand slid into the front pocket of his jeans and drew out a ring.

"It's...oh...I love citrine. It's absolutely gorgeous."

She lifted her left hand, and he slid it onto her ring finger then leaned down to kiss her knuckles. "It was my great-great grandmother's."

Mia closed her eyes. "Nadia," she murmured. "She married Alberto. It was an arranged wedding. He loved her almost at first sight. She didn't fall in love with him until the next winter. He was a fisherman and lost at sea for three days during a storm. The whole village thought the men were dead, but Nadia somehow knew and waited on the beach, refusing to go home. The boat arrived on the horizon right at sunrise. When Alberto saw her at the dock, he jumped off and swam the last few hundred feet. They conceived their first child that night."

"You're amazing," he said, pulling her to her feet. "It's no wonder I love you."

By now the dogs had found their way into the greenhouse. Sensing the giddy atmosphere, they swarmed the area, displacing rose petals and bumping into one another and occasionally the candlesticks.

"Guys, hey, calm down," Mia said. "We just got the greenhouse back. Let's not burn it down on the first night."

"It's a full moon. Why don't we take them for a nice moonlit walk?"

They blew out the candles then, hand in hand, led the exuberant dogs across the front lawn and out to the field along the edge of the property.

Chapter Two

Hanging back, the man followed Mia along Main Street in Dalton. He couldn't for the life of him figure out her game. This town was so small there was no way she could be running cons here. Especially after last year and all the news coverage surrounding her abduction by the Emerald Ring killer. Everyone in the area must know her by name. Why hadn't she moved on?

He watched while she chatted with a woman coming out of Pizza Hut before turning into the local coffee place. He casually stopped and pretended to browse in the window of a gift shop. The stuff looked like junk. He shook his head. Hell, the store wasn't even worth robbing.

Well, whatever she had up her sleeve it must be some kind of long con because this place was a nightmare to his eyes.

When he strolled by the Bean Time coffee shop, he glanced in and saw it boasted a bustling clientele. He couldn't immediately see where she was sitting but figured it would be safe enough. Once inside, he ordered a coffee and a plain bagel. His stomach usually felt better when he put a little something in it. Pretending to keep his eyes down while he added sugar and milk, he scanned the room and spotted her sitting at one of the back tables with another woman about her age. He sighed when she didn't so much as glance his way.

God, what had happened to her? At least she sat with her back to the wall. Still, it hardly mattered when she was so engrossed in the conversation that she didn't even look up as he brushed by and claimed a seat two tables away. Those sharp eyes of hers should be sweeping the room. Keeping watch for opportunities. Or danger.

While biding his time, he sat back and blew on the steaming coffee before taking a small sip.

Brooke Adams shook her head, her soft blue eyes sparkling. "I still can't believe you and Roman are engaged. It's so romantic."

Mia tried to tone down her smile, but it felt impossible, like attempting to stop the sun from shining. "To be honest, it feels kind of weird but in a good way. I was never one of those girls who imagined her wedding day or being married. It wasn't on my radar at all."

Brooke put a hand to her chest and patted her heart. "Oh, I totally imagined mine. The flowers. The food. And especially the dress. I'll admit the grooms changed over time, but I've always wanted a big, fancy wedding. What are you guys planning?"

"Um...actually, we haven't talked much about it. We've only been engaged for a little over twenty-four hours. I need to get used to it first, then I'll start thinking about the wedding. Please, you have to promise to keep this on the down low, okay? We're not telling Roman's parents until tomorrow tonight."

"Oh, they're going to be so excited."

"I hope so," Mia muttered then took a sip of her latte.

Brooke squeezed her arm. "They will be. You know they love you. Sure, it was hard after everything that happened last year but that's all in the past. You told me things were better, right?"

Mia nodded, but her eyebrows scrunched together. "Things are fine between me and them but…you know." She rolled her hand. "It's still there."

"Don't worry about Roman's parents. They'll be thrilled. You know the only thing they want is for Roman to be happy. And you, my reluctantly romantic friend, make him happier than he's ever been in his entire life. When are you telling your parents?"

Mia stared down at the table and chuckled. "Yeah. No need. I never knew my mother. Not sure if she's even alive. As for my dad, we parted ways a long time ago. I doubt he'd care that I was engaged."

"Oh…I'm sorry. I guess we've never discussed your family before. That sounds sad. Do you have any brothers or sisters?"

"Nope. I'm the only one. Don't look at me like that. I don't want your pity."

"It's not pity. Try empathy. It must have been a hard way to grow up. Good thing you have us now. You'll never have to feel alone."

"Ain't that the truth. Okay, enough wedding talk. What's going on with you?"

Brooke smiled. "The usual. Teaching my dance classes. Getting ready for the Summer Dance Gala in Nashville. I have one girl who's superb. I think she might go all the way."

"That'll be great advertising for your school, won't it? Still dating the dentist from Walkerton?"

"That would be a hard no. He seemed pretty cool on the first two dates and then things just got weird really fast. I'm not into S & M games, you know? Why can't I find a nice and incredibly hot guy like Roman? Is that too much to ask?"

"You can't give up." Mia patted her arm. "If I can find someone, you can for sure. Trust me."

"Yeah, well, let's just say I'm not going to worry about it right now." She paused and glanced down at her watch. "Darn it, I've got to go. Okay. We'll talk later. And don't you dare think about shopping for a wedding dress without me."

Mia raised her right hand as though swearing an oath. "I wouldn't dream of it."

They left the table together and exited the café.

"I'm parked down here," Brooke pointed around the corner. "Mia, I'm really happy for you." She grabbed Mia's arm and pulled her in for a hug.

"Thanks. I'm happy for me, too. See you later."

After hitting the unlock on the remote, Mia opened the back door of her Escape and retrieved the box on the seat. She'd promised Meredith at Treasure Chest she'd bring in more earrings and bracelets since the last batch had sold out in less than two weeks.

Mia's jewelry business, Healing Crystals, was going gangbusters this year. Even better than the year before when she'd thought she'd reached the absolute pinnacle of success. Last month she finally hired a part-time assistant to deal with packing shipments and overseeing the website and online store. That freed her up to make the jewelry, which was what she loved best anyway.

She had a few celebrity clients who were bringing more of their friends into the fold, and consequently, her star continued to rise. Even after a substantial price increase across the board, the orders kept pouring in. It gave Mia enormous pleasure to see she was on track to make mid-six figures this year. Best of all, she knew it was earned legitimately.

When she'd first turned her back on the past, she'd never imagined earning this kind of money while living the straight life. And the kicker was it gave her so much more satisfaction than any of the con games she'd run.

Once Mia had finished her business in Treasure Chest, she treated herself to a gorgeous wooden bowl she'd had her eye on for some time. She wandered down Main Street, noting Gino's Bakery had fresh rosemary bread in the window. That would be perfect to go with the minestrone she'd left in the slow cooker at home.

Loaded down with the bowl and two loaves of bread, she decided to get back to her workroom at home before she got dangerously behind on today's orders. She took a few steps backward and gazed upstairs from the bakery at what was now Roman's office window.

He wasn't there. Earlier this morning, he'd filled his to-go cup with coffee and kissed her on the cheek, left for Walkerton to find furnishings and office supplies to equip the new space. His excitement had been palatable, and she mentally crossed her fingers that this new venture would be everything he'd hoped for.

Roman needed this. He'd been on shaky emotional footing ever since resigning from the Dalton police department. She'd been there for him as best she could but knew from personal experience, he was the only one who could figure out his new path.

He'd make a brilliant PI. Of that, she was sure. What worried her was the location. Dalton was as *small town* as it got, and she couldn't imagine there'd be much need for a private investigator. Nashville would be better or Atlanta even more so. Well, they could always move, couldn't they? Her jewelry business was nothing if not portable.

Except she loved her log house and the land. She shook her head and pushed the thought away. No point in borrowing trouble. Especially right now when her life was as close to perfect as it got. So, she'd just let herself be happy.

She fumbled in her back pocket for the car keys and nearly dropped one of the loaves of bread.

"Here, Jenny. Let me help you with that."

The shock was intense. For a moment, she felt completely disconnected from her body. Her face had gone numb and her limbs useless, as though no longer controlled by her brain. The bread tumbled to the ground, and she took a step back, almost falling off the sidewalk onto the road.

"Careful, don't want to twist your ankle. Aren't you a sight for sore eyes," the man said.

In the next instant, a lifetime of training kicked in. Standing tall and turning to face him, her smile was automatically in place. "Well, talk about a blast from the past? Hi, Pops. I go by the name Mia now."

Danny Dawson nodded. He was a short man with a wiry build. His red hair was faded now and shot through with grey. He seemed so much smaller than she'd remembered, but his blue eyes still twinkled.

"Oh, well, names come and go, but you'll always be Jenny Dawson. Let me look at you." He tipped his head and smiled his charming smile. "Such a beauty. You always had the looks, but my how you've grown into them. Lost some of your skills, though, haven't you? You know better than to walk the streets without keeping an eye out. I wasn't even trying to get the drop on you."

He stooped down and picked up the bread, handing it over to her.

"Dalton isn't the kind of place you need to keep an eye out. What are you doing here, Pops? Small towns have never been your scene."

"Can't a man come to see his only daughter?"

"Sure. Except if that man hasn't bothered with his daughter in more than ten years it seems kinda suspicious. Do you need money?"

Danny's head snapped up, and he took a step back. "No. I wouldn't come begging."

"You did when I was seventeen, and you were in deep to Dirty Jake."

"That was another time. It was different. I stopped with the cards and the horses a few months ago."

"Wow. Now there's something I haven't heard before. Do you go to meetings and everything? Wait. Is this some kind of twelve steps thing where you have to make amends?"

"Naw." He thumped his chest. "I did it on my own."

He smiled at her, and for a moment the world went away, and she was six years old again. She and her father had spent the morning running cons on a string of variety stores. He'd been coaching her for weeks on exactly what to say and how to act, and she'd performed her role to perfection. They'd netted over four thousand dollars.

He'd picked her up and twirled her around, raining down kisses on her cheeks. They went to the movies, where he let her pick whatever she wanted at the concession stand. It was a happy childhood memory. Even now, the sense of making her father proud washed over her.

"Well, good for you," Mia said. "If it's not money, what do you want?"

"I saw you on the TV a few months back. That maniac serial killer. He didn't hurt you?"

She stared at him. "That was ages ago. And if you saw me on the news, you knew I was fine so what gives?"

He shuffled and stared down at his feet. "I guess I wanted to see you for myself. Make sure you were okay. What're you doing living in this place? You were always better in cities."

"You mean because it's easier to find marks and easier to hide? I don't do that anymore. I'm living the straight life. Have been for almost six years now."

"What?" he gasped, hand over his heart. "You mean working for a living like all the other suckers? You must be bored to death and poor as a church mouse."

She stiffened and dug out her keys, clicking the locks on the Escape. "Actually, I'm doing pretty darn well for myself. My jewelry business is thriving. I love the work, and I'm my own boss. And big bonus, I don't have to worry about getting caught or anyone taking it away from me."

"Don't you miss the rush?"

"Nope. I get a rush every time I put a big fat check in the bank. That's all I need these days."

"I can't believe it. My little Jenny's walking the line. I never expected that." He rubbed a hand back and forth over his face.

"Pops, you're making it sound like I'm the crazy one here. Having a business and living a quiet life is completely normal, which brings me back to my original question. What exactly do you want?"

He seemed lost for a moment, looking down at the ground and muttering something she couldn't hear. Behind her, on Main Street, someone tooted their horn. Her father startled, and his eyes snapped up, scanning left and right. His hand clamped on her arm.

"Get in your car. I made a mistake coming here. I'm sorry. It was so good to see you, Jenny. I'm proud of you." He kissed her on the cheek then swung around and pulled open the door to the Escape. "Off you go. I love you, baby girl."

He shoved her onto the driver's seat and sprinted away before she could get a word out. After dumping the bread and bowl inside, she scrabbled to her feet. Her father had disappeared down the alley beyond Pizza Hut. She ran after him, but by the time she'd made it to the back parking lot, all she saw was a glimpse of the taillights of a Nissan Altima speeding away along Market Street.

Chapter Three

Mia put the incident with her father out of her mind. If he'd gotten himself in trouble again, there was nothing she could do about it. It was doubtful he simply wanted to connect, but if it was somehow true, she honestly didn't have much to say to him.

Her childhood had been tumultuous at best. Not all bad, of course. There were some good memories mixed in, but on too many occasions she'd been woken in the dead of night so they could skip out on rent or disappear after some deal had gone sour. Twice before she was fifteen, her father served time for theft and fraud, and with no mother to fall back on, she was forced into the foster system.

The first time was the day after her seventh birthday. She hadn't yet learned to hide her telepathic abilities and her foster family was deeply religious. They immediately became convinced she was possessed by Satan.

The officers of Child Services took a more traditional approach and Mia found herself in the psych ward of Pittsburgh General. Doctors didn't know what to do with her, especially once she started relaying personal and intimate details from their lives. Instead, they wrote script after script until she was so doped up a zombie would have seemed more lively.

She was shunted from hospital to hospital with no one to advocate for her until her father was released from prison almost three years later. He signed her out against doctor's orders, took her off the pills, though not without selling them to a skinny, pock-marked man in a back alley in Miami, and told her she would be perfectly fine.

"You have a gift, baby doll. All those losers will never understand someone like you. From now on you keep it to yourself, and you'll be right as rain."

He'd patted her head while she'd stared groggily up at him. With the money he'd made on the drugs, he got them a room at a Motel 6, and they holed up for a week or so while her body went through withdrawal from lithium and various other anti-psychotics. She lay there twitching and hallucinating on the bed while her father spent the time reaching out to old contacts and setting up the groundwork to get back in the game.

During the next two years, Danny Dawson gradually began including Mia in his various schemes. She'd always had quick hands, and he had her practice lifting wallets on the streets every day until her technique was flawless.

She learned how to case out a place, making notes on routines and general security. He often gave her roles to play, including costumes, which was the part she loved best. Soon enough she could handle hotel maids, security people in coat rooms at restaurants, and anyone else when Danny needed a distraction while snatching up portable goods.

Hotels were the best. She'd hang out in the lobby and watch for women with big ticket shoes and purses or businessmen with lots of electronics. It wasn't hard to figure out which room they were staying in. Mia would then set up in the hotel coffee shop or across the street and keep an eye on their comings and goings. Often times, she'd even trail them outside the hotel and manage to lift the key card for their room.

If not, her father would hide out of sight, and seconds after the maid had opened the targeted room, Mia would distract her until he'd slipped inside. From there, it was easy for him to send the maid away while he appropriated everything of value in the room. They'd hit two or three hotels in the high-end district of a city over the course of a week. Combined with lifted wallets and purses, they could easily clear tens of thousands of dollars. Then it would be time to move on.

At that age, it all seemed like a grand game to her. She didn't question what happened to the people they stole from, nor did she wonder if suspicion would be cast on the poor maids or security people. Her father saw everyone as a mark, a sucker, and if people were too trusting or stupid to hold onto their cash and possessions, well, he was doing them a favor. They'd be more careful next time, wouldn't they?

Later, when she was older, she'd managed to push aside any moralizations. After all, she'd been trained for this the whole of her young life, and she didn't know any other way. School had been little more than a passing thought in her father's mind. During her stints in the foster system, she'd missed more days of class than she'd attended and only managed to pass what she did by reaching out into the minds of her fellow students and copying the answers.

There were two reasons she finally made it out of that life. The first being she fell for the wrong guy. A thief and con artist like herself, Dean Chambers was handsome and charming and sexy as sin. They teamed up together for close to a year. Picking marks, working scams, and loving one another. Or so she thought.

But it turned out Dean didn't love anyone but himself.

He disappeared one night leaving their joint bank account with a lowly balance of twelve dollars and taking everything they'd *acquired* on a recent long-term con along with the jewelry he'd given her. As a final parting gift, he'd racked up close to thirty grand on her credit cards.

When she ran into him six months later, he had a new partner. A sultry brunette with whiskey eyes and a Southern drawl. Mia had almost warned the woman, but then deciding everyone got what they deserved in this life, walked away without a backward glance.

After the shock of Dean's betrayal, Mia decided to work alone, and it went wonderfully well for quite some time. It didn't take her long to bounce back financially, especially since there was no partner with whom to split the proceeds. She managed to quickly grow her nest egg to a cool million and lived the lifestyle of the rich and famous complete with clothes, jewelry, and cars.

The downside to working without a partner, of course, was that there was no one to bail her out if things got rough. And with Nicholas Hanson, a seemingly nice man with unlimited funds, the situation got very rough indeed. Although she'd vetted him with her usual attention to detail, even her special psychic abilities somehow missed his connection to the Italian Mafia.

She escaped with her life, barely, and not much else. And that had marked the end of her criminal ways. Well, except for one last round of working the poker tables in Las Vegas and Atlantic City to plump up her barren cash reserves after the Nicholas fiasco. And really, fleecing rich tourists was hardly a crime. They were practically begging someone to come along and relieve them of their big fat stacks of bills.

Shortly after, Mia began her Healing Crystals jewelry business on a lark and was thrilled when it quickly gained traction. She continued bumping around the country for a couple of years, making jewelry, collecting dogs, until ultimately landing in Dalton, Tennessee. Home, sweet home, at last.

She'd never expected to be this happy. Or this fulfilled. Even before meeting Roman, she'd been ridiculously content in her straight, law-abiding life. Now, experiencing real love for the first time, she could no longer even remember why she'd been so resistant in the first place. It wasn't just that she felt stronger and more complete with Roman in her life, but she actually felt bullet-proof, and a hundred times better than she'd ever thought possible.

"Hey, you're awfully quiet," Roman said, jolting her from her thoughts. "You worried about the dinner?"

"What? No, not really…okay, maybe a little," she admitted. "Your parents are great, and you know I love them but after Tony…and everything. It's a weird situation. You get that, right?"

"Listen to me. It wasn't your fault. Nobody blames you, least of all my folks. And they do love you. It's just that they're still really sad. Tony was their child in every way that mattered, and they'd been grieving Anita for so long I think it wore them out. Plus, Lina's upcoming divorce is a tough blow seeing as they're so entrenched in the values of the Catholic church. If anything, I think our engagement will give them a huge boost. It'll be something to look forward to."

"I hope so." She looked out across the lawn to where Layla and Tucker were playing a spirited game of tug the rope. "It's almost time to go. I'd better get changed. Bring the dogs in when you come?"

"Of course."

He watched her scoop up her empty lemonade glass and step across the deck to the sliding door. He could accept she was apprehensive about his parents but that wasn't all. There was something else. Something bigger.

A part of him worried it was their engagement. What if she was having second thoughts? Should he ask her, or would that come off as desperate and needy? God help him, but when it came to her, he sometimes was desperate and needy. He didn't often envy her gift, but it would sure come in handy right now if he could dip into her mind and figure out what the heck was going on.

"Come on, guys, time to go in," he called to the dogs.

Mac, ever vigilante, was by his side before he'd fully exhaled with Fifi joining barely two beats later. But the lab and the dachshund continued to wrestle in the grass even when he called a second and third time.

"Layla. Tucker. Come. Now," he said, raising his voice on the final word.

Two pairs of eyes fixed on him, assessing. Realizing Roman meant business, they abandoned the rope and trotted straight over to him as though demonstrating extreme obedience.

"Yeah, yeah. Good dogs," Roman said, fighting back a smile when they pranced along beside him.

"All set?" Mia asked when he and the pack came into the kitchen.

Seeing her dress with its long flowy skirt and fitted halter top, he whistled. "Aren't you a picture?" He pointed to the floor beside him. "Mia. Come. Now," he said using the same tone he had with the delinquent dogs seconds ago.

"Sorry, bud. But that won't work on me."

He shrugged. "Okay, then." And stepping over to her, wrapped his arms around her shoulders and swept her low. "You look amazing," he said, and kissed her long and deep.

"You say the nicest things," she said against his mouth.

He lingered another few seconds before pulling her upright again. "Well, that got me good and stirred up. Maybe we could be a few minutes late?"

She pushed him away. "No because if we were...a few minutes late...I'd have to redo my makeup which would make us criminally late. Plus, I'll spend the night worrying your mom could somehow sense that we had sex, and I'm already worried enough as it is."

"I'm pretty sure my mom knows we've had sex," Roman pointed out.

"Yeah, but that's not the same as doing the deed minutes before arriving at their house."

"Okay. Fine. Be that way." He sighed, then paused, and the sexy smile she loved so much burst across his face. "You know, I don't think we'll be staying all that late. I'll wager there'll still be plenty of time to get you out of that dress later."

"Plus, since I'm not wearing panties it'll be real easy to undress me."

He blinked at her. "Why did you have to tell me that?"

"It just seemed like the right thing to do," she said, laughing at his pained expression.

Molly Mancini's eyes flicked to Mia then back to her son. A smile, not the polite, restrained one Mia had seen of late, but a full outburst of joy spread across her face.

"Is this true?" she demanded. "My son is ready to settle down and take a wife. Start a family. This makes me so happy."

She launched herself at Roman, and he leaned down and hugged tight, his eyes finding Mia's. She clearly read the smug 'I told you so' in them but could only smile in return, relieved that their engagement news was being taken so well by his parents.

Roman's father, Frank, gripped her arm. "Such good news," he said, pumping her hand before stooping to hug. "I can see how happy you make my son. No father could want anything more."

"Let me have her," Molly demanded, pushing in between Mia and Frank. Reaching up, she patted Mia's cheek. "You are a beautiful, wonderful girl. This news...it lifts my heart. Gives me hope. Your babies will be magnificent. All dark and fiery."

"We're not…I mean…we haven't…" Mia stepped back, stumbling against Roman.

"Easy Ma. Take a breath. We just got engaged. Plenty of time to talk about kids later."

"Later?" Molly's eyebrows drew together. "You're thirty-five. That's no spring chicken. And I know Mia's not as old but the longer you wait the more difficult it will be. Children are blessed gifts, but make no mistake, they are hard work. You want to be young and full of energy. Besides, after all this business in our family, we know better than anyone that life is short, and tomorrow is not guaranteed. We have to live right now. Not put off important decisions for later."

"Come Molly, I think they know all this." Frank slung an arm around his wife's shoulder. "And things are different than when we were young. Nowadays, couples build their careers first then start having families. Roman will want to put a lot of work into his private investigation business."

"Business is no reason to put off having children. Lina had the same attitude, and look where she is now. Maybe if they'd started their family right away there would be no divorce."

"Okay. I think you're scaring off my bride to be," Roman said, squeezing Mia's hand. "Besides, I'm pretty sure we have to get married first before we start popping out babies. Isn't that what the good Lord says?"

"In this instance, I would happily welcome a new Mancini into the world whether in or out of wedlock. I'm sure God would understand."

Frank caught Roman's eye and gave him a nod.

"So, the wedding?" Frank said easily. "Have you set a date?"

"Not yet." Roman shrugged and turned to Mia. "We still have a lot to decide."

"But it must be soon. Maybe later this year," Molly said. "It will be such a happy occasion and we all need some happy in our lives." She clapped her hands. "Frank, pour another drink. We need to toast the newly engaged couple."

Once they'd drunk to their health and happiness, Mia settled back into her chair at the dining room table and let out a silent breath of relief. It was nice to see Frank and Molly so excited about their wedding even if it came with all the baby talk.

"We will organize an engagement party here at the house," Molly decided. "You must invite your parents. We are all family now."

"Um...see..."

Roman jumped into the silence. "Mia's parents aren't around, and she's an only child."

Mia could feel the pity radiating from Molly and Frank. "I'm very sorry to hear that," Frank said. "And sorry that we've been so wrapped up in our own family problems we never asked about yours."

"But you must have cousins and aunts and uncles?" Molly asked.

"No. There's no one. Just me."

Molly's eyes shined with moisture. "You poor, poor girl. Well, we are your family now. You never have to be alone because we will be there for you."

"Thank you," Mia said, swallowing down the lump in her throat.

It had been ages since she'd dreamed of having a loving, supportive family surrounding her. She could still remember the terrible longing she'd felt as a little girl walking by playgrounds and seeing children with their parents. There had been no family outings or playdates in her childhood. What there had been were late nights at the racetrack with her father betting away their rent money or long hours spent sitting in the back room of some smoky, beer soaked bar while he played poker.

"We should push off," Roman said, tapping her foot under the table. "It's been a great night. Thanks for dinner."

"I'll call tomorrow to sort out dates for the engagement party. Lina will come home," Molly said.

At the door, Frank turned and embraced Roman first then Mia. "You have made your Mama and me so happy."

On the drive home, Mia turned to look out the window. "You know, I'm not sure I'm ready to have children."

"Sorry about my mom. She's very old-fashioned in her thinking."

"It's all right. I mean, it's good she brought up the subject because it's something we should talk about. Do you want kids?"

"Yes. I do. I always imagined having children. How about you?"

"Honestly? I'm not sure. Maybe. It's not something I've ever thought seriously about. I never really expected to get married, let alone have children."

"But you'll think about it now? I'm not saying right away on the kids thing but my ma's right, we can't wait forever."

She shifted to study his face. "This sounds like it's a deal breaker for you?"

He paused a beat. "I wouldn't say kids are a deal breaker, but I think I'd regret not having them."

"Then I'd better hurry up and decide one way or the other because a lifetime of regret is no way to live."

Chapter Four

Over the next week, Roman set up his office in town and began reaching out to contacts in the local police departments in the hopes of drumming up business.

Mia dug into her ever-growing pile of jewelry orders. She took the dogs for long walks around the property. And she thought about babies.

It's not that she didn't like kids because she did. Or at least she thought she did. Actually, when it came right down to it, she hadn't spent much time with children over the years. But still, she liked the idea of them. The thing that held her back, though, was the worry she'd be an epic failure as a mother.

She wondered, as she sometimes had over the last twenty-eight years, what had happened to her mother. And what kind of woman abandoned her baby? Surely not a nurturing one. Since half of Mia's genes came from that woman maybe she wasn't maternal either.

Setting down the amethyst and her wire cutters, Mia shook her head and pushed back from the worktable. There was no way she'd ever walk away from her child...no matter what the circumstances. Especially to leave him or her with someone like Danny Dawson, even if he was the biological father.

Thinking about fathers, her heart softened. Roman would be an amazing one. She could already picture him with a baby tucked up in his arm.

Holding a little boy on his shoulders or reading to his daughter every night. He was such a good man. Loyal, dependable, and fierce protector all rolled into one. Not to mention seriously hot. Though a child wouldn't care about the hot part, she supposed.

And the more she imagined having children with Roman, the more she realized she wanted it. All of it. The sleepless nights during babyhood, the toddler tantrums, the cringe-worthy school plays. Everything about it seemed wonderful.

She glanced around the room at the scatter of dogs lying in sunbeams. "You guys would love having children around," she said, nudging Tucker with her foot. "Always someone to play with. Plus, they'd have their friends over so even more little ones. And I've heard kids are pretty messy. Lots of spills and dropped food. You could help with the clean-up."

She continued talking aloud while stretching her arms overhead. "And if any of them inherited my telepathic abilities, I would be there to help them through. Unlike when I was left on my own to figure it out."

All at once, her blood froze. Should she even have children if there was a chance she could pass this on? Everything about being a psychic had made her life more difficult, sometimes brutally so. It would be cruel to subject her offspring to such a thing. Like purposely passing down a grim and lifelong disease.

By the time Roman came home a few hours later, Mia was practically in tears, and she didn't cry easily. Somehow, the imagined children had been real to her, and the idea they were being snatched away by the cruelties of fate was too much to bear. Especially when coupled with the possibility Roman might now very well reconsider their marriage.

"So, you see, we can't have kids," she said quietly, having explained her worries. "It wouldn't be fair to knowingly put that on a child."

Roman sat back in his chair and tried not to smile. "Okay, let's look at this from a different angle. You see what you have as a curse, and I see it as a gift. What if instead of telepathy, you were really smart? Like Stephen Hawking's smart. I'd say with that kind of intellect, it might be tough relating to the average Joe on the street. Meaning, socially, things would be more difficult for you. Would you then refuse to have children because they might inherit your intellect?"

Mia blinked at him. "It's not the same. Intelligence is valued by society while what I have is not. You can't imagine what it was like growing up, everyone either being scared of me or thinking I was a freak. All that time spent in psychiatric wards and all the drugs they fed me." She shook her head and dropped her eyes to where Mac pressed in against her leg. "It was…I can't even describe how awful it was."

Reaching forward, he took her hand. "Hey, what happened to you was a crime. I swear if I ever meet your parents, I'm going to give them a piece of my mind. But our children will have us. Both of us. And if they should inherit your gifts, well, you'll be able to help them every step of the way. In fact, it might be totally awesome to have psychic kids. Man, I see them killing it in soccer and baseball. And don't even get me started on spelling bees."

Thankfully he hadn't noticed her shocked stillness when the mention of meeting her parents had her flashing back to Danny Dawson standing on Dalton's Main Street. Now she matched his smile and squeezed his hand.

"I guess I hadn't thought of it like that. You're totally okay with all this?"

"More than okay. What about you? Sure you want kids? If you're only agreeing because you know I want them it would be a bad idea. I think my mom was spot on about kids being a lot of work, and if you're not all the way in, you'll come to resent me pretty darn soon."

She blew out a breath. "I've thought about it all week and discovered I really, really want them. I guess I never let myself imagine it before. Kids just seemed like one more thing I shouldn't wish for. I'm thinking two. It's lonely growing up without a sibling."

"Two sounds awesome. But not right away. It'd be nice if we have a couple of years just for ourselves."

"We shouldn't wait too long though. What if we have trouble conceiving?"

Roman tugged her hand, pulled her onto his lap and wrapped his arms around her. "Well, I guess we'll just have to enjoy trying. I think that's something I can get behind."

"Or on top of. Or underneath for that matter," she said, turning to brush her lips against his neck. "And really, we can probably never get enough practice."

He sighed and brushed his fingertips across her breast. "Practice makes perfect."

"So, you and Roman, huh?" Sheryl said the next morning as she printed out packing slips for that day's FedEx shipments. "I almost got married a couple of times. Lucky misses, I'd say. The first guy ended up in jail. The second one has five kids by four different mothers and get this, he still lives with his own mother."

Mia tried hard not to laugh out loud, but a muffled snicker escaped. She'd become used to Sheryl with her frizzy grey hair, her dour face, and her general air of life being nothing but one big disappointment.

"Fingers crossed, Roman and I don't end up living out of a wardrobe box while dodging his various baby mamas."

Sheryl shrugged. "Stranger things have happened, but I think you'll be all right. You're smart and Roman's a decent man. No bad blood in him."

Now, she did laugh. "Thanks...I guess."

"If anything were to happen, I'd take care of your babies for you." The older woman bent to where Tucker lay on his back and rubbed a hand along his belly. "Especially this sweet boy. No way I'd see him living on the streets."

"Good to know." Mia lifted the earrings and inspected them in the sunlight. "I think these are ready to go, which means I'm officially ahead of schedule."

"Those the ones for that lady in Montana? I can probably have them sent out today."

"Excellent. I have to say, Sheryl, you're nothing if not efficient."

"No point in doing a job badly," Sheryl said with a shrug.

Smiling, Mia tapped the keyboard on her laptop and brought up the next order. "No point indeed."

Once Mike from FedEx had departed with the outgoing shipments, Sheryl turned her attention to unpacking the newest inventory items.

"We're going to need more containers," she said to Mia. "The way your business is booming, there's so much more of these rocks around." She pointed to the jade stones spilling out of their box. "I could do a run to the office supply store tomorrow before I come in."

"That would be fantastic. You really are a treasure."

"I don't know about that. Lots of common sense, that's what I have." She sliced through the tape on a small box and frowned down at the contents. "You planning to do something with keys? This one's pretty ugly.

Can't imagine anyone buying a necklace with this piece of junk hanging from it."

"What? I didn't order a key," Mia said, looking up from where she'd been arranging tourmaline on the work desk.

Sheryl closed the flap on the box and peered at the return address. "From Michael Carlyle Gems in Indianapolis. Name doesn't ring a bell. Not one of your usual suppliers."

Heart hammering, Mia put out her hand. "Give it to me right now."

"Don't get yourself in a state. Probably a mix-up of some kind," Sheryl said, passing the box over.

Mia stared down at her father's familiar handwriting with the extravagant loops on the M and the H. She'd lived in Indianapolis for a while when she was eleven or maybe twelve. It was hard to keep track of all the places she'd been.

She reached for the key nestled in bubble wrap. Small with multiple scratches and a green plastic covering over the rounded handle. It sparked a memory of chlorine and Mac'n'Cheese. She closed her eyes and exhaled, opening her mind.

She saw it then. The YMCA with the huge indoor pool and the high diving board. It had taken her two weeks to find the courage to climb up the ladder. Visions of rooms with walls of mirrors for aerobic classes and barre ballet. And best of all, the cafeteria and the sweet Mrs. Danley who always asked how Mia was doing and put extra food in her bowl.

Because the YMCA worked on a sliding scale of earnings, Mia had easily been able to steal enough money to pay for the low monthly membership rate. Many a week had been spent hanging around in the warmth and eating at least one solid meal a day.

The key must be to one of the lockers in the changing area. Why on earth had Pops sent this to her? Well, whatever the reason, she wasn't getting involved, that was for sure. In the old days she would have been intrigued, but the past was the past, and she had no interest in his undoubtedly criminal activities. Because it surely was something shady. Normal law-abiding people didn't use aliases to send locker keys to their estranged daughters.

"Yeah, this is definitely a mistake," she said to Sheryl. "I didn't order anything from Michael Carlyle Gems."

"You want me to contact them?"

"Nah, they'll probably try and sell us something. I'll bet it's one of those stupid marketing tactics. You can throw it out."

"Okay. You're the boss."

She forced it from her mind and returned to the necklace in progress on her worktable. Still, later that day, after Sheryl had gone home, Mia found herself rooting through the trash can and retrieving the dented metal key with the green plastic coating. Turning it over in her hand, she frowned, then tucked it away at the bottom of the container holding her jewelry making tools.

Roman cleared his throat. "Ma is going to call you tomorrow. She's all a flutter about our engagement party. Says she has some things she wants to go over with you."

"Oh...sure. I'm pretty easy though. She can do whatever she wants."

He smiled full out. "That's good because easy is the last thing my mother is when it comes to parties. She has very definite ideas. I should warn you, don't get into any wedding details right now or she'll have you agreeing to a whole whack of stuff you don't want. And once it's in her mind you can bet she won't be happy to let it go.

"I'll be careful. Besides, you and I haven't even talked about our wedding day and what we want. I think it's up to us to decide."

"I'm the boy. My part is the proposal then showing up on the day. I thought the wedding details were exclusive girl territory. And that would be you."

"You think I'm going to organize our entire wedding by myself? Think again, buster. It's your wedding too."

"But don't you have the maid of honor and bridesmaids and whoever else to help you?"

"What bridesmaids? The only person I know well enough to ask is Brooke. I suppose I should include your sister, but I don't get the feeling Lina likes me all that much. And considering she's in the middle of a divorce, I hardly think she'll be interested anyway."

"Oh…" His eyes flicked away and then back to her. "I guess we can keep it small. Kevin is the main guy I want standing up with me anyway."

Mia sighed. "Is this going to be weird? Me having no family or friends at our wedding? Maybe we should elope or something. Remind me again why you want to marry me in the first place."

His smile came lightning fast. "Because I literally can't imagine a single day without you in my life."

Mia's lips curved before she even realized she was smiling. She poked him in the stomach. "Good answer, hot shot. All right, I'll clean up, and then we need to eat. I'm starving. I have vegetables marinating and ready to grill, and I thought we could throw on burgers and russet potatoes."

"As long as my burger is made from beef."

She rolled her eyes. "Of course, my carnivore friend. I learned my lesson the last time I tried to feed you a vegan burger. Won't be doing that again any time soon."

He slapped playfully at her butt. "That's what I like to hear. A compliant woman is good wife material."

"Aw, sucks." She shrugged and pretended to be bashful. "One of my dreams finally realized."

As Roman had predicted, Molly Mancini called Mia the next morning.

"Your engagement party is coming along beautifully," Molly said. "Most people have already RSVP'd. The head count is at just over two hundred. Everyone seems very excited. Are you sure you don't have anyone else to add to the guest list?"

"Wow. I didn't realize it was going to be so big."

"We've lived in this town a long time and know most everyone. It was hard keeping the numbers down. Don't want anyone to get their feelings hurt."

Mia swallowed and wondered why they needed to have an engagement party at all. "This sounds like a lot of work. Maybe we should just have a family dinner?"

Molly tsked. "Don't be silly. We have to celebrate this happiest of occasions. Now, let's talk about flowers and music. And the menu, of course..."

By the time Mia hung up from the call almost thirty minutes later, her head was pounding. Good God, what had they done?

When her cell signaled again a few seconds later, she considered running away. Instead, she sighed, closed her eyes, and took in a deep breath.

"Hello, Molly," she said.

"Good morning, Baby Doll. It's not Molly though."

Her heart galloped in her chest and her eyes sprang open. "Pops? What do you want?"

"Just thought I'd say 'hi' and see how your week's going." He paused and when Mia didn't respond, chuckled. "Not feeling chatty? That's okay. Plenty of time for us to catch up. I see my package was delivered. It gives me piece of mind knowing you're taking care of the key."

"That was from you?" Mia said, getting her equilibrium back. "Huh? I figured it was a mistake and had my assistant throw it away."

"Come on, little girl. You can't kid a kidder. No way you dumped it. In fact, I'd bet a thousand bucks the minute you touched it you knew exactly where it was from. And I'll go double or nothing you kept that little key somewhere safe. It may be a while since we've spent time together, but I know you inside out."

"Okay, fine. I have it. What did you hide in a locker in Indianapolis for Pete's sake?"

"Shush. No details over the phone. You can never be too careful. Let's just say I stashed a bread crumb. Something that Claudia would remember."

Internally, Mia sighed. For a short period of time after her father got out of prison the first time, he'd used the alias Frank Giles and she was Claudia. If she remembered correctly, they'd been in Orlando at the time.

"Great. But what does the bread crumb lead to?"

"Ah, well. All I can tell you is it's well worth following the trail. Now, my pet, I need you to go and retrieve the first crumb and bring it to me."

Mia's laugh was hash. "Right. Of course. You want me to drop everything, fly to Indianapolis and..."

"Don't say it," he warned. "But yes. That's precisely what I want. It'll be like old times. You must miss the rush. And I'll cut you in. Trust me, it will be ten times worth your while."

"I told you. I'm out of that life and nothing could tempt me to go back."

"Hmm...I see. Well, then, we have a problem."

"Don't you mean you have a problem?"

He sighed. "No, it's definitely we. I can't come to you because there's a very good...no, I'd say an excellent chance some extremely bad men might tail me to your little town. And if they do, I'm afraid you'd pique their interest, and they'd wonder what you might know. They're not the kind of guys to back down once they have a thread to pull on."

"But I don't know anything."

"You know a little but even still, they won't be satisfied that's all you know. I'd have to guess they'll try and pull it out of you, and you know how those things usually go."

"I always knew you were shifty, but I never thought of you as cruel. What kind of father sets violent criminals on his own daughter? It's despicable."

"Now, Jenny. It's only I'm in a spot of trouble here, and I need your help. You'll be handsomely rewarded."

"I don't want to be rewarded. What I want is for you to never, ever, under any circumstances, contact me again."

"Okay, sure," he said reassuringly. "As soon as we sort this out, I can promise to let you be. Even though the way you're living is such a waste of your talent. It makes me sad."

Mia growled. "Look. I'll mail the damn key to you."

"No can do. I've gone off the grid for a bit. And it's not only the key. I need that breadcrumb. Can't go in there myself just in case."

"Let me get this straight. You want me to fly...to the previously discussed city then go to...the place where the key will open something. Next I scoop up whatever's inside and bring it to you at another location? And if I don't follow your plan, you'll basically turn me over to the bad guys?"

"Not turn you over. It's just that I can't see any way of picking up the key without them following me. I'm afraid I'm a hunted man."

"What did you do?"

"A bit of this and a bit of that. I always said people are suckers. Even the ones who think they aren't. These particular suckers are connected, if you know what I mean."

Mia sighed. "Just give them back whatever you took. It's ridiculous that you're still running around ripping people off at your age."

"My age is part of the reason I did it. It seems your dear old dad is having some medical problems. The kind that cost a lot of money to treat. I'm doing all this to try and save my life. I thought, as an added bonus, I could see my baby girl again plus give her a financial boost at the same time. I guess I'm getting sentimental."

"What's wrong with you?" Mia asked flatly. "Or are you just trying to tug on my heartstrings?"

"Fraid not. It's the big C. You remember how I hated doctors? Well, the tumors were found late. There's still a chance though, but it ain't gonna be cheap. And it's not like I have health insurance to fall back on. When I looked around for an opportunity, this one fell straight into my lap as if coming directly from God himself. The main guy heading it up is someone from the old days. In fact, you—"

"Pops," Mia cut him off. "Enough. You always could talk the hind legs off a donkey. I can't...it's just...why are you putting this on me? I told you I was out. I've made a whole new life for myself and I'm really happy."

"The truth is I hate having to ask. It's a pride thing I guess. But it comes down to the fact I don't have anyone else. At least no one I can trust like I trust you. Hearing how happy you are, even if it is in the straight life, it makes my heart squeeze with joy. Can't you just do this one thing for me, baby girl? It won't cause you any harm, and you'd be saving my life twice over."

"I'll have to think about it, okay? I have responsibilities and my business and...other stuff. I can't disappear."

"And Roman will wonder where you've gone, I suppose."

The muscles in Mia's shoulders went to rock. "How do you know about Roman?"

"Oh, please. Anyone who followed the Emerald Ring Story knows you and Roman had a thing going. When I visited Dalton, it wasn't hard to get the locals talking about it. I soon learned the two of you are living together and, if I'm not mistaken, probably engaged by now. I'll bet the greenhouse was gorgeous all lit up with candles. I'd like to meet the man who finally tamed my fiery Jenny girl."

"I'm not going to talk to you about Roman," she said in a dangerously quiet voice. "He's a good man. Nothing like us. And forget about meeting him because it'll never happen." She unclenched her fist and blew out a breath. "Okay. I'll help you this one time on this small part of the plan, but that's it. If there's more trouble or things don't go your way, you'd better not call me again. Do you understand?"

"Sure, sure. I hear what you're saying. There won't be trouble though. I've got the whole thing figured. I think you'll be real happy with your cut. It's more money than either of us ever saw in the good old days."

"No cut. I'm not doing it for the money. I'm doing it for you, and because I know you tried, the best you knew how, to take care of me when I was little."

"Sweet Jenny. You always were a good girl. "

"I'm not so sweet. So help me God, if you mess things up for me, I'll turn you in faster than you can believe. Call me tomorrow afternoon. I'll have everything sorted out by then."

"Bless you, child. I won't forget this."

Mia's hands shook when she clicked off and placed the phone on the counter.

What the hell was she doing? Helping her father was absolute and complete lunacy. Whatever he'd gotten himself into sounded much more dangerous than his usual cons and thieving schemes. This was serious. High level crime serious. And men who did high level stuff usually had no problem torturing and killing anyone who got in their way.

By agreeing, hadn't she just gone and put herself directly in the crosshairs?

No. She'd be fine, she reasoned. In and out within forty-eight hours. End of story.

Outside, Layla barked, and when Mia glanced over at the sliding door, she saw Mac and Fifi waiting patiently to be let in. Numbly, she walked over and opened the door, calling Layla and Tucker when they didn't immediately come.

Roman could look after the dogs while she was gone. It had worked out well when she'd traveled to the Trade Fair in Jacksonville last week and this time it would only be for one or two nights. If he was busy with work during the day surely Sheryl could be hired to stay longer and watch over them into the afternoon. Mia knew she was probably being overly fussy, but if anything happened to her dogs she would lose her mind.

Her stomach pitched when her thoughts circled back to Roman. She obviously couldn't tell him. It had only been a few months ago she'd sworn up and down that she'd severed all ties to her previous life and was a brand new, law-abiding person. How could she now explain she was helping her father—a lifelong criminal—retrieve whatever he'd stolen from a bunch of other criminals?

Besides, this was an exception. A special case. Never to be repeated. And what he didn't know couldn't hurt him.

She sighed and rubbed a hand over her eyes. Mac leaned against her leg, offering his support. She patted his head and stared down into his adoring eyes.

"I'm pretty sure lying to my fiancé is a big no-no." She sighed again. "But what can I do? I don't feel right not helping Pops even though he's a fool and it's his own fault he's in this mess. And if he really is dying...well...it's one small thing I can do to ease my conscience. Somehow, I don't think Roman would understand. And I'm glad because if he was the kind of man who understood, I wouldn't want to be with him in the first place."

Mac snuffled against her hand and put his paw on her foot as though agreeing with her. She bent and kissed the top of his head. "You get it, right? We'll call this trip my final act of letting go of the past. Besides, I really don't want the bad men coming to Dalton. This way I keep all of you guys safe."

Chapter Five

"You must be excited?" Roman said the next night.

Her mind a million miles away and scrambling through all the details of the trip, she stilled in the act of folding a T-shirt. "Why would I be excited?" she asked cautiously.

"A big job with a brand new client who has deep pockets. Also, being able to charge extra for agreeing to travel to her."

"Right. Of course. But I don't think I'll make this traveling thing a habit. It's too disruptive…" She glanced over to where all four dogs lay forlornly around the bedroom. "For everyone. Thanks again for holding down the fort. What would I do without you?"

He stroked a hand down her back. "No worries on that front because you'll never have to find out."

The guilt hit like a blow to her stomach. This was harder than she'd thought. Why did he have to be so darn agreeable about everything? It would be easier if he was pissy at being left in charge of the house and the dogs because then they could snap at one another, and she could march away in a righteous huff.

This way all she could do was try and swallow down the ickiness of what she was doing. She'd never realized exactly how wrenching it felt to lie to someone she loved. Because of the lie, there was now something awful between Roman and her, pushing them apart. She could never go back to the perfect and pure closeness they'd once shared. Sure, in time it would fade, but she'd always know she'd tainted their love.

I'll never do this again, she silently vowed.

Later, when Roman curled around her in bed and held her close, she shut her eyes against the threatening tears and fought to keep her breathing slow and even. Deep in her chest, it hurt. As though her body was doing its darnedest to expel the guilt and shame.

"You're trembling," he said softly. "What's wrong?"

"Nothing. Only that I hate leaving you guys. Especially so soon after my last trip. From now on, I travel nowhere without you."

"I'll miss you too, baby." He exhaled slowly, his breath ruffling the hair against her face. "This is going to sound kinda weird, but I love hearing you say that. I know a lot of times in relationships one person has stronger feelings than the other. With us, that's me, and I'm okay with it. I love you so much I sometimes feel like I might burst. But what you said just now, it gives me peace, you know?"

There was no stopping her tears now. "That's not true," she said on a shaky breath. "I love you with everything I have. I guess I maybe have a harder time expressing it than you do. I'm sorry. I don't ever want you to think you're not loved...because you are. So much."

Turning in his arms, she kissed him. Fiercely. Possessively. Her hands stroking along his chest then lifting to his head until she could weave her fingers through his hair and hold him hard to her. She poured everything into the kiss, her worry and guilt, her love and joy, her longing. He moaned into her mouth, and she threw a leg over his hip and pressed against him, center to center.

Minutes later, when they were both naked and vibrating with need, she straddled him and lowered down taking him all the way into her in one smooth push. Her fingertips traced over his cheeks, and she kissed him softly, while inside her muscles quaked in anticipation of release.

"I love you, Roman Mancini. With all my heart. With all my soul. I give you my body. It's yours now and for always."

He rose up, his arms wrapping around her back then rolled them until she was under him. He began slowly, almost reverently, with long, smooth strokes, stopping to rock against her, to taste her neck, to slide fingertips between their joining and rub gentle circles. Her head fell back and her eyes fluttered closed, and she let herself feel everything. The heat. The friction. The sense of urgency. And when she might have otherwise wanted to speed toward the crashing end, she forced herself to wait and let it build deeper and stronger though it seemed impossible she could last.

Gritting her teeth, she exhaled in sharp bursts, holding on the edge for another moment. Another second even. Reaching out with her mind, Roman's desperate clawing need poured into her, and she clamped around him. Like a wild stallion, the groan came from deep inside his chest. His head snapped up, and his eyes locked on hers.

When she pushed up against him and began pistoning her hips, his breath sucked in, and he matched her pace. Faster. Harder. His hands gripping her hips. His weight pressing her into the mattress. She flew up like a rocket, heartbeat pounding in her ears, breath rasping out, everything at the core of her hard and tight like a wire pulled to the point of maximum tension.

She held there for a beat, then another, and finally broke apart and released into the glorious shuddering fall. Light burst across her eyelids, and a flash of heat raced over her skin. Vaguely she felt Roman thrust into her again before collapsing onto her chest.

Within minutes, Roman slept. Beside him, she lay awake well into the night trying to convince herself what she was doing wasn't a betrayal.

It was still dark the next morning when Mia left for the airport. Roman kissed her goodbye inside the screened porch, holding the dogs so she could slip outside. When she glanced back, he stood surrounded by her pack, his hand caught in a half wave, his hair tousled from sleep.

The sick feeling in her stomach wouldn't let up, and her conscience nattered at her all the way to Nashville and through the flight to Indianapolis. It was mid-morning when she landed and made her way to the car rental desk. Once behind the wheel, she punched the address into the nav system and started the car. Then swearing under her breath, she pulled out her cell.

Roman answered on the second ring. "How was the flight?"

"Fine. No delays." She paused, gathering herself. "So, here's the thing. I lied to you. I'm not in Miami for a client. I'm...it's hard to explain."

She heard him draw in a breath.

"Whatever it is, baby, just tell me. Lies are no good. Not for us."

She nodded even though he couldn't see her. "I know. I didn't want to lie, but I honestly wasn't sure how to handle things. My father sent me a key a couple of days ago...then he called. Said he was in trouble and needed help."

"Your father?" Roman said incredulously. "He has no right to ask anything after the childhood you suffered. Tell me you're not helping him?"

"I didn't want to. I said no." She rubbed at a tear on her cheek. God, when had she become such a crybaby? "But he's really sick and he's on the run from some bad men. The scary kind. All I'm doing is picking something up and bringing it to him. That's it. I promise."

"Why the hell didn't you tell me?"

"Because...honestly? I didn't think you'd understand. I barely understand myself. I just feel I have to do it. One last thing to help my pops. I know it's stupid, and I'm sorry. I won't ever lie to you again. It hurt too much. I feel like I got an ulcer from agonizing about it."

"That's why you were so...I don't know...different last night. Distracted and intense at the same time."

"The guilt was brutal. I used to literally lie for a living, but the guilt of lying to you just about tore me apart."

He sighed, and she could imagine the way his eyebrows were probably scrunched together, and his lips pulled back tight against his mouth.

"Is it illegal?" When she hesitated, he growled into the phone. "Come on. You know this is not okay."

"I'm not committing a crime, at least not a new crime," she said all in a rush. "Though technically I guess it would be considered accessory after the fact. Sort of. I won't be touching the stolen merchandise, just bringing my father a key or a lock or something."

"Don't do it, Mia. Just come back, okay? This is not a good idea."

"It'll be fine," she said soothingly. "I'll be home by tomorrow afternoon. No harm no foul. And this way there's no chance my father leads any of his...let's call them associates...to us in Dalton. It's safer this way."

"No, what's safer is you having nothing to do with your father," Roman shot back. "Are you in Miami or was that a lie too?"

"En route to Miami. Don't worry. I've got everything under control."

"Uh...no you don't because I'm not good with this. The lying...or what you're doing for your dad. You and I will be having a serious talk when you get back."

She fought to swallow over the lump in her throat. "Sure. Okay. I'm sorry, Roman. No more lies, I promise. Take good care of the pack and yourself. I love you."

When he clicked off without another word, she stared down at the phone. Shit. He was really pissed. Was this the kind of thing that could break them up? she wondered. Surely not. Especially after everything they'd been through during the past year.

She hoped when she could properly explain her side in person, it would be easier to make him understand. Anyway, she was partly doing this to keep them safe. The lying part...well, yeah, she'd been totally in the wrong there. All she could do was cross her fingers and hope Roman would trust her again.

She glanced over at the navigation screen and shook her head. There was nothing to be done about Roman right now. Time to concentrate on the job at hand. She needed to get through the hand-off with her father.

After leaving the airport, she picked up route 70 toward Indianapolis. It was a short journey into the city and the traffic wasn't bad, all things considered. She only had a vague recollection of the area. The YMCA she remembered very well along with the Four Seasons downtown where she and her father had set up shop once a month or so. They'd done very well for themselves picking off wealthy out-of-towners. She could sort of picture the house they'd stayed in for a time.

When she exited onto Washington Street, instead of going east into the Market District she found herself turning right and heading west toward Tuxedo Park. It all looked different with the small strip malls and auto parts stores, which had sprung up on practically every block. She remembered a 7-Eleven at the corner of Chester but now a Mexican restaurant had risen in its place.

Turning left onto Chester she slowed and thought back to all the days she'd walked home from the bus stop, not sure if her father would show up that night. If he'd been deep in a poker game, she might not see him for days at a time. On the flipside, he sometimes waited on her, a new plan pinging around in his mind for the two of them to make some quick cash bilking people at a Colts game or some other big event downtown.

She could see the route now. Walk to the next road. Turn right. Left on the following one. Then hallway up the block on the right-hand side to number forty-four with the broken piece of sidewalk and the green tarp covering a hole in the roof above the front window. She signaled and pulled the car over and put it in park.

The house was still there. Nothing more than a one-story shack with four tiny rooms. The tarp was no longer in place but glancing at the roof, she decided it might well be needed any time since the shingles were peeling back and, in some spots, missing altogether. The lawn, and really that was a generous term for a patch of dirt with scrubby grass, was only about six feet wide. Although the house was technically detached, it stood so close to each neighboring structure there was only a scant few inches between.

Still, at the time it had been fine with Mia. She had had her own bedroom. The bus stop was an easy walk. And though the neighborhood itself had been one of the worst for poverty and crime, she'd known how to take care of herself on the mean streets of any city.

A shudder rolled through her as she continued gazing at the house from her childhood. Thinking back, she had to wonder how she'd survived...let alone come to a place in her life where she ran a six-figure-a-year business and owned a beautiful log house in the country complete with a babbling brook. Not to mention having a sexy and decent man in her life.

That was assuming, of course, she still had Roman.

Two men approached along the sidewalk. One tall, skinny, seeming to jitter with every step, his eyes darting left and right. The other was overweight with sleeve tattoos on both arms, plus ink on his neck and shaved head. Tattoo man stared hard at Mia. He licked his lips and winked at her.

Mia shifted the car to drive and eased away. Memory lane was done for today. She needed to get on with the task at hand so she could get back to Roman and the dogs.

Ten minutes later, she parked in the lot beside the YMCA. It had been renovated considerably since she'd last seen it. The exterior was now a sunny, yellow brick, and a wall of glass allowed a full view of the indoor pool.

Inside, she paid for a day pass, took her backpack into the change area and retrieved the key from her wallet before slotting it into locker number seventy-seven and opening the door. She pulled out the small cloth bag and stuffed it into her backpack. Once in the bathroom, she shut herself into one of the stalls and examined the contents of the bag. A pair of ladies black workout pants with a pink stripe up the side, a matching pink top, and a jacket.

Feeling along the waistband of the pants, she found the hidden inner pocket. As she pushed fingers in, she located two keys on a small silver keychain. From the jacket, she pulled out a Nokia phone. When she powered it on and scrolled to the messages, found the text with the Miami address. Shoving everything back into her backpack, she zipped it closed and walked out to the rental car. She checked the time and noted she was right on schedule and would easily make the flight out of Indianapolis.

Four hours later, stepping outside through the sliding door at Miami International Airport, the hot muggy air hit with a punch. Mia stripped off her cardigan and shoved it in the backpack while waiting for the shuttle to the Hertz rental car location.

Her stomach rumbled, and she realized she'd eaten little during the day beyond a Jamba Juice smoothie she'd grabbed in the Nashville airport hours earlier. As soon as she retrieved the next package, she was going to indulge herself with something yummy.

Taking the 112 highway, she picked up I-195 and drove across the causeway toward Miami Beach. The sun was sinking into the water, and the sky turning to shades of lavender and candy floss pink. It was a truly glorious night. Deciding she might as well make the most of things, she opened the windows, turned up the radio, and sang along to Keith Urban.

Traffic slowed when she turned south on Alton Drive, but she didn't mind crawling along beside the water and gazing at all the bustling activity on the sidewalk. After turning east again, she continued another two blocks, then swung into the parking area at Flamingo Park. She remembered how bitterly disappointed she'd been as a child to discover there weren't actually any flamingos.

The park was popular with families, and the area was filled with mothers and fathers and their small ones. Some making use of the playground, others splashing in the pool, and several on the tennis courts. It had changed quite a bit in the fifteen or so years since she'd been here. The play structure was massive, whereas before there had been little more than swings and slides. She only remembered two tennis courts, but she now counted six, and there was a new second pool catering to the tiny children.

Mia paid the ten-dollar entrance fee and made her way across the grass to the lockers on the far side of the full-sized pool. Checking the key, she chuckled. Seventy-seven again. Her father had always claimed seven was his lucky number and certainly double sevens had to bring even better fortunes. She wondered idly what he would have done if his favorite locker had been in use.

She paused to wait when she noticed a woman putting clothing into a locker on the next row. When she was finally alone, Mia slotted in the key and opened the door. Inside, she found a woman's one-piece bathing suit. Pink and black like the workout clothes from Indianapolis. Plus goggles and a pink rubber swim cap.

She ran her fingers over the suit, finding nothing, and then examined the goggles before turning her attention to the swim cap. Sure enough, a brass key with a slim plastic toggle had been taped inside. Gathering everything in her arms, she stuffed the lot into her backpack, turned, and retraced her steps to the rental car.

The sky was growing dark but cruising along Collins Avenue, the night was only beginning to come alive. Restaurant and hotel lights shone, and people filled the sidewalks as though it was a holiday and not just a regular Thursday night in May. Even at this early hour, music pumped out of night clubs, and lines snaked beside buildings, everyone patiently waiting to be admitted entrance. The energy was infectious. With most of the hard work of the day completed, Mia felt like celebrating.

A place called the Pink Lotus Bar seemed appropriate, so she ordered a starter of guacamole and homemade tortilla chips and a Cajun vegan burger with a side of balsamic glazed broccoli. Taking it with her, she walked the boardwalk alongside South Pointe Beach before settling down at a picnic table and spreading out her food. It was calmer here compared to the frenzied activity in the restaurant district, and she sank into the quiet. It had been quite the day, after all, and this small pocket of peace was welcomed.

When she reached for her phone, she saw it was almost eight. Roman and the dogs would be settled in for the evening. She'd left out a shepherd's pie from the freezer for his dinner. If she remembered correctly, the Braves were playing the Mets in Atlanta. He was most likely eating on the couch while glued to the TV. Layla would be lying at his feet, and the other three spread around the room. She hoped the Braves were winning.

She sat for some time enjoying the night air and trying to convince herself she wasn't bone-weary from a day of non-stop travel. Almost done now, she reminded herself. A short drive to Lauderdale, do the hand-off with Pops, then grab a few hours of rest in a hotel by the airport.

Thinking of her father's crazy game of hide and seek, she shook her head. He always was one for the drama. Whoever was trying to track him would have had an exceedingly hard time making it even this far. And where had he come up with Fort Lauderdale? As far as she knew, he'd never lived there, though of course he could have settled into the town sometime after she'd parted ways with him. Still, it didn't seem like his sort of place since it tended to attract college kids looking for fun rather than wealthy tourists ripe for the fleecing.

Whatever. It didn't matter to her. Her part was almost done. Then she could figure out how to patch things up with Roman. Her cell pinged, and as if she had somehow summoned him, Roman's name popped up on the screen. She blew out a breath and tried to calm her racing heart.

"Hi. I was just thinking about you," she said. "How was your day? Are all the canines behaving beautifully?"

The pause was brief but she felt it like a shove to the chest. "We're fine. No problems. I wanted to make sure you're okay. Where are you?"

"Sitting on the beach in Miami. It's a beautiful night. I just had dinner."

"No trouble?"

"None. I told you this wasn't dangerous."

"Are you finished?"

"Almost. I'm meeting Pops in Fort Lauderdale in a couple of hours, and then I'm out."

"Okay. Text me when it's over and let me know you're safe."

"Sure. I'm sorry Roman. I feel terrible about everything. You still sound kind of mad."

"Kind of mad?" he said, his voice deceptively soft. "No, I'm not kind of mad. What I am is fucking furious. I can't believe you'd disregard us and what we've built together the minute your low-life father comes calling. It says a lot."

"No. It says nothing. This is a one-time thing. A kind of closure. And part of the reason I'm doing it is for us. To keep us safe, so I have no regrets about my past."

"I'm not talking about this now. Text me when you're finished. Be careful, Mia."

When he clicked off, she stared down at the phone and shook her head. Oh boy, did she have a lot of bridges to mend.

After snoozing in her car for an hour or so, she made a stop at the Starbucks on Second Street, ordered a venti chai tea latte then got back behind the wheel and began the drive to Fort Lauderdale. The navigation system estimated it would take an hour and five minutes, which would put her there early, but she figured it didn't matter all that much. Since her father was supposedly in hiding, it wasn't as if he had anything else on his schedule.

Fort Lauderdale was much quieter than Miami Beach had been. No frenetic energy pumping off the sidewalks. Much less in the way of eye-bleeding neon signs. And certainly no music blaring. Not knowing the city, she followed the nav screen, winding through the small downtown area and out toward the ocean. Passing by the larger hotels, she turned onto the next street and pulled over at 131 Grace Drive.

She stared at the building. Lake Largo Motel. It looked the sort of place students would hang out and party. Kind of an odd choice for this particular venture. Glancing down the street, she spotted a CVS on the opposite corner all lit up like a welcoming beacon.

For a moment she debated the merits of simply parking at the motel but shrugged and rolled her eyes before executing a neat U-turn and found a spot at the back of the CVS. Call it a lifetime of training...courtesy of Danny Dawson...or simply his recent paranoia leaking into her headspace, but it did feel better knowing she had taken every precaution. She opened the side pocket of her backpack and fished out the second key from the locker in Indianapolis. Early or not, she was going in and getting this over and done with.

The night air was soupy and felt too thick to breathe. Or maybe the breathing thing was just nerves. Either way, for a minute she struggled to get enough oxygen. In her old life, this day would have been a walk in the park, but, man, she felt tired and strung out.

Guess I've lost my life-of-crime chops, she thought. *And I'm not sorry for it.*

Keeping to the shadows, she jogged down the road and made her way across to the motel parking lot. She took the stairs to the second level and walked along the outdoor corridor to number twenty-seven. He had to pick a room with a seven in it, of course. She knocked once then used the key to unlock the door. Inside, the room was dark.

"Pops?" she called out softly.

There was no response. As she eased away from the open doorway and positioned herself against the wall, she slid a hand in and groped until she found the light switch. She flicked it on and quickly retracted her arm. Waiting several beats, she cautiously inched her face to the opening and peered inside. The small room was empty. Searching the corridor and casting a glance around the parking area below to be certain no one was watching, she slipped into the room leaving the door slightly ajar.

Silently, she approached the bathroom, pushed the door open and hit the lights. No one lurked behind the shower curtain. She catalogued the room. Double bed. TV. Small table and two chairs. Tiny kitchenette with sink, fridge, and microwave.

Mia hurried back to the door, checked outside once more then shut it and turned the deadbolt. She repositioned the curtains and made sure there were no handy gaps for spying eyes. Then she searched the room.

And found nothing.

After settling on the bed, she propped a pillow behind her back before closing her eyes. She cleared her mind, working to slow her breathing and fully open herself. She saw flashes of all sorts of people, and as she'd suspected, most of them were young. None were her father. She picked up the TV remote and held it to her chest not finding him there, either. Nope, he hadn't been in the room.

She checked the time. Just shy of eleven p.m. which meant she was an hour early for their rendezvous. She'd assumed he would've been holed up here, but this motel room was obviously another ruse to confuse the men perusing him. She couldn't remember a time he'd gone to such lengths, and it made her distinctly uneasy. Maybe she should dump the key and be on her way.

She removed the backpack and unzipped the main compartment before sifting through until she found the pink swim cap with the key taped inside. Outside, she heard a vehicle pull into the lot below. Headlights cut across the parking lot illuminating a rising layer of dust before abruptly cutting out. The driver's door opened and a man lurched out and hurried toward the stairs and out of sight.

She waited breathlessly until the knock came. Three taps in rapid succession, pause, two taps, pause, one tap.

The first thing she saw was her father's cocky smile. Though once she'd pulled him into the room, she noted he was pale, and sweat beaded on his forehead. Still, his smile widened, and he opened his arms, pulling her into a hug and kissing the side of her head.

"Jenny, girl. I knew I could count on you. We always made a great team. Tell me the truth now. You've been having the time of your life today, haven't you?"

Mia stepped back and out of reach. "Hardly. Can't say I miss any of this."

"You parked away from here?"

She nodded. "Just like old times. Anyway, I got the key from Flamingo Park, so I've done my part."

He clapped his hands. "Brilliant work. No trouble?"

"None." She paused and gazed into those familiar blue eyes. "The cancer is bad?"

"Don't you worry your head about it. Once I collect all my bits and pieces and turn them into cash, I'll be able to start on a new experimental treatment. They say it's giving good results. Plus, I'll be living like a king."

"Where will you be?"

Lifting his index finger in the air, he shook his head. "Better that you don't know. If you want, I can contact you once I'm settled. Let you know how things are going."

She thought of Roman. His anger and disappointment. She thought about her quiet life in Dalton.

"Sure, I'd appreciate you keeping me in the loop," she said, handing him the pink swim cap. "So…I think I'll take off. Good luck with everything. I hope it works out."

"It will. You'll see. I'll be right as rain in a few months and a wealthy man to boot. Maybe then we can talk about you taking a cut. I'd like to be able to give you something. It would mean a lot to me."

"Yeah...I don't think so, but I appreciate the offer. Bye, Pops."

"Goodbye, my beautiful darling."

She'd barely slipped her backpack in place when the sound of squealing tires cut through the night. Danny killed the lights and carefully pulled back the edge of the curtain, peering out. The light from the parking lot shone on his face.

"Trouble," he said under his breath.

She pressed in beside him. "What kind of trouble?"

"The bad kind. I knew they were tailing me, but I thought I'd given them the slip." She heard him swallow in a gulp. "I guess they followed me after all." He leaned his head against the door frame and briefly closed his eyes before turning to face her. "I'll distract them, and you make a run for it. Take the key, and we can meet up later. You still have the phone from the first locker?"

She nodded. "I've got it, but why don't we just call the police?"

"No police. I'll figure this out. Quick as a cat, that's me. I'll make it through. You drive south on I-95 and get off at Exit 38. There's a Sunoco on the right. Drive around back, and pull over to the picnic area behind the trees. I'll call you when I've shaken them off and tell you where to meet. Give me a couple of minutes, then go left out of the door and take the far stairs. You can sneak around the side and get farther down the road before darting across to wherever you stashed your ride."

"I'm not leaving you here. Come with me, Pops. I'm guessing these men are dangerous."

"They are, love. They most definitely are." He patted her cheek. "But they won't kill me because otherwise how will they recover the diamonds? I'm going out now so be ready."

Chapter Six

Danny was gone so quickly Mia didn't have time to say another word. She slid along the wall until she reached the window and could watch out. Three men stepped out of a large SUV, their heads turning left and right as they scanned the area. She couldn't see her father.

One of the men stayed with the vehicle, and the other two split up, each walking to one end of the row of rooms. They disappeared below the balcony for several seconds, then she heard shouting. The man by the SUV whirled around and pointed behind him, and the other two men took off running toward the neighboring parking lot.

Mia eased the door open and slipped out. She could still see the man by the SUV, but his attention was firmly fixed off in the distance. Thankful that several of the lights above the room doors were burned out, she crawled along the floor as quietly as she could keeping close to the wall.

"Over there, Jimmy," one of the men shouted from below. "I can see that bastard near the green Toyota. Get 'im."

Faster now, Mia crabbed along. When she reached the stairs, she stopped short at the sound of a car door slamming. An engine roared and tires squealed. Glancing down through the railing she caught sight of the SUV flying out onto the road then skidding as it turned into the next driveway. She bolted down the stairs and ran under the balcony trying to see where her father had gone.

The building next door was a dive bar with a faded and peeling sign proclaiming it to be Seb's Seafood and Spirits. There were only a handful of cars parked outside. In the corner by the door, two of the men chased Danny Dawson along the back until he disappeared into some shrubbery.

"Hey, over here," Mia yelled, waving her arms.

The men turned, one of them raising a gun and pointing it in her direction. Even though they were at least eighty feet away, she started to shake. She spun and fled toward the stairs she'd come down. Behind her the SUV's engine gunned.

Noticing a light on in reception, she pounded her fist against the glass. "Call the police. These men are going to bust up the motel." A pair of startled eyes met hers, and the man leapt off his chair and charged toward the door. "Don't come out. Call the police," she repeated as she ran past.

She took a quick glance over her shoulder, just in time to see the SUV jerk to a stop only a few feet away. The man stared at her, and in that brief second, she recognized the face of the driver even though it had been half a dozen years.

"Go, go, go," she chanted under her breath, turned and sprinted away.

Past the end of the building, over a rickety fence, through a parking lot with a lone car, along a dirt path and into another parking lot, she realized this one was packed to the gills. She crouched between two cars, gasping, sweat running down her back, and inched along until she had a view of the way she'd come. She appeared to be alone for the moment. Shaking with relief, she sank to the ground.

Music drifted out from the nightclub. A techno beat. People laughed. Two couples stood smoking by the front door, one of the women more than a little tipsy and leaning on her date for support. In the distance, sirens sounded.

Slowly, she eased up and glanced toward the motel. Headlights shone out, pointing toward the road. She carefully retraced her steps until she came to the parking lot with the single car. Using it for cover, she strained through the darkness to see what was happening with her father and the men.

"I called the police," someone shouted. "You'd better get gone, and don't come back."

A gunshot rang out in the night. Mia's breath caught. Three more shots came in quick succession.

Sneaking along the back of the motel now, she pushed through overgrown weeds and garbage, hoping the noise didn't give her away. On the other side, she stepped onto the property of Seb's Seafood and Spirits. Choosing a pickup truck to use for cover, she scuttled toward it. A vehicle sounded on the road. She risked a glance and was rewarded to see the SUV peel away.

Standing upright now, she surveyed the mostly empty lot, then looked back toward the motel. Where the hell was her father? She walked to the back of the bar and searched the area where she'd last seen him disappear...but found nothing. Two wailing police cars raced down the road to the motel, and she squatted down again. No way could she afford to get caught up in this mess.

People had started coming out of various rooms at the motel and were gathering by the front office. The police cars parked askew so they blocked the exit. Four officers stepped out onto the asphalt. The strobing blue lights colored the night.

Behind her, something sounded and a creeping sensation spread across her skin. She made her way into the bushes again, blinking to clear her vision after looking at the lights by the motel. The sound came again. A sort of wet gasping noise, and she pushed her way toward the source.

Her foot bumped up against something, and she shifted lower, reaching out with her hand. The object was firm, As she felt along the side she encountered bare flesh. Risking discovery, she fished her phone from her pocket and switched it on, using the backlight from the screen. Aiming it up the body, her heartbeat pounded inside her head when she saw her father.

Blood covered the left side of his chest and pooled below him. He was gasping for air, and a thin line of blood trickled from his mouth. His eyes rolled side-to-side then fixed on her. He smiled, his teeth stained red.

"Jenny, my girl," he began to speak between breaths, each word an effort. "I'm in a...spot of...trouble. Go now. Take the key. The diamonds...yours. Find Lou." He coughed and clutched at his chest. "Lou needs...just...go. Jenny...I love...you."

Mia dropped the phone and put her hands against where the blood was gushing out and pressed hard, desperate to stop the bleeding. "No, Pops. Listen to me. The police are here. I'll get help. Hang on."

His eyes fluttered closed. "Too late." She leaned closer, struggling to hear the words. "Run...get...away. It's Dean and..."

"Come on. Stay with me," she sobbed.

She could no longer hear his breathing. Her hands were now slick with blood, but she grabbed the phone and clicked it on again. Her father's face was slack and his eyes empty, staring up into the night sky. Reaching out with her mind...she felt nothing. He was gone. Bowing over him, she gulped against the pain while tears poured down her cheeks.

"Oh, Pops. Why did you have to do this?"

Slowly she became aware of the activity from the Lake Largo Motel parking lot. People talking. Doors opening and closing. Flashlight beams crisscrossing the area. Two of the cops were poking around the perimeter.

It surely wouldn't be long before they widened the search. She couldn't do anything for her father now. But she could still get herself gone.

Swiping at her tears, she fought down the sobs then gently bent over him and closed his eyelids. She hated leaving him but he, more than anyone, would understand. Her mind began clicking back into gear, and she pushed her hands into the pockets of his shorts.

No wallet. He was a careful man to the end. But she did find another key. She shoved it in her pocket with her phone. Then patting her father's cheek, bent down and kissed his forehead.

"Goodbye, Pops. I'm sorry it ended this way."

She stood and carefully made her way behind the bar. Continuing on past an office building and another motel, she found shelter behind a tree and sank to the ground to regroup. She could no longer see the Lake Largo Motel, but there was increased activity on Grace Street with cars driving past both directions.

There was no doubt in her mind the police would search the properties on either side of the motel. Surely it wouldn't be long before they stumbled across her father's body. And what of the men? They'd still want to find her. Especially Dean. If Pops had double-crossed them, there'd be no giving up until they got their merchandise back. It was crystal clear, they didn't mind killing to get it.

Maybe she should come out of hiding and make herself known to the police. She hadn't really done anything wrong. Unless they were going to get sticky about her aiding and abetting a known criminal after he'd committed grand larceny.

But what could she really tell the cops anyway? She didn't know anything about where they'd stolen the diamonds. They could have been lifted from a jewelry store or a museum or even a single individual. Hell, it could be some kind of smuggling operation, for all she knew. Since Danny

Dawson had never run in those high stakes circles while she'd been with him, it wasn't as if she knew much about the players involved.

Except Dean. The driver of the SUV. She knew all about him.

Once, long ago, she'd thought she'd loved him, but he'd turned out to be her greatest mistake. It didn't surprise her one bit to learn he was swimming with the big fish now. He'd always dreamed big.

If she went to the cops, all she could really tell them was there were diamonds...somewhere...stolen from...she didn't know who. And she'd been working with her father to double-cross his partners and keep them for himself. One of the men had killed him. And Dean Chambers was involved. Though it was doubtful he still went by that name.

Really, there was little the cops could do with such scant information. Added to that, other than her father's murder, it was highly unlikely any of this took place in Fort Lauderdale or the surrounding area.

Besides, if those men discovered she'd gone to the police, she was as good as dead. Just like her father. No, the only way through this mess was to keep her mouth shut. Maybe Dean hadn't recognized her. Or if he had, he might not be able to find her. She was pretty well hidden, after all.

Pops found me.

But that was different. For all she knew, Pops may have been keeping tabs on her this past few years. It was unlikely Dean had given her more than a passing thought since they'd parted ways six or seven years ago.

So, it was decided then. No police. Instead, she'd bide her time and slowly make her way back to the CVS while keeping her eyes peeled for the cops and the three men. Once she deemed it safe enough, she'd drive away. Except not to the Fort Lauderdale airport. That was the obvious place to look. And not back to Miami either on the off chance they somehow tracked her flight into Florida.

Should she instead drive home? No. It would take, what, twelve or thirteen hours and she was already exhausted. No way she wanted to hole up in a hotel either just in case. Visualizing the cities north of there, she settled on Tampa. Once on the road she should be able to make it in a few hours. That she could handle.

Her cell vibrated in the pocket of her jeans and she pulled it out. The text was from Roman.

What's the deal? Are you safe?

She paused, hands shaking, and slowly exhaled. There was no point in telling him what was going on. He couldn't help her from Dalton, and it would only cause more worry. Scratch that, he'd be terrified for her.

I'm fine. Just about to head out. I'll text again when I board the plane. Love you.

Three dots popped up on the screen indicating Roman was typing. They disappeared for a few seconds, returned again for close to a minute, before going away again. She waited, hoping like crazy, but when several minutes passed she realized he wasn't going to respond.

She wished she didn't have to tell him what happened. It would only infuriate him further, but hadn't she vowed only last night there'd be no more lies? Besides, he needed to know in case Dean and his cohorts somehow found their way to her house.

More than anything, she regretted agreeing to help her father. He might still be alive if she'd said no. And Roman wouldn't be so mad he could barely text her a one-line message. And she wouldn't be hiding behind a tree in the middle of the night trying to avoid the police.

Nor would she be covered in blood, either, she realized noticing the sticky dampness on the front of her jeans. No way she could walk up to the well-lit drugstore looking like she'd been in a cage fight. Not to mention getting through the airport without attracting attention.

Why hadn't she thought to bring a change of clothes? Stupid. So stupid. Suddenly she remembered the workout gear from the locker in Indianapolis and quietly eased off her backpack. Pushing her phone inside the main compartment, she clicked it on and examined the black pants and pink top. Ladies small. They should do the trick.

She stripped off her blouse and used it to clean her hands then pulled on the new top. A little tight in the boobs but it would work. The pants fit her like a glove, and thankfully she was wearing running shoes so the outfit would look complete. While digging around in the pack, she found the mostly full bottle of water from the plane. She carefully poured some into her hand and splashed her face before again using the blouse as a towel. That would have to hold her for now. Once back in the car she could do more damage control if necessary.

Sometime later, three more police cars careened down Grace Drive. By then, Mia had made it all the way to where Grace crossed Ocean Street. She waited until Ocean was clear of cars, crossed and then crossed back over to the far side of Grace. Down the street, the cops had set up a blockade, and she could see shadowy figures walking along the side of the road.

Skirting around the far side of the CVS and approaching the lot from the back to avoid the security cameras, she slid behind the wheel of the rental. With shaky hands, she readjusted the rearview mirror and studied herself. A smudge of blood darkened the side of her neck, and there was more still under her chin. She quickly pulled out the water bottle and blouse again, dabbing at the stains.

Blood caked around her fingernails, but she couldn't worry about that now. The priority was getting out of there before the police widened the search area. Adrenaline coursed through her veins, and she started the engine and pulled slowly out of the parking lot then made a right onto Ocean Street.

As soon as she could, she cut west, weaving and turning, until she saw the signs for I-95. It didn't seem that anyone followed her. Wary still, she sped along for almost ten miles, then began a series of exits and entrances onto the freeway, going a bit north, then back south, before assuring herself she'd done everything she could to shake a tail.

Finally merging back onto the northbound freeway, she settled into the fast lane. The muscles in her arms and back relaxed a smidgeon. It was almost three o'clock by the time she jumped over to I-75 on the west border of Florida. She began to yawn. Great big, jaw-cracking motions that had her eyes watering. She knew it wasn't only fatigue. With the adrenaline finally drained away, she was left running on fumes.

Exiting close to the airport, she arrowed toward the golden arches and pulled in as close to the door as she could get lest she need to make a speedy getaway. Inside, she made her way to the bathroom. There she used her travel toothbrush and plenty of soap, scrubbing her fingernails until they were squeaky clean. Realizing strands of her hair and her right ear were also caked in red, she used the water bottle and poured it over her head then pulled out the cardigan she'd worn at the start of her trip and mopped up the wetness as best she could.

Finally, she pried off the blood-encrusted case of her phone and ran it under the hot water tap, pulled out the clothes she'd been wearing and placed the lot inside the wet cardigan, fastening up the buttons and tying the arms around the bundle of them. Back in the restaurant, she ordered a coffee to go. Exiting out of the parking lot, she drove another block to a Burger King, found the dumpster bin in the back, and disposed of the incriminating clothing.

Tampa International Airport was busier than she'd expected given the early hour. After finding an appropriate chair off to the side, she used her phone to bring up the Expedia site and began looking for flights all the while keeping a watch on the pedestrian traffic.

She wished she'd been able to get a better look at the two men with Dean. As it was, all she could say with certainty was they were Caucasian or possibly Hispanic and both had medium builds. It wasn't much to go on, that was for sure.

With full attention back to the phone, she scrolled down the screen searching for the earliest available flight to Nashville. In the terminal, someone shouted, "Over here," and running feet slapped against the tile floor. Heart thumping, she shrank back and prepared to flee, but the man continued toward a woman with a pile of luggage. Mia exhaled slowly and deliberately and closed her eyes.

You won't feel safe until you book the damned ticket and get through security. So do it already.

Her finger hovered over the Buy Now button of a Nashville bound United flight leaving in just over an hour. Glancing around again, she resubmitted the search, this time for LaGuardia. She knew it was foolish since the odds of Dean and the thugs following her here had to be tiny but routing home through New York felt safer. And she'd do whatever it took to protect her new life.

After purchasing her seat, she quickly made her way through security and out to the gates. Thankful to find a Ron Jon Surf Shop open, she bought a baseball cap with a *Love and Peace* patch sewn above the bill. She bundled her hair up under the cap and pulled out her sunglasses, then hunkered down at the gate and counted the minutes until the boarding process started.

She stalled until the very end of the line before stepping up with her phone screen displaying the boarding pass. Once inside the plane, she waited patiently as those ahead struggled to stuff carry-on luggage into overhead compartments and find their seats.

Using the time, she scanned the passengers. Definitely no Dean. His blonde hair was easy to spot. There were a few men who might possibly have been his companions, but she was quickly able to rule out all of them except for one as they appeared to be traveling with women or children or both.

The lone man in question had an aisle seat three rows in front of hers. He looked up when she approached, and she smiled nice and big.

"These early morning flights are a killer, right?" she said.

"You said it. Wouldn't make it through without my latte." He lifted a Starbucks cup as if in salute.

"Lucky you. I was running late and didn't have time to get mine yet. Have a good flight."

As she inched by him, she decided it was unlikely he was one of the bad guys. First of all, he had on loafers. And secondly, she'd bet her SUV the tie he was wearing with the paisley pattern was a genuine Hermes. That was a lot of money to spend on creating a cover.

Anyway, he couldn't do anything to her on the plane, and when they disembarked in New York she'd watch him carefully. Still, it didn't hurt to make certain. She pretended to trip and putting out a hand on the seatback for support, rested her fingers on his shoulder and let her mind go. His mind was so open it was like reading a book.

His name was Jared and he worked for Deloitte Touche. He was returning home to New York after a forensic accounting conference. It was his girlfriend's birthday tomorrow. Kate was her name. And tonight he had a dinner reservation at The Empire Rooftop and tickets to the ballet.

Mia continued on to her seat and sank down with relief. She was safe. At least as far as she could tell. Eyes gritty with fatigue, she pushed her backpack under the seat in front, buckled her seatbelt, and fell into sleep even before the plane had taxied away from the gate.

Two hours of downtime in a cramped airplane didn't put a dent in her exhaustion. In fact, she felt worse when they touched down in New York. As she trudged off the plane, she realized she'd forgotten to text Roman. Shrugging, she decided it probably made more sense to wait until she'd booked the next flight since then she could tell him exactly what time she'd be home.

Inside the terminal, her pulse quickened as she scanned faces and tried to read the energy. No one darted out to grab her. No one looked her way. No shifty-eyed hoodlum began following her to Starbucks. Using a large woman in line behind her as a shield from the people walking by, Mia shrank back and let out a relieved breath.

She pulled out her phone and began scrolling the options for getting to Nashville and was dismayed to discover the next few planes were completely full. The first flight she could snag wasn't due to leave for four hours.

Great. Super. Because there was nothing more fun than hanging around an airport when you were running on two hours of sleep while worried for your safety because your father had just been killed practically in front of you. Her eyes filled with tears, and she blinked at them furiously.

"Welcome to Starbucks. What can I get started for you?" The woman behind the counter beamed out a smile.

"Um...venti soy Chai tea latte. Extra hot," Mia said, trying not to sob.

"Name?" the woman asked.

"Mi...Martha," Mia corrected herself quickly.

She walked to the end of the counter to wait for the latte, grabbed a napkin, dabbed at her eyes and took stock.

You have got to pull it together, girl. You're tougher than this. You know you are. And in a few hours, you'll be home.

Thinking of home reminded her of Roman, and she looked down at her phone again with a sigh.

Plane was delayed. Won't touch down until 5:15. Miss you.

The response text pinged back within seconds. Um…engagement party…you remember that right?! Thought we promised my parents we'd arrive early…guess I'll head over as planned, and you'll get there when you get there.

Shit. Shit. Shit. With everything that had happened in the last twenty-four hours the party had gone right out of her mind. It seemed this New York detour wasn't the best idea after all. She shook her head. No, it had been more than worthwhile because if there was even the slightest chance Dean traced her leaving the scene this would hopefully throw him off the trail.

Sorry. I'll get there as soon as I can. Promise.

I'd be careful throwing around words like 'promise' right now.

In a flash her temper rose wild and ferocious.

Back off. I'm doing the best I can.

Guess we have different definitions of best. See you at the party if it's not too much bother.

Bite me.

She clicked off the phone without checking to see if he responded.

"Is there a Martha here? I have a Chai latte for Martha."

Mia raised her hand. "That's me."

Still furious about the exchange with Roman, she took a gulp and promptly burned the roof of her mouth. Shit burgers. It hurt. Would this stupid, awful trip ever end?

It was almost 7:30 when Mia pulled up to her house that night. Murphy's Law meant the flight home from LaGuardia had been delayed for God knows what reason, and then she'd hit traffic coming out of Nashville. She'd called straight through to Molly and Frank as soon as she landed, explaining the situation, but she hadn't bothered contacting Roman. Her mood was dark enough without another run-in with him. The dumb jerk.

The minute she stepped inside the front door, she was attacked by a pile of wagging wiggly dogs, and it melted her heart.

"Oh, my goodness, I missed you guys like crazy. Were you good babies? Did you take care of the house for me?"

Tucker yipped his response while Mac took possession of Mia's lap and pressed his face to hers and the other two ran and leaped about. She breathed them in. Their doggy scent and the joy of the reunion buoyed her immensely. Now if only she didn't have to go to this stupid party.

She kissed the top of Mac's head and ran a hand along Layla's side before pushing to her feet and squaring her shoulders. But she did have to go to the stupid party, and though she felt as if she'd been trampled by elephants, she'd do her darnedest to put on a good show. She'd smile and chat and fawn over Molly and Frank and act like there was nowhere else she'd rather be.

And Roman could be damned.

Chapter Seven

Roman nodded and smiled at Kevin, a detective from the Dalton police department. Kevin's girlfriend, Lisa, nattered on and on while he frantically tried to pick up the thread of the conversation.

"It sounds like a great time," he ventured.

Lisa's face went stiff. "My mother had food poisoning so badly she had to be hospitalized. We were all sick. Not sure how that's a great time."

Roman swallowed and caught Kevin's smirk. "I meant before the food poisoning. When everyone was having fun on the …um…cruise?"

"We were at the beach house." She punched his arm and smiled. "Clearly I must be boring you to tears, so I'll shut up now."

He shook his head. "No, of course not. Sorry, Lisa. I'm having trouble concentrating."

"Is everything okay?" Kevin asked.

"Sure. Sure. Of course. Just a lot going on tonight. And I've never been one for big, fancy parties."

"Look." Lisa clapped her hands. "There's Mia. She made it. Love her outfit. Very classy."

Roman followed Lisa's gaze and saw Mia standing with his mother and another woman. Mia was stunning in black dress pants and a green shimmery top that hugged her curves. Her fiery hair had been tamed into an up-do and green stones sparkled at her throat and ears. Her lips moved into a smile, and she bent down and kissed his mother on the cheek.

These last twenty-four hours had been an emotional maelstrom of epic proportions. He'd been so frightened for her then later furious that she'd put herself in unnecessary danger on top of the lying. Now, seeing her standing there, her breathtaking beauty and that warm smile beaming out, it was a punch to the gut. Her eyes tracked over to him, and her lips went flat as she tipped her head and nodded.

Fuck that, he thought, pushing past Kevin and making his way toward her.

"Wow. Ten after eight. So glad you could join us," he said, keeping his tone neutral.

"Now, Roman, it couldn't be helped. Mia's business is important and plane schedules are out of our control," Molly said soothingly. "She's here now, and that's all that matters."

He nodded. "Yeah. Of course."

"How are you?" Mia asked. "Did you have a good day?" Her smile hit solidly on the middle of the polite meter and her eyes flicked over him and across to a group beyond his right shoulder.

"I had a great day, thanks for asking." He took her arm and pulled her away from his mother. "As guests of honor, we should mingle."

"Are you trying to piss me off?" she asked in an undertone, the perfect smile still in place.

"No."

"Then stop tugging at me."

He dropped her arm with a thud. "Fine. No contact then."

She turned until her eyes met his, and he saw the fury flashing there. "Good idea because I'm this close to punching you in the face."

"Oh, man. That was the wrong thing to say."

"Roman, I'm pretty sure you don't want to make a scene at your parents' party in front of a good portion of the town. So, I'd suggest you leash the crazy, smile like you mean it, and take me around to meet everyone. Think you can do that?"

She was pushing every one of his buttons, and she knew it. Scratch that, she was glorying in it. He gritted his teeth and shoved his hands in his pockets. He wasn't the one in the wrong here. Where was the apology? The contrition? How dare she come waltzing back as if butter didn't melt in her fucking mouth and talk to him that way.

Except she was right about causing a scene. Dammit all to hell.

Fine. He could pretend to make nice. But later, oh Lordy, they were going to have it out.

He smiled and nodded. "Darling," he drawled. "Let's go meet some people."

Since Roman stayed behind at the end of the party to help his father wrestle some furniture back into place, Mia had beaten him home. Lights blazed throughout the house, and Layla waited inside the front door.

He stormed in, ready to do battle. The vice grip he'd been using to keep his emotions in check all night, loosened notch by notch until the temper ran wild and free once again. Oh, he was so ready for this. Not seeing her on the couch where he'd expected, or in the kitchen, and realizing the rest of the dogs were nowhere around, he ran up the stairs.

"I'm home," he called out. "And you have a hell of a lot of explaining to do."

Stomping down the corridor, he turned into the bedroom and stopped short. She lay, fully clothed and curled in the fetal position, facing away from him. A full glass of wine sat on the bedside table. Mac stood beside the bed, apparently guarding his mistress, while Tucker and Fifi had settled down at her feet on the duvet even though they normally slept in one of the multitudes of dog beds scattered around the floor.

No way, he thought, his vision going red with fury. She couldn't pretend to sleep her way out of this argument. He strode up to the bed as Mac watched him, the corner of his lip lifting into the barest hint of a snarl.

"Sit," he snapped out, pointing to the floor. "She ain't hiding behind you tonight. Go on, sit."

The Doberman's butt sank slowly to the ground, but, like a laser, his entire being remained focused on Roman. Reaching down, Roman nudged Mia's shoulder. Her head flopped to the side. He did it again, with the same result. Then, with his anger reaching crescendo, he grasped her elbow and gave her one hard shake.

Her eyes opened, bleary and bloodshot, and swiveled up to him. She smiled and patted his hand. "Hey, baby," she mumbled. "Gonna sleep some more."

She was gone again in the next second, and Mac pushed in and licked her hand before turning accusing eyes on Roman. Defeated, depressed beyond reason, he lowered down onto the bed beside her and stroked a hand across her cheek. The jewelry was gone, and her face was bare of makeup.

"Why do you have to be so beautiful?" he whispered. "And why do I have to love you so much it terrifies me?"

After a moment, he reached over and drank down her wine in greedy gulps. Then he made his way back downstairs and dealt with the lights before stripping off and curling around her. In the darkness, he heard Mac sigh and flop down onto his cushion at the side of the bed. He thought of the previous night and how he'd been beside himself with worry, tossing and turning into the early morning hours. Now, wrapping an arm around her shoulders, he drifted off to sleep within seconds.

Mia woke first and carefully shimmied out of bed. Still tired but with her sleep deficit more than partway restored, she stripped off last night's clothes and decided comfort would rule the day, picking out a pair of yoga pants and matching hoodie. Though she longed for a shower, she wanted her quiet kitchen and dogs more, so she quickly brushed her teeth and splashed water on her face.

As she slipped through the bedroom, the dogs hurried ahead down the hall, but she paused by the door and gazed back at the bed. Roman lay on his back, chest rising and falling rhythmically. His hair sleep-tousled and the lines of his face soft. Her heart squeezed. She might still be mad as all get out but, God help her, she loved him like crazy.

Reaching out with her mind, she sighed just a little. He was awake.

Guess he wants some alone time before we throw down.

Fine with her. She could use the peace and quiet to regroup.

Downstairs, she fed the dogs and let them out the back door into the run. Once she'd steeped a pot of peppermint tea, she sat out on the deck with her mug and phone. While taking a moment to breathe in the soft morning air, she watched the dogs sniff and play in the grass before turning her attention to the screen of her phone. It was time to see what was going on in Florida.

She found the story first up in the *Fort Lauderdale Sun Sentinel*. **Trouble at Lake Largo Motel** the headline screamed. Scrolling down, she read that police had responded to manager Brandon Michaels' call about three men acting suspiciously just before midnight at the motel. Once on scene, four gunshots were heard in the vacant land behind the neighboring bar where they subsequently found the body of a man.

The Fort Lauderdale Police Department was asking for assistance from anyone who witnessed the incident or had any information on either the dark Escalade SUV or the men who were seen in the vicinity.

The dead man was described as mid-sixties with light red hair. Approximately five-foot-nine inches. Slim build. No identification. Police were continuing to investigate the scene and gather information from the Lake Largo Motel. Clicking another page online, Mia found a similar story on the first page of the *South Florida Times*.

Her heart squeezed with grief. Poor Pops. Always living on the edge and now it had gotten him killed. She dropped the phone in her lap and rubbed her palms together remembering the feel of his blood covering her hands.

Beside her, the door opened and Roman stepped out. His hair was wet from the shower, but he hadn't bothered to shave. He stood barefoot with eyes heavily shadowed.

"Hey," he said.

"Hey." She grasped her phone again and met his gaze. "I guess we should talk?"

He shrugged. "If we're going to get into it I think I'd better get caffeinated first. Give me a minute."

She gazed over to where the greenhouse sparkled in the morning sun and remembered the night of the proposal when she'd thought she had it all. How had things gone so terribly wrong in...what...surely it was more than ten days? She counted back. Nope. Ten whole days. That's how fast she'd screwed everything up. Maybe, in the end, she wasn't cut out for relationships, she thought, brooding into her tea.

When Roman returned and made his way over to the chair beside her, she shifted to face him. "Okay, let me start by saying I'm sorry about showing up late to our engagement party and even more sorry about lying. I won't do it again."

He sighed. "We need to talk about the *why*. It worries me you felt you had to lie in the first place. Have I ever been unreasonable or hard to talk to?"

"No. Not especially. It's difficult to explain." She shrugged. "You may not be on the force any longer but you're a cop to the bone. Most everything's black and white to you. I already made you wiggle your moral compass when I told you my real identity, and you found the outstanding warrants for some of my aliases. I didn't want to put you in that position again."

"I thought the plan going forward was for you to stay on the right side of the law."

"I am. Really. This was a one-time thing, and it was for my father. I know he wasn't the best parent in the world, but he was all I had, and he loved me in his way."

He nodded slowly. "Okay. I get that. From my end, though, it felt like you chose him over me. A man who, even though you say he tried his best, hardly gave you much of a life. And worse than that, turned you into a criminal well before your tenth birthday. Let's not forget you've been estranged from him for years. What about the next time he calls for help? How do I know you won't go trotting off again?"

She took in a breath and stared out over the lawn again toward the greenhouse. "I won't because he's dead."

Roman shot straight up out of his chair. "What the hell? When? Were you there? Tell me what happened."

Still gazing away, she clicked on her phone and handed it to him. She heard him pace across the deck. The dogs, sensing the change in atmosphere, scrambled up the stairs beside her. Roman's breath came out in angry bursts, and Layla whined.

"It's okay girl," Mia crooned.

"It's not okay," Roman countered. "Tell me you weren't at the Lake Largo Motel last night?"

She shook her head. "They killed Pops, and there was nothing I could do. He was gone so fast." A tear teetered on the edge of her eyelid, finally plopping onto her cheek. Another one followed.

Roman crouched beside her, his hand reaching for hers. "Tell me everything, baby."

When she'd finished recounting the awful story, he sat back on his heels. "I don't even know what to say. That is some serious shit. This Dean guy. Do you think he recognized you?"

She swiped at her eyes. "I don't know. My hope is he's long forgotten all about me, but with Pops in the mix, I can't rule it out. I'm certain no one followed me back here, but that doesn't mean Dean won't find me."

Roman's fist tapped against the armrest of the chair. "What a fucking mess. I wish like hell you hadn't gone. It'd probably be best to come clean with the police."

"What? No. That's a terrible idea. I bet they'd be pretty interested in what I was doing there, don't you think? And if those men find out I went to the police, I'm as good as dead."

"You can be protected."

"By the cops? Come on. You and I both know that isn't a solution. A properly motivated person can get to anyone."

"You have a better plan?" he asked, an edge to his voice.

"Not yet. I'm working on it. The police will probably figure out Pops' identity by the end of the day. How long will they keep an unclaimed body?"

"Every state is different, but I would guess sixty days is the minimum. Why? You don't want to come forward as next of kin?"

"Not right now. It'll be a way for Dean and those jerks to track me."

"Tell me about this Dean guy. What's his story?"

Mia rubbed a hand over her face. "Talking about all this stuff is getting me wound up again. Let's walk."

He opened the gate, and they made their way across the lawn and began strolling along the tree line at the edge of the field. The dogs, delighted with the turn of events, ran with noses to the ground before circling back to the humans.

"It's a nice morning," Mia said, lifting her face to the sky. "And it's so darn good to be home." They walked on in silence for several minutes before she sighed. "Dean and I were a thing back in the day. We ran cons together and we were...you know...together."

Roman tried not to react but the muscles in his shoulders turned to concrete. "When was this?"

"Nine. Ten years ago. I was eighteen, and I'd been doing fine on my own, but then I ran into him in New Orleans. He'd been around here and there when I was young. His dad knew Pops though they never worked together. Anyway, Dean and I went for a drink in New Orleans and things built from there. It was nice having a partner again. Better than when it had been me and Pops."

Roman stopped and turned to her. "And what exactly did you and Dean do for money?"

Shifting her gaze to his face, she cocked an eyebrow. "You really want to know?"

His head shook slowly back and forth. "Nope. But I think I've gotta hear it so I have an idea of what and who we're dealing with."

She exhaled in a gust then shrugged. "We'd picked out a guy. A rich guy. Dean did recon and I'd sort of...befriended him. I'd string him along for a couple of weeks until I'd figured out alarm codes, safe combos, stuff like that. Then we'd clean him out. After, I'd try to stick with the guy for a bit to blow off any suspicion."

"And when you befriended these men did it include...um...physical benefits?" Roman's eyes slid away from hers, and he began walking again.

You vowed only the truth from here on in, she reminded herself.

"Yes. Sometimes. I did whatever was necessary to work the con. It was strictly business," she said, her tone forceful. Then she sighed, and when she spoke again her voice had softened. "Trust me, I'm not proud of what I did. That particular part of my life fills me with shame, but I can't go back and fix it, so it is what it is."

"And Dean, your supposed boyfriend, was okay with you sleeping with these men?"

Heat shot into Mia's cheeks. "He knew it was probably happening, but we never talked about it."

"Is that why you two split?"

"No." She sighed and looked away. "I guess it's probably the oldest story in the world. He played me for a fool, relieved me of all my money—which was considerable, I might add—then took up with a new partner. Another woman. A sultry brunette with a pouty mouth and huge brown eyes. I saw them in a bar about a month later. When I marched up to him full of fire and fury, he didn't apologize or even have the decency to look contrite. He just introduced me to Belinda with a smirking smile. I wanted to warn her but then I figured, what comes around goes around, so I gritted my teeth and smiled and walked away."

"And that was the last time you saw him?"

She shook her head. "No, I ran into him a few times after. Always with a different woman. The last time was in a restaurant in New York, he followed me to the restroom and said he missed me. That he'd made a mistake doing what he had and couldn't we try again? I told him there wasn't a chance in hell of us getting back together. The next morning he sent flowers to my hotel room and a card saying he was sorry. I went to Europe after that and didn't see him again. At least not until the night my father was killed."

Roman's pace quickened, and she had to jog to catch up. "I think that's enough for now," he said. "I need a break. I'm gonna head into town for a couple of hours and work on setting up my office. The furniture came yesterday."

"That's great, Roman. I can help. Or bring you lunch. It'd be—"

"No," he cut her off, his hand slicing through the air. "I don't want...it's best if I'm alone right now."

"It doesn't take a mind reader to see you're pissed. I already told you about my past, so this can hardly be a surprise."

He whirled to face her. "It's one thing hearing about something that happened a long time ago, but now you've gone and invited your past into our lives. Excuse me if I'm not doing cartwheels over the idea of spending quality time with your psychopathic ex-boyfriend and his gang."

She blinked at him. "I didn't invite any of this. It just happened."

His smile was brief. "No, baby, you made a choice to help your father, and now here we are."

"But that's not the only thing bothering you, is it?" She paused and studied his face. "I thought we'd already cleared this hurdle. You told me you could deal with who I was before, but you're actually not fine with it at all."

She backed away, and they stood staring at one another.

"Give me a break, okay?" Roman said. "Your past is a lot to swallow."

"Does this mean it's always going to be there between us and every time I make the smallest mistake, you'll throw it in my face? Because if so, I don't see how we're going to work." Her hand flicked back and forth between them. "I can't live the rest of my life being made to feel like a second-class citizen and constantly having to apologize for who I am. I think you'd better figure this out and get back to me."

Roman's shoulders slumped, and he rubbed a hand across his eyes. "This whole thing took me by surprise. That's all. I think I should be given a little latitude to catch my breath. So, I'm going into town to put my desk together, and we'll finish talking later. Over dinner maybe. Why don't I pick something up?"

"Fine. We'll talk later. I have lots of work to do anyway. I'm going to keep walking the dogs a bit longer. I'll see you tonight."

"Okay." Roman turned and took a few steps away before stopping and glancing back. "Hey, I'm really sorry about your father. It must have been horrible. I wish you hadn't been there to see it. You have your cell?"

She nodded numbly. "Yeah."

"Good. Keep it with you, okay?"

Mia didn't respond. Instead, she whistled for Tucker and Layla, who had made their way to the far side of the field and began walking toward the forest at the back of her property.

Later that afternoon, Roman turned at the sound of a knock on the open door of his office.

Kevin stood on the threshold and gave him a two-fingered salute. "There's Dalton's very own hot shot private eye in action. Are you solving the case of how come when you put one of these bastards together there're always leftover screws? It's a nice desk, bro."

"Thanks. Thought it would suit the décor."

"You mean the 'I'm a one man show and not wasting money on ambience' décor?"

Roman pointed a finger at him. "You got it in one. So, what's happening?"

"Not much. Just picking up some stuff from the hardware store. I have a DIY project myself. Lisa wants window boxes, and I told her I was the man for the job."

"Have you ever built anything?"

"Not unless you count the bird feeder from eleventh grade shop class."

"And it was such a thing of beauty." Roman chuckled. "I seem to remember you almost failed shop."

"Yeah, well, the teacher had it in for me. Besides, they're window boxes. How hard can it be?"

"Says every man right before he tries to build something to impress his lady. Aren't you past the impressing stage yet? You and Lisa have been together for almost two years."

Kevin exhaled on a nod. "I know. Time flies, man. I'm thinking of taking the plunge like you did with Mia. When you're with 'the one' and you know it, there's no reason to hold back, right?"

Roman tested the desk with his hand then shrugged and lowered a hip down. "No reason. Especially since you and Lisa know everything about each other. That's one great thing about growing up in the same town together."

"Sure. But, when it's a stranger like Mia, it can't hurt to have all that mystery swirling around the other person. Keeps it interesting."

"Too interesting," Roman muttered. "Hey, hypothetical question. Do you think people can change? I'm talking about the deep-down core elements. Aren't they pretty much set at birth?"

Kevin studied his friend's face. "What's going on, bro? I thought you seemed off at the party last night. You and Mia having problems?"

"I don't know. Maybe. This is on the down low, right?"

"Of course." Kevin made a scoffing sound in his throat. "What do you take me for—the town gossip?"

"No. Just...it's weird talking about it. Anyway, you know some of it from the thing before with my sister when we ran background on Mia. She basically started out on the wrong side of the law and stayed there for a lot of years. Not violent stuff, though. You understand?"

Kevin nodded slowly, his eyes intent on Roman. "Sure. Fraud and theft. That kind of thing, right?"

"Yep. But like I said, she did it for a while even when she was old enough to know right from wrong. Now it's years later and here we are in Dalton. Mia's living the good life, a respectable businesswoman, taxpayer, the whole nine yards. But isn't all that stuff from before still in her? How do I know she won't switch sides again?"

"Whoa. This is some serious wondering. Did something happen that's got your antennae buzzing?"

"She didn't do anything, if that's what you mean but…let's just say her past has come calling, and I'm worried she might be in trouble again."

"Well." Kevin rubbed a hand along his jaw. "If it was Lisa, I have to say I'd still want to be with her. At least as long as she wasn't actively embracing her dark side. Everyone has a dark side, man. With Mia, though, she was trained from birth to act on hers. I'd say her turning it around later was a big deal. Bigger than just us regular Joes living quiet lives and never being tested. Walking away like she did when it was the only thing she knew took flat-out guts. I take my hat off to her."

"Yeah. I do too." Roman nodded. "Most of the time. But right now, I'm pissed at having to deal with this crap from her past. Pissed that it's infringing on our life when all I want to do is find my damned footing again." He sighed. "It's been tough getting going after Anita and Tony…"

"Hey, I know. That was a shit hand you got dealt. And Mia was great through the whole thing. I guess she's cooler with your family and history than you are with hers, huh?"

Roman frowned. "I guess."

"Anyway, I'd better book. Those window boxes won't build themselves. Plus, I see a pretty great sexual reward coming my way tonight."

"Well…enjoy. Hey, we should go out for a beer sometime."

"Absolutely. I'm around whenever. Later."

"See ya."

Chapter Eight

Mia had long since settled her emotions by the time Roman arrived home with beer and pizza. She'd even managed to get some work done, which was a bonus since she'd missed two days going to Florida and was now considerably behind on orders. She still had one more piece to finish for tomorrow morning and was determined to stay up as long as it took to meet the deadline. She'd worked too darn hard building this business to let it start slipping now.

"How was your day?" she asked.

"Fine. And yours?"

"Good enough." She slid the pizza box across the counter and lifted the lid before nodding approvingly. "I'm starved."

"Me too." Roman reached into the cupboard and pulled down two plates. "You want a beer?"

"No thanks. I've got passion fruit iced tea on the go."

"Yuck."

They each loaded their plate with pizza slices, and Mia handed Roman a napkin before sitting at the bistro table in the bay window. She took a bite and moaned.

"So good. Why don't we get pizza more often?"

"Cause you're always cooking that healthy stuff." He put up a hand when a line dug in between her brows. "Hey, I'm not complaining. I like the healthy stuff just fine, but you did ask."

She nodded. "Your point." Wiping her mouth with a napkin, she cleared her throat. "I've been thinking. For now, let's put aside whatever trouble you're having with me and my past. And since you came back, and brought pizza to boot, I'm assuming you're not breaking up with me?"

Roman reached over and squeezed her hand. "No. Of course not. I'm trying—"

"So," she cut him off. "We're both still in this thing, but there are problems with our relationship. Big problems, apparently. Fine. But right now I think we should focus on dealing with the 'Dean and his thugs' situation. After, when we have some breathing room, we'll tackle the other."

He nodded, his hand still covering hers. "I guess that makes sense, but I don't think we should leave the other thing too long, do you?"

"No. Of course not. It's important."

"I agree. What do you propose for our Dean problem?"

"We need to find the diamonds."

"What?"

"Yeah. Think about it. If we turn the diamonds over to the police it takes care of two things. Firstly, the cops won't be all that inclined to come after me. At least I don't think they will. And number two, I'll be useless to Dean, and he won't have any reason to hunt me down." She shrugged. "Unless he just wants a straight-out revenge kill—in which case I can't think of what to do other than moving to some remote island in the West Indies. Plus, I'm not sure he's the revenge-kill kind of guy."

"It could work. The West Indies, I mean. Would you be topless and wearing a grass skirt every day? Because if so then I think it will more than work."

"Not with my fair skin. I'll likely be covered from head to toe and slathered in way too much sunscreen."

"Huh? In that case I guess we'd better find the shiny rocks. Do you know where they are?"

"Not really. I know Pops split them out and stashed them in at least two places. I still have the key from the locker in Miami though."

"Any idea what it opens?"

"Not sure. Thought I'd try and get a reading from it. Pops also mentioned something about this Lou person, so that's another angle to pursue."

She paused and took a bite of pizza. Roman sat back and studied her, a smile blooming on his face.

"And who is this Lou guy?"

"Lou is a woman. Mary Lou. I think she and my dad were together. I got a flash of a blonde with lots of makeup and big boobs. I'm guessing if we figure out his home base, Lou will be somewhere around. I just want to be really careful about exposing her to Dean. I have to think Pops was keeping her well-hidden."

"Okay. Sounds like we at least have a couple of starting points."

Once the pizzas had been demolished, Mia sat back and stretched her arms overhead. She let out a sigh. "Guess I might as well give it a whirl right now and see what I can get."

When she retrieved the backpack from the bedroom closet, she brought it downstairs to the kitchen table. She dug out the key she'd recovered from her father's pocket and the pink bathing cap and laid them in front of her. Then she closed her eyes and exhaled in a slow, steady stream while she cleared her mind. Opposite, Roman watched quietly.

She blinked her eyes open and reached for the bathing cap, pulling the tape off and removing the key. It was silver, small, and looked relatively new with no scratches. Placing the key on her palm, she closed her hand over it and opened herself fully.

The flash came immediately. She saw her father again. Alive. Smiling. Whistling "It's a Small World" and swinging his arm as he walked quickly along a dock. Beside him, the water sparkled under an intense blue sky. Seagulls swooped and cawed.

"Pops is in a shipyard...no, that's not the right term. It's a marina," she mumbled.

"What's he doing?"

"He's..." She paused, watching the vision roll forward. "He's carrying something. Sort of a bulky box but not that heavy. A man is cleaning a fish, and the birds are lining up on the edge of the pier because he's throwing them scraps. Shoot, it's gone. That's all I saw."

Roman leaned toward her. "Could you tell where? Did it seem like Florida?"

"I don't know. It was a long dock with lots of boats. It felt like the ocean, but I suppose it could have been a really large lake."

"How about names on the boats?"

Mia closed her eyes, her teeth worrying along her bottom lip. "No. The boats were off to my right, but the scene was oriented left to where the man was set up on a picnic table with the fish. Oh, he had a dog. A really cute dog. She was sitting under the table at his feet. A Cairn terrier like Toto from *The Wizard of Oz*."

Roman turned everything over in his mind. "Doesn't seem like there's much to go on. Do you even get the sense the boats or the marina have anything to do with whatever the key is for? Could it be your dad just happened to have it with him when he went to visit someone?"

"I don't know. He might own a boat for all I know. Maybe live on one? I sort of remember being on one at some stage when I was really young, and

I think my dad was driving or captaining or whatever it's called. Maybe. Ugh. This is frustrating."

"Think you'll be able to get more, or is it usually a one-shot deal?"

"I absolutely could get more. I'll try again later and for sure first thing tomorrow. I find I'm more open as soon as I wake. Must be because the subconscious mind is so close to the surface. If there's nothing new at that point, I'll try the other key. I don't want to do it now and contaminate my connection to the first one."

"Okay. On my end, I'm going to dig around some and see what I can turn up on Dean. You said his last name was Chambers?"

"Yeah, though I have no idea what he's going by now."

Roman nodded. "I want you to do something for me. Jot down a list of all the aliases he used when you two were working together plus the places you went. I'll track him through that time period and see what details I can gather. Also, go back to the times you ran into him later on and give me the cities and any names of people he was acquainted with."

"Why?"

"Because we need all the info we can get. He might still be associated with people from back then or maybe he's using an old alias. Hopefully, we can find him before he finds you."

"Okay. I'll put it together and shoot you an email." She stood, picking up her backpack and the keys.

"I have a necklace to finish up for the morning, so I'm going to keep working."

It was after midnight before she put down her tools and pushed back from the worktable. Upstairs, Roman was already in bed though he had his laptop balanced on his thighs. The light from the screen illuminated his face in the darkened room. While the dogs settled onto the various beds scattered around the floor, she slipped in beside him.

"I'm so tired I could hardly walk up the stairs," she said on a yawn.

"Will it bother you if I work for a bit longer?"

"I'm already asleep," she said, snuggling against him.

He glanced down at her, stroking a hand briefly across her head. "Goodnight."

"Goodnight."

He shifted, inching away until they were no longer touching. She squeezed her eyes shut while her heart hammered in her chest. Roman was a physically demonstrative person. At least he always had been with her. Normally, there was hugging and kissing. Often, he massaged tired shoulders and cramped hands from long hours of jewelry making. Always, he wrapped himself around her until she could feel his heartbeat against her shoulder.

It was frightening to realize there was nothing she could do, no easy fix, for the thing that was driving them apart. She couldn't go back in time and undo her past, after all. And would she even want to?

The answer was no. So much of what she had done in her early years was shameful, but at the same time, she had to believe it was all part and parcel of who she was today. It had been hard and lonely work turning her life around. And the years of struggle only made her more proud of the person she'd become.

No matter how much she cared for Roman, she couldn't live her life forever apologizing. And it felt harmful to her psyche to be with someone who didn't love her all the way through. She'd rather be alone—forever alone—than slowly have her self-worth chipped away. But lordy, if it came down to the crunch, it would be hard to let him go. She loved Roman, probably always would. And that was a love that went all the way through.

She rubbed her fingers over the engagement ring. *Please don't let this thing break us apart,* she prayed silently into the night.

When Roman came down the stairs the next morning, he found Mia sitting in the kitchen with her eyes closed and her cupped hands resting on the table in front of her. Mac, as usual, sat close by and looked adoringly at his master while Fifi, also a slave to hero worshiping, was pressed against the Doberman's flank. The other two dogs were nowhere to be seen. Likely outside playing, he decided.

He stood watching. Her hair was swept up in a messy bun with loose pieces framing her face, her generous mouth curved into a slight smile. God, she was beautiful. Sometimes when he looked at her, he couldn't believe she was his.

But then his stupid mind flashed to images of her with a bunch of faceless men. Letting them do whatever they wanted with her body so she and her psychopath of a boyfriend could rob them blind. As far as he was concerned, it was no different than being a prostitute. Except at least with that, it was a fair and honest exchange. The way she'd done it was somehow worse.

Mia isn't like that anymore and hasn't been for a long time.

He exhaled and shook it off as best he could. When she blinked and her eyes—soft in the morning light—met his gaze, his stomach clutched. He had to get past this. Let it go. Because as God was his witness, he loved her with everything he had.

"The marina was in San Francisco," she said. "I could see the Golden Gate Bridge in the distance."

"That's a start." He nodded. "Still, I'm betting there are a hell of a lot of marinas in the Bay Area. A name would be good."

She shrugged. "That's all I've got right now. I'm hoping when I go there, something will spark."

"When you *go* there?" he repeated slowly.

"Yes. As I suspected, the Fort Lauderdale police have identified Pops. That'll put Dean on edge and make him determined to find the diamonds as quickly as possible. I'm thinking I'll leave tomorrow. The sooner the better, really."

"I'm coming with you."

She smiled. "I was hoping you'd say that."

"What about the dogs?"

"I've found a decent kennel outside of Nashville. It's actually really cool. They have rooms sort of like a motel except the walls are glass. There are even beds and toys and a TV. I thought I could put Mac and Fifi in one and Layla and Tucker next door. I can arrange to have the dogs walked twice a day plus they get playtime on top of that. I hate leaving them, but I figure this is safer for everyone. You know…in case Dean shows up while we're gone."

"Makes sense." He cocked his head to the side and rubbed a hand along his jaw. "You know. We can go together but not 'go' together."

"What do you mean?"

"I'll be your surveillance guy. We drive separately. Don't sit together on the plane. Different hotel rooms. And I'll sort of follow along in your footsteps and look out for anyone tracking you. It'll be safer for you. If Dean or his men are somehow there, I can turn the tables and follow them."

"Wow. Look at you with your PI hat on. You're going to be a natural."

"I'd say that remains to be seen. I'm heading into town to hang at my office on the off chance anyone strolls in with a case. Send me the flight and hotel info when you've got it, and I'll book my passage west."

"Don't you want breakfast?"

"Nah. I'll grab something at Gabe's."

"Okay. Talk to you later," she said, smiling brightly. "Thanks for agreeing to come."

"There's nowhere else I'd rather be than with you."

She heard the jingle of his keys in the front hall. Then the door opened and shut, and all was quiet. Her smile faded.

With me but not 'with' me, she thought sadly.

Chapter Nine

Mia found it to be an odd experience being at the airport and traveling to San Francisco and knowing Roman was there, lots of time even seeing him, but pretending they were strangers. Keeping her eyes from straying to him was a constant battle of wills. The only saving grace was the cell phones.

"Anything?" she asked when he answered her call.

"All is quiet on the western front," he said. "How're you doing? After the dogs, I mean?"

She strolled around the food court trying to decide if she was hungry enough to eat a chickpea and veggie wrap. It looked like a lot of food.

"I'm okay, I guess. I hated leaving them there, especially Mac. I could feel how scared he was. This is the first time I've put him in a kennel. At least he has Fifi to comfort him."

"I'm sure he'll be fine once he settles in, and we'll only be gone a couple of days."

"I texted the kennel after I dropped off my car, and they say he's doing fine. Layla and Tucker are apparently doing better than fine and tearing around their room playing with all the toys. Let's hope I can find the marina quickly so we can get back home. Are you getting anything to eat?"

"Lining up at Subway right now. There's a foot-long roast beef calling my name."

"Extra horse radish?"

"You know it. Okay. Talk later."

"Bye."

She slid the phone back into her pocket and snagged an apple and a banana. That should fill the void for the time being. When the flight was called, she noticed Roman hung back. She slipped on her backpack and joined the line.

Roman had a seat near the back of the plane, and he passed by her on his way. She paid him no notice, instead continued scanning her fellow passengers. She couldn't see anyone suspicious. Her phone signaled, and she glanced down.

Don't think you were followed. We should be safe enough until we land in San Fran.

She texted back.

Dean is definitely not on the flight. Miss you. Have a good trip.

Back at you.

Upon landing in San Francisco, they kept up the charade, getting separate cars at two different car rental companies. He followed her out onto U.S. Route 101 then dropped back, putting extra distance between them. She moseyed along, looking out across the bay as she drove along Embarcadero. The day was overcast and foggy, lending a mystical air to the area as she passed under the Bay Bridge.

It didn't take long to check into the Bayside Motel on, appropriately enough, Bay Street. It hit dead center on the low end of basic, still it was cheap and had free Wi-Fi. Not as if they were there for a holiday. She didn't glimpse Roman anywhere in the vicinity, but he texted when she got to her room.

What's the plan?

Thought I'd start along this side of the bay and hit all the piers. You're going to follow?

Don't worry about me. Just do your thing. If I lose you I'll let you know. Feel anything yet?

Not so far. Okay. I'm heading out.

Mia soon realized that the majority of the piers off Embarcadero were not for small boats or boats at all really. Mostly there were restaurants, stores, aquariums, museums, and all the other attractions found in places that draw high volumes of tourists. She spotted a bench partway along Pier 7 and, disheartened and out of ideas, sank down onto it. To make matters worse, it had been raining off and on for the last few hours, and she was soaked through.

Her secret hope had been that once she arrived in San Francisco, she'd somehow know exactly where to go, or better yet, another vision would come to her. But she felt nothing from the area. It was almost as if her father had never been there at all. She shook her head. He had. She'd seen it with her own eyes. Boats. Sparkling water. Golden Gate Bridge over his right shoulder.

Now that she thought about it, it didn't make sense for the vision to have originated on this side of the bay. It had to have come from over by Oakland or maybe Berkeley. Mia pulled out her phone and brought up a map. As she zoomed in, she sighed with frustration. There were so many docks and marinas. It could take the better part of a week to search through every one.

She called Roman. "I'm going to head back. It'll be dark soon, and I'm starving. I saw a restaurant on the same block as our motel, so I'll pick something up and go back to my room."

"Sounds good. I'll meet you there. What's your room number?"

"Two eleven. See you in a bit."

They dug into burgers...veggie for Mia...and fries, they said little until the food was gone.

"I should have spent more time researching the area," Mia admitted. "I'm starting to worry this is a fool's errand."

Roman shrugged. "Maybe. But you had to try. You know, I was thinking we should come back here sometime when we can enjoy the place. It seems like a cool city."

"We should," Mia said, trying not to show how desperately pleased she was to hear that Roman still thought about a future for them as a couple. "Also, it'd be nice to see the area when the sun comes out. I'll bet it's spectacular."

"Yeah. The weather was not our friend today, that's for sure. Where do you want to start tomorrow?"

"I'm not sure yet. I'll spend some time studying maps tonight, and maybe Google Street View will help. If nothing strikes, I figure I'll drive across the Bay Bridge and cruise up and down to get a feel for the area. Then I guess all that's left is to pick an end and start going through the marinas one by one."

"Sounds logical. But I have to believe your intuition will kick in and give you a clue."

"Man, I hope so because otherwise I see us being here awhile. And even if we do find the place or the boat or whatever that vision is leading me to, it doesn't guarantee it'll have anything to do with the diamonds."

"Okay, Debbie Downer. I think someone needs a nap."

She sighed. "I'm sorry. I guess I am tired and a little stressed."

"Let's chill out and watch some TV for a bit. If you fall asleep, so be it. You can always do your research in the morning. I think sleep should be priority one tonight." He tipped back his head and yawned. "Don't think I'll be up for much longer myself."

"Are you going to stay in my room tonight?"

"Might as well. I haven't seen a hint of suspicious activity all day."

"That's good. I'll sleep better knowing you're here with me," she said, gathering up food wrappers and pushing back from the table. "I'm going to hop in the shower first, if that's okay?"

"Be my guest."

Later, after clicking off the TV, Roman turned to where Mia lay sleeping beside him. He stroked her damp hair and very softly ran a fingertip along her cheek. Her eyelids flickered but she didn't wake. He shifted down under the sheets until he was lying flat, tucked himself around her and closed his eyes.

Though it was still overcast the next morning, the fog had mostly lifted, and the air seemed lighter and cleaner to Mia. While driving across the Bay Bridge, her spirits soared. She'd been buzzing with energy ever since she woke early this morning to find Roman's arm across her back, and his face pressed into the side of her neck.

It may have happened while he was asleep, but she still took the physical contact as a good sign. It must mean that subconsciously Roman was starting to let go of the resentment or judgment or whatever it was that caused him to hold back from her. These last two days, she'd found it excruciating being with him yet feeling the disconnect.

She was dying to kiss him, hug him, simply run her fingers through his hair, but knew he wouldn't welcome her touch. And it hurt. Worse than she'd expected. She now understood if they couldn't fix their relationship, it wouldn't be possible for her to be around him even casually. This kind of unrequited yearning would tear her apart an inch at a time.

Concentrate on the key, she scolded herself as she exited the Bay Bridge and continued east on I-80. For a mile or so, she kept her eyes peeled, glancing left and right along the busy stretch where three freeways merged. When she saw the sign for Garner Street, her stomach quivered, and a sizzle of electricity shot across the nape of her neck. Without thinking, she signaled and exited, turning left toward the bay.

The traffic thinned out, and she slowed and glanced in her rearview mirror searching for Roman. There he was three cars behind. Letting out a breath, she continued on past the Hilton and the Berkeley Research Center following the road as it hugged the edge of the land beside the water. Everywhere she looked, boats and yachts were docked, bobbing in the choppy waves.

She pulled into a lot by the Markdale Marina and sat for a time, swiveling her head back and forth and taking in the area. This felt right somehow. She parked the car and continued on foot walking by the boats, smelling the fishy, seaweed air, and hearing the overpowering cry of seagulls circling overhead.

The Markdale Marina wasn't the place. Neither was Sunny Sails Cove or On the Bay. She kept going, walking along piers and docks while frequently glancing across to the Golden Gate Bridge and trying to reconcile her vision with what she saw in person.

Time passed. She had no idea where Roman was but figured since the phone had stayed quiet he wasn't lost. Stepping off yet another pier, she wished she'd thought to bring a snack. With lunch missed and breakfast nothing more than a distant memory, she was seriously famished.

She could take a break, she supposed. There had been plenty of food places closer to the freeway. But despite the hunger, something drove her on. She walked along a path with blue metal benches on one side and large grey stones on the other.

A little girl ran laughing, a pink balloon trailing behind and a small dog following at her heels. Mia turned to watch, the joyful child automatically bringing a smile to her face. And how cute was that dog? Totally adorable, of course. It was a Cairn terrier. When she was little, she'd wanted one just like it after falling in love with Dorothy and Toto.

She stopped. Heart racing. And stared at the dog. Exactly like the dog she'd seen in her vision sitting under the picnic table while the man cleaned fish. She whirled around and once again stared at the bridge. Pretty close to right, she thought.

Up ahead was a sign for Myrtle's Marina. The sign was faded, and the paint was peeling across the first M. She marched up to the pier and her breath caught in her throat. This seemed so familiar. The girl and dog raced by her and down almost to the end before darting along a small plank and jumping onto a boat with a red stripe along the side and a flower painted by the back. Lily's Dream was stenciled beside the flower in red and gold.

Approaching cautiously, Mia stood by the narrow walkway then shook her head. Not Lily's Dream. She didn't get any familiar ping when she looked at it. Slowly, she walked on. The Wayfinder was next with royal blue script. Then Rosalind where a man on a ladder attended to something on the main pole near the front of the boat. Journey Man was larger than the others and had patches of a putty-like substance on the side.

At the very end stood *Heart's Desire* and Mia got a hit. She studied the boat. On the smaller side compared to the others docked here. It had a cabin, and there were a few chairs scattered about on the deck. No music sounded from below as some of the others had.

"Can I help you?"

Mia gasped, a hand to her heart, and whirled around. "I didn't hear you come up," she said, blowing out a breath.

The man was youngish, somewhere in his early thirties, and though his face was set in stern lines, she'd bet he was more inclined to be friendly.

"Are you looking for someone?" he asked.

"No. Well, maybe. A friend of a friend has a boat somewhere along here, and I thought I'd see if I could track him down."

"I know most of the people in the area. What's his name?"

"Frank Wells. He's fortyish. Tall. Dark hair. I can't remember the name of the boat, but I thought it had Heart in it."

"I've never heard of Frank Wells, and this isn't his boat. Are you sure he docks on this pier?"

"That's the thing. I'm not sure at all. I somehow thought I could stroll around and just magically find it. I had no idea there were so many boats. I'll check in with my friend later and find out for sure before I come back next time."

"Probably be best. It's a busy spot. Do you sail?"

"No. I've never even been on a boat. Well, a ferry sure, but not a boat like any of these. It must be fun."

The man smiled. "It is. Every day I get out on the water is a good day."

"Do you live on your boat?"

"Not right now but maybe one day. Can't do it here in any case. They don't allow liveaboard."

"Liveaboard?"

"Means pretty much what is says. If you want to live-a-board your boat certain marinas will let you, but it costs more. They usually have better security and hookups for electrics and the like."

"Huh." She looked around as though fascinated. "It might be fun to do for a while. Probably cheaper than owning a house."

"Especially in the Bay Area. Anyway, I'd better get back to it. Just so you know, some people don't take kindly to folks hanging around their boats. Now Jerry here, the guy who owns *Heart's Desire*, he'd probably be okay but still, we all look out for one another."

"Oh my gosh. I'm so sorry. I didn't know. Okay. I'm leaving. Have a nice day."

"You too. And if you can't track down your friend, come and hit me up. I'll take you for a tour on the Rosalind."

Roman and Mia waited until well after dark before approaching *Heart's Desire*. They had to shimmy through the slats of a metal gate to get out to the boats but thankfully there were no surveillance cameras. Mia had made sure of that when she'd left earlier that afternoon.

It was quiet and mostly dark on the pier and as far as they could tell, no one was on board any of the boats. They hurried along to the end and scrambled onto the deck of *Heart's Desire*. Earlier, when the sun set, the wind had died down. Now the water was serene with the gentlest of swells rocking the boat.

Making their way to the cabin, Mia tried the small silver key in the lock, but it wasn't even close to a good fit.

"Shoot, I was hoping it would be as easy as opening the door and walking in," she whispered.

"Here, let me look," Roman said, pushing in beside her and aiming a pen light at the door. "I've been working on my lock picking skills."

"Really?"

"Yep. Figured it might come in handy in my line of work."

He unzipped his windbreaker and reached into the inside pocket, pulling out a small leather case. When he opened it, Mia saw a row of silver tools.

"I can't believe that you, former detective Roman Mancini, own a set of lock picks."

"I know. Who'd have thunk it? Okay, give me a minute here."

Roman pushed a tension wrench into the lock then chose a tool with a small hook on the end. Holding the wrench in place, he gently probed with the hook managing to press it roughly halfway in. After several minutes had ticked by, he let out a frustrated sigh.

Aiming the pen light at the leather case on the floor, Mia inspected the remaining tools, choosing one with a serrated edge. "Let me try. I used to be pretty decent back in the day."

Roman handed her the wrench and taking the flashlight, stepped to the side. Mia positioned the wrench in the opening, playing back and forth a few times until she decided it gave slightly more to the right. Holding it with gentle pressure, she inserted the raking tool and began dragging it in and out of the opening. All at once, the wrench turned the lock and the door opened.

"And that, my friend, is how it's done," she said smugly, holding the tools out to him.

Roman blinked at her. "Okay. Can I just say wow. That was lightning fast. Maybe you could give me lessons?"

"Sure. Anytime." She blew out a breath and pushed the door open. "Okay. Here we go."

Four steps down, she stopped to get her bearings. Roman followed close behind, his light slowly arcing over the space. Immediately to the left they saw a cushioned bench seat and a small table. Directly across was the kitchen area with a tiny sink and two hot plates. They walked along the narrow aisle in the living space and found a double bed behind an accordion type plastic divider. Tucked in on the right was a small portable toilet.

It was untidy. The bed clothes had been left in a jumble. Plates strewn about on the small counter. Books and papers spread across the table and various other surfaces. From the smell of things, the toilet needed to be emptied.

"This is gross," Mia said, trying not to breathe in through her nose.

Roman shrugged. "Could be worse. Okay, I'm going to crouch on the deck and keep watch and you start looking for a lock box or a safe or something hidden away. Here, take the light."

Mia checked all the cupboards on the right side. They were filled with a selection of non-perishable foods and kitchen items such as plates and cups. The storage around the table held more books along with clothing and jugs of water. She crawled up onto the bed and pushed her hands down beside the mattress. Nothing but hair and dirt which had her gagging. A cupboard beside the divider had been used for toiletries.

She sat at the table and considered. This was definitely her father's boat. Once past the toilet stench, she was picking up hints of Old Spice, his favorite cologne. Plus, she could feel his energy in the clothes and the books. A Jack Reacher novel lay on the table. She closed her eyes and pushed out with her mind.

Her father sat on the deck with a beer in his hand, the book resting face down on his thigh. Beside him, a portable radio played Duke Ellington.

The flash was gone in an instant, but it confirmed her theory. Danny Dawson had spent time here. Which was great and all, but what did it have to do with the silver key she'd found in Miami?

"How's it going?" Roman called down softly.

"Not too well. I've gone through the place, and there's nothing here. No safe. No locked cubby for valuables. Nothing."

His head appeared at the top of the doorway. "Let's switch and see if I have any luck."

"Okay," she said, leaving the flashlight on the table.

Outside, the night air was refreshing after the confines of the cabin. She sat cross legged on the deck and gazed up toward the sky. It was still overcast, and the sliver of the moon was mostly obscured by the clouds. No stars showed through.

Farther out in the bay, a few boats cruised by. She glanced along the pier toward the land and was relieved to see continued darkness in the other cabins. A car rolled past, and a few moments later, two women walked a Labrador along Garner Street. Otherwise, all was quiet.

Beneath her, the boat rocked slightly, and she found it soothing. In fact, after a few minutes, she struggled to keep her eyes open. Muffling a yawn, she shook her head back and forth trying to throw off the lethargy. As disappointed as she was not to find anything, she wouldn't be sorry to see her bed.

The vision was upon her before she even realized it. Her father wearing a swimming mask and a headlamp with a neon yellow elastic strap. He clutched a small black box in his arm as he shimmied over the side of the boat into the water. Taking a deep breath, he dove down and began swimming. His light cut through the dark water, and he lifted his head illuminating the underside of the boat.

"Hey, what is it?" Roman was kneeling beside her. "Did you see something?"

She nodded and sighed. "Yeah. Feel like going for a swim?"

***

In the end, they had to risk coming back a second night for the underwater excursion.

On the deck, they'd searched the compartments under the bench seat and found the face mask and underwater headlamp Mia had seen in the vision. Unfortunately, there was no sign of the wet suit. When Roman leaned over the side and trailed a hand in the water, he quickly snatched it back.

"Jes-sus. That's cold. No way either of us is going in without a suit."

Mia had frowned. "I'm sure I can handle it."

But when she, too, had tested the water, she'd been forced to agree with him, and they'd called it a night.

They'd spent part of the next morning going to dive shops and scouting out the best deals before finally settling on a place called In The Deep on Fisherman's Wharf. Roman had insisted he be the one in the water while Mia stayed on lookout.

"It might take a lot of strength to wrestle the box off the hull." He'd put up a hand to stop her protest. "Now don't get all uppity with me. I know you're plenty tough, but a man is always going to beat out a woman in the strength department."

She'd blown out an angry breath. "I know, and it pisses me off."

"Hey, men can't have babies, so I'd say it evens out in the end."

"It doesn't always feel so even."

Now, though, Mia secretly admitted to herself she was plenty glad to be the one staying warm and dry on the boat. It was a windy night and cool enough for a light jacket. The waves chopped, lifting the boat up and down, and it looked mighty dark down there in the water.

Roman finished tying one end of a rope to a hook beside the bench seat then passed the other to Mia and turned around. She fed it through a loop on the back of his wetsuit and not knowing any actual sailor's knots, hoped a conventional double knot would do the trick. She passed him the lamp, and he pulled the Velcro tight as he fitted it over his head.

"Wish me luck," he said, his smile tight.

A chill of apprehension shot through her. Patting his cheek, she stepped up and kissed him on the lips. "Luck," she whispered.

He turned on the lamp and swung his legs over the side of the boat before dropping neatly into the water. She leaned over, and he glanced up at her, the headlamp making her blink.

"Man. The water's alive down here," he called out.

He took a deep breath, glanced at her once more, then dove under. She started counting. One Mississippi. Two Mississippi. The rope continued slipping over the side, the neat coils disappearing one by one.

When she reached forty, she heard splashing close to the front of the boat and hurried over. Roman's head bobbed above the surface, the lamp still shining.

"Did you find anything?"

"Yeah. But I couldn't pry it off. I'm going to catch my breath and go down again. Have you been keeping a watch?"

"Um...sure." She glanced over her shoulder at the dark pier beyond. "Nobody out there."

Roman dove down several times only to return to the surface empty handed.

"I've shifted it closer to this side, but I can't get the damned thing off."

Mia searched through the tools in a compartment they'd discovered near the steering wheel and came up with a small hammer and a crowbar.

"Will either of these be useful?"

He took the crowbar, shoving it through the rope around his waist before disappearing underwater once again. He seemed to be down there for a long time, and Mia gathered up some of the rope. When there was still plenty of slack she relaxed slightly.

Finally, he surfaced, coughing and sputtering. With obvious effort, he raised his right arm, and she saw the small black box dangling from his hand.

Chapter Ten

Mia leaned down as far as she dared and managed to grab the handle of the black box and haul it out of the water before tugging the rope to help Roman slither up and onto the deck.

"Holy shit, I can't believe you got it," she said, then slapped a hand over her mouth when she realized she'd practically shouted.

Roman rolled over and struggled to the bench seat where they'd left a small pile of hotel towels. He quickly stripped off the wetsuit, roughly dried himself, then slid into a pair of sweatpants and T-shirt before zipping on a padded jacket. His teeth chattered and his fingers shook when he attempted to get into his Nikes.

Mia knelt before him. "Here. Let me. You okay?"

"Nothing a hot shower and a shot of rum won't fix. We should get moving."

"Yeah. The sooner the better."

They'd decided to wait until safely back in their room before opening the box. By the time they jogged down the walkway of the motel they were all but bursting with excitement.

"You want to shower first?" Mia asked.

"Hell, no. Open that thing already," he said.

Mia fished out the small silver key from her purse. "It would totally suck if this doesn't fit," she said on a half laugh.

But it did fit, slotting in smoothly and turning the lock so the lid sprang up. She stared inside, noting it was bone dry before the disappointment hit at seeing a plastic coke bottle. Scowling, she pulled it out.

"Pops, you have got to be kidding me," she said in disgust.

"Wait. Hold the phone. There's something in there. Give it over."

She handed him the bottle, gasping when he held it up to the light. In the bottom was a small patch of fabric. Roman upended the bottle, shaking until the fabric dropped into the narrow neck then unscrewed the cap and attempted to catch hold of the end and pull it through.

It was no use as it had lodged at the base of the neck and his fingers wouldn't fit in. Mia tried, but although her fingers were small enough to reach the cloth, she couldn't properly grasp it. She handed the bottle back to Roman.

"I have tweezers in my makeup bag. I bet that'll do the trick."

She returned seconds later and Roman held the bottle steady while she pushed the ends of the tweezers inside. Pinching them tight over the fabric, she slowly withdrew her hand, and though the cloth fought to stay put, she eventually began to make headway.

"It keeps catching. There's something in there," she mumbled, repositioning the tweezers.

When part of the fabric finally poked out through the opening, Roman grasped it between his thumb and forefinger, pulling hard. It came out with a whoosh and thudded to the floor. Mia grabbed it up, noticing the weight, and placed it on the table in front of her.

"It's a pouch," Roman said, pointing to the chord.

She untied the double bow and pushed the fabric apart. The gemstones caught the light, sparkling like miniature suns against the black cloth.

"Are those...they can't be...I think they're diamonds," she said in a hushed tone.

"Let's see."

Roman picked up the pouch and carefully poured the stones into his palm, making a small mound about the size of a half lime. He poked his finger into the pile and shifted them around then looked over to Mia.

"I've been around a lot of gemstones over the years, but unless you have a loupe and proper training, there's no sure way to tell if they're the real thing." She shook her head. "Okay. We'll have to get them appraised."

"Um…I think if we walk into a jewelry store with a handful of diamonds, it's going to raise some questions."

"Yeah…you're right. Okay. One or two of the smaller ones then."

"It's my turn to hold them." She giggled when he poured them into her cupped hands. "Oh, so pretty. Look how shiny they are? If they are the real deal, this pile is worth a small fortune."

Roman picked up his phone and began tapping the screen.

"It says here a twenty carat diamond is about the size of a nickel and worth anywhere from five hundred K all the way up to two million depending on the quality. There's got to be." He gestured toward her hands. "What? Maybe forty or fifty carats there so we're looking at a minimum of a couple of million but likely much, much more."

"I can't believe it. Pops was always small time. Sure, he dreamed big, but the reality was nothing like this."

"You sound proud?"

"Not proud exactly. More awestruck. And yes, I know whatever he did to get them was wrong. But Jeez Louise, this is something."

"Yeah. Something that got him killed."

She nodded before pouring the stones back into the pouch. "You're right. We need to be careful."

"I don't think it's a good idea to fly home with them. What if, for some crazy reason, we get searched at security? It'd be hard to explain a handful of diamonds."

"I can send them with FedEx. I get packages all the time, so if anyone is watching the house they'd never suspect."

"Good idea. We'll do that first thing in the morning then hop on a flight. I don't think we should get anything appraised in San Francisco just in case I somehow missed a tail. It'll only tip them off."

"Going to a jeweler close to Dalton doesn't seem like a good idea either," Mia said. "How about we route the flight home through…I don't know…Las Vegas or somewhere like that leaving enough of a layover we can hop in a cab and have a couple of the small diamonds looked at?"

"Perfect. Let's see if we can book something right now."

They were easily able to arrange a stop-over in Las Vegas with more than enough time to zip out to jewelry stores on the strip and still have them arriving home at a reasonable hour. Inside the FedEx office, Mia found it tougher than she'd expected to hand over the small box containing the diamonds to the woman behind the counter.

"They'll be there by tomorrow, guaranteed?" she asked nervously.

"Yes, ma'am. Here's your tracking number. You can check online every step of the journey."

Mia looked down at the familiar invoice slip then over to the box. "Okay. Thank you. It's just really important it gets there safely. You don't lose many packages, right?"

The woman eyed her then worked up a polite smile. "Ma'am, our company loses approximately zero point five-five percent of packages. That's less than one percent. Short of a fire, Tsunami, or armed robbery, your package will be delivered by eight p.m. tomorrow. Is there anything else I can help you with this morning?"

"No. That's all. Thank you again."

"Have a nice day."

"I'll bet that woman thought you had some kind of obsessive disorder," Roman mumbled as they left the office.

"As far as those diamonds are concerned, I absolutely do."

"Well, they're gone for now so let's concentrate on getting to Vegas and finding out what we actually have."

She blew out a breath. "Yeah. Okay."

Even though it probably wasn't necessary, Roman and Mia decided to stick with their routine of traveling as strangers. Upon landing at McCarran International, they took separate taxis to the Strip. They each had one of the small diamonds and having researched online, went directly to the jewelry stores. Mia had chosen The Gemstones Gallery while Roman went with Diamond Sea.

Afterward, they met outside the MGM Grand and compared notes while walking along the Strip.

"Well?" she asked.

"You first."

"Okay. The man took me into his office and put the stone on a light board then looked at it using his loupes." She fanned a hand in front of her face. "Man, it's hot here."

"Come on." Roman rolled his hand impatiently.

"Well, looks like we have a winner. He said it was definitely a diamond, and he gave it a quality rating of IF which stands for internally flawless. Also, he told me it would be rated nearly colorless, another thing in the plus column for appraisal value. Then he weighed and measured the stone and it's approximately point eight five carats. According to him he would put the value at ten grand."

Roman nodded. "It was pretty much the same with me. Except my jeweler was a woman. Anyway, like yours, she gave it top ratings on clarity and color, but this one weighed in at one point two-five carats so she estimated it to be worth between twenty-two and twenty-five thousand."

"Wow. So our little pile is definitely hitting into the millions."

"I'd say so."

"Man, this better not be the zero point five-five percent of times that FedEx loses a friggin' package."

Roman rubbed her shoulder. "Don't worry. They won't. Come on, we'd better get back to the airport."

After a short delay leaving Las Vegas, Roman and Mia landed in Nashville and made their way to their separate vehicles. Roman headed straight home while Mia detoured to the kennel and picked up four delighted dogs.

She was half an hour from home when Roman called. "The house is secure. Doesn't look like anyone's been here. I talked to Kevin on the quiet, and he checked the place himself twice a day while we've been gone."

"You didn't tell me Kevin was involved."

"Well, only involved in the sense I told him someone from your past might be looking to make trouble."

"Okay. I guess that's good. Especially the part about the house being fine. I don't feel up to dealing with anything tonight beyond filling my face and passing out."

"Since you're probably still twenty minutes out, why don't I zip into town and get takeout."

"No. I can make a stir fry or pasta or something," she protested.

"Mia, come on. After finding the you-know-whats, neither of us slept more than five minutes last night. Cut yourself a break, okay?"

She sighed. "All right. Get me a quinoa and beet salad. The dogs say 'hi' by the way."

"I'll bet they do. It'll be nice to take them for a walk tonight."

"Yeah. It will. See you soon."

The sun was setting when Mia and the dogs waited on the front lawn while Roman locked the house.

"From now on, you lock every time," he said, when he joined her and they began walking across the driveway. "Even if you're only going out to garden."

"But won't they just break in anyway?"

"Sure, but it's usually noisier that way, and even if you don't hear it these guys will," Roman said, pointing to Mac and Fifi who had stayed by Mia's side.

"I guess. It's a pain though."

"So is getting taken by some men who might be connected to Russian Mafia. In fact, I'll wager that's more of a pain. At least it is for me because then I'll have to go and chase after you."

"Aw. That's so sweet." She patted his cheek. "Such a romantic."

When Roman smiled, her heart soared. Ever since they'd found the diamonds, she'd felt closer to him again. Not as strong as before, but so much better than it had been after the engagement party. She knew there was still much to be resolved but at least this gave her hope.

"We need to talk about what we're going to do with the diamonds when they arrive tomorrow," he said.

"Please don't say 'take them to the police'. We can't. Not until we're sure we've found all of them."

"I agree." When she flashed a surprised look at him, he shrugged. "What?"

"I guess I thought you'd be all 'cop' about this."

"We might need them for leverage. Though I'm going to do my damnedest to make sure it doesn't come to that. In the meantime, we'll have to come up with a safe place."

"What about a safety deposit box?"

He nodded. "Maybe. The only problem is we can't access it twenty-four seven and there'd be no sneaking in and out. It'll take seeing a bank employee and all that jazz. Still, that could also be a plus because if they somehow steal the key away from us, they won't be able to get in and out undetected either."

"I guess we could bury them somewhere on my property...or hide them in the lake near your parent's cottage..." she trailed off.

"Let's think about what would be best. I'm not inclined to go with the lake. I don't want my family getting pulled into this."

She nodded. "Yeah. You're right. Stupid idea."

"I'm kinda liking the idea of burying them here. You have lots of land and it's so secluded in the woods at the back. As long as there isn't a flood or something, I could see it working out as a hiding spot."

"Provided we remember exactly where we put them."

He took her hand in his and interlaced their fingers. "That's why we have you. No way you'll forget. Not with that freaky, deaky mind of yours."

"Um...thanks...I think." She swung their joined hands. "This is nice. Us walking together with the dogs on such a gorgeous evening. Even if we are bone tired."

Chocolate brown eyes latched onto hers. "It is. Almost feels normal, doesn't it?"

"Does that mean you're not mad anymore?"

His smile was slow, but when it bloomed she felt the warmth of it. "I wouldn't say I'm not still partially pissed, but I'm working my way through it."

"Good. I'm glad to hear it." She paused "It was kinda exciting being on the diamond hunt in San Francisco, wasn't it."

"Actually...yeah...I have to admit I had a pretty good time."

She sighed. "I keep thinking about Pops stuck in some morgue in Florida with no one claiming his body."

"Hopefully soon, baby. Do you think he would want a service or anything?"

"God." She covered her mouth with her hand and shook her head. "I hadn't even thought about that. I don't know what he'd want, and I seriously doubt he'll have a will. That wasn't Pops' way. Even with stage IV cancer, I'll bet he didn't figure he was going to die. He was all about seeing the glass half full even when it strayed into delusional territory. Maybe Lou will have an idea of what he'd like for a memorial or whatever. Assuming I can find her."

Roman slung his arm around her shoulders and pulled her close. "You'll find her. I have utmost faith in you. But put it aside for tonight. Let's finish our walk and hit the hay. I'm seriously bagged."

"Yeah. Me too."

The next morning, Mia sat on the back deck and meditated for twenty minutes while the sun rose and the dogs played. Once her mind was suitably clear, she retrieved the key she'd found in her father's pocket the night he died and cupped it gently in her palm. She closed her eyes and focused on her breathing while inviting the energy into her but nothing came. No flashes. No visions. The key felt lifeless in her hand.

"Maybe I'll get a reading from the diamonds themselves," she said to Roman when he asked how it had gone.

"Later today, right?"

"I checked the tracking code this morning. Apparently, some time before five p.m."

"Let's hope you get a reading from them because we're almost out of leads."

"I could always go to Florida and talk my way into seeing Pops' affects. Except it'd be easy for Dean to track me. He probably paid off one of the clerks in the office to keep a watch. I'll definitely try the stones first. Anyway, what are you up to today?"

"I'm heading into town for a meeting. I might have my first case."

"What? Really? You never said anything."

"It only came up last night. Kevin contacted me. A friend of a friend needs a background check. It's pretty straight forward and not all that lucrative but gotta start somewhere."

"Roman, that's awesome. I'm so happy for you."

"Sure you'll be okay alone?"

"Of course. I might as well get some work done until I figure out where to go next for the diamonds."

"While I'm at the office I'll put in a couple of hours on the computer working through your father's aliases. See if I can pinpoint a current address."

"Great. That would really help."

"You want take-out tonight?"

"No. I'm making black bean taco salad with fresh salsa and guacamole."

"Yum." Leaning down, he pressed his lips lightly to hers. "Don't work too hard."

"Yeah. Yeah. Get out of here. Good luck with your first client."

Mia spent the day trying not to worry, but it was hard since there was so damn much to worry about. At least Roman had moved down on the list. The last day or so, things felt decidedly more normal between them.

Although they might not be a hundred percent on track, they were making gains in the right direction. And thank God for that. It had killed her when she thought her stupid past was going to come between them, especially after they'd fought so hard to put this relationship together.

Now if she could only figure a way through this mess her father had dragged her into. She shook her head. Roman was right. She hadn't been dragged in or had it thrust upon her. The truth was she'd made the choice to get involved, even if only in a small way.

The fact it had blown up into a mess of epic proportions, while unfortunate, was totally on her. If only she could go back in time, she'd tell her father flat-out 'no.' If she truly wanted the past to stay in the past, she couldn't open the door and invite it in, could she?

The day dragged on. She settled down at her jewelry table, determined to work steadily through until the diamonds arrived but found her mind wandering. Her progress was slower than molasses in January. In fact, by the middle of the afternoon, she'd only completed one order.

Not good, she chastised herself. At this rate, it wouldn't be long before her bottom line suffered. And oh how she cherished her bottom line. She pushed back from the table and walked across the room to the window.

"You okay," Sheryl asked.

"Yeah. I'm great," Mia said. She put on a bright smile and turned to the desk in the corner where her assistant worked. "How's it going?"

"Good. I've finished updating the website and responded to all the outstanding inquiries. Um…things are getting a little backed up…"

Mia sighed. "I know. I'm behind schedule. Hopefully I'll catch up over the next few days. For any orders coming in, can you let people know the revised timeline? Maybe you should email Meredith at Hidden Treasures and tell her I'm about ten days out from delivering any new products."

"Will do. Anything else after that?"

"I'm afraid not, so you might as well take off early."

"Okay. If you're sure."

"Sure as sure can be."

Half an hour later, Sheryl picked up her purse. "Well, I'm going to push off." The driveway sensor pinged, and she glanced over her shoulder and out the window. "Looks like company. You expecting anyone?"

Mia frowned and walked to the window. A grey Audi was being driven carefully along the gravel driveway toward the house. Unfortunately, the glare of the sun on the windshield obscured the driver.

"I don't know who that is," she said, staring.

"I'll stay. Just in case."

The car swung around and parked at the side of the house by the flagstone path, but the driver remained inside. Mia racked her brain. No, she definitely didn't know the car. And living outside of town, it was unusual to get drop-in visitors. She pushed out with her energy and almost gasped aloud when she realized it was Dean.

Chapter Eleven

Mia knew it was Dean in the car like she knew the sun would rise again tomorrow. He'd opened his mind and thought of her exactly the way he used to do in the old days when they were together. It was a technique they'd employed to find one another in new locations without using cell phones or, back in the early days, pagers. It was quick, efficient, and left no electronic trace. Plus, Dean had thought it way cool.

And now here he was at her house in Dalton, sitting in his car and giving her a heads up. "I...um...I'm good. I think it might be an old friend, so no worries."

"You sure? You look kind of shook up."

"It's only that I forgot he was coming and...you know...I'm surprised."

"Okay," Sheryl said doubtfully. "Still, I'm gonna stay until we make certain."

Mia grabbed her phone and shoved it in her pocket, then she and Sheryl walked out to the sun room. She opened the screen door, letting the dogs out, and stood on the front step, studying the Audi. Dean was alone. He raised his hand to wave, and she stared at him for several seconds before returning the gesture.

The dogs rushed to Dean's car, circling and barking, as was their custom with unfamiliar vehicles.

"That's your friend?" Sheryl asked.

"Yeah. That's him."

"I think he's afraid of the dogs."

"Maybe you're right."

Except Mia knew Dean wasn't because in her head, clear as a bell, she heard him say 'whoa, awesome dogs, babes'. Mia whistled anyway and Mac, always obedient, trotted straight up the steps and sat by her feet with Fifi barely a second behind. The other two continued with their attack dog routine until she called them a second time.

Dean opened the driver's door and got out and stood beside the car while his eyes locked with Mia's. "Hey, pretty lady. Long time no see," he called out.

"If I had a guy friend who looked like that, I sure as heck wouldn't forget he was coming," Sheryl said under her breath.

He was tall and still lean though he'd put on some muscle since they'd last met. His golden hair shone like a halo around his head, and when he smiled over at her, her heart beat thickly in her ear. Dean had always been a looker, that was for sure, and the passage of time hadn't changed that one bit.

"Hi, come on up," she called out.

It was probably foolish to invite him in, but since he was alone, and she couldn't sense him harboring any evil intent, she might as well see what was what. He'd tracked her down, after all, so this meeting was going to happen sooner or later. And since it was going to happen, better when Roman wasn't around.

"Hi, I'm Sheryl." Mia's assistant stuck out her hand and shook Dean's enthusiastically. "It's real nice to meet you."

Mia had to stifle a laugh. Even Sheryl, with her dour temperament, wasn't immune to the powers of the opposite sex. And Dean had always had fearsome powers when it came to attracting women.

"Dean. Enchanted to meet you."

He bowed low and brushed his lips across Sheryl's knuckles before smiling down at her as if she were the only person in the whole wide world. To Mia's astonishment, Sheryl giggled then pushed at her hair while a faint line of color rose up her neck. Good grief, the woman was getting all fluttery.

"Aren't you something," Sheryl managed. "I hear you're a friend of Mia's?"

Dean turned to Mia, his smile wide and bright. "We go way back, don't we babes? I must say, you're looking mighty fine."

He reached for her hand, but before Mia realized what was happening, he'd dipped her low and laid a warm kiss on her lips.

After a second of shock, she turned her face away and pushed against his chest. "Hey...let me up."

Dean chuckled and hugged her close before finally releasing her. "Sorry. I couldn't help myself."

"Oh...well..." Sheryl rubbed her nose then her mouth before clasping her hands in front of her as if not sure what to do with them.

Mia stepped back from Dean, crossing her arms over her chest. She turned to Sheryl. "Thanks again for all the help. I'll see you the day after tomorrow."

"Isn't she a peach," Dean said brightly when Sheryl drove away.

He squatted down and rubbed his hands along Layla and Tucker who had left a small pile of balls and sticks at his feet in the hopes he might be convinced to play. Beside her, Mac quivered, his eyes fixed on the visitor.

"Come inside, I'll get you something cold to drink."

Mia turned and stepped back in through the screen door letting it slam once Mac and Fifi had followed her inside. She heard Tucker bark then the thud of paws racing across the lawn. Seemed like Dean had been coerced into a game after all.

In the kitchen, she exhaled slowly and held her hand flat in front of her. Pretty darn steady. Clearly, she hadn't lost her touch under pressure. Though in all honesty, she'd always known she'd end up here—meeting with Dean. She hadn't been able to see any other scenario as far as the diamonds were concerned. Still, she had hoped it would happen later and be on her terms.

After pouring two glasses of iced tea, she brought them to the sun room and sat watching Dean play with the dogs outside. She suspected he was giving her extra time to settle, but she also knew it wasn't only for show. He'd always liked dogs. She remembered they'd talked about maybe getting a couple once they had a proper home base.

When he joined her a few minutes later, Mac growled low in his throat and little Fifi whined worriedly.

"Shush, guys," she said, patting Mac's head.

"Those two don't like me, huh? Oh well, can't win 'em all. You look great, Jenny. Beautiful as always. I lost track of you for a while there."

"How did you find me now?"

"Danny." He leaned toward her, ocean blue eyes earnest. "I'm sorry about what happened. I never meant for him to die. I only wanted the rocks back. He pulled a gun on the guys. Didn't think Danny ever carried. Could have sworn he was allergic to guns."

Mia swallowed and looked away. "I was with him when he died."

"I know. I saw you at the motel. Figured you were helping him with the diamonds."

Steeling herself, she shook her head then turned and stared him straight in the eye. "I wasn't. He told me a week or so before that he was sick. When he called from Florida saying it was the end of the road, I couldn't stand to think of him being alone, so I went there. Turns out he had a whole other thing in mind. I was about to walk away when you showed up and...well, you know what happened."

"Yeah. It was a tough night."

He didn't say anything for a time, and Mia studied him as he sipped his iced tea, his hand idly stroking Layla's head. "Why are you here?"

Putting down the glass, he spread his arms wide. "Believe it or not, I'm coming with my hat in hand, begging for your help. I need you. Your dad stashed those diamonds God knows where and you're probably the only person who can find them."

She blew out a breath and formed the next lie. "I have no idea what he did with them."

"Come on. Even if he didn't tell you, we both know with your special talents, you can find them."

"Maybe. But I don't want to. I'm out of that life now."

"Babes, seriously? It's me. I know you. Long term, you'll never be happy living straight. It's not who you are. Would you try and turn a hot-blooded thoroughbred into a cart horse? Or a jaguar into a house cat?"

"Those are stupid analogies. People can be whoever they want to be."

"On the surface, sure, people can change. How they talk, manners, things like that. But deep down, in the core of their personality, they are who they are. And you, my beauty, are a brilliant thief."

She shook her head stubbornly. "Not anymore."

He scooted his chair closer. "I've missed you. I thought about you so often over the years. We were such a great team, and I've always believed we were destined to be together. Now here we are, lives intersecting once again."

"Dean. Listen to me. I have a whole new life which I love. My business is growing every year." She paused, her fingers rubbing across the antique citrine ring. "I'm engaged now."

He chuckled but took her hand and gazed down at the engagement ring. "Congratulations. It's lovely, I'm sure. And no doubt all kinds of sentimental, but please forgive me if I think you look better in diamonds and rubies. I gather he's a cop. Well, ex-cop. Though I suppose the same as you being a thief, Roman Mancini will always be a cop. It can't have been easy getting him to swallow your back story?"

She snatched her hand away. "Roman loves me, and he's fine with my past."

"Well, that's excellent news. Since he's all hunky dory with your past, he shouldn't mind you helping me out. I'll reward you handsomely for your time, of course. You must remember I was always more than generous especially when it came to you." When Mia didn't respond, he continued on. "I'll bet once you and I are working together again it will all come back to you. The rush. The excitement. The glory of the hunt. You're going to swallow your tongue when you see the diamonds because they are spectacular. And as for me, well, I hate to brag but I have to say I'm pretty much prime."

He stood and began unbuttoning his shirt.

"What the hell are you doing?" Mia asked in exasperation.

His smile was lazy now as he undid the last button and spread his shirt wide, baring his chest. "Giving you a sneak peak of coming attractions. When we were together before, I was still a boy. I'm all man now, baby, and this body was made for loving you."

She told herself she wouldn't look, but somehow her eyes flicked over and latched onto his abs, six perfect planes of muscle veeing down toward the top button of his jeans. Above that, his pecs were well defined and highlighted by a sprinkling of downy hair that begged to be explored by her fingers. She blinked and finally glanced away.

"Put your shirt back on."

"Looks like someone's working up to a blush. Okay. All right. Closing up the shirt. It's all safe now."

Resisting the urge to rub her hand across her brow, Mia swallowed. "I'm sorry I can't help you. Best of luck with the diamonds." She stood and smiled, the perfect hostess. "It was nice seeing you again."

Dean shook his head and leaned back in the chair. "Playing hard to get, huh? Okay. Here's the thing. I was hoping you'd come on board for old time's sake and because I'm sure in your heart of hearts you agree with everything I said. Especially about us being together. But the truth is, there are other ways to convince you."

Her heart thudded in her chest. "What do you mean?"

"I mean I might have something the police would be interested in. You remember Charles Boorman III?"

Mia sank back down to the chair. "The Monet and the rubies," she muttered.

"That's my clever girl. Never one to forget a detail. I'll bet you recall how we propped up the painting on the headboard, and you lay yourself out across the bed wearing that big assed necklace. Could be I still have the pictures. And could be, if you don't help me, they'll find their way to the Charleston police department."

"Hey, you drag me down...I'll take you with me."

"How? There's no evidence I was ever there. But I'm darn sure good ol' Charlie will remember you. That sweet young thing he wined and dined around the city for almost two weeks."

"But...you wouldn't..."

"How will Roman feel when his fiancé is sent away for three to five? Will he still be waiting for you when you come out of the slammer? Just so you know, I'll still be here for you."

"You're a sadistic bastard."

Dean sighed. "Maybe. Please understand, I take no pleasure in backing you up against the wall, but you made your choice. And I need the diamonds."

As one, the dogs leaped to their feet and rushed over to the screen door. Hearing the tell-tale rattle coming from the driveway, Mia glanced over her shoulder and all but froze. FedEx was here. The perfect cosmic joke.

"Looks like another shipment. Excuse me, I'll just get that," she said as casually as she could.

On legs that felt loose and unwieldy like a newborn foal standing moments after birth, she somehow managed to make her way outside to meet the driver at the bottom of the steps. Although her hand shook when she wrote her signature on the tablet, she could already feel a lifetime of training kicking in. By the time she'd walked the small box across the sun porch and dropped in unceremoniously by the front door, she was back in control.

"Jenny—"

"It's Mia," she snapped, cutting him off. "Jenny is dead and gone."

He smiled and set the glass down and stood. "Be that as it may, I've given you plenty to think about, and you'll no doubt want to get a few things in order. I'll pick you up at nine a.m. sharp. Now, since I figured there was little chance you'd invite me to stay, I'm off to somewhere called the Dalton Inn and Tavern." He shuddered as though the very thought of small-town accommodations was too much to bear.

She stared at him blankly, her mind still processing the nine a.m. sharp comment.

"Perhaps you could recommend a place to eat?" he said.

"Gabe's Diner," she answered without thinking. "Decent food though not fancy. Dean, I can't just leave with you."

"My darling, I'm afraid you have to. Since you say you don't know where the diamonds are, I suggest we start at Danny's place in New York and let that phenomenal gift of yours loose. I'm betting you'll come up with a nice solid lead. If not," he shrugged. "I have a lineup of other places to take you. We keep looking until the job is done. Whatever you're planning to do with the dogs, I suggest you keep it open ended because this might take a while."

"I could just run."

"Sure you could. Pack up the dogs. Maybe the fiancé—if he'll come. And steal away in the dead of night. Except then you'll always be running because if you're not here tomorrow, those photos are going straight to the cops along with a note vis a vie your last known alias and Roman's name. Doesn't sound like you'll be living a quiet, ordinary life after that."

"Get out," she hissed, suddenly so furious she felt capable of bludgeoning him to death.

He lifted his hands in surrender. "There's my exit cue. Sleep tight, Jenny. I can't tell you how much I'm looking forward to teaming up with you again."

In a shocked daze, she watched Dean leave. Surely he was bluffing. Turning in a partner to the cops was against their code. Or at least it had been. Who knew what kind of code Dean was living by these days.

She remembered the night they'd taken those pictures. It had been their first really big con. Oh, the exhilaration, the sheer and absolute giddy joy she'd felt in that hotel room with their spoils. Dean had ordered champagne, and they'd toasted themselves and the perfect execution of their plan. He'd draped the twenty-carat ruby around her neck and told her he loved her for the first time. She'd thought nothing in her whole life would ever compare to that moment.

Her mind raced like a hamster on a wheel, always coming back to the same answer—she was going to have to help him find the diamonds. She already had some of them, though Dean didn't need to know that right now. It never hurt to have an ace up her sleeve.

Hopefully her dad had only split the stash into two lots. With any luck, she might be able to quickly zero in on the second location. Maybe in the end, it would be a short two- or three-day trip. Over and done with in the blink of an eye.

What about Roman? No way he'd believe she had to go out of town for work. Not when they were in the thick of the diamond hunt and she was supposedly worried about Dean finding her. And yet, if she told him the truth...well, she had no idea how he'd react, but the odds were not in her favor.

And really, how could he wholeheartedly embrace the idea of his fiancé traipsing off with her criminal ex-boyfriend who was threatening to send her to prison? The whole thing was ludicrous, like some half-baked plot from a B-movie. It didn't happen in real life to good, decent people.

Which meant, in all likelihood, she was going to lose Roman. But hopefully keep her freedom. If their relationship was doomed anyway, maybe there was no need to get into the whole Dean mess. Maybe she should just break up with Roman, clean and simple, no explanation necessary.

That way she wouldn't have to be humiliated yet again because of her past indiscretions.

She shook her head. That wasn't fair to Roman. He deserved the truth. And she deserved to hold herself to a higher standard. No cowardly, bullshit breakup. She'd stand there and speak her truth, come what may.

Still trembling, but resolved to her decision, Mia struggled to her feet and made her way back inside the house, retrieving the FedEx box as she went. So much to do now. She needed to hide the diamonds. Make arrangements for the dogs and pack all their things.

In town, Roman looked up in surprise at the tap on his office door then smiled when Mia stepped in.

"Hey there, beautiful," he said, not noticing when she stiffened. "To what do I owe the honor?"

"Hey, yourself."

When her smile didn't stay in place, the first tickle of apprehension skittered across the back of his neck. "Everything okay?"

"Not really. I have something to tell you."

"I was about to head home. Why don't we talk there?"

She sighed and looked down. "I think here is better. That way, after, I can leave you to your space."

"You're starting to scare me. Come here and give me a kiss first."

He stood and held out a hand. Reluctantly, she skirted around the desk and stepped up to him, her eyes not meeting his even when she leaned in to peck him on the lips. He wrapped his arms around her tight shoulders and held her close, exhaling slowly in the hopes she'd relax against him. She didn't.

"Baby, I'm sure whatever it is, it can't be that bad."

"It's bad," she said, pushing against his chest until he released her. "Sit, okay? And I'll just tell you straight out. It's easier that way."

When he lowered to the chair, he saw how pale her cheeks were and the way her teeth clamped onto her bottom lip. He wished she wouldn't tell him. Cowardly, sure, but they were barely getting their footing back after the mess with her father. Why couldn't they have some goddamn peace and quiet for once in their relationship.

"Okay," she said then cleared her throat. "Dean came to the house this afternoon—"

"What?" Roman surged to his feet. "Did he hurt you? Where is that bastard right now?"

"I'm fine. He didn't lay a finger on me. He played with Layla and Tucker. We had iced tea on the sun porch. And he asked me to help him find the diamonds."

"He can ask all he wants," Roman growled, stalking across the small space to the window before spinning around to face her. "No way you're helping him. He killed your father for fuck's sake."

Mia lowered down to the corner of the desk looking small and defeated. "He said it was an accident. And besides, he didn't pull the trigger. It was one of the guys with him."

"So what. He's still responsible for his death. Why are you defending him?"

"I'm not. But I am going to have to work with him. I leave in the morning. Hopefully it won't take long."

Roman felt like his head was going to explode. "Are you out of your mind," he shouted, then seeing her flinch, worked to lower his voice. "Why would you want to help that piece of garbage? Is it some stupid old time's sake deal? Because you'd better get over that right now."

"I don't want to do it. I have to," Mia said calmly. "Dean has photographs that link me to a job we did in Charleston. I help him now and it all goes away."

"And if you don't?"

"I guess I'll be spending some time in a lovely federal institution."

"But surely you can turn around and point the finger right back at Dean?"

"I can try but I'm the only one in the photo, so I don't have any proof."

Roman hissed then rubbed a hand along his jaw. "Any chance he's bluffing? I mean, with you in prison there's no way he finds the diamonds."

Mia shrugged. "Hard to say. Not sure I'm willing to risk it though."

"You didn't tell him about the ones we found?"

"Nope. Just in case I can somehow use them against him."

He sat beside her on the edge of the desk. "Good girl. So what are we going to do?"

"There's no *we*. I'm going to help Dean, and I'll see how it goes. I've arranged for the dogs to go to the same kennel as before. It seemed to work out okay…even for Mac."

Her voice hitched, and she blinked furiously then cleared her throat again. "Anyway, I wanted to give this back to you." Slipping her hand into the pocket of her jeans, she handed him the engagement ring.

"Mia. Why?"

"Because I can't be engaged to you while I'm traipsing around helping Dean recover his stolen goods. And I don't want anything to happen to it. That ring is a family heirloom. But I'm mostly giving it back because it doesn't seem like you and I are destined to work out. Apparently, the demons of my past are not letting go any time soon. I'm really sorry."

"Hey. We'll figure it out. Somehow." He paused and slowly exhaled. "Maybe I should take the ring though only to be sure it stays safe, like you said. But we're still engaged. I'm nowhere near ready to give up."

She turned and stared at him. "I thought you'd be pitching a fit right about now. Why aren't you upset?"

"I'm furious and sick to my stomach, but it's not your fault. The important thing is you told me the truth, and that gives me more hope than you can imagine."

"It actually is kind of my fault since I did help steal the ruby and the Monet."

"That wasn't—wait. You stole an original Monet painting?"

"And a ginormous ruby. It was bigger than my thumb. Apparently, it once belonged to the queen of Sweden."

Roman whistled. "Wowzer. That's impressive." He shook his head. "I can't believe I'm congratulating you on federal grand larceny. Anyway, what I'm trying to say is that I'm somehow okay with it."

He took a couple of breaths to test that what he'd said was true. Then sighed to himself. Yes, he truly was okay with the fact Mia had once lifted a rare and valuable painting along with royal jewels. Since he'd already known she was a thief, what she'd stolen seemed of little importance as long as it didn't involve violence.

Suddenly, it dawned on him what he was feeling was something close to pride in her accomplishment. He supposed it was nice knowing she'd been great at her job. And that thought scared the hell out of him. Was he officially crossing over to the dark side?

"I'm coming with you," he said.

"That's crazy."

"Not any crazier than you going in the first place. No way I'm letting this Dean guy take you…where exactly is he taking you?"

"He didn't say and it's not as if I can point him in any particular direction."

"Let's go back to your place and have a look at the diamonds," Roman said. "Could be you'll know where to go once those shiny stones whisper in your ear."

"Oh my God, I completely forgot about trying them." She paused, nodding her head. "I'm thinking take-out might be a good idea after all."

"I could go for Chinese."

"Fine. I'll swing by The Red Dragon and pick some up on the way home."

"I'll be right behind you."

Back at the log house, Mia opened the FedEx box. The fabric pouch was perfectly nested in bubble wrap exactly as she'd packed it. Upon releasing the cord, she peeked in at the diamonds. Still glittery, she noted, and still thrilling to know they were worth a couple of million dollars.

She'd planned to wait until Roman arrived but found herself tipping them into her palm. Cupping both hands around them, she exhaled slowly and gazed down at the gemstones before closing her eyes. Oh, yes, the diamonds were alive with energy and indeed they heated her hands.

The visions came to her immediately.

Chapter Twelve

"I know where to go next," Mia said when Roman stepped into the kitchen.

"The diamonds were talkative?"

"Yep. They had plenty to say. The main thing being they were with Pops in Savanah before they went to San Francisco. So, I figure maybe he left some of the others there. Or if not, I should be able to get some kind of sense from the place itself."

He leaned in and kissed her forehead. "You're awesome as always. And Savanah isn't too far."

"I looked it up. Eight hours or so by car."

"Food smells good. I'm starved."

"I'll dish it up though I have to admit my stomach's so jumpy I don't know if I can eat."

"Try. We need to bring our A game on this trip with Dean. Part of that, Missy, is eating at regular intervals."

"Okay. All right. I'll give it a shot."

They sat together at the kitchen table and Roman dug in enthusiastically while Mia did her best to swallow a few mouthfuls of steamed veggies. Once they'd started eating, Mac who'd been on serious alert, finally allowed himself to lie on the rug in the next room. Mia stared over at him and Roman could see the worry in her eyes.

"He'll be fine. They all will. The kennel is the safest place for them."

"I know. Only it's so hard leaving them when I can't explain that it's not forever. I feel like I'm abandoning them."

"Sure, I know it's hard." He inhaled another forkful of chicken chow mein. "Do we have a plan or are we going to go ahead and hand over all the diamonds to Dean?"

"I don't know. I'm still trying to figure it out. It seems with the threat of those stupid pictures, I might have to." She gestured to the pouch on the counter. "And that reminds me, we need to hide these babies for now."

"I guess burying them in the woods is off...in case Dean's watching."

"How about we bury them indoors?" Mia smiled and glanced over to the front room. "That Jade plant has a nice big pot and it's not exactly the first place anyone would think to look."

"I like how your mind works."

"What if Dean won't let you go tomorrow?"

"He'll have to because otherwise you won't be finding any diamonds, will you? It wouldn't be smart to blow his trump card just because the trump card's fiancé insists on coming."

Mia nodded. "Yeah. He'll complain plenty, but he'll likely give in."

They'd been on the road for almost an hour. Mia was behind the wheel while Roman rode shot gun and Dean sat in the back directly behind the driver's seat. It was a clever setup, Mia mused. Neither she nor Roman could easily get to Dean. The only way to put a kink in his plans was by causing a traffic accident. Which she had no plans of doing because, hello, incriminating photos.

Besides, it wasn't as if Dean had a gun pointed directly at her head or anything. He did have a gun though. He'd pulled it out and shown them the business end when she and Roman had walked out the front door of her house. It wasn't until Roman reluctantly dropped both his shoulder holster and ankle weapon that Dean had tucked his own pistol in the back of his jeans like bad guys in the movies always did.

After that, he'd searched both of them for wiretapping equipment and relieved them of their cell phones.

"What's Mister Dark and Broody doing here?" Dean had asked Mia. "You should know if anything were to happen to me, I've left instructions for the pictures to be immediately sent to the police."

"I go where Mia goes," Roman had said flatly.

"Oh, really." Dean had chuckled. "Not happening."

But in the end, it had only taken a few minutes to convince Dean that it was, in fact, happening or he lost Mia's help with the diamond hunt. And now here they were, the three musketeers—all for one and one for all—driving down the road of action and adventure to certain riches, at least that was Dean's version of events. From Mia's perspective, there was no 'three' anything and the road they were driving on was I-24 plain and simple.

"Where'd the diamonds come from," Roman asked, breaking the silence.

"Deepest, darkest Russia," Dean said. "They were smuggled over on a container ship carrying Vodka."

"By you?" Roman asked.

"Nope. But Danny got wind of it and brought me in on the sting. Worked perfectly too until he went rogue."

"You stole the diamonds from the Russian Mafia?" Mia said in horror, her eyes meeting his in the rearview mirror.

"So, what if I did?"

"Wait. Hold the phone," Roman said, turning toward the back seat. "How are you not dead already?"

"Because I'm smart, and I always land on my feet."

"But they know it was you?" Mia pressed.

"I doubt it."

Roman kept his eyes fixed on Dean's face. "What about the other two men working with you?"

"Jimmy and Karl? They'll never talk. Besides, they have stars in their eyes over the money. No way they'll give that up."

"And you could always ensure their silence by threatening to pin my father's murder on them," Mia said.

He pointed his finger at her and made a clicking sound. "You said it. Trust me, there's nothing for you folks to worry about."

Mia chewed on her bottom lip. "Maybe Savannah isn't such a great idea. Won't the mob guys be keeping an eye out?"

"Pretty sure they're scouring South Florida right about now. You worry about finding the rocks. Let me worry about the Ruskies. No more talking."

Roman raised his eyebrow at Mia, and she shook her head. In the back, Dean turned and stared out the window. Although she returned her eyes to the road, she sent the majority of her energy back toward the man behind her.

Dean knew well enough how to block her probing, but must have forgotten to erect a mental barrier, for she slipped easily into his mind. And as she wormed through the doubt and worry circling his brain, she realized all the talk had been bravado. He was, in fact, quite frightened.

Likely the original plan had been to get as far away as quickly as he could once the heist was completed. Now though, he was stuck scrambling around the scene of the crime and knew he walked a tightrope of danger. Millions of dollars were great and all, but surely it couldn't be worth risking his life? Her father had already paid the ultimate price. Wasn't one death enough?

She didn't say any of this, of course. Putting Dean's manhood on the line in front of Roman wasn't the way to make him see reason. She'd wait until she had some one-on-one time with him. Maybe if she gave Dean the diamonds she and Roman had already found, that would be enough to back him off the hunt.

Or not. Dean had always been the 'go big or go home' type even in his younger days. She doubted much had changed.

It struck Mia then that when Dean had arrived at her house yesterday with his blackmail scheme, she hadn't actually been afraid. Pissed off, sure. But not truly scared he would physically hurt her. Now that she knew about the Russian Mafia connection, adrenaline coursed through her veins. She had to concentrate on keeping her breathing steady because her own fear was strong and deep.

Her eyes flicked across to Roman. He must have sensed something, for his arm slowly slid along the console and rested on the top of her thigh. Even through her jeans, she could feel the heat of him, and it comforted more than she'd expected. After a quick check of her side mirror, she pressed down on the accelerator and guided the car into the fast lane and past a line of dawdling traffic. The sooner this was over with the better, as far as she was concerned.

It was coming on six o'clock by the time they arrived in Savannah. Dean instructed Mia off the I-16 and onto the 37th Connector before taking several smaller streets and pulling into an Applebee's. They'd only stopped one other time during the drive. When she stepped out of the car, she put her hands on her hips, and with a groan, stretched her shoulders and back.

Roman stood with his arms crossed over his chest. "What now?"

Dean smiled and patted Mia on the back. "Now we eat, drink, and make merry. Once it's dark we'll head to Danny's place."

"Where are we staying tonight?"

Now Dean slung an arm around Mia's shoulders. "That depends entirely on Jenny...I mean, Mia. I'll never get used to the new name, babes."

He smiled down at her as though they were the best of friends. She reached up and grabbed his hand, removing it from her body before stepping to the side and out of reach.

"Anyway," Dean continued. "If Mia senses the rest of the diamonds are close by, we keep looking. If she gets nothing or a faraway destination, we can hole up here for the night and recalibrate our plan."

Inside, Applebee's was bustling with diners...mostly families with small children while the second largest demographic appeared to be older couples. Dean, all smiles and flattery, convinced the hostess to seat them at a booth. Roman slid in beside Mia, his hand resting along the back of the bench seat. Once their orders had been placed, they sat in silence with Dean's eyes intent on Mia's face. Roman's gaze was fixed on Dean.

Mia sensed the warring energy at the table, especially from Roman. It had been a long day for her fiancé, and his restraint had been admirable. Now she worried his leash might be ready to snap. When the waiter finally returned with their drinks, she sighed and reached for her Perrier.

Dean held his cabernet aloft. "To old friends, reunited at last," he said in toast. He stretched across the table to clink Mia's cup then tipped his glass toward Roman. "And to new, and somewhat surly, acquaintances."

Roman stared down at Dean's wine, shrugged, and lifted his beer. "And to being blackmailed and dragged across state lines," he said with the hint of a smile.

Dean's blue eyes seemed to sparkle, and he threw back his head and laughed. "Yes, we mustn't forget that," he said and took a measured sip of his wine. "A cop, through and through, aren't you?"

Roman didn't respond, instead he drank some beer and wiped his mouth with the back of his hand.

"Speaking of cops." Dean set his glass down and leaned toward Mia. "Do you remember the time in Seattle after we'd relieved Dustin Fredricks of his gold bars and an officer of the law stopped us in the hotel hallway?"

Mia remembered perfectly but gave a half shake of her head. "There were so many hotels and more than enough cops," she said.

"We were attempting to leave with the gold and the wheels on the rolling suitcase broke so we had to carry it out." He turned his smile on Roman. "You've probably never had occasion to lift a solid gold bar, but I'll tell you, it weighs a whole heck of lot. And we had thirty of them. As luck would have it, some small-time hood had been hitting the rooms in the hotel and stealing trinkets. And this lovely policeman was very concerned about our belongings and making sure we didn't leave anything of value unattended."

Dean's eyes rested on Mia's face, and she found she couldn't help smiling.

"Meanwhile," he continued. "There we are holding this outrageously heavy bag of stolen gold. We didn't want to put it down and draw any attention to what we were carrying and Jen...I mean, Mia and I had to stand there cool as cucumbers while our arms and shoulders screamed. I swear that cop didn't stop talking for a good ten minutes."

"That's a great story," Roman said, his face set in stone.

"Wait. I have a better one." Dean's eyes shifted back to Mia. "You ever tell him about Santa Fe?"

She sighed and dropped her head. "How about a new topic? Um...seen any good movies lately?"

Dean made a tsking sound. "Aw, babes, you shouldn't be afraid to talk about your past. If Roman loves you, he'll understand, right?"

Roman's arm came around Mia's shoulders in a show of support, but she could easily feel the dark emotions bubbling just under the surface.

"Hey, you two can reminisce all night. It doesn't bother me," Roman said.

Dean smiled triumphantly at Mia. "See, there you go. So anyway, Mia had been working on this guy for about a week. Um...Wentworth Holden was his name. Talk about pretentious, right? He had a stamp collection which doesn't sound impressive but they're worth a boat load of cash with the bonus of being easily portable. And he also had these goats."

"Billy, Bobby, and Betty," Mia mumbled.

The waiter approached and set a plate of food down in front of each of them, asked about refills on drinks, and departed.

"Yeah, they were something else," Dean continued, ignoring his steak and fries. "And it turned out their main goal in life was to get into that house."

Mia nodded in agreement. "They used to throw themselves at the glass doors. It was pretty annoying. Wentworth called them incorrigible, but he never penned them up or anything. Just let them wander around the grounds peeking in the windows. He said it made him feel wanted," she said mostly to herself. It was funny the things you remembered about people.

Roman had removed his arm from Mia's shoulders when the food arrived and now turned to study her face.

"So, there I was in the empty house working on opening the locked case of stamps," Dean continued. "And these frickin' goats were flinging themselves at the sliding door. I wasn't worried, though, because my partner had already told me all about their antics. What I didn't realize was that you had to make sure that sliding door was all the way closed. Since it wasn't, the goats popped it off the track and burst into the house like frat boys raiding a sorority. Scared the hell out of me."

The laugh burst out of Mia like a song, and she quickly covered her mouth with her hand, but her shoulders continued to shake. Roman wanted to be disapproving but found himself so drawn into the story, he was smiling before he realized it.

"What happened?" Roman asked.

"I got the goods," Dean said proudly. "And managed to make my getaway with only a few minor head butts from the goats."

"Wentworth and I arrived home later. We'd been at the opera," Mia jumped in. "And the place was trashed. I literally stood there with my mouth hanging open like a guppy fish. The damage those three little tyrants did was so complete and total it was hard to believe. They somehow pulled art off the wall, ripped the antique couch and chairs, broke dishes in the kitchen, pooped and peed everywhere including in the middle of a bed. And there they were strutting around like they owned the place. Drunk with power and not an ounce of remorse on any of those tiny goat faces."

Roman chuckled and nodded. "Actually, it's the perfect cover for a crime. You couldn't have planned it better if you tried. Destroyed the crime scene good and proper. I'll bet it took Wentworth a while to realize his stamps were missing?"

Mia remembered. "At least a week because he refused to stay in the house until it had been cleaned. He even talked about getting rid of the goats, but

I'll bet he didn't. I was gone before he went back home, so I wasn't even around when he discovered the theft."

"Yeah. It turned out great," Dean said, cutting off a corner of his steak. "We even joked about getting our own goats. We'd be the goat thieves. Or the thieves with goats."

"Good old Billy, Bobby, and Betty. It was the highlight of their goaty existence," Mia said, laughing again. "I'll bet they relived that night for the rest of their days. I wonder how long goats live?"

Both men shrugged, and Mia took a bite of her veggie pizza.

"How close are we to Danny Dawson's room?" Roman asked.

"Five minutes."

"Where are Karl and Jimmy?" Mia asked.

"Keeping an eye on things in Lauderdale."

"Things like the Russian guys showing up?"

"Yeah. We need to know because if they're on to Danny then they're on to all of us. So far, no sign of anyone poking around."

"That's good news," she said.

"Could be. Or maybe they're staying well out of sight and waiting until someone shows up," Roman said.

"Yeah. Hard to say. Still, I'm taking it as a good sign."

They loitered in the restaurant until it was fully dark, then Dean instructed Roman to get behind the wheel.

"Sorry, babes. But it doesn't hurt to have someone with Roman's training drive us in. You never know, right?"

"I'm an excellent driver." Mia sniffed. "And I got us out of plenty of tight spots back in the day, or have you forgotten?"

"Trust me, I haven't forgotten a single thing about you," Dean said in a silky, soft voice.

"Don't be weird," Mia snapped.

"Just telling it like it is," Dean said.

Roman started the engine. "Let's go," he called out.

Dean smirked at Mia then slid onto the back seat behind Roman. Shaking her head, she opened the car door and settled in the front, quickly fastening her seatbelt when Roman immediately began backing out of the parking space.

After a moment of quiet in the car, Dean cleared his throat. "Is this a frosty silence I'm sensing?"

"Nope," Roman said, keeping his eyes on the road. "Where to next?"

"Right onto Conklin. And good because I'd hate to see you two love birds having a spat."

"No spat," Mia said, purposefully shifting closer to Roman.

The Airbnb was located on a quiet tree-lined street. Dean instructed Roman to continue past and park at the corner 7-Eleven and they walked the half block back. The air was hot and humid, and Mia's shirt clung to her back. Pulling an elastic tie from her back pocket, she quickly gathered her hair into a ponytail. A woman hurried by never lifting her eyes from the sidewalk.

"We have it rented for another two weeks," Dean said softly. "We should be good to walk right on in."

"You have a key?" Roman asked.

"Naturally." Dean's teeth flashed white in the darkness, and he clapped a hand on Roman's shoulder. "You, my good friend, are going to stand lookout. It's pretty handy having a third person."

"Whew. And here I was worried I wouldn't be able to help," Roman deadpanned.

Leaving Roman standing guard on the driveway at the side of the house, they walked to the back of the bungalow and took a set of stairs down to the basement. Dean opened the door and ushered Mia in. She stepped slowly, already buffeted by the turbulent energy. When Dean flicked on the lights, she wasn't the least bit surprised to see the place had been tossed.

"Shit," Dean said, taking in the mess of ruined furniture. "How the hell did they trace us to this place? I used an alias, as usual, and we were barely here. We only rented it for a month because it was less hassle with the owners."

"Well, they certainly found you," Mia said.

She walked through to the next room and saw the bedclothes had been removed and the mattress slashed. Even the pillows had been relieved of their stuffing. The small dresser stood without drawers. They'd been pulled apart and left on the floor in a heap of broken wood.

"Danny slept in here a few nights, and I took the other room," Dean said, coming to stand beside her and stare down at the bed. "Jeez Louise, I wonder if the diamonds were here?"

"What about Jimmy and Karl?"

"They stayed somewhere else. It seemed better to split up. You think you'll be able to get anything from in here?"

Mia blew out a breath. "I dunno. The other energy is very strong. I might not be able to see through it. All I can do is try."

"Try fast, okay? It probably isn't safe for us to hang too long."

She sank to the floor, sitting cross-legged and closing her eyes. Beside her, Dean shifted nervously, his breathing audible. She blocked it out. Immediately, she was in the scene with two men. They held machete type knives and hacked at the mattress before getting on their hands and knees and searching the closet. A third man entered with a crowbar and pried up sections of the floor.

"They aren't speaking Russian," she said, her eyes still closed.

Dean's voice came from close by. "What do they look like?"

"Tall, dark brown hair and flat blue eyes. He has a thin scar running from his left ear down along his jaw."

"That's Niko. Who else do you see?"

"Shorter. Maybe five eight. Reddish brown hair. Husky build. And the other guy is a little taller but skinny with dark eyes. Jumpy. His hands constantly moving. And he's chewing gum."

"Not sure about the husky guy but the other one is Alex."

"They didn't find the diamonds here." She blinked her eyes open and glanced to where Dean sat on the floor beside her. "Their accents were American."

"Yeah, they were sent here for education and acclimatization starting in high school. Trust me when I say their roots are all Russian. Did you get any echo from Danny?"

"Let me try again."

She rubbed a hand across her forehead then settled herself and pushed out with her mind. After several minutes, she shook her head.

"Crap," Dean said. "Now what?"

"Now we get out of here. This place is creeping me out."

He put out a hand to help her to her feet.

"Guess I'm not getting my deposit back," he said as they continued through the small sitting room and to the door at the back.

"Oh, please. I'm sure you used a forged card to secure the booking."

"Still, it's the principle of the thing."

He unlocked the door. Mia was relieved to make her way out into the night air after the claustrophobic atmosphere inside the house. Dean grabbed her arm, pulling her back against the bungalow.

"Did you hear Roman's whistle?" he whispered in her ear.

"What? No. Are you sure?"

They huddled quietly, straining to hear. Sure enough the two-note whistle came through the night sounding very much like a chickadee. Mia's stomach flip-flopped and sparks of electricity raced across her skin.

Beside her, Dean repeated the whistle. It seemed much too loud in the still night and Mia's eyes combed the area, convinced they were about to be discovered. Sweat trickled down her back.

Dean put his mouth against her ear. "Okay. Let's take the backyard route down the street until we're close to the 7-Eleven. Hopefully Roman will have the car revved and ready to go."

They kept to the back of the house until they reached the far side before scooting across to the next building, thankful it was only a few scant feet away. This worked fine for the next few houses, but eventually they reached a yard which was fenced.

"They have a dog. A Rottweiler," Mia hissed when Dean began climbing the wooden slats. "What if they let it out?"

"It's not out now so hurry, and we should be fine."

"I heard something," Mia said, tugging on Dean's sleeve a couple of houses past. They stopped, crouching low by a car. "There it is again. Someone's running."

"Could be Roman."

"No way. He knows how to keep quiet," Mia said.

"Okay. Let's hang here a second."

The footsteps continued past their location, and they waited for another minute or so until they were sure.

"It only sounded like one person," Dean said. "I'll bet there are at least two, so don't let your guard down."

"As if."

They returned to sneaking across back yards including climbing a few more fences. Mia lost count of how many times she rapped a knee or shin against a hidden object in her path. Lifting her head, she strained to see through the darkness. She thought she could just about make out a concrete wall. Surely that must be the border of the parking lot? They were almost there. A couple more back yards and thankfully no fences.

At the last house, they sidled along the driveway and kept low, scanning the street. Empty. In the parking lot to their right, an engine sprang to life. From time to time, headlights from traffic on the next street over swept across the road.

"This wall is too high to climb, so we'll have to go along the sidewalk to the corner," Dean said.

Mia's breath sounded harsh in her ears. She swallowed and nodded. "Okay. Here we go."

She stood and checked both ways for signs of lurking machete-wielding Russian mobsters with American accents, then stepped onto the sidewalk. Dean grabbed her hand, slowing her hurried steps, and linked his fingers through hers.

"Hey, here we are, the perfect love-struck couple going for an evening stroll."

"Okay. Right. Strolling." Mia exhaled. "Why does the corner look so far away?"

"We'll be there in two shakes of a stick, babes. Just relax."

"Sure. Relax. Good idea," she whispered back. "Why didn't I think of that?"

"Can you sense if Roman is up ahead?"

"Um..." She slowed...letting her vision go to a soft focus...until, up ahead, the traffic lights bled into one another, and the streetlights seemed like glowing orbs. "I can't feel him. There's something—oh, no."

Mia whirled around pulling Dean with her and tugged at his arm urging him to run. When he looked back over his shoulder, he saw the silhouette of two men moving briskly around the side of the building and starting down the street toward them. Dean dragged Mia along with him as he turned down the driveway of the first house they came to. They sprinted to the back and continued running through the yards retracing their steps from moments ago.

"We need to hide," Dean said.

"How about the place with the play structure in the yard?"

"Hey, that looks like a shed over there."

He flung his arm out pointing off to their left and, still running, Mia turned her head and spotted the dark object at the back of the property. Slapping footsteps sounded from up ahead, and someone shouted something, but she couldn't make out the words. She and Dean cut through the long grass toward the corner while a beam of light played across the area to their right.

"Flashlights," Mia hissed.

"We're almost there," Dean said breathlessly.

The air seemed as heavy as syrup, and Mia found it increasingly difficult to take in a breath. She struggled to keep up with Dean. Glancing to the right, she saw one of the men advancing into the yard beside them and swinging a flashlight back and forth.

Dean grabbed her hand again, propelling her along then shoving her in front of him when they reached the small garden shed. Crouching down, she tried to push in between the wall and a hedge, but her path was blocked by pieces of wood and other debris.

"I can't get through," she whispered.

"Let me try," Dean said, crawling in past her and working on the obstacle.

"Hey, over here," a man called out.

"I'm going around to the other side," Mia said.

"No, wait. I've almost got it," Dean hissed.

Mia continued along the front of the shed and started down the other side toward the back. The air went out of her completely when she became aware of movement in the yard behind her. Her skin was now crawling with thousands of pinpricks of electricity, and she scuttled as quickly as she could across the grass.

"Well, well, what do we have here?" The voice came from practically on top of her. "Hey, lady. I've got a gun pointed straight at your head, so you'd better stop crawling away."

She froze in place, too terrified to look at the man or the gun.

"Where is he?" another voice called from the left.

"Don't know yet but I've snagged myself a woman. Come on, sweetheart, stand up and let me see you."

A hand came down on her shoulder. When she didn't respond, the same hand grabbed her hair, yanking her head back and pulling her up while she cried out in pain. As she got her legs under her, he spun her around. She clamped a hand to the back of her head where her scalp screamed from the insult.

The second man joined them and shone his flashlight in Mia's face, momentarily blinding her. "Who the hell is this?" he asked.

"Don't know but she's the one we saw on the camera with Dean in the Bnb," the first man said, pressing the gun forward so it pointed at her chest. "Tell us where he is, and we'll let you go."

Trembling from head to toe, struggling to control her breathing, Mia shook her head. "I don't know what you're talking about. I was out for my evening stroll."

"Then why'd you run?" The second man said, pushing his face in close to hers. His skin was mottled with pockmarks, and he had big fishy lips.

"I saw you running, and you had a gun. I was understandably scared," she said, trying for a reasonable tone.

"Hey, I know her. She's Dawson's kid. I seen pictures in his wallet." The second man, who's pointy incisors reminded her of Ricky Gervais, lowered his gun and grabbed her arm. "Maybe we don't need Dean. She probably knows where her old man stashed the rocks."

"Your dad cheated us," fish lips said. "Double-crossing a partner is the worst thing a man can do. Total lack of morals."

"As opposed to holding a woman at gunpoint," Mia returned.

"I want Dean, too. Where is that son of a bitch?" fish lips asked.

Mia attempted to shrug as much as the restraining hand would allow. "We split up, and he crossed the road. Guess I chose the unlucky side."

Out on the street, tires squealed, and someone laid on their horn.

"That's probably him. Come on," Ricky Gervais said.

Fish lips whirled around and ran through the grass while Ricky Gervais tugged Mia along. For her part, she dug her heels into the ground and tried to stall his progress as much as possible, terrified because she sensed it was Roman out on the street, and he wouldn't realize the men had guns.

"Guess who?" Dean's voice sing-songed from behind them. "Stop right there because now you're the one with a gun pointed at your head."

Ricky Gervais stiffened, and his arm came around Mia's waist, pulling her tight against his chest. "Well, I've got a gun on the little lady, so looks like we have ourselves a Mexican standoff."

Slowly, he spun them around to face Dean.

"Let her go, and you can have me," Dean said. "And FYI, you doofus, a Mexican standoff means three guys pointing guns at each other."

"Jimmy," Ricky Gervais called out. "I need some help back here."

"Come on, it's a simple transaction. Let her step to the side nice and slow. As soon as she's clear, I'll drop the gun."

"No way. You must think I'm stupid. Toss the gun over here and lay on the ground, face down."

Realizing Ricky Gervais was unsure of his next move, Mia squirmed in his arms and kicked at his shins. He tightened his hold and elbowed her hard in the side. In return she stomped on his foot, but when he pressed the gun to her temple she stilled again.

In that moment, the flash came to her strong and true. Ricky Gervais pointing this same gun at her father. Danny Dawson had scrambled to pull out his own gun, but Ricky fired so quickly he immediately slumped to the ground.

"You'll never find them, Karl," her father had said to Ricky Gervais. "They're gone."

Then Ricky Gervais-Karl had kicked him hard in the chest before Jimmy pulled him away and the police sirens sounded in the background.

"He killed my father," Mia cried. "Pops didn't even have his gun out, and Karl, here, shot him in cold blood."

Dean stared at him. "Is that true?"

"No way, man. The bitch is lying."

"That means it's your fault we can't find the diamonds. You and your stupid temper." Dean waved the gun back and forth.

"Shut up. Me and Jimmy know you threw in with Danny and double-crossed us too. You gotta pay for that, man."

"Let her go," Dean said, his voice quiet but firm. "She had nothing to do with any of it."

"Cept she was there, right? Or how else did she see me shoot her old man? So she musta been in on it," Karl said.

As Karl continued sniping back and forth with Dean, Mia noticed his gun hand relaxed against her throat. She shifted slightly, mouthing 'get ready' at Dean then slumped in Karl's arms letting her weight fall against him as though she had fainted.

Karl shuffled to the side to counterbalance the load of her. Taking advantage, she turned her head and bit down as hard as she could on the wrist of his gun hand while simultaneously kicking straight up with the back of her heel between his legs.

"Arrgh," Karl squealed.

His other arm clamped around her all but making it impossible to breathe, but she didn't let go of his wrist even as he attempted to yank his arm away. Karl's body jerked, and he groaned. It jerked again, and the pressure around her midsection loosened. All at once he began shrinking to the ground.

"Let go, babes," Dean said. "He's out."

Dean pulled her free, and she whirled around staring down at her captor who had collapsed on his side with one leg bent under him. His eyes were rolled back in his head and blood poured from a wound to his temple.

Dean tapped her shoulder. "Run," he urged.

She turned and followed him into the next yard. She was so lightheaded spots swam in her vision, and she still couldn't catch her breath. It felt as if she were moving in slow motion, her legs barely covering any distance with each stride and her feet heavy on the ground.

"Hey. Cut it out. I've got you. Don't make me shoot," Jimmy's voice came from her right side.

Mia didn't look, didn't stop, just kept struggling to race across the yard, which seemed to stretch on forever.

"Look out," Dean said, grabbing her arm.

"What?"

When she turned to him in confusion, he pushed her to the side. His body jolted twice as though he'd been hit with an electric shock and sank to his knees. It was only in that instant she registered the noise she'd heard had been gunfire. She crawled toward him and reached for his gun, which had fallen from his hand. But before she could pick it up, Jimmy kicked it away and pressed the barrel of his gun against the top of her head.

"It's over, sweetheart."

Beside her, Dean's breath came out in gasps. At least he was alive, she thought numbly. Slowly, she raised her hands in surrender.

Chapter Thirteen

Jimmy picked up Dean's gun and shoved it in his shoulder holster before hauling Mia to her feet. His hand clamped over her elbow, and he dragged her across the lawn to where Karl still lay in a heap...though he was moaning, and his eyes blinked slowly.

"Pistol whipped," he muttered. "Figures. Dean never was much on shooting. Come on, Karl, you great lump, get up."

Jimmy kicked him lightly in the shin then reached down into the man's shirt pocket and pulled out a handful of zip ties. Spinning Mia around, he wrestled her other arm behind her and secured her wrists together at the small of her back.

How was it possible that for the second time in her life a man was zip tying her?

"I need to help Dean," she pleaded.

Jimmy sighed and pushed her forward until she was walking. He guided her back to Dean who was bent over and clutching his left arm to his body. Dean rocked back and forth ever so slightly as though soothing himself.

"Lemme see," Jimmy said, pulling Dean's right arm away.

"You shot me, you stupid son of a bitch," Dean said through clenched teeth.

"Shoulda stopped when I told you," Jimmy said without sympathy. "You'll be fine. I aimed for your shoulder, and I'm a good shot."

"We should try and stop the bleeding," Mia said.

"Later." He reached down and took Dean's good arm and helped him to his feet. "You two stand right there and don't move, or I'll shoot you again."

"Dean, oh my God," Mia whispered. "Are you okay?"

"It hurts like hellfire, and it's still bleeding pretty steady," he said, his voice roughened and his breathing uneven. "Where's Roman?"

Mia exhaled. "I sensed him out on the street a few minutes ago but now...I don't know. He's probably watching and trying to figure out how to get to us. Too bad you took away his guns."

Dean didn't respond. He stood with his head down, breathing through his nose and holding his left arm across his stomach while blood dripped from the elbow. She glanced over to Jimmy and saw he'd managed to get Karl on his feet and walking an unsteady line back toward them.

"What will they do with us?" she asked.

"No idea. Hopefully, I can convince them I didn't throw in with Danny."

"Let's go," Jimmy said, taking Mia's elbow and guiding her toward the driveway beside the nearest house.

She stared up at the darkened windows wondering how on Earth no one heard gunshots or noticed four people scrambling through the back yards. What would happen if she screamed? Probably Jimmy would shoot her in the shoulder same as he'd done to Dean. She wondered if Dean still had his cell phone.

"Okay, princess. Move it. We don't have all night." Jimmy poked her in the back with the gun, and she shot forward.

When they reached the sidewalk, Mia's eyes flicked left and right hoping to see Roman, but the street was empty. Karl grumbled that his head hurt.

A thud sounded, Dean cried out, and Jimmy glanced back and growled in his throat.

"Karl, don't be an ass wipe. Stop pounding on him. We need to get 'em off the street."

A car cruised slowly toward them. Not Roman in the Audi but a red Nissan. Jimmy stepped over to Mia and slung an arm around her shoulders. Up ahead a black van beeped, and the running lights flashed once.

Jimmy increased his stride sweeping Mia along with him until they reached the van. He opened the back door wide and motioned for her to get inside. With no other option presenting itself, Mia reluctantly clambered in.

"Come on. Come on," Jimmy muttered under his breath.

Soon enough, Dean was shoved in next to her, and the door slammed shut. Karl slumped in the passenger seat, hand clutching the side of this head, and Jimmy started the engine and pulled smoothly away from the curb. There were no windows in the back of the van. The seats had been removed and the area was covered with a rough cloth.

Mia scooted against the wall beside Dean. It was uncomfortable sitting on the barely padded floor with her hands tied behind her back. Her shoulders were already mighty unhappy. She studied Dean. His head was tipped back against the metal wall, and his eyes were closed. Blood continued dripping down from his shoulder though it was a small stream rather than a gushing arterial burst. When headlights played across his face, she noticed his skin was as pale as milk, and his lips pinched together.

"Hang in there," she whispered.

"I'm trying," he muttered.

"No talking," Karl roared, clearly in a bad mood.

Mia closed her eyes and stilled her mind. Reaching out, she searched for Roman. He had to be somewhere nearby, she reasoned. But all she sensed was Dean's pain and fear. Shifting closer, she closed her hand over his.

The van continued through the city, slowing, turning, stopping at red lights, until Mia had lost all sense of where they were going. Eventually, Jimmy eased over several speed bumps and into a parking lot by a row of warehouses. Angling toward the end building, he hit a remote on the dashboard and the bay door began to slowly roll up. He swung the vehicle around, backed in, parked, and set the door to close before stepping out of the van. Karl sat watching the two of them as if they were going to make a break for it…bullet wounds and zip ties notwithstanding.

The main space of the warehouse was filled with cars. All jammed so closely together Mia couldn't figure out how they'd managed to park them that way. Jimmy took her elbow and directed her between the van and a black Mercedes and toward a short hallway.

He pushed by her and took out a key fob then unlocked the first door on the right. It was a small office with a couple of desks holding laptops and a long, orange couch pushed against the far wall. There were no windows. The room reeked of cigarette smoke.

Karl shoved Dean onto the couch and turned to Jimmy. "I need a fucking drink."

"Pour me one, too," Jimmy said.

Karl disappeared back out to the hallway, and Jimmy eyed Mia.

"I'd like to look at Dean's wound," she said calmly, keeping her eyes steady on his. "Do you have any medical supplies?"

"Some. They're in the bathroom at the back."

He nodded to the corner beyond the couch, and she saw a door she'd missed in her initial scan of the room. She turned slightly and lifted her bound hands away from her back.

"Come on. It's not like I'm going anywhere. There're two of you, and you're armed."

"And you know I'll shoot you if you cause one bit of trouble."

Mia nodded then stood stock still when he produced a switch blade from his pocket, the metal glinting under the fluorescent lights. He sliced off the zip tie in one quick move before pocketing the knife and walking to the desk by the door.

She rubbed her tender wrists and rolled her shoulders.

"Okay, let me see how bad it is," she said, sitting next to Dean on the hideous orange couch.

"I thought you guys were supposed to be in Lauderdale keeping an eye out," Dean said bitterly.

"Yeah, well. The whole thing smelled fishy and me and Karl decided you were the one that needed watching. Turns out we was right."

Mia gently tugged at Dean's shirt, undoing the buttons and pushing his right arm to the side. Some of the blood had dripped onto the seat cushion. His grey cotton shirt was soaked in red, and she pulled it away from his chest and bared his left shoulder.

Once she was able to wipe the area clean, she found the small circular wound just above his collar bone. She urged him to lean forward, which he did, hissing against the pain when he moved, and she saw the exit wound was slightly lower on his body but had luckily managed to avoid any bones.

"Looks like it caught the meat and not much else," she said reassuring him.

"I also took one in the arm. That's what's killing me," he muttered.

"I need to slip the shirt off and have a look." She worked the fabric carefully down his left side while he closed his eyes and panted. "Oh, here it is. No exit wound on this one, so the bullet must still be in there."

"No shit, Sherlock," Dean gasped.

"Hey, I'm not the bad guy here," she reminded him.

On a shaky exhale, his eyes met hers, still brilliantly blue despite the shadow of pain. "Sorry. Didn't mean it. It sucks getting shot."

"Apology accepted." She patted his cheek. "I'll see what I can find to patch you up. You're going to be okay. Hang in there."

He nodded and eased back against the couch, his right arm coming across to cradle the injured one.

Mia hurried to the bathroom. It was bigger than she'd expected and even contained a bathtub. She rooted through the medicine cabinet behind the mirror, but there was little beyond cough drops and—ew, gross—condoms.

In a narrow floor-to-ceiling cupboard beside the tub she found what she was looking for in the form of a white plastic box with a big red cross on the lid. Inside was sterile gauze and bandages, rubbing alcohol, antibiotic ointment, scissors, tweezers, pressure wraps, and the kind of cold compresses that activated when shaken.

Closing the lid down with a snap, she turned back to the cupboard and grabbed several towels. Then deciding it would be best to bring Dean into the bathroom rather than treat him on the filthy couch, she went out to the main room and coaxed him to follow her.

The shoulder wound was a straightforward case of applying pressure for several minutes until the bleeding slowed. Next Mia cleaned both holes with plenty of water and a small splash of the rubbing alcohol.

"Shit. Shit. Shit," Dean wheezed.

"Sorry. It's not always best to use this stuff, but I'm worried about bacteria."

She covered the wounds with ointment and gauze and using a hand towel front and back, managed to wrap the entire shoulder with a couple of Ace bandages. Next, she instructed Dean to sit on the toilet while she inspected the bullet hole in his upper arm. It continued to bleed more aggressively than the other wounds had.

"Um...do you think I should try and pull the bullet out?" she asked, biting her lower lip.

"That sounds painful," Dean said, his face somehow even paler than before.

"You know, it's probably best to leave it be for now since I have no idea what I'm doing. We can at least work on the bleeding and clean it up."

She took another towel and placed it around his arm and over the wound, pressing down hard. Dean winced. "Did you happen to see any heavy-duty pain meds?"

"Only Tylenol and ibuprofen. They'll at least take some of the sting out and help with the swelling." She paused and tipped her head toward the door, trying to make out what Jimmy and Karl were saying. "Any ideas on escaping?" she asked.

"Unless we can get hold of the guns, I don't see us getting away. And with me like this it isn't likely we'll disarm them, is it?"

Mia shook her head and repositioned the towel making sure to keep the pressure nice and firm. "Probably not. What do you think Jimmy will do with us? It sort of seems like he's the leader of the two."

"Yeah, I'd say he's definitely the one in charge. If we could find the diamonds, he might be convinced to let us walk though it pisses me off since I never double-crossed him in the first place."

"What about the Russian guys I saw going through the Airbnb? I wonder if Jimmy's working with them."

"Doubt it. The mob isn't likely to let Jimmy and Karl run loose after they stole from them."

"Which means we could potentially have two sets of men after us?"

"I guess so. Where the hell is Roman?"

"Without a gun or weapon of some sort, I don't know what he can do besides call the police? And he might be too worried about you and the blackmail pictures to get them involved," she said, letting some of the bitterness she felt creep into her voice.

"We'll have to hope we get lucky then. Don't suppose you've had any flashes of inspiration on where your father hid the damn diamonds?"

"Nope. Hey, I never asked. How much did you steal?"

"A couple of hundred carats. The only other place I can think of taking you is his apartment in New York. You ever been there?"

"To the city? Yes. Didn't know Pops had an apartment. Was that his home base?"

"Not really, He had a bunch of different places. Said he liked to move around and stay loose. I think he mighta had a boat too, but I couldn't find it."

Mia shrugged nonchalantly. "He always did like being on the water." She sighed, thinking about the diamonds she and Roman had already found. "Even if we could find some of them, maybe it would be enough to appease Jimmy and Karl."

"Maybe. Though they were pretty amped up about millions and millions coming their way, so I don't know if they'd be willing to settle."

"Then I guess I'll have to find all of them," Mia said. "And that means next stop New York City. Hey, the bleeding has slowed down. Let's get you cleaned up."

Mia continued to work on Dean's arm wound and gave him some Advil before helping him back to the couch. Karl paced back and forth by the desks, a bottle of Maker's Mark in his hand. Jimmy sat sipping from a glass and staring at the screen of his laptop.

"Here's the thing," Mia said. "I think I might know how to find the diamonds."

Both men snapped to attention and Karl rushed to her, grabbing her elbow and shaking her hard. "I knew you was lying."

"Hey, back off, buster," Mia snarled, stepping to the side and yanking her arm away.

"Karl," Jimmy warned. "Cool it." His muddy brown eyes swung back to Mia. "Where'd you say they are?"

"I didn't but if we go to my father's apartment, I'll bet I find something in his safe that will point the way. I know how his mind worked and the kinds of places he hid things. He used to do stuff like that when I was a kid."

"And where would this safe be?"

"New York."

Jimmy blinked and nodded. "That's a clip from here. I'd say a solid day's drive." He pushed away from the table and slowly walked to the back of the room, his glass of whiskey still in hand. "Feeling okay?" he asked Dean when he passed by.

Dean snorted. "Oh, yeah. I feel great. Never better."

"You get what you get," Jimmy said placidly.

"I didn't take the diamonds," Dean exploded. "You think if I knew where they were I'd be sitting on this ugly ass couch with a bullet in my arm?"

"Danny brought you to us, so far as I'm concerned his double-crossing is on you," Karl said, whirling around and kicking the leg of the desk. "I should be on an island soaking up the rays by now. Instead I'm chasing around after your sorry mug."

"Right now, I don't much care if you did or didn't cross us," Jimmy said. "But I want those stones back. One way or another I'm gonna get them." His eyes shifted from Mia to Dean and then back again, resting on her face.

"Here's what we're gonna do. Karl stays and watches over Dean. You and me hit the road for the big city."

"No way," Karl exploded. "I'm not staying here with this traitor."

Mia crossed her arms over her chest. "And I'm not going anywhere without Dean."

Jimmy's smile lacked warmth. "It's funny how you think you can bargain with me. You're going. He stays. End of story. I suggest you use the restroom before we leave cause I ain't stopping every five minutes."

"I don't trust Karl. He has no self-control," Mia said. "What's to stop him from smacking Dean around or even killing him as soon as you walk out the door?"

"Hey, I can control myself fine," Karl said, lifting his lip in a sneer.

"Karl won't touch Dean," Jimmy said. "He knows how to keep his eyes on the prize."

"Why can't we all go?" Mia pressed

"Cause I need Karl here. The diamonds ain't the only thing we got going on. And it's harder being on the road with a guy who's all shot up. It raises questions. People remember. Trust me, it's better this way."

"Are you a man of your word?" Mia asked.

"Course. You ain't got your word then you ain't got nothing."

"Okay. Give me your word that nothing happens to Dean, and I'll go with you to my father's apartment and figure out where the diamonds are. When I find them, you release both of us."

Jimmy studied her face for several seconds before nodding. "It's a deal. But if you don't find them, I own both your asses."

"Mia will find them, and when she does, I want my cut," Dean said. "Because I didn't do anything wrong here."

"You'll get half your original cut and that's it," Jimmy said. He lifted his glass and drained the whiskey then turned back to Mia. "We leave in five minutes, so do what you need to do and wait by the door."

Chapter Fourteen

Roman crept around the perimeter of the warehouse. Other than the bay door and a small metal walkout door beside it, there weren't any other entrances. He knew his lock picking skills were no match for the door and besides, he'd already spotted the security camera which meant it was probably also wired in with an alarm. The few windows on the back of the building were set high up just below the roof. Even if he could somehow climb to them, he wasn't sure they were big enough to fit through.

As time ticked by, his anxiety notched up until he was vibrating with the need to do something, anything, to get Mia the hell out of there. It had been fifteen minutes since he'd seen the van disappear into the warehouse. Try as he might to keep his focus clear, his mind continually showed him scenes of Mia being tortured. Or worse.

He began searching the area for a weapon of some sort. Preferably a large rock or better yet a discarded gun and a box of bullets. Sadly, all he found were pebbles scattered on the asphalt parking lot. Shrugging, he sat and took off his shoe and his sock. He filled the sock with as many of the pebbles and small rocks as he could find.

There were also pieces of broken glass and he threw them in for good measure until half of the foot area was filled. He knotted the end of the sock and swung it in a circle in front of him liking the weight of it. Not bad, he figured. And certainly better than nothing.

A grating noise sounded behind him. He whirled around and realized the bay door was lifting, so he ran to the far side of the building out of sight. Carefully easing his head around the corner, he saw the van back out, followed by a black Mercedes with Mia behind the wheel.

She must have sensed his presence because she turned her head and looked directly at him. He could see her mouth moving, but it was too dark to make out what she was trying to tell him. She turned to the passenger seat and the man beside her motioned to keep backing the car away from the building.

Glancing toward Roman again, she repeatedly tipped her head at the warehouse urging him to run inside. Then she took her foot off the brake, and the car began rolling again. Meanwhile, the man driving the van swung around and positioned the vehicle to re-enter the building once the Mercedes was clear of the door.

Heart thudding, mind rabbiting, Roman's only instinct was to follow Mia's car. He calculated how long it would take him to run down the street to where he'd stashed Dean's Audi and pick up the chase but immediately realized they'd likely be long gone by that time.

He watched the sedan clear the parking area and head north along the service road. To his left, the van was nearly halfway into the building. Clutching the weighted sock, he ran along the wall to the opening. Already the door was slowly rolling down.

Since the regular door was on the far side, Roman had to hope the guy behind the wheel would also be heading off in that direction. Ducking slightly, he passed under the lowering door and flung himself to the left, almost ramming into the back of a car. He crouched down and crawled between the bumper of the car and the brick wall, his breath sounding way too loud in his ears.

The door of the van slammed shut and footsteps receded across the concrete floor. Thankfully, the light was dim enough in the warehouse that Roman figured he'd be hard to spot. He crawled out and made his way along the side of the van until he could see the man disappearing into a hallway.

Once standing fully upright, he peered into the van hoping for a better weapon. All he saw were fast food wrappers and a couple of packs of Marlboro Lights. He peered through to the back and could just about make out that the seats had been removed...but little else. His hands itched to pull the door open, but he cautioned himself, worried the interior light would shine like a beacon pointing the way straight to him. Looked like he'd have to go with the sock weapon.

And now that he stopped to think about it, why the hell had Mia motioned him in here in the first place? Did she figure he could torture this second man until he revealed her destination? His hand thunked against his forehead. Of course not. Mia wasn't the torturing kind. Clearly Dean must still be in here somewhere, and she wanted Roman to rescue him.

The only trouble was Roman didn't care one lick about Dean or what happened to him. As far as he was concerned, the man had made his bed and now he had to lie in it. But...Dean would probably know where Mia was going, wouldn't he? He nodded to himself. Yep. He could do that—rescue the stupid son of a bitch—if it meant saving Mia.

Carefully squeezing in between two cars, he made his way to the hallway and inched along until he came to the first door. He pressed his ear to the cold metal, then he heard a male voice. And though he couldn't make out the words, the man seemed to be ranting. And possibly kicking something, given the irregular thudding sounds.

Even though Roman only heard the one voice, it stood to reason there might be a second person in the room because who ranted to an empty space? A crazy person, that's who.

Or someone on the phone, he realized.

Shit.

Okay. Impossible to tell if Dean was in there or not. But this wasn't the only room in the hallway. He made it to the next door, also metal, and tried the handle. It was locked. But the door after that opened with a creak that made Roman's heart lurch. He paused, staring back toward the first door, and waited. When he counted to sixty and no one came running out, he slowly released his breath.

The room was large and though he didn't dare flip on the light, he could see well enough. It contained four bunk beds pressed up against the back wall, a large table with plastic chairs and a small kitchenette. As quietly as he could, he searched the drawers, feeling practically giddy when he located a steak knife.

Hello, Mr. Sharp, he thought, testing the blade with his thumb.

Roman eased out of the room and tiptoed across the hall to the last door but, alas, it was also locked. After sneaking back to the room nearest the garage area, he listened again but could no longer hear any voices. He inspected the door carefully. Solid metal with a sturdy round knob. The frame was also metal. There was no way he'd be able to force it open, so he had to somehow get the guy—and hopefully it was just the single guy—out of the room.

He could bang on the door, but then he'd lose the element of surprise. Ditto if he caused a ruckus in the hallway. He stepped quietly back to the main body of the warehouse and gazed at the multitude of cars packed into the place. Definitely some kind of auto theft ring...man, wouldn't he just love to sick the cops on these thugs?

His attention drifted to the garage door. Likely as not, there was a sensor or monitor alerting when it was activated. That would get Mr. Thug's attention. Roman sidled between the vehicles and searched the area by the door looking for a switch.

Bingo. Two big yellow buttons with an up arrow on one and the down arrow on the second. Perfect. Okay. So what was his plan? He couldn't simply stand out here waiting for the guy because there was no doubt in Roman's mind he'd come with gun drawn.

He turned and stared at the hallway, then he gauged the distance and the easiest route through the cars. He stopped to listen for several seconds ensuring all was quiet before testing the route back to the hallway and making his way along to the unlocked door. Yeah. He figured he could get back there before Mr. Thug had gathered his wits and come out to investigate.

Roman checked that the knife was easily accessible from his front pocket. He wrapped the end of the sock around his hand then returned to the bay door. This had to work. Mia was out there on her own, and he was going to get her back or die trying.

Exhaling in one long whoosh, he raised his fist and tapped it against the yellow up button. The motor above him began grinding. He turned and scooted toward the hallway. It remained empty. Sprinting almost to the end, he yanked the unlocked door open and dove inside, making sure it didn't slam behind him.

He opened the door a bare inch and tried to hear over the frantic pounding of his heart.

"That better not be you, Jimmy," the man said flinging the door wide when he stepped into the hallway.

He lifted his gun, cocking it, and walked toward the garage section. The motor of the door had stopped by the time he reached the threshold.

Roman continued watching while the man paused and surveyed the area then turned left, walking toward the overhead door. Wasting no time, Roman ran to the first room and pulled the door open partway before carefully poking his head in.

"Where the fuck have you been?" Dean said.

In the brief few seconds Roman's eyes flicked to him, he noted that Dean's right hand was tied to the handle of a door at the back of the room and his other arm was bandaged and hung in a makeshift sling.

"Don't suppose you have a gun?" Roman said, slipping into the room.

Dean shook his head. "Got a bullet if you want to dig it out of my arm."

Roman shook his head. "Just the one guy with you?"

"Yep. Good ol' Karl."

He ran across the room to Dean and slid out his knife and cut the zip tie, freeing him. "I'm going to jump Karl when he comes back. Any idea what I can use to take him down?"

"There's a toilet in here," Dean said, motioning to the door he'd been tied to. "The top of the tank should do the trick."

It seemed to take forever for Karl to return. Dean remained by the bathroom door so it appeared he was still tied where he'd been left while Roman stood by the main door. Finally, the handle turned and the door opened smoothly.

"Wasn't nothing. Stupid door musta—" Karl started to say.

The sentence ended abruptly when Roman slammed the heavy piece of porcelain against the back of the man's head. Karl made a sort of 'glugging' sound before slumping to the floor. Roman immediately dropped the toilet top and crouched down by the felled man. Once he grabbed the gun, he slid the safety on and slipped it into his jeans pocket then checked Karl's neck for a pulse.

"Not dead, thank God," he said to Dean. "We need to tie him."

"Should be some zip ties in his back pocket." Dean sat down gingerly on the couch, carefully cradling his injured arm.

"Excellent."

Within minutes, Roman had Karl's hands secured behind his back and his ankles bound together. He searched the rest of his pockets, finding a cell phone and a set of keys. Then leaning down and grasping the man's shoulders, dragged him along the concrete floor and into the bathroom. Hauling and rolling, he managed to get him into the tub before sitting back on his heels and catching his breath.

He used more zip ties, then attached Karl's wrists to the hot tap faucet. Carefully tipping his head against the wall, he checked that the man was still breathing before returning to the main room.

"Where's Mia going?"

"New York to Danny's apartment."

"You know where it is?"

"Uh huh."

"Get up. We're leaving. She's only about fifteen minutes ahead."

"We need supplies," Dean said, struggling to his feet. "Like another gun."

"Gee. I don't think the gun store will be open right now," Roman said, turning his attention to the door of the bathroom.

"So now you're a wise guy?" Dean walked over to watch while Roman dragged one of the desks across the floor and jammed it under the handle of the bathroom door. "I have a couple stashed away. Plus, I need some better drugs."

"Okay. But we have to be quick," Roman said reluctantly. "I don't want anything to happen to her."

"Jenny will be fine." He paused and rubbed his hand across his forehead. "I mean Mia. She knows how to take care of herself, and Jimmy has his eye on the prize. As long as he gets his diamonds, he won't hurt her."

"He better not," Roman muttered. He walked over to the second desk and picked up Karl's phone. "Any idea what his passcode is?"

"Try 'big dick' all one word."

Roman lifted his eyebrows. "You're kidding me?"

"Nope. It suits him, don't you think?"

Roman said nothing, simply tapping in the code and smiling when it unlocked the screen. He scrolled through the contacts noting Jimmy's number. "You think they track one another?"

"No idea but not worth the risk in case."

"Yeah. You're right. No point in tipping Jimmy off that Karl's been taken out. Where's your cell?"

"Don't know. Jimmy took it off me first thing. Knowing him, he probably still has it."

Roman held the phone above his head and let it drop onto the concrete floor before repeatedly smashing it with the heel of his shoe until the screen was cracked beyond repair and small pieces of plastic littered the floor.

He tested the power button. "That baby is toast. Come on, let's get out of here."

It was at least twenty minutes later when they'd cleared Savannah and were headed north on I-95. Roman worked to keep his mind from racing while Dean slumped in the passenger seat, occasionally sipping from a bottle of rum.

They'd hit a twenty-four hour Rite Aid and along with the rum, had grabbed some snack food, Tylenol, more bandages, and a proper sling. The guns had been retrieved from a basement easement in an alleyway a few blocks from the Airbnb. Two Glocks, a Berretta, and a Colt with plenty of ammo.

Knowing they were well armed left Roman battling with his conscience. Was he really on board with killing a man? As a police officer, he'd always been mentally prepared to do whatever was necessary to serve and protect. But this was different, and he was no longer a cop.

He thought about Danny Dawson. Karl and Jimmy had apparently had no problem taking him out. And despite what Dean said, it stood to reason Mia was in a great deal of danger whether or not she found the diamonds. Thinking of Mia, his mind crystallized. If the situation came down to it, Roman knew he wouldn't hesitate to shoot Jimmy. Or even Dean, should he get in the way. He would keep her safe no matter the cost.

"How'd you get shot?" he asked Dean.

Dean sighed, tipped the bottle up and took another swig. "Mia and me got away from Karl, but Jimmy came back as we were making our escape. He called out, warning us to stop, but Mia kept running. When I looked back, I saw he was aiming at her and..." He gave a half shrug then winced.

Roman stared over at him. "You jumped in front of her?"

"Yeah, I guess I did. Look. Don't make a big deal out of it, okay?"

"Not gonna, considering you're the reason someone was pointing a gun at Mia in the first place." He paused and blew out a breath. "Still, I gotta say thanks."

"Sure. Whatever. I don't want anything to happen to her either. We had a lot of history together."

"Which was the point you were making at dinner with all the back-in-the-day stories. It doesn't worry me. Mia is done with it. She'd never go back to this life."

"Sure she says that and probably even believes it. But you didn't see how good she was at the game. That girl could work a con in her sleep and loved every minute of it. It's in the blood. You can't turn your back on something like that."

Roman hated that Dean's words sent a chill down his spine. Still, he curled his lip in contempt and kept his eyes steadily on the road. "Well, last I looked, she has turned her back."

"It'll be real interesting to see what happens when we find the diamonds and she gets her cut. Nothing works so well to whet the appetite like a good payday."

"You really think Jimmy and Karl are giving you a piece of this? Man, you're dumber than I thought. You're cut out of the game, buddy boy. With the diamonds and with Mia."

Dean didn't respond and Roman clicked on the radio. Finding a station with old rock was easy, and he settled back against the seat and dug in for the long drive ahead. Over the coming hours, he pushed the speed as much as dared. He figured Mia would do her best to dawdle in the hopes he wasn't too far behind. Since the car was likely stolen, Jimmy wouldn't be eager to attract the attention of the police.

Roman only stopped twice during the dash up the East coast and even then, it was less than five minutes while he and Dean relieved themselves on the side of the freeway. He'd taken so many caffeine pills by the time they hit the outskirts of New York City that his hands were shaking.

He reached across the console and punched Dean's thigh. "Where to?"

Dean blinked and wiped his face. "Um...Ramone Street in Brooklyn. I'll program the nav."

Almost noon by now, the traffic was predictably heavy, and Roman had to keep from thumping the steering wheel in frustration as they crawled along and the minutes ticked by.

"You ever been to this place?" he asked Dean.

"A couple of times. Small apartment block. He's on the top floor, which isn't saying much since it's only, I don't know, like eight stories or so. Security is pretty lax. It's the usual buzz-in deal at the main door."

"Any chance you have a key?"

"Fraid not."

"Well, I guess we'll have to figure it out when we get there."

They drove on while the female voice of the navigation system guided Roman. As expected, there were no empty street slots, but after circling the building, they discovered the garage door to the underground car park was up. Roman stopped at the key slot and studied the protruding wires.

"Looks like somebody knows their way around electronics."

"That would be Jimmy's specialty. Smart to leave it open in case they have to book out of here for some reason. And they won't be up there long enough for the super to get down here and deal with it."

There were no vacant spots, but Roman managed to jam the Audi into a corner by a post. Scanning the other vehicles in the tiny garage, he smiled and pointed over Dean's shoulder. "Say, do you suppose that's Jimmy's car? Not too many Mercedes in the area."

"I don't know, since I never got a look at what they were driving." He opened his door and leaned out. "Hot damn. Those are Georgia plates."

Roman shut off the engine and stepped out. "She must still be here. Thank you, God," he said, his eyes swinging briefly heavenward. "You keep watch, and I'm gonna make sure no one can drive that baby away."

Turning back to the car, he retrieved the steak knife and walked across the lot to the Mercedes. After quickly looking around to make sure no one was watching, he crouched down and stabbed at the front driver's side tire.

The knife was sturdy and reasonably sharp, but even still, he was hacking away for close to a minute before he heard a satisfying whoosh of air. Roman repeated the process on both of the back tires for good measure before standing and massaging his wrist. Turns out being a bad guy was a lot of work.

Back at the Audi, he opened the trunk and picked up one of the Glocks. He released the magazine to check the bullets and reloaded it again. "What do you want?" he asked Dean.

"I'll take the other Glock. And an extra mag because you never know."

"He's only one guy," Roman said. "And the guns are for insurance. I'm hoping to do this thing without firing a single shot."

Dean took the gun and second magazine from Roman. He slide the magazine into his front pocket and the gun down the back of his pants. His face was ashen and sticky with sweat.

"Hey, you sure you're up to this? You don't look so hot," Roman said.

"I'm fine. Hang on." He walked around the car and opened the passenger door, then reached into the glove compartment. Turning back to Roman he handed him a cell phone. "I always keep spare burners just in case. Come on. Let's get going."

The keypad on the door into the building had also been compromised, and luckily Jimmy must have felt certain he wasn't followed since he hadn't bothered to secure it once he and Mia had passed through. Roman and Dean made their way to the elevators. One was at the lobby level. The other on the eighth floor.

"This just gets better and better," Roman said. "Okay, here's our plan. I say we take him here. The building's small, and it's the middle of the day. Little chance anyone else will happen along. Since you're...shall we say...compromised, you go up and watch Danny's door. Get off on the seventh floor and walk up so Jimmy doesn't think it's hinky that both elevators are stopped on eight. Give me a heads up when they leave, then follow them down. Hopefully I'll have it under control by the time you get here."

Dean studied Roman's face, blinking slowly, then nodded. "Okay. It sounds solid."

Once the elevator doors closed behind Dean, Roman fixed his eyes on the second elevator in case the timing was off and Dean missed them leaving. After five minutes or so had passed, he walked back out to the parking garage and scoped the area. To Roman's eye, an SUV parked between the Mercedes and the garage door would provide the best concealment.

Standing by the vehicle, he could just about see through the glass door to the bank of elevators and make out the illuminated floor lights above. He leaned on the hood, set the phone down beside his elbow, and slowed his breathing. The fact he was about to possibly assault...certainly restrain...a man was seriously insane. He felt for the Glock in his waistband and wondered what other crimes this gun had been used to commit.

During the last twenty-four hours, Roman had done a number of things that weighed heavily, but he realized, for him, this was the moment he'd officially crossed the line and joined up with the bad guys. How the hell had it come to this? The whole thing made his skin crawl and he could only hope he'd find a way to live with whatever was about to happen.

God damn, Mia. This was her fault.

He sighed. Not true. Much the same as Mia had made the decision to help her father, Roman had been the one to insist on accompanying her with Dean. His choice. His consequences. The phone pinged and his eyes darted to the screen.

They're out.

Chapter Fifteen

Seconds later, the elevator indicator began showing progress of its descent, and Roman's heart jackhammered against his ribs. He reached for the gun, chambered a bullet, and crouched down by the front tire.

He saw their feet first. Jimmy's housed in black boots and Mia wearing her favorite blue and pink New Balance sneakers. Jimmy was speaking loudly.

"Come on, man. Where the hell are you? Stop messing around and take care of business. Karl, I swear, when I get back to Savannah I'm gonna..."

Roman scooted along the front of the SUV then reared up practically right behind him and cocked the gun. Jimmy stopped short and shot a glance over his shoulder at Roman, the phone still pressed against his ear, his other hand gripping Mia's arm.

"Karl can't come to the phone right now," Roman drawled. "He's tied up in the john." He pressed the barrel of the gun against the side of Jimmy's head. "Let her go."

Mia yanked her arm away and smiling, turned to Roman. "I knew you'd come," she said, as though they were doing nothing more than meeting for dinner at a nice restaurant. "Where's Dean?"

Roman kept his eyes trained on Jimmy. "He should be along any minute. Take Jimmy's phone, would you babe? He won't be needing it."

Once Mia had secured the phone, Roman grabbed Jimmy's shoulder and spun him, pressing him against the SUV. "Assume the position, asshole."

Calmly, Jimmy spread his legs and bent over resting his palms on the hood of the vehicle. He turned his head slowly and fixed cold, brown eyes on Roman. "You're making a big mistake here. You don't want me as an enemy."

Roman kicked Jimmy's legs farther apart and leaned in close to the man's ear. "The minute you took Mia we were already enemies, so I'd say you're a little too late on that score."

Slipping the Glock in at the small of his back, he patted Jimmy down and relieved him of a switch blade, a Berretta, and a Colt. Beside him, Mia exclaimed in delight and rushed away.

"Oh, Dean. How're you doing?" Roman heard her say.

"Give me your wrists, nice and slow. Left one first," Roman said to Jimmy.

Roman grasped the left wrist and pressed it into the small of the man's back. When the right arm released from the hood of the car, Jimmy shoved his hips straight into Roman and managed to push him back a step. His right arm continued arcing around and connected with the side of Roman's neck while Roman fought to hold the left wrist in place and press Jimmy against the metal grill.

They struggled until a foot shot out to the side and slammed against Roman's calf, unbalancing him enough that Jimmy was able to roll him and reverse their positions. Now Roman was the one pinned against the unforgiving metal. Jimmy tried to reach around him and grab the gun in the waistband of his jeans. When he twisted away, Jimmy began punching, his large meaty hands smashing into Roman's shoulders.

Roman timed the punches and shot his fist straight out, catching Jimmy in the throat. The other man gulped and coughed while Roman was already gripping his right arm and twisting it behind his back.

"Zip ties," he called out to Dean, gasping at the effort of containing the still struggling man.

Eventually, with a little more sweat and a few chosen curse words, Roman secured Jimmy's hands behind his back.

He stepped back and blew out a breath. "Stupid bastard. Where the hell did he think he was going?"

"You're an optimist, aren't you Jimmy?" Mia said. "Thanks for the ride, but it looks like we'll be parting ways now. Give my regards to Karl."

She reached up and patted Jimmy's cheeks while the man glowered at her. Then she snagged the car keys from his back pocket, walked over to the Mercedes, and opened the trunk.

"You can't be serious," Roman said.

"Best place for him. He won't come to any harm, and it might be awhile before someone needs their car. Even if it's only a few minutes, that's enough for us to make our getaway. Besides, it's not that bad."

"Says the girl who was locked in a trunk less than a year ago."

"Come on. What's the big deal?" Dean said. "Besides, the longer we hang out talking about it, the more chance we're discovered."

Roman looked from one to the other then sighed. "Okay. Yeah. You're right. Come on, Jimmy."

He tugged on his elbow, and after a brief pause, Jimmy walked toward the Mercedes.

"Youse guys are gonna pay for this," he said. As he turned his head, he spat on Roman's shoe. "Nobody crosses Jimmy G and gets away with it."

"Just get in already," Dean said, standing beside Mia. He pulled out his gun and pointed it at Jimmy, gesturing him into the trunk. "I never crossed you over the diamonds, and you still came after me. Seems like justice has been served."

Jimmy lifted his gaze to Dean. "You're a dead man, you hear me? I'll be outta here in two minutes, and I'll catch you faster than that. I know where you're going."

Mia smiled full on. "Actually, I may have lied a teensy little bit back there. Pops didn't hide the diamonds in Los Angeles."

"No more talking," Roman said and helped Jimmy swing his legs into the trunk.

He put a protective hand over Jimmy's head when the man lowered his torso down then closed the lid of the trunk with a small satisfying bang.

Roman immediately turned and grabbed Mia for a hug, and, for a moment, she worried he might crack her ribs.

"I'm okay. I'm all right," she patted his back. "Except I can't breathe, and all my internal organs are being displaced."

"I don't care." His arms hugged her tighter then after a beat the pressure eased. "You sure you're fine?"

"One hundred percent."

She beamed up at him but before she could say anything else, his mouth crushed down on hers, stealing her breath. His lips parted, taking her deeper, and his hands cupped the back of her head. She stepped all the way into him, taking the anguish and fear and sending back love and light.

When a fine tremor ran across the muscles of his chest, she once again patted his back then rubbed slow, lazy circles letting her hands fall lower and lower until she finally grasped his hips and pulled him hard against her, center to center.

"Don't worry, baby," she murmured against his mouth. "Everything's going to be okay."

Behind her, Dean cleared his throat. "As much as I'm loving this happy reunion, we'd best skedaddle. Don't want to be caught standing outside the trunk of our captive."

Eyes never leaving Mia's face, Roman stroked fingertips across her cheeks and along the side of her neck sending skitters of desire racing down her spine. "Yeah. We should hit the road." He lowered his face and brushed her lips with his one last time. "Okay. Let's move on out."

Mia sighed then let him take her hand and lead her to the Audi.

"I'll drive," she said. "Jimmy took over for the last few hours, and I got to sleep some which I'm guessing is more than either of you managed."

Dean settled across the back seat carefully cradling his right arm while Mia and Roman buckled in up front.

"Now what?" Roman asked.

She eased the car away from the corner post and executed a three-point turn before glancing over her shoulder. "First things first, we have to get that bullet out of Dean's arm, and since the hospital is out of the question, I'm waiting for him to tell me where to go."

Dean's painfilled eyes met hers. He shrugged and shook his head.

"Come on, man. Mia's right. You can't walk around like that. And no doubt you know a guy who can help, so spit it out already. Time's a wasting."

Dean blew out a breath and rested his head back against the seat. "Okay. Alright. Maybe I do know someone who might know someone. I gotta make a call, and in the meantime, I suggest we hit the road before Jimmy gets himself out of the trunk."

"Fine. I'll start driving," Mia said, putting the car in gear and exiting the parking garage.

After picking a destination at random, she programmed the nav for Williamsburg and made her way to Marcy Avenue. In the back, Dean made his call, identifying himself as Charlie Waters, and asked for a medic hookup in New York City. When he hung up, Roman shot him a look.

"Charlie Waters, huh?"

"Yeah. I have a couple of aliases on the go. It's safer. For me, and for the others. That way whoever they send me to won't even know my real name."

"How long will it take?" Mia asked.

"Don't know. This is my first time needing a doc. Hope it'll be my last, too. Can't say I'm loving the whole getting shot thing."

"And Jimmy and Karl don't use the same guy?" Roman asked.

"Not that I know of. In case you didn't notice, we aren't exactly pals."

They drove in silence for several minutes until Roman tapped Mia's thigh. "There's a convenience store up ahead. Pull over. We need phones."

She double-parked outside of Snacks'N'Stuff, and Roman got out of the car.

She called out to him, "Get some food, too. I'm starved." Then she turned sideways in her seat and studied Dean. "How're you doing?"

"Just peachy."

"Since this is totally your fault, I shouldn't feel sorry for you, but I do."

"My fault? I literally took a bullet for you. Two of them, in fact," he said, squinting his eyes open.

"Yeah. It was nice of you. But, and it's a big *but*, I wouldn't have been there if you hadn't forced me to go with you. So still your fault."

Dean's lips quirked into a smile. "You always were a hard ass. I don't know any other chick who would say that to the guy who saved her life."

She reached back and squeezed his knee. "Thanks. For the life-saving part. I mean it, sincerely." She paused and studied the bandage on his arm. "That's bleeding again. It'll soak through pretty soon. Hope your guy hurries up and calls back." He glanced down at the bandage and shrugged while she continued studying him. "You never used to need bullet removal services. What happened to you?"

"Got bored with the long scams. And the truth is, I never found anyone as good as you, so half the time, the take was pretty lousy."

"Guess you shouldn't have walked out on me, huh?"

Dean sighed heavily. "You could say that was the biggest mistake of my life. I'm sorry, Peanut."

Mia stiffened at the long-forgotten pet name. "Yeah, well, it was the best thing that ever happened to me. Otherwise, I wouldn't have ended up all but broken in a back alley after getting on the wrong side of Nunzio and his gang, and I never would've gotten out. In a way, I have you to thank for the life I have now."

"You're welcome, I guess."

Roman opened the car door and slid onto the passenger seat clutching two large plastic bags. "We'd better go. You're double parked and there's a uniform down the road writing tickets. We don't need to draw any extra attention to ourselves, do we?"

While Mia drove, Roman rummaged around in the bag and came out with bottles of water. He opened one and handed it back to Dean before doing the same for Mia.

Mia took a long drink then rolled her shoulders and sighed. "Are you okay? I saw Jimmy get some shots in while you were dealing with him."

"I'm fine. We should find a place to park until Dean's guy calls. No point in driving around wasting gas. It's not like Jimmy would have any way of tracking us."

"Yeah. Okay." After a bit, they came across a strip mall, and she swung into the lot before parking facing out and turning off the engine. "What are we going to do after the doctor?"

"I don't know. Quite the mess we're in, wouldn't you say? Can't see the way out yet either."

Mia leaned toward him. "I might have an idea," she said in an undertone.

"Hey, why'd we stop?" Dean mumbled, shifting in his seat.

"Cause it's the best move right now. You hanging in?" Roman said.

"Sure. No problem."

"One thing I've been wondering," Mia said, turning sideways in her seat again. "How'd my dad get involved in this? Did you bring him in?"

"It was the other way around. He called me. I guess he did another job with Jimmy a few months ago, and it went good. You know those auto transport trailers that haul new cars around the country? Your dad figured out a way to jack them from dealership lots and supply Jimmy with a bunch of primo product for his chop shop operation. Then the diamond thing fell into their laps when one of the Russian guys got shitfaced and ran his mouth in the exact bar Danny happened to be in. They needed a fourth guy, so he brought me on board. I knew of Jimmy G, of course, but I'd never worked with him before."

"And now you never will again," Roman said.

"We'll see. Lots can be washed under the bridge if I get the rest of our stock back from wherever Danny stashed it. I'll split it with the guys, and all will be right in the world, just you see. Now that I've got Jenny—I mean Mia—on my side, I'm gonna get lucky. I can just feel it."

"You always were an optimist," Mia said at the same time Dean's phone pinged. She waved her hand. "See. Point in case. Everything's coming up roses for Dean Chambers."

"Yo." Dean said into the phone. "I'm Charlie. Yep. GSW to upper arm. Okay. Sure. Of course."

When he clicked off, Roman gestured with his hand. "What's the plan?"

"We need to go to 1134 Westney Ave in Queens. He'll take me in as soon as I get there."

"Just out of curiosity, how much does something like this set you back?" asked Roman.

"I paid twenty-five large on retainer to my contact guy. Once the doc assesses me, he'll give the final price. Take it or leave it. No haggling. Anything over the twenty-five thousand, I have forty-eight hours to make good on or they send out the leg breakers. Don't worry. I have enough stashed away if need be."

Mia had already started the car and punched in the address. "Looks like it'll take thirty-six minutes. Let's go."

Dean dozed off and on during the drive. Roman fished out a large bag of barbeque chips, and he and Mia had eaten the whole thing down by the time they got to Westney Avenue. The nav directed them to a red brick building that had been refurbished with big, shiny new windows. Dean roused, looking pale and heavy-eyed. He told Mia to go into the underground parking and head down to the second level and take spot number twenty-two.

Once the Audi was parked, Dean pushed open his door and struggled out of the car. He staggered a little after he got to his feet and leaned against the car, clutching his arm while exhaling through tight lips.

"I'm going in with you," Mia said, unbuckling her seatbelt.

"No way. It's bad enough we drove Dean here. I don't want some crooked doctor being able to ID you," Roman said.

"He's right, Peanut. I'll be fine." Dean pushed away from the car and trudged toward the bank of elevators.

Mia hissed out a breath. "He looks like he's going to collapse. I have to help him."

"Fine. We'll all go. But only as far as the doc's floor. We ain't walking him in, and we damn well ain't meeting this guy."

"Okay. Fine. Come on."

They hurried across to Dean, and Mia tucked in beside him and put her arm around his waist to lend support.

"What floor?" Roman demanded.

"Penthouse. You need a code. It's nine two, four two, eight six," Dean said.

Roman sprinted ahead, and by the time Mia had helped Dean to the elevator, Roman was already inside with his finger on the 'hold open' button.

"I don't get why it hurts more now," Dean said, slumping against the wall.

"Because the shock's worn off," Roman said bluntly. "You know, you really should consider a different line of work. You'd kill it in sales or something."

Dean snorted. "Thanks, but no way. I could never be a working shmuck."

"You'd get shot a lot less," Mia said.

The doors pinged open, and Mia guided Dean onto a well-lit hallway that stretched about a hundred feet long. "How far?"

"There's only four units up here, and he's number one in the far right-hand corner. I've got it from here. Thanks."

Roman and Mia watched while Dean slowly made his way toward the door, then they quickly backed into the elevator and hit the button for the parking garage before Dean raised his good hand to knock.

"There're cameras in here," Roman said, tipping his head to the right.

"Yeah. I figured. But I couldn't leave the poor guy on his own. I was afraid he'd pass out or something."

"I think he's playing it up. And besides, if you can't do the time then don't commit the crime."

Mia nodded. "I know, and I one hundred percent agree." She paused. "Anyway, I did get something in my dad's apartment. A little glimpse, shall we say."

Roman shook his head. "Let's wait until we're outside, okay. It's safer."

Mia nodded and bumped her shoulder against Roman's. "Good thinking. You can never be too careful, right?"

"Right."

He shifted away until they were no longer touching. In the parking garage, Roman strode ahead and reached the Audi first. He walked around to the passenger seat and waited until Mia clicked the locks. Once they were both inside, he gestured at her with his hand.

"What'd you find at your dad's?"

"Not so much find as see. I think Lou—Mary Lou Adler—is in Atlantic City. They were looking at condos on the boardwalk and Pops was telling her it was only for a short while, and she had to stay safe."

Roman nodded. "Okay. And you think she might be able to help us."

"I don't know," Mia said shrugging. "It's the only thing I can figure to do. Unless you have a better idea?"

"Nope. I've been thinking about it nonstop, of course, but can't see a way through yet. If Jimmy's any kind of decent thug, he'll be able to figure out where you live pretty quick, so we should avoid your house for the time being. We're not going back until we have a good plan. I'm assuming the Russian guys won't know to look for you?"

Again Mia shrugged. "I doubt it, but who the hell knows."

"Which means right now, Jimmy is our biggest problem."

"Don't forget about Karl," Mia said.

"Yeah. But from what you and Dean have said he's hardly the brains of the operation."

"No. But he's not steady like Jimmy. Karl is all over the map emotionally. Plus, he's the one who killed my dad."

Roman's eyes widened. "You know that for sure?"

"I saw it when he touched me. Pops didn't even have his gun out, and Karl just point blank put a bullet in his heart."

"I wish we could nail that guy, but we don't have any proof. If we could implicate him in some other crime and the police are legally allowed to seize his gun, then they could do a ballistics match. Until then..." He let out a growl. "Except I took Karl's gun. I'm the one with the murder weapon. God, this is so frustrating. What about Dean? How long before he drops this nice guy act and gets violent with us?"

"He's not the violent type. Okay, okay," she hurried on when Roman's face creased in annoyance. "I know he had a gun on us before, but he was never going to use it. It isn't his style."

"And you know this...how? Because he never did in the past. Sweetheart, that was ten years ago. A lot can happen in a decade."

"Let's not argue about it," Mia said. "Since we're going to ditch Dean and find Lou he won't be a problem. Even though I fully believe he'd never hurt us, I can't guarantee he wouldn't bring Jimmy to Lou if enough pressure was applied. I don't want anything to happen to her because of us."

Roman exhaled. "Okay. Sounds good. We can't take his car though. Jimmy knows it."

"Yeah. I thought of that. We'll have to rent one. I don't think it's far to Atlantic City, but I don't want to punch it into the nav and basically give Dean a trail to follow."

"Okay. Let's walk out and Uber it to a rental," Roman said collecting up the two bags of supplies.

"I'll leave the keys under the driver's mat. Not the safest but best we can do."

"I sure hope this Lou person can help us, or it'll be a big waste of time," Roman said once they were outside waiting for their ride.

"Maybe but it's not like we have any other ideas right now." She stroked a hand down his arm, and when he shifted away yet again, turned to face him. "What's going on with you? That's the second time you've shaken me off."

"I guess the fact we're aiding and abetting a felon is starting to piss me off all over again. And maybe it seems like you can't help sticking up for him at every turn."

Her eyes widened. "You think I still have a little something for Dean? Come on. Get real."

"Maybe not a little something," he said, using his fingers as air quotes. "But it seems your bond runs deep. This is a guy who encouraged you to whore yourself for the cons then took off with your money, leaving you high and dry while he picked up with another woman. I'm having a hard time wrapping my head around why you're still so loyal to him."

"I'm not...it isn't..." She blew out a breath. "Look. He's a means to an end. That's it. We have to solve this problem of the diamonds and Jimmy and Karl and a bunch of Russian Mafia thugs. And Dean might be able to help us. If not, at least he isn't actively working against us. So what if I helped him into the building? Call it common decency. If you can't get over yourself then maybe you need to get out of my way."

The challenge lay between them like a gauntlet thrown down. They stared at one another, Mia's face flushed, and her breath came fast while

Roman was expressionless, stiff and tight as though carved from stone. Finally, he nodded.

"Let's just find this Mary Lou and figure out the next thing, okay."

"Fine."

Mia turned away and stared across the street to where a mother walked slowing carrying a baby against her chest and holding the hand of an unsteady toddler. She wondered if the woman was having a better day than she was.

Chapter Sixteen

They rented a tan colored Nissan Sentra. Nice and non-descript. This time Roman took the wheel, and Mia sat turned away from him with her head back and her eyes closed. It took almost two and a half hours to reach Atlantic City and during that time, she and Roman didn't exchange a single word.

When he pulled the car over into a parking spot on the street just before the boardwalk, she finally turned to him.

"What's our plan here?" he asked.

"I don't have much of one. I guess we'll start hitting the buildings and hope to get lucky. Could be a long haul," she said, gazing at the numerous condos dotted along the boardwalk."

"How can you be sure they didn't rent a house or something?"

"Because in my vision that's what they were looking at on the computer. And Pops would have thought a building was safer. More security for sure. Neighbors close by. And I'll bet he installed a doorway cam so she could check for any sketchy looking characters."

Roman blew out a breath and rubbed a hand back and forth across his forehead. His face was showing signs of the abuse it had suffered at the hands of Jimmy. Luckily there were no cuts, but his cheek was bruised, and he was going to have a beauty of a shiner on his left eye.

There'd been talk of setting up engagement pictures. Mia chuckled to herself at the thought of Molly's horror if and when she saw Roman's face. Looks like they'd have to wait a couple of weeks on the photo shoot. Assuming Roman still wanted to go ahead with the wedding.

She'd done a lot of thinking on the drive and how it'd been a hell of a week or so. Frankly, she wouldn't totally blame him should he decide to back away. If the positions were reversed, and they were running around getting into all kinds of trouble with Roman's ex-girlfriend, she couldn't honestly say how she'd be feeling and surely shouldn't condemn him for being pissed off and frustrated.

And she'd never forget that he'd really come through for her. God, he'd been magnificent back there in that underground parking garage. So tough and strong and completely calm while he dealt with Jimmy the thug. She could admit to herself seeing him in action had been a serious turn on.

"In case I didn't say it before, thanks for rescuing me from Jimmy. You were amazing," she said softly.

He blinked at her and nodded. "You're welcome. I'd say anytime, but I seriously don't want this to become a habit. Come on, let's hit Dunkin' Donuts. I need some caffeine before we start the 'needle in the haystack' portion of our day."

With large coffees in hand, they decided to split up and cover twice the real estate at once. After they'd programmed each other's numbers into the new phones, Mia shoved hers into her back pocket.

"We check in every thirty minutes, okay?" Roman said and waited for Mia to nod her agreement. "Who am I looking for?"

"Lou," she said then put up an index finger. "Sorry. Make that Loretta Maples. At least that's the ID I saw on the desk during my glimpse."

"Loretta Maples," he repeated. "Okay. Let's do this. Stay sharp. Chances of Jimmy tracking us here are dead low but not zero."

With that, he dropped sunglasses over his eyes, took a sip of coffee, and strolled across the street toward the nearest building.

They pounded the pavement for four hours before stopping for food. Inside a booth at Denny's, Roman slumped against the back of the seat and flashed a huge yawn.

"You need a nap," Mia said.

"Yeah or twelve hours facedown, but we don't have time for either. Good thing I'm used to shift work and long hauls on my feet."

"This is taking a lot longer than I thought. We may have to stay overnight."

He tapped a finger to his temple. "Great minds. I was thinking the same thing. And we do have to stay somewhere, so Atlantic City is as safe as any, right?" His face lit up. "Here comes our food. Praise Jesus because I'm about ready to gnaw off my own arm."

Once the waitress had deposited heaping plates of steaming food in front of them, all was quiet at the table for a time. Roman shoveled in mouthfuls of fried chicken and chewed furiously, only pausing occasionally to gulp down some of his Coke. Mia ate enthusiastically though not quite mirroring Roman's full-on caveman style, and soon her bowl of stir fry was down to the last few scraps. Leaning back, she patted her stomach.

"That feels so much better. I was actually getting dizzy before. Should we ask for some ice for your face?"

"Naw. I'm good for now. You ready to get back out there?"

"I guess." She squared her shoulders. "All I've been thinking about these last few hours is how great it would be to drive back to Dalton, pick up the dogs, and go home. You don't think Jimmy will find the dogs, do you?"

Roman studied her face. "Honestly? Yeah. He probably will. It wouldn't take much to stroll around Dalton telling everyone he's a good friend of

Mia Reeves, town hero, and get them to spill stories about you. I'll bet the dogs come up pretty fast. The townsfolk are a chatty lot."

"Shit. I hadn't thought of that. I'm going to call Renee. Give her a heads up and make sure she doesn't release them to anyone but me." She stared down at her phone. "I can't remember the number. Man, I need my old phone back."

She dialed information and got the number for Wag'A'Way Kennels. "Hi, Renee, it's Mia. How are my babies?"

"Seem to be enjoying their getaway. Lots of playing and barking and happy dog sounds. Except the big guy, of course. He's constantly on watch."

Her heart clutched at the thought of Mac worried he'd been abandoned again. "I'm glad they're okay. Um…listen…I'm not exactly sure when I'll get back. Hopefully tomorrow, but it might be the day after. Do you have room for them to stay?"

"Of course. Don't worry about it."

She blew out a breath. "Good. And there's one other thing…please don't release them to anyone but me, okay?"

"I would never do that," Renee said, her voice filled with shock.

"I know. Of course, you wouldn't. Just wanted to put it out there. If I can't make it back tomorrow, I'll give you a call and let you know. Thanks a million. You're the best."

After hanging up, she shook her head. "I don't like this. If anything happens to them, I'm going to shoot Jimmy myself. I wish I'd never agreed to help my dad."

"You and me both," Roman mumbled. "Come on. Let's get going. The sooner we find Lou the better."

But they didn't find her. At least not during the next few hours. It was dark when they finally decided to quit for the day. They grabbed a pizza and booked themselves into a motel. The shower stall was tiny, barely enough room for one person, and Mia insisted that Roman go first.

After her turn under the water, she found him sprawled across the bed dead asleep in nothing but his boxers. She eased down beside him and rubbed a hand across his bare chest. Poor guy. He'd been up for the better part of thirty-six hours by now. She'd at least managed to snatch a few hours in the car with Jimmy...was that only today? She couldn't even remember anymore.

The pizza smelled heavenly, but the box was all the way across the room, and it was just too darn far. Sighing and slipping down until she was lying on the bed, she tucked in beside Roman and was asleep two seconds later.

It turned out the pizza was just as good for breakfast. Maybe even better since they both woke ravenously hungry. The rest of the morning was spent covering the final condo buildings on the boardwalk with zero success. Still tired, and feeling defeated, they met up at the same Denny's as the previous day to regroup and refuel.

"Maybe they did end up renting a house," Mia said dejectedly. "If so, how the hell will we find her?"

"Don't know," Roman said. "Did I tell you I called information yesterday, and there's no listings for a Loretta Maples or a Daniel Dawson. They must have used a different alias."

She slumped against the back of her seat. "Great. Just great. Other than finding Lou, I don't have any other ideas. Do you?"

"Nothing good. I guess we could always go back and hole up at your house. Fortify things and lean on Kevin for some extra patrols. Except he's gonna press me for details and want to run background checks. He is a cop after all. I don't think saying 'some random bad guy from Mia's past' will cut it with him."

"Or we could get a room close to Dalton and stake out my house maybe?"

"Yeah. That could work. But it might be a long stakeout. Days or even weeks. And what about the dogs? Can't keep four of them in a motel. I'm also worried about Dean. Who knows what the hell he'll get up to. He's a loose cannon in all of this."

"We do have some of the diamonds," Mia reminded him. "Maybe it'll be enough to bargain with."

"It might have been before I trussed Jimmy up and locked him in his truck. I kinda doubt it'll do the trick now."

"Shit. We're nowhere. And this isn't even the worst-case scenario. If the Russians get wind of me, it's game over. We can't even run because they'll go after your family."

"I know," Roman said grimly. "There's no running in this scenario. At least not for me. I've gotta figure a way to get all of them out of the picture."

"Yeah. But how?"

"Working on it. I don't want to talk anymore. Let's just eat, okay?"

Mia's stomach was in knots, and it took all her effort to force down some of the steamed veggies. Roman, on the other hand, cleaned his plate. She pushed her fries toward him.

"Help yourself. I'm pretty much done."

Shrugging, he finished the rest of her fries and drained his drink before tapping his chest and turning his head to the side to let out a small burp. Mia took one last bite then chewed slowly and thoroughly before wiping her mouth.

"That hit the spot but now I could go for something sweet. I think there's a piece of apple pie with my name on it," he said, raising his hand for the waitress.

"Seriously? You're going to make yourself..." She trailed off, and her eyes fixed on the window beside them.

"What? Is it Jimmy?" Instantly on guard, Roman sprang to his feet and swung to face the door with his hand reaching to the small of his back where he'd tucked the gun.

"It's...I don't know. I just got a funny feeling like skitters up my spine." She leaned closer to the window, turning her head left and right then gasped. "Holy Hanukkah. I think that might be Lou."

Chapter Seventeen

"Mary Lou? Where? Are you sure?" Roman asked, rushing to the window and staring out.

"No. Not sure. But maybe." She pointed across the street to a woman strolling along the boardwalk.

Roman pulled out his wallet and threw down a fifty then grabbed Mia's elbow and steered her through the restaurant. Outside, they paused and watched the woman. She was about five-foot-five or six, large chested with slim hips and blonde hair teased into a bouffant style do. Apparently in no hurry, she slowed to gaze inside store windows as she passed then stopped at a pottery shop to study the wares before going inside.

"Perfect," Roman breathed. "She's just walked herself straight into a trap. Come on. You go in and talk to her. I'll stay outside and watch the door. Make sure to put yourself between her and the back exit if there is one."

Mia shot him a smug smile. "This isn't my first rodeo. Don't worry, I know what to do."

Inside the store, Mia assessed the layout. There was, indeed, a second exit leading out to a parking area. Glancing over her shoulder, she saw Roman had taken up his station right outside the main door. Keeping it casual, she sauntered toward the back and paused for a moment while pretending to study a collection of glazed bowls.

Meanwhile, Lou or Loretta or whatever she was calling herself, chatted happily to the store clerk.

"Oh, I just love these plates. The colors are to die for. I could get soft, green napkins to make the whole thing pop."

Her accent held a slight southern twang, and Mia could smell her perfume from all the way across the store. Something musky and sexy and wholly overpowering.

"We just got them in yesterday. One of a kind and all handmade. I was telling Tandy they won't last long."

"They certainly won't because I'm going to buy them right now. The whole set," Lou said.

"Great. I'll box it up for you. What about the coffee collection?"

"Hm...I hadn't even noticed them. Look at those delicate handles. Yes, I want them too."

"I can have everything delivered this afternoon if that's easier," the clerk said.

"Can't say no to that, can I? I'm going to keep browsing for a minute, sweetie."

"Take your time." The clerk turned to Mia. "Can I help you find something?"

"No. Just looking."

The salesperson set the armload of items on the counter then disappeared through a door beside the exit. Mia strolled over to where Lou was inspecting an adobe ice bucket with fat, purple grapes painted on the side.

"That's pretty," Mia said.

"I know. I think I'm going to get it too. At this rate, I may buy up the whole store," Lou said, patting her ample bosom.

Up close, there were fine lines around her mouth and eyes; her hair was clearly bleached blonde because a hint of dark brown showed at the hairline. She had a pretty face with large grey eyes and a small pert nose. Her makeup, though heavy, was expertly applied, and a set of huge false lashes fluttered every time she blinked. Mia guessed she was somewhere in her early forties, so maybe ten years or so older than she was and at least that much younger than her father had been.

"Lou?" When the woman jerked slightly, Mia gently grasped her elbow. "You're Mary Lou, right?"

"What? No. My name is Edith. I'm sorry. You've made a mistake."

Though it was subtle, Mia sensed a tremor run through the woman.

"Almost packed up here," the shop clerk called out. "Is there anything else you want to add to the order?"

"Um...gosh, I just realized I'm late for an appointment." Lou shoved the ice bucket back on the shelf. "Can you put it on my account, Donna?"

"Yes...of course," the woman said hesitantly, her eyes flicking between Mia and Lou. "Is everything all right?"

Lou forced out a little laugh. "Absolutely. Thanks so much for your help." She shifted her attention to Mia. "Like I said before, you've got the wrong person. Goodbye now."

With the clerk's eyes on her, Mia decided it was best to let Lou leave the store. She tipped her head toward Roman who immediately stepped to the left and disappeared from view. After a few seconds had passed, she nonchalantly walked out of the store after Lou.

On the sidewalk, Roman had his arm around the woman and held her up against his side. Lou pushed against him, straining to free herself while at the same time her head twisted side-to-side as she surveyed the street. Mia immediately trotted over and tucked in on the other side of Lou so she was sandwiched in between them.

"I'll scream," Lou warned.

"No, you won't because I'm Mia...or Jenny if you like. I'm Danny's daughter. He told me to come and find you."

Lou stopped abruptly and stared at Mia. Then her face broke into a smile. "Oh my gosh, I didn't recognize you at first. Of course, you're Jenny. I saw the pictures from the Emerald Ring killer story. You poor thing. That must have been so scary."

"It...um...was," Mia said, easing to the side to give Lou a bit of space.

Lou glanced over at Roman and nodded several times. "And you must be Detective Roman Mancini. Even more handsome in person than you were on the TV, except look what happened to your poor face. Well, gosh, this is something. I wondered if I'd ever meet you, Jenny. I mean Mia." She paused and tipped her head while her teeth worried her plump bottom lip. "Which name do you prefer?"

"Mia," Mia said. "Is there somewhere we can talk?"

"Yes. Of course. We can go back to my place. It's not far. Is Danny coming home soon? He said it would probably be a couple of months, so this is a bit of a surprise. A happy surprise of course." Her laugh tinkled out, and she squeezed Mia's hand. "I miss your dad like crazy. He's the best man I've ever known. I cried buckets of tears when he told me he had to go to Europe for work."

Mia's heart sank, and she flicked a glance at Roman.

"Your place would be perfect, as long as you don't mind," Roman said.

"Mind? You're practically family. And lucky you, I made cookies this morning. Not to toot my own horn but they're so good you'll be weeping like a baby when you taste them. I'll brew us up some tea because what's better than tea and cookies? Oh, what a wonderful day this is turning out to be. I have to admit, I've been lonely since I moved to Atlantic City. It's hard being in a new place all by yourself."

Lou chattered on while they walked halfway along the boardwalk to a silver and glass building on the side Mia had searched only a few hours before. Lou punched a code into the lobby keypad then led them to the elevator. The whole time, Mia's stomach pinched with anxiety. How could she tell this sweet woman that Danny was dead?

"How is my man?" Lou asked, turning to Mia. "When did you talk to him? Or were you in Europe too? He always dreamed you'd work together again."

"How long have you and Danny been together?" Roman said quickly before Mia had a chance to squirm.

"It'll be a year next month. Can you believe it? I've never had anyone treat me so good. I feel like I've won the lottery or something. And I don't mean for the money part. I mean emotionally," she said, patting her heart.

The elevator pinged and the doors opened onto a brightly lit corridor with royal blue carpeting and silver walls.

"Not much farther," Lou said, stepping out and turning left. "I got a corner unit. Windows on both sides."

She led them into the light and bright condo, owing to the expanse of glass along the front wall. Through it was a soaring view of the Atlantic Ocean. Mia quickly scanned the room and saw the space had been decorated with a heavily feminine hand. The couch was floral and a huge print of soft pink lilies hung on the wall to the right. Lacey material had been draped over the table lamps, and the rug centered under the coffee table was white and fluffy and looked like a cloud.

In among the books on the shelves were photos, knickknacks, and arrangements of dried flowers. In front of the floor-to-ceiling glass, a large collection of plants had been placed to maximize sun exposure. A knee-high jungle in front of the gorgeous view.

The kitchen was small and ruthlessly clean. No dishes in the sink. No crumbs on the counters. No fingerprints on the fridge. All the appliances shone silver, and a wooden bowl held a small mound of lemons and limes on the narrow breakfast bar next to a vase of pink roses.

Lou gestured them to the couch. "Please, be comfortable. I'll make tea."

Mia shot Roman a look then turned and walked the three steps to the breakfast bar, placing her hands on the counter. Meanwhile, Lou bustled around putting the kettle on to boil and pulling a glass container from the fridge.

"Let's talk tea," Lou said, her gaze landing on Mia's face. "I have Earl Grey and English breakfast tea. Also, a bunch of herbals. Peppermint might be nice."

"Lou, where did my father tell you he was going?" Mia asked.

"Well, now, I don't remember all the places. I do know he said the first job was in Paris. At the Louvre. He's been in such high demand these past few months. But then, he is the world's foremost expert in art of the Impressionism era."

Roman stepped up beside Mia. "And you moved recently? Why was that?"

Lou pursed her bright pink lips and blew out a breath. "Yes. It was for my safety. Danny was called in to appraise a painting at a museum in...ah...I think it was in Savannah and it turned out to be a fake. The gentleman who was selling it—well, he wasn't really a gentleman since it turned out he had connections to the Russian Mafia—was very unhappy, and he made threats against my Danny. Can you believe it? Poor Danny was just doing his job, and this jerk came along and upended our lives."

"When was this?" Mia asked.

"Almost two months ago now. A very stressful time, let me tell you. I've lived in Vegas practically my whole life. You might not believe it now, but

I used to be a dancer on the strip." Her cheeks pinked up, and she shook her head slightly. "I had a hard upbringing, and it was easy money for a girl like me. But it wasn't an easy life, that's for sure. Anyway, Danny was so worried for my safety after the fake Degas incident he insisted I move and change my name for a while. So now I'm Edith Carter of Atlantic City."

"And then he went to Europe for work a couple of weeks ago. Have you talked to him since he left?" Roman asked

"Not hardly. He wanted to make sure there was no connection between me and him in case somehow this hooligan got hold of his phone. No calls or texts just to be safe. He has been sending me flowers though." She turned and delicately ran a fingertip across the pink roses. "These came a week or ten days ago with a sweet little card. Have you talked to him?"

Mia shook her head and gazed down at the countertop. It was soft grey with black marbling. She traced her finger along one of the dark lines, back and forth, back and forth, while her mind screamed not to do it. Not to shatter this lovely woman's life with the news about her father.

"Mary Lou, I'm so sorry but Danny died," she said softly still staring at the counter.

Lou gasped, and when Mia looked up again, she saw the woman back away until she hit the pantry cupboard behind her. Both her hands were at the base of her throat and her fingers fluttered against her skin.

"It happened a few days ago. He was shot."

Lou's mouth opened and closed like a fish, and her eyes darted all around, anywhere but at Mia. Finally, she turned to Roman, her eyes wide and pleading.

"Is this true? Is he really dead?"

Roman nodded slowly, his gaze never leaving her face. "I'm afraid so. I'm really sorry for your loss."

The woman gulped twice, her breath catching in her throat, and her eyes brimming over with tears. Mia watched as the pain washed over Lou like a tidal wave and wondered why she herself still felt so little when she thought of her father's death. In fact, she mostly just felt numb. So numb even Lou's pain wasn't penetrating her.

Roman sprinted around the counter and gathered Lou in his arms. "There now. Take it easy," he mumbled while patting her shoulder. "I'm so sorry. So sorry."

He kept talking in a low tone and rubbing her back while Lou let out an unending string of great big wracking sobs that echoed off the walls of the small condo. She sounded like an animal being torn apart by wolves.

"Let's sit you down," Roman was saying to Lou, his voice sounding faraway. "Is there anyone we can call? A family member or friend perhaps?"

"I don't know..." Lou hiccupped. "I can't think. What happened to him? How did he die?"

Roman guided her into the living room and onto the couch while Mia searched through the cupboards until she found a glass and filled it with water. By the time she returned to the sitting area, Lou was perched on the couch with Roman beside her, holding her hand. She set the water down on a coaster beside the crying woman and lowered to the coffee table.

Mia exhaled silently then looked into Lou's devastated eyes. "Danny was shot. I was with him. He didn't suffer. It all happened very quickly. Your name was the last thing he said."

"It was that Mafia man, wasn't it? We have to find him. Make him pay for what he's done." Lou glanced between Roman and Mia. "Where did it happen? We'll have to bring Danny home."

"He was in Florida. I couldn't claim his body because it wasn't safe. And you can't get him either. At least not yet," Mia said.

"Florida? But I don't understand. Danny told me all the work was in Europe." She nodded and turned to Roman. "But of course. The Degas thug must have lured him back to the East coast with a phony job so he could kill him."

"Lou, now listen to me. I have to tell you some things. Hard things. I don't do it to hurt you but to protect you. This situation is dangerous, and you need to understand why," Roman said gently.

Lou's eyes stayed riveted to his face. "Okay," she said shakily. "I'm listening."

"Danny wasn't an art appraiser. He was a con artist and a thief. He got in with some bad men, and then he double-crossed them. Definitely not his best move. The men are trying to find what Danny took, and they'll do anything to get it. Including hurt a lovely woman like you."

Lou sprang to her feet and put her hands on her hips. "You are a horrible man. How dare you say these things about Danny. He's a kind and gentle soul. He'd never do anything that was against the law. He's decent and moral and you're nothing but a liar." She turned to Mia. "How can you let him talk about your father that way?"

"Because it's the truth. I'm sorry, Lou. It doesn't mean my dad didn't love you because he obviously did. Otherwise, he wouldn't have gone to so much trouble to get you in a safe place. And he was never a violent man. He mostly ran con games and stole things. He always had some scam or other on the go. This time, though, he got in too deep and made some really bad choices. He told me he was desperate because of the cancer and not being able to pay for the treatment."

Lou's face went slack, and she stood there blinking uncertainly. Her makeup was ruined. The mascara had run down her cheeks leaving thin black pathways. A large portion of the foundation on the lower half of her face was rubbed away and gave her skin a splotchy look.

"Danny didn't have cancer," she said slowly, shaking her head. "I'd have known."

Mia sighed. "He told me he did. Pretty advanced. He was trying to raise the money to start an expensive new treatment."

"How could I not have known? He seemed fine. Maybe a little tired but he said it was from working so much. And he had lost some weight, I guess. When I pointed it out, he patted his stomach and said he was getting in better shape for me so I wouldn't start staring at the young guys. Oh, God."

She collapsed forward into her hands and sobbed quietly. Roman flicked Mia a glance then patted the crying woman's shoulder.

"Come now," Roman said quietly. "This is hard. The hardest news anyone has to face."

"I just don't understand why Danny never told me any of this. I loved him, and I thought he loved me, but I guess I was in love with a lie," she said slowly between sobs.

They sat that way for a few minutes. Mia on the coffee table. Lou folded over, crying into her hands while Roman continued rubbing her back as though she was a colicky baby. Finally, the crying quieted, and Lou got her breathing back under control and sat back against the couch dabbing at her eyes.

"Lou," Mia said. "Did my dad leave anything for me? Maybe a key? It's important. There are some very bad men after me, and I have to find what they need or...well, I don't know exactly what they'll do, but it won't be good, that's for sure."

"And this is because of Danny? He put you in danger?" Lou's ruined eyes slid away from Mia's face as though she couldn't bear to hear the answer.

"It doesn't matter why this happened. What matters is dealing with the situation so if there's anything here you think might help, I'd be grateful if you give it to me."

"I don't remember Danny setting anything aside for you. I'm sorry."

"Could I see his things?" Mia pressed. "Something might spark an answer."

Lou shook her head slowly side-to-side. "I doubt there's anything to find but be my guest." She swept her right arm to the side. "Search the whole place if you want. I really don't care."

Mia walked slowly through the kitchen and sitting area while Lou stayed slumped on the couch with Roman by her side talking in low tones. She didn't want to start yanking open cupboards in front of the grieving woman and had to hope something would jump out at her and point the way. Beyond the main living area were two bedrooms and one bath.

The second and smaller room was set up as a craft area. A table spanned the far wall and, in the center, sat a squat white machine. Beside the machine were a mound of tiny plastic flowers along with clear acrylic boxes of various stones, beads, and string. Lou must be a fellow jewelry maker.

A larger bedroom had a queen-sized bed done up in soft greens and pinks. A print of a sun sinking into the water hung above the bed with more shades of pink and purple. Mia sat on the edge of the bed and closed her eyes. She breathed in deeply through her nose and slowly exhaled while she worked to quiet her mind.

Nothing came to her. At least nothing of her father. She saw a series of glimpses of Lou walking through the area, coming out of the bathroom, sitting on the bed and watching TV. Always alone. Maybe Danny really hadn't been here that often.

Still, she opened drawers and walked through the closet, letting her fingers trail across the few items of clothing belonging to her father. There were only four shirts and two pairs of pants. Nothing in the pockets. And certainly nothing that sparked any visions.

Back in the sitting room, Lou stood by the window and looked out across the water with her arms hugging her stomach. Roman was in the kitchen making tea. His eyes met Mia's, and after taking in her expression, his head dropped and he sighed.

"How are you doing, Lou?" Mia asked.

"I don't know." Lou turned toward her. "I'm a complete wreck. I feel like I'm the one who's been shot."

"It's likely shock," Roman said, walking out holding a mug. He set it down on a coaster on the coffee table. "What can we do to help?"

Lou glanced around the room as though seeing it for the first time. Her eyes fell on Mia for a few seconds then skittered away again. "I don't know. There's nothing anyone can do, is there? Danny's gone, and he isn't coming back. There's no happy ever after scenario in this story. I should have known. A girl like me doesn't ever get the fairytale."

"That's not true," Mia said, stepping up to her. "Everyone deserves a chance at happiness. And I know you made my father happy. I'm only sorry he never told you what was going on. It wasn't fair of him."

Lou let out a shuddering breath and sank onto the couch. "What happens now? You say we can't even bury Danny yet. When can we?"

Mia shrugged and glanced at Roman.

"We're not sure," Roman said. "Until we find the missing diamonds and get these guys off our back everything's up in the air. Did Danny every introduce you to his...um...partners or workmates?"

"No. Only a man named Dean. He seemed very nice." She paused, and her brows scrunched together. "Except he isn't nice, is he? He's probably one of the bad guys. What if he finds me?"

Roman crouched in front of her. "When did you meet Dean? Did he come here?"

She shook her head. "No. Not here. It was at a restaurant in Vegas about six or seven months ago. Before the so-called 'Degas Incident' which I'm now coming to see must have been when Danny was plotting to double-cross his partners."

"And Dean met you as Mary Lou and not Edith?" Mia asked.

"That's right. I only met him once, and it was before Danny wanted to move me." Her breath caught in her throat. "Will Dean find me? Or the other men?"

"I don't think so," Roman said. "He hasn't mentioned you so far, but if the Russian guys get hold of him and he's being…shall we say, 'pressured'…there's no guarantee he won't blurt your name out."

"We need to find the jewels," Mia said. "Otherwise, this will never end. Think hard, Lou. Did Danny say anything about a hiding place or a special key or…I don't know…maybe a deposit box at the bank?"

"No. Nothing like that. I swear. Though he did leave behind his old appraising tools." She stopped and shook her head then sighed. "I can't get my brain to believe the truth. He wasn't an expert art appraiser. Anyway, he had a small box of supposed tools which I stored in my crafts room. I thought it was odd, but he told me he was buying new ones for this job. He wanted to class himself up a little."

"Please, let there be a clue or message or something because I've got nothing so far," she said to Roman when Lou hurried out of the room.

The woman returned with a small wooden box. It looked well used. The corners were rubbed soft, and a couple of shallow gouges showed along the front. Lou placed it on the table and flicked the brass clasp to lift the lid. She rooted around inside then shook her head.

"Nothing but a bunch of tools," she said in disgust.

"May I?" Mia asked then reached out and picked up the box when Lou nodded.

She placed it beside her on the couch and removed each of the small items and laid them along the cushion. The tools were metal with fine carved wooden handles. Each had a short blade of varying thickness. A few flecks of dried paint clung on here and there. Good old Pops, he always knew how to look the part when he was running a con. He'd probably picked up the kit for next to nothing in a pawn shop somewhere.

Glancing inside the empty box, Mia felt around with the pads of her fingers hoping for any irregularity which might point to a hidden compartment. But there was nothing. Just smooth, flat surfaces dovetailing into neat corners. She reached out with her mind and found nothing there either. It was as if her father hadn't ever handled the box or tools.

Shaking her head at Roman, she blew out a breath. "Looks like this is a dead end, and I don't have any other ideas."

"So now what?"

"With no lead to follow, it seems pointless wandering around hoping we'll stumble into a clue. I guess we might as well go home."

Lou glanced back and forth between them. "What about me? Am I in danger?"

Roman patted her arm. "Probably not. But if you do have somewhere else to go—somewhere you're sure Dean wouldn't know about—it wouldn't hurt to relocate."

She rubbed a finger back and forth along her lower lip. "I'm not sure...I mean...I have friends, of course, but it'd be weird asking if I could move in with one of them. And if Dean or those other horrid men somehow find me, I don't want to put anyone at risk. I guess I could pick another city at random and get a short-term lease or something." She gazed around at the cozy sitting area. "If I'm doing it in secret, I can hardly bring all my things, can I?"

"Better not to," Roman said.

She blinked and when a single tear rolled down her cheek, dabbed at her eye. "I'm sorry. After everything that's happened with Danny and...everything...it's stupid to be upset about all my silly things, but I spent ages putting this place together and making it nice."

"It's really lovely. I can see that you're very comfortable here," Roman said in a soothing tone. "Lou, I promise you Mia and I are doing everything in our power to get these guys out of the picture. Hopefully, you won't have to worry for much longer. If you give us a way to contact you, we'll get in touch once the coast is clear so you don't have to keep worrying."

Lou exhaled in a gust and patted at her chest. "Okay. That would be good. Thank you. But I should probably get a new cell phone, right? One of those untraceable ones. Where do I go for that?"

Roman glanced at Mia then pulled his burner phone out of his back pocket. "Here. Take this one. I only activated it yesterday so none of the bad guys have this number. Don't use it for anything but contacting us, okay? And when everything's sorted out, we'll call, so keep it with you at all times."

Lou cradled the phone in her hands and looking down at it, rocked slightly while nodding her head. "Thank you. You've been so kind to me. Both of you. I guess I should start figuring out where I'm gonna hide...and get my clothes, at least, packed up."

Mia heard the slight hiccup in her voice and saw the way she was sort of curled toward the cell phone as though it was a baby. Or a puppy. Or something so delicate and precious she had to guard it from the world. And in a way, Lou did have to guard that cell phone because it was her only way of knowing she wasn't alone against this threat. And it was the only way word would get to her when she was finally safe.

She pictured Lou, grieving and scared for her life, with nothing but a suitcase, arriving alone in some unknown city. Her heart twisted in her chest, and she looked over at Roman who must have clearly read the expression on her face because he frowned and shook his head. When she glanced back at Lou, she saw her biting her lip and working to slow her breathing.

"Do you want to come with us?" Mia blurted out.

"Mia," Roman warned.

Lou's head snapped up and her eyes locked on Mia's face, big and round and hopeful as a child's. "Really? That would be...oh, my...so wonderful. I hate admitting it, even to myself, but I'm scared right down to the bone and so, so tired of being alone. These last few months..." She trailed off and stared down at her lap. "It's been hard—and now with Danny gone..." She shook her head and lifted her gaze again. "I don't want to have to go through this by myself."

"Hang on a minute, Lou. I think Mia and I need to have a little chat," Roman said.

She reached out and clamped a hand over his wrist. "I won't get in the way. I won't even talk if you don't want me to. I'll be quiet as a mouse. I promise. Just please let me go with you."

He sighed. "It's not that I don't want you to come. You have to understand the situation. Dean knows where Mia lives. We have no idea what we'll be walking into when we get back to Dalton. Also, I...let's call it...incapacitated...one of the other guys, Jimmy. I can guarantee he'll make it his mission in life to track me down and make me pay. I don't want to put you in unnecessary danger. It's so much safer if you stay as far away from

Mia and me as possible. Go hide out somewhere on your own. They'll never find you."

"Roman's right," Mia said softly. "I don't know what I was thinking bringing you into the eye of the storm."

"But you offered. You invited me," Lou said quickly. "And I know the risks because you've explained it straight out. I'm a grown woman, and I can make up my own mind. I want to go with you. Maybe I can even help."

Chapter Eighteen

After a little more back and forth, Lou convinced Roman and Mia to take her with them. Despite assuring she could be packed up and ready in a flash, it was more than two hours before they hit the road.

All had agreed driving was the better option. It might be a twelve-hour journey but harder to be traced in a rental car and, with three of them rotating the driving, they could go straight through. Lou took the first shift behind the wheel with Mia beside her, and Roman sprawled across the back seat. A forest of plants were carefully arranged at his feet since Lou had become tearful at the thought of leaving them, and neither Roman nor Mia had the heart to tell her no.

The drive was uneventful, and it was a little after four in the morning when Roman, now behind the wheel, saw the exit sign for Dalton which was some twenty miles ahead. He continued along the freeway and pulled into a twenty-four-hour gas station. Mia was already awake, but Lou jolted from the back seat and rubbed her eyes.

"Oh, we're still not there?" she said.

"Close though," Roman said. "I thought we should fuel up and talk about the next step."

"Snacks would be a good idea. For later," Mia clarified when Lou looked queasy. "Who knows how this day will go, and it's always good to have provisions."

"Great. You ladies deal with that. I'll get gas then we'll put our heads together and figure out our next step."

"So," Roman said once everyone was back in the car. "I think our first priority is seeing if the house has been breached. I suggest we park on Tenth Street directly at the back of the property, and I'll do some recon while the two of you wait for me to give the 'all clear' sign."

"No, way. Nah-uh. I'm coming with you," Mia said. "The most dangerous area will be at the house, and I don't want you going in alone. Plus, I might be able to...sense...things that you won't. Lou, you'll be fine acting as our getaway driver, right? You still have the burner phone, and we'll make contact once we know what's what."

Lou swallowed once then nodded her head. "Yes. Of course, I'll be fine."

"Wait. What about Kevin? He could come as backup," Mia said.

"Too soon for Kevin. We may need him later once we have the lay of the land, but I don't want him walking into an unknown situation on my behalf. Added to that, he'd be there in official police capacity, which involves certain protocols we might not want to happen. It takes away our choices."

"I guess," Mia said.

"Who is Kevin?" Lou asked.

"Kevin was my partner when I was on the Dalton police force." Roman started the car. "All right, let's do this."

"But you're not a police officer anymore?" Lou said.

"That's right. I resigned about a year ago."

"After you found your sister, God rest her soul," Lou said softly and crossed herself. "That must have been hard. I'm really sorry."

"Thanks."

"Roman's starting a private investigation service," Mia said. "He's going to be so great at it."

"Time will tell, I guess," Roman said, pulling back onto the freeway.

They entered Dalton from the east and cruised slowly through the small town. It was surreal to Mia the way it all looked so quiet and normal after everything she and Roman had been through in the last few days.

"Oh, this is such a darling little place," Lou said, clapping her hands together. "It's like something from a Hallmark movie."

"Hopefully, at some point, you'll get to see more of it," Mia said.

By the time Roman eased over onto the shoulder of Tenth Street, a thin sliver of light showed along the edge of the horizon. Mia waited for Lou to slide behind the wheel before leaning in.

"It'll take us about ten minutes or so to get onto my property and another five will bring us close to the house. Don't worry if you don't hear anything from us for a bit, okay?" Mia said.

"Okay. I'll hang tight until you give me a sign."

The nearest house was at least a quarter mile down the road and thankfully no lights shone in the windows. Roman pushed his way through a hedge and into the neighboring field. Mia quickly scampered after him and, sticking close to the tree line, they made their way north. The sky was cloudy and obscuring the moon, which made it tough trekking across the uneven ground. Still, once they got close to the log house, the lack of light would work in their favor.

"We need to hurry," Roman said softly. "Gotta get there before sunrise."

"We will. Not much farther now. Look, that's the back corner of my land right where those trees start."

They'd walked the small, forested section of her property on a regular basis and were familiar with the terrain but even still managed to trip on rocks and roots and whack a shin here and there as they hurried onward. Once through and onto the open section of land, they paused, and Mia closed her eyes and reached out with her mind.

"I don't sense anyone," she said then fell silent again for another minute before opening her eyes and smiling at Roman. "It feels empty and peaceful."

"Great. But we're still proceeding in stealth mode. I want you behind me, okay?"

"Fine. Whatever. No one's here, so it doesn't matter anyway."

They approached the house via the shed which had been repurposed as a garage. Roman eased the door open and stepped inside. Both cars squatted silently and appeared undamaged. He slipped out again and motioned to the house.

"You stay here. I'm going in through the dog run and the sliding door. Don't come until I flash the kitchen lights. Got it?"

Mia rolled her eyes. "Yeah. Yeah. I got it. Just so you know, if there was someone in the house, there's no way I'd let you go in alone."

It took less than five minutes before the lights in the kitchen flashed three times. She pushed off the wall and walked into the house via the front porch. Roman stood at the base of the stairs waiting for her.

"All clear just like you said. The place looks untouched as far as I can see. Let's keep the lights off though. They could be watching and waiting for our return."

"Jimmy and Karl?"

"Yeah. Or Dean. Or all three of them. Or the Mafia guys," Roman said, counting off on his fingers. "Or some other bad guy that we don't even know about yet."

She studied his face, noting the shadows of fatigue around his eyes and that the left one now had a full-on shiner. The bruise on his cheek bloomed in shades of purple and black, and the dark stubble on his jawline was well past the five o'clock stage. He looked exhausted and scruffy and wholly disreputable. She wondered what it said about her that all she wanted to do right now was jump his bones.

"Yeah. We've got a lot to figure out. But at least we're home. I'll text Lou and tell her the coast is clear. Why don't you go up and catch some sleep. I'll keep watch for a while, okay?"

He blinked a couple of times and rubbed a hand over his forehead. "Sleep sounds good. Only for a couple of hours though."

In the end, she let him sleep for almost six hours. He needed it and Lord only knew what they'd be facing in the coming day or two. Lou was thrilled to get herself set up in the spare bedroom surrounded by her plants and soon she, too, was lost in dreamland.

After rooting around in the pot of the jade plant and finding the small stash of diamonds untouched, Mia breathed a massive sigh of relief. She then spent a while wandering the silent house and stroking her crystals and books and photos. It helped ground her and bring her back to herself after the last few days of dealing with Dean and his scummy partners in crime. It might have been a normal part of her life in the past, but she could admit being back in that world had shaken her to the core.

Turning her life around had been a long and, at times, brutal path. She'd had to struggle daily to put away the dark side of herself and sometimes still marveled she'd manage to do so. From early childhood, she'd been taught to embrace things that were despicable and amoral. Lying, cheating, stealing. Not to mention the persistent cons. And the fact she'd taken to it like a duck to water still filled her with shame.

She shook her head clearing out the negative thoughts. She wasn't that person anymore. And because of all her hard work, she'd built an amazing new life. All she had to do was keep walking the line.

Deciding everyone in the house needed some optimum nutrition, she set about making a hearty feast. With one eye constantly flicking to the driveway monitor, she roasted vegetables, made a potato salad, and marinated chicken breasts before cooking and slicing them thinly. For herself, she baked thick slices of tofu slathered in a homemade barbeque sauce.

And the entire time, she pined for her pack of dogs. They loved to help out in the kitchen and normally crowded around her feet in the hopes of treats. God. She missed them so much it hurt. But she couldn't bring them home yet. Not when so much was up in the air. Putting her dogs in danger was not an option.

Even though it was a beautiful day, they ate inside in case someone was watching.

"You're quite a cook," Lou said. "This chicken is wonderful. Everything is great."

"Thanks. I like doing it."

"Me too. There's something so soothing about preparing food. Especially for loved ones," Lou said.

"I like preparing takeout," Roman said.

"And you're so good at it," Mia said. She paused and cleared her throat. "I've been thinking. We can't stay shut up in the house just waiting for one of the bad guys to show up."

"I agree." Roman nodded then took another bite of chicken and chewed quickly. "Though if we want to be in a position of strength to negotiate with them, we still need to find the rest of the diamonds."

"Where would Danny hide them?" Lou asked.

"I don't know. I've wracked my brain and come up with nothing. Pops loved his little games so there has to be a clue somewhere. If only I could find it," Mia said.

"Now that you've had time to process everything from yesterday, can you think of any place he'd hide something like that?" Roman asked Lou.

She frowned, and when a tear leaked from the corner of her eye, rubbed it away. "I just can't. The man I knew didn't go around hiding things. He had no special nooks and crannies or secret pockets. Well...I mean, he hid his whole entire self from me. But in our day-to-day life, I never found anything tucked away."

A small sob escaped and Lou's shoulders shook with the effort of fighting back tears. "I'm sorry for being so emotional. I thought I loved him and he loved me. But if someone hides their true self from you that means you don't even know them. They're basically a stranger. How can you love a stranger? You can't."

Mia leaned toward Lou. "Listen to me. He did love you. I know he did. I...well...I felt it when he talked about you. You may not have known everything about him, but it can still be love all the same."

Lou sniffled and lifted teary eyes to Roman. "Do you think what Mia says is true?"

Roman hesitated, and Mia could see the doubt settle over his face. "Sure. Of course. Love is love, right? I guess you don't always have to know everything about the other person."

An icy ball of dread settled in Mia's stomach. Although she'd promised herself not to go poking around in Roman's mind, she reached out with her senses and clearly felt the disgust Roman had for her father.

"Oh my gosh. I never thought—" Lou stopped and brought a hand to her mouth as though in shock. "This could be something. Right before he left, Danny gave me a brooch. A butterfly with blue and pink stones. Just costume jewelry but still lovely. And it was in a sweet little jewelry box. He said it was some kind of puzzle but once I found the brooch in the main compartment, I never looked any further. I figured he was just being sweet to me, but maybe there was something else hidden inside."

"Where is it?" Roman asked, his eyes fixed on Lou's face.

"Upstairs in my room. Even after everything you told me yesterday, I couldn't bear to leave it behind." She pushed back from the table and got unsteadily to her feet. "I'll be right back."

"This could be it," Mia said, surging to her feet.

"Or it could be nothing. Let's not get too excited until we know," Roman warned.

When Lou returned, she set a box on the table. It was about the size of a deck of cards and the wood shone rich and dark. She pressed the middle of one of the longer sides and a small section lifted revealing a compartment about half as deep as the box itself. Inside, nestled in cotton batten lay the brooch Lou had described.

"Do you mind?" Mia asked.

"Be my guest," Lou said.

Mia plucked out the brooch and studied it. The blue and pink stones were definitely glass and the base of the butterfly was some kind of mixed metal that had been made to look like gold.

"It's pretty," she said before passing it to Roman.

"He used to give me sweet little things like this all the time," Lou said. "That's why it never occurred to me there was anything strange going on."

The box had weight Mia realized when she lifted it off the table. She slowly raised and lowered the lid to the brooch compartment, noting there were no visible hinges. The wood had been fitted smoothly together and feathered at the meeting point. Whether there was some internal mechanism acting as a hinge or it was simply superior craftmanship of the join, she had no way of knowing since she had little wood-working experience.

She closed the lid down firmly until it fitted back into place and the joints all but disappeared. After examining each side of the box, she could just about make out faint lines of other possible compartments but no matter how many places she pushed, nothing popped open.

Finally, struck with a flash of intuition, she placed her thumb along one bottom edge and her index finger on the other and squeezed. When the bottom compartment slid out, it revealed a piece of paper folded into a small square. Lou's eyes went to saucers.

"Holy moly, I can't believe it," she said.

Roman carefully pulled the paper out and unfolded it, smoothing it on the table between them. Three pairs of eyes stared down.

"Diamonds are a girl's best friend.

But diamonds need light to shine.

What's better than an antique glow?

From a ceiling in the town's historic row."

"Why that sneaky bastard," Mia said with more than a hint of pride in her voice.

Chapter Nineteen

"What did Danny do?" Roman asked.

"I'll bet you dollars to donuts Pops hid the diamonds in among the crystals of that antique chandelier at city hall. You know the big one in the room to the left of the foyer where they hold meetings and winter socials? They had the Sweetheart Dance there this past Valentine's."

Lou stared at Mia. "How could you possibly know that from such a strange clue?"

Since it wasn't so much what had been written on the paper as the massive flash of her father on a ladder under the chandelier that tipped her off, Mia simply shrugged.

Roman jumped into the awkward silence. "The important thing is what do we do now?"

"I guess it'd be best to verify just in case I'm wrong," Mia said. "If they are there, though, doesn't that mean we're in the driver's seat?"

"It sure does," Roman said.

"Won't you hand the diamonds over to the police?" Lou asked.

Mia nodded. "That's what we originally planned, but it's more complicated than I expected. For Jimmy and Karl, it's personal now. If we give the diamonds to the cops, their heads are gonna explode with revenge fantasies. Then there's the Russians. In my experience, these aren't typically the kind of guys who'll just shrug it off and walk away. Examples must be made and someone always has to pay."

"First things first," Roman said. "We need to be sure we're playing with a full deck of diamonds. I think it's time for a trip to town. Only one of us though. It's important we keep a strong force at the house."

"I'll go to town," Mia said.

"And Lou and I will stay here."

"Oh, but I'd like to see the town, and isn't it safer if two of us go in case all these bad guys are roaming around Main Street," Lou said.

"I don't like Mia going alone either, but it's the best option. You'll take a cell phone and let me know when you pull into City Hall and as soon as you're out," Roman said, turning to face Mia. "If something happens here, I'll text and you don't come home. Okay? Go to Pine Lodge Hotel outside Walkerton and wait there."

"Guys, no one has to worry about me. I've got this," Mia said, instantly deciding she'd ignore Roman's suggestion to run away at the first sign of trouble. She stood with a groan and stretched her arms over her head. "Might as well make tracks. The sooner we know where we stand the better."

"Take the rental. It's doubtful any of the players know about it so you should be able to slip into town unnoticed."

With her hair bundled up in a baseball cap and sunglasses covering almost half of her face, Mia stepped out of the Nissan Sentra onto the sidewalk in front of City Hall. It was a large two-story stone building with black shutters and a big shiny black door.

Relieved no one loitered outside, Mia hurried up the half dozen steps and pulled the heavy door open. Inside, all hopes of quickly slipping in and out unnoticed went up in smoke when Melanie Gamble, wife of Mayor Jett Gamble, smiled and beckoned her over to the small reception nook.

She slipped off her sunglasses and hooked them in the front of her T-shirt before approaching Melanie.

"Well, hello, Mia. I almost didn't recognize you. So nice to see you. Now what can I help you with today?"

"I was hoping I could get a feel for the space in the special events room. I'm thinking of hosting an event—a jewelry festival—sometime next year and wondered about booking a place right here in town."

"It's a lovely room. So much history. Did you know John F. Kennedy himself once gave a speech there? If only these walls could talk." She paused and gazed around the foyer as though expecting half a dozen ghosts to materialize before walking out from behind her desk. "I'll show you through."

"Oh, no. You must be busy, and I don't want to take up any of your precious time. I can give myself the tour."

"Nonsense. I'm happy to help. It is part of my job, after all. I haven't seen you around much lately. Not since your engagement party. Congratulations again."

Mia quickly pushed her ringless left hand into her pocket in case Melanie was one of those women who liked to ooh and ah over engagement rings.

"Thanks. I guess I've just been slammed. You know how it goes."

"Of course. Of course. And what with a wedding to plan your plate is surely overflowing. Here we are."

She stepped into the events room and flicked on the light switch. Mia resisted the impulse to immediately fix her gaze on the chandelier, instead walking slowly around the large area while Melanie talked on and on about different wedding themes and where to get the best deal on dresses.

"Both of my daughters went to Lydia's Boutique. Now I may be biased but I have to say they were two of the most beautiful brides I've ever seen. If you go, tell Lydia I sent you."

"Yes. Thank you. Melanie," she turned to the woman and placed a hand on her arm before smiling big and bright. "Would you mind if I spent a few moments just wandering quietly to take in the space. Atmosphere is so important at these events, and I want to make sure this room is exactly right."

"I couldn't agree more. So many people disregard the feel of their environment but it's everything. I swear after I began a serious study of feng shui and moved my living room sofa to face south, my whole life changed. I'm so much more positive now and even Jett is less anxious."

Mia held her smile and nodded. "I'll only be a couple of minutes. I appreciate you letting me do this."

Once she was finally and blessedly alone, Mia blew out a breath and took a step over until she stood directly under the massive antique crystal chandelier. The ceiling was high, probably twelve or fourteen feet but the chain on the chandelier was long, so the light fixture hung only a few feet above her head. It didn't take more than thirty seconds to spot the first bundle of shiny hitchhikers secured to the inner portion of one of the large rectangular cuts of stone.

She counted a handful more before she dropped her gaze and walked slowly to the window to lean her head against the glass. Without painstakingly examining the entire chandelier, she couldn't be certain how much of the stolen bounty was hidden in plain sight, but her intuition told her this portion was much larger than what she and Roman had already found.

Mia turned when Melanie walked briskly back into the room. "How're you getting on in here? Thought I'd save you a step and printed out the forms you'll need if you decide to go ahead with renting the space."

"Thanks. I'm going to think about it, but I'll definitely take the forms. I appreciated all your help." Mia folded the papers and tucked them in a back pocket. "Well, I'd best get going. Good to see you again."

"Same. Give my regards to Roman. Such a good man. The mayor and I would sure like to see him back working for the Dalton Police Department."

"Maybe someday," Mia mumbled. "Okay, bye now."

In the foyer, she paused and pretended to fumble getting her phone out of her pocket. She tilted her head so it appeared she stared down at the screen all the while studying the alarm pad on the wall. It was the standard type on which a code was punched to arm and disarm the security system.

Ever so casually, she moved over to the wall and rested her forearm against the pad hoping she was going to get lucky. Barely more than a few seconds had passed before the flashes filled her mind's eye. An ongoing montage of arms reaching toward the keypad and fingers punching in a five-digit code.

She quickly typed the code into the notes app on her phone. Not that she was likely to forget but it didn't hurt to be extra careful. After everything she'd done to live a good and law-abiding life, it would just blow if she got caught breaking into City Hall in the town she now called home. After pushing open the door, she paused and snapped a picture of the handle and lock before slipping on her sunglasses and stepping outside.

Turning her head left and right, she studied the street but couldn't see any signs of anyone lurking or watching out for her. When she pushed out with her mind, the energy around her felt calm and stable with no hints of malice directed her way. Still, she walked slowly back to the rental and continued scanning the area until she was safely behind the wheel.

By the time she'd made the short drive back home, the effects of the past few days coupled with the long night were catching up with her. She blinked gritty eyes while she parked the rental car out of sight behind the garage and staggered to the house. Roman, waiting by the kitchen slider, pulled her into his arms.

"Awesome job, babes. You are a rock star," he said against the top of her head.

She sighed and melted into him. Inside her heart swelled in her chest. Although only a few days had passed, it felt like a lifetime since he'd shown her any physical affection.

"It was no big deal," she said, snuggling closer and breathing him in.

"You need to sleep," he said when she began yawning against his chest.

"Yeah. I'm definitely feeling like I've been run over by a train. Shouldn't we decide on a plan first?"

"Hey, I'm already working on it." He led her to the stairs and gently pushed her up the first step. "We can talk later when you're rested. Lou's up in the spare room keeping watch. Maybe poke your head in on your way by and say 'hi.' She was worried the whole time you were gone."

"Aw. That's sweet." She took another step then turned back to face Roman. "I've got some ideas about our situation so promise not to do anything until later, okay?"

"Of course. We're a team, right?"

"Yeah. We're a team."

It was dark when Mia jolted awake. Her heart beat like a warning drum in her head and all the hairs on the back of her neck stood at attention. She'd barely had a chance to glance around the bedroom when Roman stepped into the doorway.

"What is it? What happened?" she asked.

"Looks like our timeline just moved up," Roman said, lifting his cell. "Last night when we were driving home, I set up a Google alert for Jimmy. And I just got a hit. His chop shop in Savannah was burned to the ground. They're speculating arson. And a man, Karl Joseph Bonner, was found dead outside the building tied to a chair and sporting numerous injuries. It sounds suspiciously like torture from what I'm reading. Now, big picture,

Jimmy was no saint so he could've pissed off any number of guys, but this smells like organized crime to me."

"The Russians finally found him. Do you think Jimmy's still alive?"

Roman shrugged. "Impossible to say. Since Karl was the only body mentioned, I'd have to say yes. Though whether or not the Russians actually have Jimmy is a whole other question."

"Nothing about Dean?" she asked.

"Nope." He paused then walked over and sat beside her on the bed. "If they tortured Karl, we have to assume the Russians know about our involvement and likely where we live. They'll be gathering forces and coming our way. I'd guess we probably have twenty-four hours or so before they have boots on the ground in Dalton."

"And if Jimmy's still a free man, he'll be doing the same except trying to get to us first. Maybe twelve hours on his clock," Mia added.

"Well. I think we both knew it was always going to come down to this. And now, at least, we have a bigger chunk of the stones." He patted her hand then stood. "What we need is a team meeting. I'm going to wake Lou."

Mia rolled off the bed, rubbed her eyes, and patted her hair into place. "I'll go down and make coffee."

They convened in the kitchen. Although Roman laid the driveway monitor on the counter, nobody paid much attention to the screen.

"Should we run?" Lou asked. Since she'd left Atlantic City, she hadn't bothered with makeup or much in the way of hairstyling and looked tired and very pale. "I have to admit I'm scared right to the bone."

"You can. In fact, you should. No one's after you. They don't even know your name. Take the rental and get as far away as possible," Roman said.

"But if we took the diamonds, we could all run and stay running for a good long time," she said.

"We can't leave," Mia said softly. "Roman's family is here. My life is here. This is my home now. You need to do what's best for you, Lou. Take a moment now and decide. I hope you'll leave because it'll be safer for you."

Roman cleared his throat. "As for us, before we get into figuring out our offense, I say we talk defense. The way I see it, we need to protect this property." He stopped and shook his head at Mia. "No. Don't say it's only a house. It's so much more than that to you, and we're not going to let them take it from us. Next there's my parents. And finally, we need to think about the dogs."

"I agree. But there're only two of us."

"Three of us," Lou said. "I'm not leaving. I may be scared, but some of these men killed my Danny, and I want to help make them pay."

"Okay. Three of us but, still, we can't deal with that many situations plus whatever plan we're going to put in place with the diamonds," Mia said.

"Yeah. I know. I've been thinking about nothing else all day. What if there were more than three us though?"

Mia shook her head. "No way. Nah-ah. We can't, in good conscience, drag anyone else into this mess. I'll even feel bad getting Kevin involved though I suspect we might have to since organized crime is about to invade his town."

"Yeah. Kevin definitely needs a heads-up on that at some point. But not yet. As for throwing more bodies at the problem, unfortunately, the Dalton PD is too small to put men on so many places while also planning for a sting operation. I figure it's up to us to bridge the gap. I'm talking about a professional security team. I contacted Mitch Fowler earlier today, and he's interested in the job."

Mia's face scrunched in concentration. "I know that name from somewhere..." She snapped her fingers. "Tightline right? They were great about helping me with all the news hounds after...well...after Tony but this is a bit more than keeping paparazzi off my lawn."

"He was a Navy Seal. So are most of his team. They usually take on jobs neutralizing verified threats against high level government types or the uber wealthy. They also work hostage and kidnapping details. This is right up their alley."

Mia tipped her head. "Huh. Really? I didn't know he was such a bad ass."

"I like the sound of this Tightline team," Lou said, smiling for the first time that day.

"He and I talked about putting two or three guys here at the house. They'll block off the driveway and lay down spike strips across the front of your property. He figures only one guy at Wag'A'Way to guard the dogs, and I'm going to do my damnedest to get my parents tucked up in a hotel somewhere outside Dalton. Walkerton maybe or better still, Nashville. Mitch will put a pair on them at the hotel. It should work." He nodded his head several times. "Yeah. It should work just fine. Though it won't be cheap."

"How scared should I be?" Mia asked.

"Definitely a little scared. If we do what I just said, that's six guys plus Mitch running the op. A thousand per guy per day with another two grand for Mitch."

"But that's eight thousand a day," Lou said. "You should keep some of the diamonds to pay him."

Mia snorted. "Something tells me Mitch won't take stolen gemstones as payment. He struck me as a straight arrow kind of guy."

"It's gotta be cash. And for something like this, a minimum three-day charge to cover getting everyone here and in place then home again. So, we're looking at, best case, around twenty-four grand."

"I've got the money to cover Mitch, so let's not worry about it right now," Mia said.

"I'd better call him and move up the timeline because we basically need him right now. And we'll take care of his bill together. Are you on board with this?" Roman asked.

Mia sighed and turning her head, stared at the wall. "Yeah. I guess so. It should work to keep everyone safe."

Roman reached across the table and placed his hand on hers. "What is it, babes?"

"I miss my dogs." She shrugged and dropped her head. "And I guess I'm just sad and seriously mad at Pops. Everything's such a mess, and it's all because of him. I know I have some responsibility here because I did agree to help him in the first place but after finding the diamonds he hid in City Hall it made me realize it was always going to come down to this. He put me in danger right from the get-go. Basically, the story of my life."

"Oh, sweetie. I'm sure he didn't mean this to happen," Lou said. "Danny probably thought he'd scoop up all the diamonds and outsmart the bad guys without anyone getting hurt."

Roman turned Mia's hand over and threaded his fingers through hers. "It's a shitshow. No question. But we're going to fix it. I promise. And after everything's over, we can finally bring the pack home where they belong. Then we're going to take a break. No work. No worries. Just you and me and the fur babies."

Mia squeezed his fingers and worked up a smile. "That sounds nice." She paused and looked around the kitchen. "What if...maybe this is crazy, but we could bring your parents and the dogs here. Make a sort of compound with the Tightline guys patrolling the property lines. We're far enough out of town it shouldn't bring danger to any of the folks in Dalton. And you'd feel better knowing your parents were with you. I know I won't be happy until I can see my dogs."

Roman leaned his head back and closed his eyes for several seconds. Slowly he began to nod. "Maybe that would be the best way to go. Instead of scattering our resources, concentrate everything here. Short of anyone hitting the house with a rocket launcher, we should be good and safe. But no way we do the diamond takedown on this property. Too much chance for things getting away from us."

"I have a great place in mind. Remote. Far from here. We can get it set up before anyone arrives in town."

"Okay. Let me contact Mitch and get him rolling. Then we'll figure out the rest of the plan."

"You mean the part where we brilliantly corral some medium-level bad guys and some really serious bad guys and hand them over to the police wrapped in a nice tidy bow so they go away for life? And all without any of us seeing the business end of a gun," Mia asked.

"That about sums it up," Roman said, his smile brilliant. "I think we're gonna need a lot more coffee."

Chapter Twenty

It was almost eleven o'clock when they finally finished their planning session around the kitchen table.

"Whew," Lou said. "We're surely ready for anything."

Roman leaned his head back to stretch his neck. "You would think but, more often than not, something ends up going sideways. And when it does, we'll have to hope we can pivot fast enough to come out on top."

"And speaking of coming out on top, I'd say now is as good a time as any to put phase one into action," Mia said, pushing back from the table."

"Are you sure you don't want me to come?" Lou asked. "Maybe it would be better if Roman held down the fort and I played getaway driver."

"You'll be fine here. I promise." Roman leaned toward Lou and placed a hand on each shoulder. "It is very, very unlikely anyone will reach us until sometime tomorrow. I'll keep you up to date by text the whole time, and we shouldn't be away much more than an hour or so. Okay?"

She swallowed once then nodded. "Okay."

Mia turned from where she was rinsing out coffee mugs in the sink. "Lou, I get it. We're asking a lot of you. You know you can still change your mind about staying. There's no shame in driving to safety before the action starts."

"No. I've made my decision. I want to see these jerks pay. More than that, I want to know I helped even if my part is really, really small. It still means something, you know."

"You're one tough lady," Roman said. He gave her shoulders a gentle squeeze before releasing her and standing. "You ready?" he asked Mia.

They quickly gathered up the supplies needed for the job then deciding to stay with the rental car, climbed into the Nissan. Roman drove carefully, sticking a shade below the posted speed limit and signaling each and every turn. He knew well enough the Dalton PD didn't normally have a huge show of force when it came to nighttime traffic duty, but he wasn't taking any chances.

"You're not saying much. Nervous?" he asked Mia.

"What? Oh. No. Not especially. I was just thinking." She turned her head and resumed looking out the window. "Remember how we talked about having children? But we can't, can we? What if something like this happens again, and we had kids? It would kill me to put them in danger."

When Roman said nothing she shifted to look at him then hurried on. "I mean, of course we might not even be together after this is over. I know you're mad about...well...everything. And I don't blame you. I'd probably be mad too. Forget I said anything about kids or...whatever. This isn't the time to talk about us. We should just concentrate on the job."

They were passing through the old section of town where big, stately homes sat on generous lots. Every single one landscaped within an inch of its life. Old-fashioned coach lights with large oval globes lit the wide and graceful street, and the whole vibe of the area was one of big-time money. Roman pulled over and put the car in park then turned to face Mia.

"Yeah. I was pissed when this all started, and there've been a couple of times here and there I've drifted back into that territory, but that doesn't mean I don't love you, Mia. Even when I don't want to, I still do. It's damn frustrating. So, you'd better believe we're going to be together after this is over. And after our next big fight. And after one of us is sick. And after every other crap thing that happens in our life together. Because that's what this is for me. It's a lifetime deal. We can figure out the kids thing later, okay? But I wanted you to be straight on the rest of it."

She didn't realize she was crying until Roman unclipped his seatbelt and inched closer to wipe the tears from her cheeks.

"Don't, baby. It kills me when you cry," he said softly.

"These are happy tears," she hiccupped. "And relieved tears. And how-did-I-get-so-damn-lucky tears. We're talking top-of-the-line, primo grade tears. I wouldn't cry them for anyone but you."

He cupped her chin and leaned in slowly until their lips met. The kiss was so sweet, so tender it took her breath away. She traced her fingers along the line of his jaw and closed her eyes, letting the love wash over her. When they finally parted, she was soothed and filled with both lust and joy. In fact, she could have sworn her skin glowed from head to toe.

These past few days she'd told herself she'd be fine if Roman ended things, but it was a flat-out lie. How could she ever be fine without this in her life? Their connection was a force so powerful, so totally consuming, everything was flat and dull and lifeless when it was gone. Like an out of focus black-and-white photo.

With his eyes still on hers, he nodded once before sliding back across the seat and fastening his seatbelt. The corners of his lips twitched; he was obviously fighting the smile, but it burst across his face anyways.

"Glad we sorted that out," he said.

"Yeah. Me too. And it was the perfect time to talk. It's not like we have anything else of importance going on right now."

His face went serious again, and he laid his hand on her thigh. "Nothing is more important than us."

"When you're right, you're right." She sighed then shook her head. "Okay. You ready to steal back some diamonds?"

"More than." He put the car back into gear and pulled out onto the street. "Sure you don't want me to come in?"

"Positive. And if anything happens, you said you'd burn out of there, right? No point in both of us getting caught. It'd be especially bad for you. You could all but kiss your PI license goodbye, plus any chance of ever working on any police force in the whole country. Besides, I'll need someone to bail me out."

"Don't even joke about getting caught," he said.

"Aw, come on. Let me have my fun. It's been a rough couple of days."

"Don't I know it."

The town wasn't totally asleep since a few of the local watering holes stayed open until two a.m. but they didn't pass any other cars on their way to City Hall. Mia glimpsed a couple strolling hand in hand and a young guy walking fast with his head down. Otherwise, the sidewalks were empty.

Roman parked in an alley behind the library and turned off the car. They each pulled out a pair of latex gloves and slipped them on. After stepping out of the car, Mia carefully clicked her door shut while Roman opened the trunk and removed the collapsible ladder. A stiff breeze swirled the warm air around them and brought along some powerful smells of garbage from the nearby dumpster.

"You sure it's not too heavy?"

She slipped a backpack over her shoulders then hoisted up the aluminum ladder. "Stop fussing. I'm fine. This ain't even close to my first rodeo. Don't forget to text Lou. I know she'll be worrying."

"Got your phone and the picks and the headlamp?"

"Check. Check. And check. Now get back in the car like a good getaway driver."

But Roman followed her to the end of the alley then stood in the shadows, peeling off the gloves and shoving them into his back pocket while he watched her make her way to the front of City Hall. There were several perimeter lights glowing, but if he hadn't been looking, he wouldn't have known she was even there.

God, she was like a cat. Slinking along the walls. Keeping low. Somehow graceful as a ballerina while carrying that damn ladder. She paused at the corner of the building by the stairs leading to the front door. She looked both ways. When she stayed in place, still and focused, for what seemed an age, he worried she'd seen something then realized she was reaching out with her mind.

He blinked a couple of times, his vision straining against the darkness, and then he caught her again, on the move now. Up the stairs she went and into the alcove by the door. To him, she all but disappeared against the black door. While he waited, every muscle strained. Finally, something caught the light, and he realized the ladder was passing through and into the building.

She was in. Damn those were some world-class lock-picking skills.

Now his heart beat like a drum. This was the most dangerous part of the entire operation. Either she had the right alarm code, or she didn't. If not, it was game over for them. At least for tonight. He knew the alarm was wired into the police station just a few blocks north of here. They'd have to get gone in five minutes or less.

He counted in his head and when he reached ninety, figured they were safe. His heart thumped hard in his chest then settled and slowed.

Keeping his arm between his body and the alley wall, he checked his phone. Five minutes past midnight. He slipped back to the car and eased inside. Suddenly remembering Lou, he fired off a quick text.

All going well. You ok?

Everything's quiet. Keeping my fingers crossed for you.

He started the car and cursed at how loud the engine sounded then reminded himself the wind would cover some of the noise. Besides, people drove cars. All the time. It was a fact of life in Dalton. Nothing to see here.

He inched along the alley until the nose of the car was barely breaching the end, and he had line of sight to City Hall. The building remained dark and quiet. He checked his phone again. How was it only six minutes had passed? It felt more like an hour. He wished he was the one on the inside because this waiting was brutal.

Out of the corner of his eye he caught movement on the street, and his breath backed up in his throat. A woman and a dog sauntered straight up to the library. He watched as she pulled open a drop box on the library wall and placed a book inside. Then a second and third one followed.

Jesus. Who the hell returned books at midnight?

The dog then proceeded to sniff all along the grass in front of the main library door while the woman stared down at her phone.

"Come on. Come on," he mumbled to himself. "Get out of here and go home."

Very slowly, the woman and dog made their way past the library and crossed the street directly in front of City Hall. Roman kept his eyes on them until they turned onto a side street and disappeared around the corner. He checked the time again while a bead of sweat rolled down between his shoulder blades.

She'd been in there almost twenty minutes now. He was so strung up with nerves he just about gasped aloud when his phone pinged in his hand. He saw it was another text from Lou, and he blew out a breath and quickly replied telling her there was no news and he'd get back to her when there was. He hoped she'd take the hint to sit tight.

He caught the sound of an approaching car, and the headlights burned bright from left of his position. Even though it was likely unnecessary, he slid down in the seat until his head was barely above the dashboard. As the car neared his lookout post in the alley, the lights bounced off each building it passed and cast crazy shadows. His breathing sounded loud in the still car. It didn't slow until the vehicle was well down the street and receding into the distance.

Jesus Christ. He couldn't take much more of this waiting.

"Hey there, any chance I could catch a ride?"

At the sound of Mia's voice, his heart all but stopped. He swung around to the open window and stared out at her. She stood cool as a cucumber, one hand resting on the ladder which she'd set down beside her and the other holding her backpack.

It took her less than a minute to stow the ladder in the trunk and climb onto the passenger seat beside him. And it took him every second of that time to get his erratic breathing under control. Reaching across, he grabbed her hand and squeezed hard.

"Success?" he asked.

"Yep. One hundred percent. Ow, you're hurting my hand."

"Sorry." He released her. "I'm just so glad you're out safe and sound."

When he continued staring at her, she tipped her head and smirked. "Should we maybe get out of here? Scene of the crime and all that."

He grinned back. "Yeah. Yeah. Okay. It may not be your first rodeo, but it sure as hell is mine. Cut me some slack."

"You have one job—getaway driver," she teased. "Let's see some driving already."

He eased the Nissan out and onto the street in front of City Hall, and she leaned across the console and waved at the building.

"You are so badass," he said with a chuckle.

Her head, very close to his, turned and their gazes locked. There was mischief in her eyes and something else. Something wholly sexy that called to him like a siren song. He went instantly hard. Wrenching his attention back to the road, he fought to drive slowly while she flipped up the arm rest between them and scooted over until they were touching.

"I'd forgotten about the sexy after-effects from pulling off a job. You're going to really like the next part of this operation," she said, her lips against his ear and her voice husky.

By the time they'd reached the outskirts of town, Roman was so filled with lust he could barely see straight. She'd pulled off her T-shirt and bra, and her lips were latched onto his neck. With every kiss and lick and nibble, he throbbed. She moaned and sucked on his earlobe while one of her hands caressed her own nipple.

"Jesus. Wait. Let me park somewhere before I drive off the road," he muttered.

"You'd better hurry up," she whispered.

He turned onto a dirt road, and the car fish-tailed before he managed to straighten it out. Mia laughed her sexy, throaty laugh and undid his seatbelt. With shaking hands he managed to steer onto the shoulder and put the car in park.

She unzipped his jeans, reached in and freed him. In the next second, she had shifted down and her mouth closed over him, warm and wet. Her tongue circled and lapped, and it felt so damn good he thought he might explode right then and there. Reaching for her head, he groaned and thrust slowly into her mouth.

He lost all track of time. Of space. Of the universe itself. There was nothing but her mouth around him. Finally, though it cost him dearly, he pushed at her shoulder.

"Easy, baby. Let's slow it down."

"I'm not in a slow mood," she said and wiggled up until their faces were level. Then she took his hands and placed them on her breasts. "Come on. Use me. Enjoy me. Make me like it."

He caressed until she was moaning. Sucked until she writhed against him. When he slowly rolled her nipple between his fingers and thumb, she begged on a breath gone ragged.

They scrambled out of the car, and he met her on the passenger side. She pulled down her jeans and turning, braced her hands against the side of the car. Then he stepped up behind her and pushed straight into all that wet and glorious heat.

They went fast and hard. She brought his hands to her breasts and cried out with every thrust all the while urging him on. When she came, he covered her mouth gently with his hand and held her while she gasped and shuddered and gradually stilled. He waited, throbbing inside her and rubbed slow circles at her core until he felt her build again.

Then he started to move. This time there was no stopping him. He caught that wave and rode it hard, chasing and chasing until the heat rose up and engulfed him. Until he knew he wouldn't last another second.

The intensity was unlike anything he'd ever felt, and he groaned out against a pleasure so deep and sweet he wondered if he was dying. When she arched her back and flexed her hips, he emptied into her with a growl, and she sobbed out a breath before collapsing onto the hood of the car.

They stayed that way, his arms wrapped around her from behind and his face buried in her hair, while bodies stilled and hearts slowed and breathing regulated. Finally, she rested her elbows on the car and looked back over her shoulder, her face silhouetted against the headlights.

"You alive back there?" she asked, rocking her hips slightly.

"I'm not sure. I may have died while having the best orgasm of my life. It would be a hell of a way to go."

"Yeah. It would be." She sighed. "Much as I'm loving this, we probably shouldn't hang out for too long. You know, just in case."

It came to him then that they were on the side of a public road, and she was mostly naked and he was still buried deep inside her. And they were on the way home from committing a felony and still had all the evidence in the car. Which was still running, for Pete's sake. He must have momentarily lost his mind.

He gently eased out of her and zipped himself up while she wriggled into her pants. Since she was still topless, he indulged himself for a moment longer and slowly ran his fingertips back and forth across her breasts.

"God, you're so beautiful," he breathed.

She patted his butt. "You're not bad yourself. Okay. I'm going to put the girls away, so say your goodbyes."

"I'll really miss you," he said solemnly before leaning down and kissing her left nipple. "And you too." His lips closed over her right one.

She laughed and pushed him aside before reaching into the car and pulling out her bra and T-shirt. While she finished dressing, he jogged around the front of the hood and got behind the wheel. When she slid in beside him, he took her hand in his and kissed the knuckles.

"I adore you, Mia Reeves."

"Why thank you, kind sir." With her free hand, she pretended to fluff her hair, then she grabbed his chin and planted a firm kiss on his lips. "And I adore you right back," she said, her voice soft and silky.

When they stepped into the house, Lou smothered Mia against her and sobbed into her shoulder. "I was so scared. I kept picturing you in handcuffs being put in the back of a police car."

"It's okay." Mia patted Lou's back. "No harm no foul. And now we have a whole bunch of diamonds to use for trapping the bad guys."

Lou pulled back and patted her eyes. "Ooh. Goody. I almost forgot about that part. Show me."

Roman put the backpack on the kitchen counter and Mia walked over and removed a small black purse. She unzipped it and turned it upside down and a collection of clear, square, plastic pouches spilled out. The flaps on the pouches were glued shut and Roman grabbed the scissors and cut slits along the tops.

By the time he was done, a small, shiny pile of gemstones about the size of a half lemon winked up at them from the counter. Lou's eyes went to saucers, and she reached out with her hand then quickly snatched it back as though feeling the heat of a flame.

"It's okay," Mia said, laughing. "You can touch them. They're likely very friendly and probably thrilled to be out of those icky plastic containers where the light can show them off and make them all pretty again."

"So beautiful," Lou murmured as she spread them out on the counter. "I can't believe I'm stroking a pile of diamonds."

"How does it feel?" Mia asked.

"Wonderful. Like magic."

"We should add the first stash to the pile," Roman said.

"First stash?" Lou squeaked. "What first stash?"

"It's a long story," Mia said when Roman disappeared into her work room.

He returned carrying the dirt-covered pouch and stood over the sink, brushing the worst of it away before opening the cord and letting the diamonds inside drop down onto the pile on the counter.

Once again, Lou oohed and aahed and played with the stones. She plucked up one of the larger pieces and held it above her ring finger.

"This would look nice right here, don't you think?" she said with a laugh.

"Stunning," Roman agreed.

"If everything goes according to plan, what will happen to all of these beauties?" Lou asked.

Roman shrugged. "They'll be taken in as evidence in the case. After that, probably sold and the proceeds funneled back into funding for the police."

"And you'll happily hand them straight over to the cops?" Lou said, frowning. "It doesn't seem right somehow."

Mia secretly agreed but didn't say anything. Roman was such a straight-arrow, law-abiding guy, and she'd already pushed him way far out of his comfort zone during this whole mess with her father. I mean, hello, they'd just come back from breaking into City Hall. She decided to say nothing for now. She was all for walking the line and everything but if a couple of those stones somehow ended up in her jewelry supplies, she figured she could live with it.

Roman carefully collected the gemstones and stowed them in a Tupperware. He checked the time on his phone. "It's not quite two yet. We should all try and get some shut eye. Mitch will be here by about seven a.m. and things will get crazy after that, so let's make the most of the time we have now."

"Shouldn't we be worried about keeping watch?" Lou asked.

"Nah. I'll keep the monitor with me on the off chance, but I think we'll be safe at least until Mitch shows up," Roman said.

Mia yawned, picked up the container of diamonds, and tucked them under her arm. "I could go for some downtime. I think every drop of adrenaline has drained straight out of my body."

In the bedroom, she stowed the Tupperware in the linen closet before slipping into a sleep shirt. She was already starting to go under by the time Roman stepped in after doing his security round of the house. When he stripped down and curled around her, she dropped straight to sleep.

Neither of them stirred until Roman's phone pinged with a text. Immediately after, came the bleat of the driveway monitor. He fumbled for the phone and squinted at the screen while Mia scrambled upright.

"Relax. It's only Mitch," he said.

Chapter Twenty-One

After lightning-fast showers, Roman and Mia emerged from the house to find the entire parking area between the sunroom and the shed filled with two large black Ford trucks each pulling a shiny black trailer with the single word 'Tightline' stenciled in green along the left side. Four men stood sipping from silver to-go cups and looking around with focused concentration etched on their faces.

One of them broke away from the group and walked over to meet Mia and Roman by the house. Mia immediately recognized the lanky, red-haired man as Mitch Fowler. He offered his hand and a quick smile.

"Roman. Mia. Good to see you. Sorry about the circumstances," he said.

Roman clasped his hand. "Thanks for coming."

"Hi, Mitch," Mia said. "The way things are going I'm starting to wonder if I should already be booking you in for next year."

He chuckled. "I don't often have repeat customers."

"What do you need from us?" Roman asked.

"We'll start assessing the property and setting up a perimeter. I have three more men on the way. They should be here by noon." His eyes flicked to Roman. "What's the status on your parents?"

"I'm going to bring them here. At least I hope I am. They're what you might call a bit 'crusty' and don't always listen, but I'll scare the bejeebers out of them if I have to. Mia's also planning to pick up the dogs. It was her idea to put everyone in a single location and not split your resources."

Mitch tipped his head toward her. "Smart. Some might say one location makes for an easy target, but I say, 'do it once and do it right.' In a couple of hours, we'll have this place locked down tighter than Quantico. The sooner we get everyone inside the perimeter, the safer it'll be. Don't want to be in the position of moving people..." He paused and smiled. "Or dogs onto the base after the enemy has reached our location."

Roman nodded. "Okay then. I guess we all have our assignments. I'll go corral my folks. Mia can pick up the pack. One more thing, there's a woman in the house. Mary Lou. She was with Mia's father before everything went to shit, and we ended up bringing her back with us. The situation has her pretty shook up, but she's sweet, and I don't think she'll be any trouble."

"Noted. Keep in touch. Both of you. I want updates when you get to the secondary locations and when you're back on route to the base. Once everyone's settled at the house, and I'm satisfied with the outside fortifications, we're going to need a sit down to go over procedures. We should also talk about any future plans the two of you have to bring this situation to a close...so stay available."

"We've got nothing else but this right now," Mia said simply before turning and stepping up into the sunroom.

"She holding up okay?" Mitch asked in an undertone.

"Yeah. Mia's tough as nails. You'll soon see what I'm talking about. I'd better get on the road. By my estimation, we could see at least one of the groups arrive sometime today, and I don't want to give them a nice easy target."

"You got armor in the vehicles?"

"Afraid not. Never anticipated needing it," Roman said.

"After today, we use my transport. Can't give it to you now cause we'll be hauling the trailers over every square inch of this land but once we're set up, they'll be at your disposal."

"Thanks, man. I mean it."

Within the hour, Mia sat on the floor of the reception area at Wag'A'Way Kennels, overrun by her dogs who insisted on licking every available part of her. Her heart felt too full. Too open and raw. She tried not to sob, but her breath hiccupped more than once.

"Okay, guys. I love you too. I'm sorry I was gone so long," she cooed. "I know it was hard. Poor babies."

She could barely contain them as she led them out to her Escape. Once everyone was finally loaded in the vehicle, she lowered her head to the steering wheel and exhaled in a long woosh. She'd known reuniting with her dogs would be emotional, but she hadn't expected to feel as though she'd somehow let them down.

"You did your job. You kept them safe," she told herself.

"Who's ready to go home?" she said aloud, and a chorus of yips and whines responded from behind her. "That sounds like a lot of yeses to me, so let's get this party started."

Mac pushed his face over the divider and rested his chin on her shoulder, and her heart went to mush. He stayed that way for the rest of the drive.

Back at the log house, Mitch and his team had already secured the front of her property. A double line of spike strips spanned the grass by the road, and the entrance to the driveway now had a sturdy concrete barricade on either side. Seeing everything that was being put into place filled her with confidence while simultaneously sparking a low-grade sense of anger that any of this was necessary.

One of the men stepped out from the back of the trailer with his hand on the butt of his gun and studied her SUV. She lowered the window and waved, and he nodded and gestured her through. Up at the house, the second truck and trailer was gone from the yard.

She parked by the path to the front door and released her jubilant dogs who ran and sniffed and marked everywhere. Mac soon returned to her side and leaned against her leg. She stroked her hand along his back and sighed. Things might be all kinds of crazy, but at least she had her dogs again.

Since she'd beaten Roman home and all appeared quiet in the house, she led the dogs behind the garage and began walking her fields. The poor things had been cooped up at the kennel for days now, and this might be the last time they were able to stretch their legs until this ridiculous mess was sorted out once and for all.

Someone had driven along by the tree line, and she followed the tracks of flattened grass. The empty vehicle was parked by the forest at the back of the property. While Mac and Fifi remained at her side, Layla and Tucker ran, zigzagging across the field and bursting by her from time to time.

She whistled to them then stepped into the treed area. Layla bounded up with a huge doggy smile on her gorgeous golden face. Knowing Tucker wouldn't stay on his own for long, Mia continued walking...and sure enough he soon fell in behind her.

Immediately, she heard the men. She couldn't make out what they were saying, but their voices were clipped and there was much rustling and hammering. She found them all the way at the back edge of her property digging a small trench along the floor of the forest. There were three of them and as one, they spun in her direction. She noticed two had drawn their guns.

"Sorry. Just me," she said, raising her hands palms out. "How's it going?"

Mitch nodded at his companions, and they holstered their weapons. "Hey there. We're making good progress. Wow. That's a lot of dogs. Are they friendly?"

"Mostly, except for this guy here. Mac takes security and protection very seriously. I guess he's sort of like you. Don't worry. I'll make sure he's good with all your guys," Mia said. "Why don't we start now?"

She walked up to the three men and held out her hand. "Hi, I'm Mia, and this is Mac."

Playing along, Mitch carefully shook her hand while keeping his eye on the Doberman. "Hi, Mia. Nice to meet you. This is Dom and Cooper."

Mia turned to face the other two men. Dom was tall, maybe six four or five, and built like a linebacker. He had dark hair cut close to his head and a sleeve tattoo containing intricate curving symbols that reminded her of Māori art. He didn't smile while they shook hands, but his grey eyes held warmth.

Cooper was a big guy too though not quite to the stature of Dom. He also sported a buzz cut but his tattoo was confined to a single dagger on his right forearm. He had a square face and tanned skin and flashed her a big smile.

"I love dogs," he said. He looked down to where Mac sniffed slowly up and down his pantleg. "He's a beauty, all right."

Mitch crouched down and both Layla and Tucker threw themselves at him. "These guys sure know how to say hello."

"Aw, look at this little one," Dom said. He was down on his knees and stroking Fifi with a hand the same size as her entire body.

Mac returned to Mia's side and looked up at her with calm eyes. "Looks like you guys passed the test."

"Do they normally wander loose like this?" Mitch asked.

"I don't let them out on their own but, yeah, we go walking every day." She shook her head. "I know what you're going to say, and I'll be keeping them in the house or the dog run until this is over."

"How big's the run?" Mitch asked.

"Um…maybe fifteen feet by thirty or so."

He took out his phone and typed something then nodded. "Okay. I'll see about securing it. We'll probably be another hour back here then we have some work to do on the east and west borders before we get to the house. Might be best if you start heading back now."

She sighed. "Okay. See you later then."

Dom, who was still down patting Fifi, stood, somewhat reluctantly to Mia's eye. "Bye little girl," he said to the dog.

Back at the house, Mia gave out treats then called Lou down to meet the dogs. She walked hesitantly into the kitchen looking scared stiff.

"They'll be in the house then?" she asked.

"Yep. They do live here after all. Don't worry. They'll soon get used to you and you to them." Mia paused and smiled. "See. Layla already thinks you're the bee's knees. You can pat her if you want."

It took some time and plenty of coaxing, but Lou gradually worked her way through the pack of dogs, patting each one and giving them treats out of her hand.

"Oh, he's so gentle," she said in surprise when Mac delicately picked a small Milk-Bone off her palm. "And look how kind his eyes are."

"He's a good guy," Mia said simply. "And once he accepts you, he'll protect you with his life."

"How's it going out there?" Lou asked.

"Okay. I think. Roman texted a couple of minutes ago. He's got his parents packed up. They should be here within a half hour or so. I'd better get a room ready for them."

"Do you need me to move?"

"That's okay. I'm going to set them up in the master. There's a pullout couch in Roman's office, so he and I will bunk in there. I'm not sure about all the men. I didn't think to ask. Oh, well. No doubt we'll find a place for everyone," Mia said.

"It's kind of exciting having all this activity. I have to admit, I already feel so much safer here."

She gave Lou's hand a squeeze. "Try not to worry. I have faith that everything will be okay in the end."

Lou's face melted into a sweet smile. "I don't think I've thanked you for letting me come here and for taking such good care of me. I really appreciate it. I would've been beside myself with nerves if I'd stayed home alone knowing those awful, awful men were on the loose."

Going with impulse, Mia wrapped her arms around Lou and rocked her side-to-side. "Don't give it a second thought. We love having you here."

Mac pushed in between the two women, and when they broke apart Mia glanced down at him. She saw he studied Lou with puzzled eyes. He circled Mia once before pressing against her and resting one of his front paws on her foot.

"It's okay, big guy. This is a lot, I know. So many new people and strange things going on." She crouched down and gave the Doberman a reassuring hug, much like she'd given Lou. "Let's go upstairs and make some beds."

Roman and his parents arrived sometime later with a collection of suitcases and boxes and bags. He looked altogether tired and fed up, but he smiled when he saw the dogs gather at his feet.

"Hello, strangers. Looks like you found your way back, huh?" He glanced over at Mia. "Everyone settling in okay?"

"Oh, yeah. It's like they were never gone. You can take that straight up. I've put your folks in our room."

Outside, Frank and Molly gathered items from the trunk of Roman's car. When they saw Mia, they immediately dropped everything and walked quickly toward her.

"We're so sorry about your father. You must be devastated," Molly said, grasping Mia's hands.

"An awful shock for you," Frank said.

"Thank you. Yes, it's been…tough," Mia said.

When they both stepped in as a unit and hugged her, she wanted to push them off and tell them she wasn't so much sad about her father as supremely angry for everything he was putting her through. Instead, she swallowed down her anger, leaned into the hug, and accepted their condolences.

"And I'm sorry you have to leave your house," Mia said when at last they released her. "I'll do everything I can to make sure you're comfortable here."

"Don't worry, child. We'll be fine," Molly said.

It was past noon by the time Frank and Molly were unpacked in the main bedroom upstairs. Roman was still up there with them. Mia stood studying the contents of the fridge and formulating a plan for feeding everyone when the driveway monitor beeped from the counter. With heart thumping, she strode to the front room and stared out the window until two black Ford trucks appeared. One was towing a large RV.

"Easy, boy," she said to Mac whose hackles had risen. "The rest of the security team has arrived."

She quickly made wraps and submarine sandwiches using some of the lunch meat Roman's parents had brought. A large salad and a platter of cut fruit rounded out the meal.

"Lunch is ready," she called out.

Since she didn't have a dedicated dining room or indeed a dining table, she cleared off her worktable and Roman helped her carry it to the sitting room off the kitchen. After sanitizing the surface, she dragged her work chair over and added the chairs from the small bistro table and sent Roman up for his office chair.

"You mustn't fuss over us," Molly said when she came down and saw Mia laying out the food.

"Hardly any fuss at all. It's a very simple meal," Mia said.

The dogs were bustling around and keeping tabs on the platters of food. Mia noticed Lou kept her distance from the four-legged members of the household and quickly shooed Layla away when the lab pushed her head onto Lou's lap.

"Be firm with her," Mia instructed. "She's the kind of girl who doesn't always take 'no' for an answer."

When a knock sounded on the front door, pandemonium broke out. All four dogs bolted and their nails scabbled against the hardwood floor as they barked and bumped against one another in their race to confront the intruder.

"Sorry guys. They're still adjusting to all the activity," Mia said.

"I'll get it," Roman said.

"And I'll come and corral the dogs," Mia said. "Please, everyone. Sit. Eat."

Mitch and Dom stood outside on the front lawn.

"I wanted to give you a progress report and go over some things. I also need to assess the house, and Mia mentioned a dog run. Is this a good time?" Mitch asked.

"Come on in," Roman said. "Both of you."

By now, Mia had the dogs sitting in a neat row and waiting politely. When the two men stepped into the house, not a single canine moved.

"They look like soldiers," Mitch said.

"I was just reminding them of the rules. They seemed to have forgotten all their manners." She walked back and forth along the line of them then made a rolling gesture with her hand and they broke formation and began sniffing at the men.

"Rules are good," Dom said, squatting down and patting Fifi.

"You guys must be hungry. I have food. Lots and lots of food. Come on back," Mia said.

While Roman made introductions, Mia quickly pulled out two more rolls and made each of them a sub sandwich. There wasn't enough room around the table to accommodate two more bodies, so she set them up on stools at the nearby kitchen counter.

"Thank you," Mitch said. "I certainly wasn't expecting to be fed."

"How does that work? You guys getting food and...um...other basic necessities," Lou asked.

"We have an RV and it's stocked with food. Mostly MREs—you know, military rations—and microwave meals. Quick stuff. Which reminds me, would you mind if we plugged in somewhere. I do have a generator, but I'd like to save the gas in case the power gets cut at some point."

"Go right ahead. There's an outlet in the shed across the parking lot," Roman said.

"You think they'll cut the electricity?" Molly asked. "These men are monsters."

Mia fought back a smile. On a scale of bad things happening, she wasn't sure she'd rate losing power anywhere near the top. "I have a generator too so no need to worry," she said.

Mitch nodded while he chewed. "Excellent. That could come in handy. This sub is seriously good, by the way. The other guys will be green with envy when they find out we got good eats."

"Maybe we don't tell them," Dom said.

"Yeah. Maybe we don't. Anyway, I wanted to let you know we're close to having a perimeter established. The guys are completing the job right now. We've got motion sensors set up at various points and cameras here and there. We concentrated most of the resources on the front and back since that's where most properties are breached. From now, I'll have one of my men blocking the driveway twenty-four seven."

"Will that be enough to stop these criminals?" Frank asked. His face was calm and his eyes steady.

"Where there's a will there's a way," Mitch said. "But we'll have plenty of warning if there is a breach, and there ain't nobody driving a vehicle onto this land. We've made sure of that. Take away their wheels, and they're more vulnerable. We also have a couple of drones and will be doing regular flyovers, so don't be alarmed when you see them. Plus, we're going to create another perimeter around the house. It'll be about a hundred feet out and act as a secondary alert."

"That sounds impressive. I already feel so much safer," Lou said.

Mia noticed that Lou looked much as she had when they'd first spotted her walking along the boardwalk of Atlantic City. She'd gone all out on her makeup, including false eyelashes, and her hair was full and fluffy around her face. Her generous and currently plum-colored lips smiled as she gazed at Mitch.

"Glad to be of service," Mitch said.

"Were you really a Navy Seal?" she asked.

"Yes, Ma'am. So was Dom. We also have a couple of Delta Forces guys on the team. Mia, I'm going to take a look at the dog run. I have some bulletproof acrylic sheets, and I'll cover as much as I can to keep them safe."

Mia smiled. "Wonderful. The dogs are very appreciative."

"From this moment on, no walking them out on the property. They can be in the house or in the run. Nowhere else. Okay?" Mitch waited for Mia to nod. "Same goes for you folks. I want everyone to essentially stay in the house."

"How sure are you these men will come?" Dom asked.

Roman and Mia exchanged a look. She nodded, and he strode out of the kitchen.

"We can't, of course, be one hundred percent sure, but I doubt either group will walk away. One member, Dean Chambers, has already been to the house back when everything started, so by now, probably everyone knows where I live."

Roman returned, carrying the small Tupperware, and walked up to the counter by Mitch and Dom. He pried off the lid and carefully upended the container letting the diamonds spread across the granite.

"Holy Mother of God," Molly said, springing up from the table. In a flash, she was at the counter and staring down at the jewels. "These cannot be real?"

"Roman and I had a couple from the first batch appraised, and they were the genuine deal," Mia said.

Molly crossed herself and mumbled something under her breath. "And for these your father died?"

Mia slowly nodded then glanced down at the stones. She scooped up a small number of them and played them across her palm while staring as though seeing them for the first time. "Yes. For these my father died," she repeated.

"But you have a plan, right?" Lou said. "You're going to get justice for Danny."

"Oh, yeah. We have a plan. And it's not only for justice but for our freedom. And yours and Molly's and Frank's."

Mitch took out his phone and laid it on the counter. He leaned his elbows on his knees, and his gaze went to Mia's face. "Maybe it's time we talked about this plan of yours."

Chapter Twenty-Two

Mia glanced to Roman then back to Mitch. "The plan isn't all the way fleshed out yet, but we have a good overview. The basic idea is we stash the diamonds at a second location to keep any danger away from our house then try to get both groups there at the same time. Hopefully, they'll have a good old-fashioned shoot-out, and we bring the cops in to sweep up whoever's left standing."

"We have a location in mind. It's about a half hour from here and remote, so it shouldn't bring danger to the citizens of Dalton or any of the surrounding communities. It's also the last property on a dead end road meaning only one escape route and easily blocked by the police," Roman said.

Mitch nodded. "We should go there now and prepare the site. You going to use the actual diamonds or a decoy?"

"The diamonds. The chance of someone stumbling across them is minimal, and if either party somehow detects we're passing off fakes, it'll add more complications. We want this done," Roman said.

Mitch tipped his head side-to-side then turned to Dom. "Any thoughts?"

"Wondering how you're going to get both groups on site simultaneously. From the info we've been given, Jimmy is on target to arrive hours before Niko and the other Russians. He likely won't sit idly by waiting happily until he's given an invitation. Especially since he's running scared from the mob."

"Yeah. It's a problem," Mia said. "Now that we have a crack security team on site, though, maybe we simply let him blunder around and try to get access to the house. You guys can keep him busy. I know nothing's foolproof, but Jimmy is a regular thug. He chops cars and runs drugs and, apparently, steals diamonds from other bad guys. He thinks he's coming to deal with me and Roman...not a bunch of highly trained men with access to military grade equipment."

"Could work," Mitch said, considering. "How many men would we be talking about?"

"Jimmy already lost his partner to the Russians. But he won't come alone, so he'll likely pull in some muscle. Maybe two or three more besides him," Roman said.

"Don't forget Dean," Mia said. "Jimmy might coerce him into coming along. He's shot though so won't be much of a threat."

Mitch pulled out his phone and checked the time. "First priority is this diamond site. I suggest we head there now and get it squared away. Both of you should come. I'll need five minutes to gather supplies and brief my men. Dom will take over while I'm in the field."

Mia lifted a finger. "Could we maybe do a quick detour on the way back? I want to stock up on food. We have a lot of bodies to feed and MRE rations or not, your men should have at least one awesome meal a day, don't you think?"

"You're the boss, and I make it a policy to never turn down a home-cooked meal," Mitch said while the corners of his mouth twitched up in a smile.

Mia glanced over to the table. "If anyone needs anything, speak now."

They were on the road in under fifteen minutes. Mia and Roman sat on the back seats of one of the big burly pickups. Mitch was behind the wheel, and he'd brought along one of his men, Jose, who was introduced as an expert in command operations.

Roman directed Mitch through the town of Dalton and beyond. No one else spoke during the drive. Nobody turned on the radio. From time to time, the phone in Jose's hand pinged, and he quickly tapped out responses to the messages. When they turned onto Shaker's Line, Mia's anxiety grew in leaps and bounds. She thought she was hiding her emotions well enough, but Roman leaned across and took her hand.

"You okay?" he asked.

"Peachy," she said.

"Problem?" Mitch asked, his eyes meeting Roman's in the rearview mirror.

"Bad memories. This is the same place Mia was brought last year by my...by the Emerald Ring Killer."

"I'm fine," Mia said.

Jose turned and looked over his shoulder. He was a small, wiry man with dusky gold skin and sharp brown eyes. "I read the story. You were brave and very resourceful."

"Um...thanks, I guess. Anyway, it's old news. We need to focus on our current situation."

"Don't worry. We've got this," Roman said.

They turned onto the dirt track and bumped along until they reached the old stone barn. It looked much the same to Mia as the last time she was there. The metal roof was still gone and a few of the trusses had shifted to lean drunkenly against their neighbors. Occasional gaps showed along the side walls where planks had gone missing. Outside, grass and weeds grew right up against the foundation and obscured the doorways.

Mitch parked the truck in the grass next to the building then turned in his seat. "You two stay here while Jose and I do recon. I want one set of eyes on the driveway and the other on the fields surrounding the barn. You carrying?" he asked Roman.

"I've got my Glock. Why don't I do the sweep with you? It'll go faster."

"No. I want you here with Mia. We'll signal when we're sure it's clear."

Mia kept her eyes focused on the driveway, and it felt like no time had passed when Roman nudged her thigh and opened his door. Inside the barn, it was as dark and dank as she remembered. Most of the loft floor was still intact, and the main source of natural light came from the doorways carved into the foundation. Both Mitch and Jose held flashlights and swept their beams back and forth

Roman walked across the open space to where two small stone rooms nestled along the back wall. "I figured one of these could provide some cover if needed."

"Yeah. About the only place," Mitch agreed.

They all crowded into the room to the left of the doorway and studied the space. A small stack of grain bags rested on a wooden pallet. Vermin had chewed holes in the burlap, and mounds of moldy grain scattered across the floor. Beside the pallet stood three plastic barrels.

Jose pried off one of the lids and leaned down. "Molasses," he said, wrinkling his nose.

"That's a lucky break," Roman said.

Mia's eyebrows scrunched together. "Why lucky?"

"They'll act as armor against bullets. A great place to hunker down if things go sideways," he said.

Now she stared at him. "Why do we care? I thought what we wanted was a bunch of really dead bad guys."

Roman shrugged and said nothing, but in a flash, Mia saw into his mind and understood.

Mitch stepped into the silence. "I think what he's trying to say is this plan hinges on getting all the players to this location at around the same time. How's that going to happen exactly? You give them both a map or something? They'll also want some assurance it's not a trap." He paused and his expression softened. "Mia, you need to prepare for the fact that one or both of you may have to accompany them here, and you'll want a safe place to shelter."

"We move the barrels from the wall and stash weapons and ammo behind them," Jose said matter-of-factly. "Maybe some body armor and shields."

"Yeah. It could work just fine. We'll put cameras on the main door and outside the barn. Sensors around the perimeter. On the dirt track coming in," Mitch said. He stepped back into the main space and shone his flashlight along the walls. "Don't forget this stone is also gonna repel bullets just fine."

A tremor went through Mia. All at once, the smell of dirt and decay sickened her. She hurried back outside and leaned a hand against the wall to steady herself. No matter what happened, she couldn't let Roman be the one to come here.

This was her father's doing and by extension, the responsibility fell to her. If Roman got hurt or…worse. Well, it wasn't happening because she simply wouldn't allow it.

"How's it going?" Mitch asked.

"Fine. Just needed some air," Mia said.

"I won't make you any promises, but we'll do everything we can to mitigate the danger. We're going to get this place wired up. You mind giving us a hand?"

They stopped at a grocery store on the way home. Although Mia would have preferred shopping alone, both Roman and Mitch insisted she be accompanied. Mitch stationed himself inside the store at the entrance while Roman took control of the cart and pushed it up and down the aisles behind her.

After several minutes of shopping in silence, Roman finally cleared his throat. "I have a good feeling about our plan. Especially after Mitch and Jose added their tweaks to the location. You've been awful quiet since we left. Having doubts?"

She pursed her lips and shook her head. "I want there to be some way neither of us has to be physically present when this goes down. Tweaks or not, it seems like a suicide mission."

He moved from behind the cart and over to where she stood in the middle of the bread aisle. "I don't think that's true. Especially if I'm the one to go in. I have training for exactly this sort of thing, and I'm damn good with a gun."

"I know you are, but I still hate the idea of it." She sighed and turned, grabbing multiple loaves of bread before tossing them in the cart.

"Maybe we will figure out another way. But it's good to be prepared for the worst, isn't it?"

"Of course. It felt weird leaving the diamonds there after everything we did to find them in the first place."

"Yeah, but it's for the best. Do we really need this much food?" he said frowning down at the cart.

"Yes. We really need this much food. There're five of us in the house plus seven from Tightline, and we have no idea how long we'll be under siege. The last thing we need is a bunch of hungry people."

He pushed the cart to the end of the aisle after her. "I just hope the assholes hurry up and get here. I want this over. It already feels like it's been going on for a decade or so."

That night, Mia cooked up a hearty beef stew with homemade rosemary bread and apple pie and ice cream for dessert. For herself, she made baked beans on toast and a simple salad. All the while, she fought down the queasy, panicky feeling that had been building in her gut all afternoon.

The main members of the household gathered around the table while the Tightline men ate in shifts sitting at the kitchen counter.

"You have been so busy all day. How did you have time for making food?" Molly asked, whispers of Italy weaving through her words.

"Cooking keeps me calm," Mia said.

"From now on, I help. You already do too much. Besides, there is nothing for me right now but to stay in the house, so it will help me to cook with you," Molly said.

"Please let her," Frank said, clasping his hands together. "Otherwise, she pokes at me all day."

"Of course, you can help. And I'm sorry. I know this situation is far from ideal, but at least you're safe," Mia said.

"And hopefully it won't last long," Roman said.

"Already counting the hours for us to leave?" Frank teased.

Roman smiled broadly. "You know it, old man."

"Howdy, folks," Mitch said as he entered the kitchen. "Mia, this is some spread you've put on. Mucho gracious."

"You're very welcome. How are things outside?"

Mitch spooned stew into a bowl and added two slices of the bread to the top. "Nothing to report other than lots of interested wildlife back in the woods. I'm always amazed at how fast they find the cameras. You'll be happy to hear we ran tests on the setup at our secondary location and everything's working like a charm."

"You really left all those diamonds in a deserted barn?" Lou asked.

"We sure did," Roman said. "But they're well protected. Mitch has all the latest in high tech."

"You mean cameras and such," she said. "But it's half an hour from here. If someone finds them they'll be long gone before any of us get there. And if we don't have the diamonds, we don't have bargaining power...so we're as good as dead."

"The diamonds are hard to find even if you know they're in the barn. The only person finding them is someone who knows exactly where to look," Mia said.

Lou frowned down at her stew. "I hope you're right because our lives depend on it."

"You've probably never spent much time in an old barn," Roman said conversationally. "First of all, the light's really bad. Even with flashlights, it's hard to make out any details. Also, all kinds of our friends from the animal kingdom make the most of whatever they can find. We're talking rats and mice of course. There was definitely some evidence of racoons around the place. And then we have the birds. Barn swallows mostly. They like to make nests right up in the ceiling against those big old barn beams. And the nests aren't all fluffy like some birds. Those industrious swallows want real sturdy homes for their babies, so they create something that sort of looks like a small mud hut. As it turns out, it's the perfect place for stashing millions of dollars' worth of diamonds."

Lou stared at him for a second then slowly smiled. "Clever. And sneaky. I like that. And you're right, no one would think to look in a bird's nest."

"Folks, I know this is hard," Mitch said. "But my team has a lot of experience with this sort of thing. I'd say, in this particular situation, we're well ahead of the curve, so try to relax. You're safe here. Short of someone dropping in from a helicopter, no one's getting through to the house. Roman. Mia. I have a couple of things to go over whenever you have a minute."

"I should probably let the dogs out. We could talk on the deck," Mia said.

Outside, the sun had set and the first few stars were twinkling in the indigo sky. The dogs happily ran the length of their run before carefully inspecting each section of the clear acrylic sheeting Mitch's men had installed against the fence. Mac lifted his leg and marked one of the sheets.

"I know that stuff is bullet proof, but I have to wonder if it's strong enough to withstand the mighty force of dog urine," Roman said.

"It'll hold. It sure is pretty country out here." Mitch rubbed a hand back and forth under his chin. "I wanted to let you know I've tapped one of my sources, and our friend Niko Davidov is a mover and shaker within the Bratva. Word is he's young and ambitious. This smuggling operation was his first big test. Obviously, he needs to save face and is gathering a team even as we speak. By my estimation, they'll arrive in Dalton sometime tomorrow."

"I'm impressed. Excellent intel. Don't suppose you know where Jimmy is?" Roman asked.

"'Fraid not. Since his shop burned, I haven't been able to track him."

"He's here. Or almost here," Mia said, her gaze fixing on the field beyond the house.

Mitch's eyes sharpened on her face. "How do you know? Have you had contact with him?"

When Mia simply shook her head and said nothing, Roman cleared his throat.

"Mia has...that is...she sometimes gets feelings about things. If she says Jimmy's close by you can take that to the bank."

"I once worked with a guy who got feelings. His feelings saved my life in Afghanistan. I'd never discount someone with that instinct. Anything else I should know?"

"There is something else. Something about the plan. I can't put my finger on it, but we're missing something." Mia shrugged. "Sorry I can't be more specific."

"That's okay. If anything else comes to you, I want to be the first to know. Okay, moving on. With most of my jobs, I typically touch base with the local authorities. Roman, what about your contact in the Dalton PD? We have credible intel that organized crime is on its way to the area. I think a heads up is in order, don't you?"

"Yeah. You're probably right. My concern is they'll take over the diamond op. I guess I don't want to lose control." Roman glanced back at the house. "There's so much at stake here."

"I get that. How about we don't clue them all the way in? If we simply let them know you're being harassed by some serious level guys...at least they'll be on alert. Let me handle it, okay. I'll drive into town right now and introduce myself."

"Except as soon as Kevin hears, he'll be burning up my cell with questions. He's a friend. I don't want to lie to him or put him in danger," Roman said.

"Can't help you there. That's what you call one of those moral quandaries," Mitch said, grinning.

"If the positions were reversed, what would you want him to do?" Mia asked.

"Tell me, of course."

"There's your answer. Give him a call and spell it out for him. He'll understand. Plus, wouldn't it be good to run the idea by someone else? He might pick up whatever we've missed," Mia said, wrapping her arms around herself.

Roman nodded slowly. "You're right."

"Of course, I'm right. Now I'll leave you men with your assignments while I clean up the kitchen. Then I think I'll get an early night because I'm just about spent, and it sounds like tomorrow's going to be a nonstop thrill ride." She whistled to the dogs and held the sliding door open while they rushed inside.

It was almost two hours later when Roman entered his office where she lay on the pull-out couch. Despite her exhaustion, anxiety continued to flood her nervous system, and she couldn't sleep.

"How's Kevin?" she asked.

"I'd say his nose is a little out of joint, but he was mostly okay by the time we were done talking. He says I can count on him to keep the diamond drop to himself until I give him the go ahead. Mitch let me know his friendly stop-in at the department went about as good as he expected. Initially lots of attitude, I'm guessing that was mostly from Schmidt and Hansen. Those guys can be real assholes sometimes. But they're on alert and said they'd also keep an eye on my parents' house, which I appreciate."

"That's good. Every little bit helps."

He sat on the bed and stroked a hand along her arm. "I'm worried about you. You've been off ever since we went to the barn on Shaker's Line. You wanna tell me about it?"

She heaved out a sigh and pushed up to a sitting position. He noticed she was wearing a T-shirt instead of her customary sleep top, and she had three beaded bracelets stacked on her wrist.

"I wish I could tell you about it, but I don't know what's wrong. Only that I have this overwhelming sense of dread our plan isn't going to work. In the old days, if I got one of these—Dean used to call it my heebie jeebie episodes—I'd pull out right away." Her voice was high, and she twisted the bracelets around and around her wrist. "Except, in this case, we can't do that because we literally have no Plan B and no time to make one. Jimmy's going to get here sometime tonight. Of that I'm certain."

"Easy now. I hear what you're saying, and I believe you." His hand closed over hers and stopped the manic twisting of the beads. "And if—or when—the plan fails, we'll adapt. You and I are both smart and quick on our feet. Plus, we have Mitch and his team, not to mention the Dalton Police Department at our disposal. We'll find a way through this. We have to. Now lie back down. Jimmy may be on his way, but he's not here yet and we need to sleep."

She wiggled down, and he helped settle the covers around her. Her face was pale and drawn, and her eyes held shadows. It made his heart squeeze. He shifted in beside her and snuggled close while he rubbed slow circles over her belly.

Her breathing gradually slowed, and she blinked more and more slowly until her eyes closed. At long last, she slept, and the tension released from her body. He sighed and closed his own eyes chasing after her into oblivion.

It was three twenty-nine when the call came from Mitch. Roman mumbled, "Mancini," into the phone as he fought to embrace consciousness.

Chapter Twenty-Three

Mitch's voice was calm and matter-of-fact. "The east border was breached almost ten minutes ago. We caught the perp on one of the perimeter cameras. Unfortunately, he escaped before we were able to detain him."

"I'm coming," was all Roman said. He tossed the phone on the bed and rubbed his hands back and forth across his face.

"I heard what he said. I'm coming too," Mia said, throwing off the covers and pushing to her feet.

The dogs, always sensitive to atmosphere, paced around the small room and managed to put themselves in the path of both Mia and Roman who hurried to pull on clothes.

"I'm not bringing the dogs, but I should at least let them out," Mia said.

"Okay. But make it quick."

They both stood on the back porch while the dogs did their business. Mia noticed Roman had his gun in his hand held down beside his leg while his eyes repeatedly scanned the area around the house. The air was warm, and the inky sky had no moon. Lights from the porch cast long shadows across the lawns. She shivered and fought off the image of an unknown, faceless man watching them through the sight of his gun.

Mac, and surprisingly, little Fifi, were bound and determined to join in on the mission. Mia gently pushed them back inside the house and bending down, kissed Mac on the head.

"You have to guard the house. You're head of security, remember?" Mia told him.

Fifi scrabbled at her leg, and she picked her up and gave her a quick cuddle before setting her down next to Mac.

"Let's go," Roman said, trying to hold onto his patience.

A Tightline man met them at the walkway and insisted on escorting them across the parking lot to the far side of the VR where one of the trailers was stationed. Inside, Mitch sat at a table holding laptops, keyboards, cell phones, com radios, a curved bracket mounted with six flat-screen monitors, and various other pieces of equipment.

Mitch nodded at the man with Mia and Roman. "Corey, go back out to sector seven and do one more sweep."

"Aye, Captain," the man said before slipping away.

"What's the situation?" Roman said.

Mitch tapped one of the keyboards then pointed to a monitor. "Here's our intruder. This is on the east border near the rocky tree line about a hundred and ten feet northwest of the residence at twenty-two Barrow Line."

They watched as the footage rolled forward, and a burly man pushed through branches and gingerly made his way across a wall of uneven rocks. He was bald with a large, bushy mustache and small, closely set eyes. The man stopped and scanned left and right then continued on for four more strides before disappearing from the camera range. The time on the screen showed three-eleven.

"I immediately dispatched two of my men to that sector. We caught him briefly on another camera, but something must have spooked him. See here."

He tapped a different screen, and they saw the same man sprinting across a field toward the neighbor's property. Now the time was three-seventeen.

"I'm guessing he's gone?" Roman said.

"Seems to be. I sent up one of the drones and saw a Mercedes sedan driving east at a high rate of speed."

"Jimmy," Mia mumbled.

Mitch turned to face her. "Did you recognize the man as one of Jimmy's?"

"No. I've never seen him before. But the last time I was with Jimmy, he had a black Mercedes sedan. And I can feel him out there."

"Not definitive proof but most likely it's him," Roman said. "Looks like the game is officially on. Now all we need is Niko to get his ass over here, and we'll finally have a chance to end this thing."

Mia clutched her hands in front of her stomach and glanced at the monitors. "Our idea was good on paper, but now that it's happening, I don't see how we'll get either of them to go to the barn on Shaker's Line. Especially after they've gotten a look at the security we've laid on here. They'll think we're way too prepared and be sure it's a big fat trap."

"It's a dilemma, all right. But let's not get all twisted up about it. Our main objective is keeping everyone here safe. So far, so good. I don't expect there'll be any more action this morning so why don't you guys head on back to the house and see if you can catch some more sleep," Mitch said.

"You manage to grab any shuteye?" Roman asked.

"Sure. I got a couple of hours down before midnight. I'll let you know if there're any more developments."

"I don't think I can sleep," Mia said on the walk back to the house.

"Me neither. I could go for some coffee, though. How about you?" He slung an arm around Mia's shoulder.

"Maybe. I'm starting to realize I might be a coffee drinker after all. At least I am while we're under siege."

They stepped into the house and were immediately enveloped by dogs.

"You guys shush," Mia whispered, casting a glance at the stairs. "We have guests, remember? I'll be very, very mad at you if anyone wakes up."

She hustled them through to the kitchen and decided the best way to keep the peace was by serving an early breakfast. While she dished out kibble and replenished water bowls, Roman set up the Keurig machine, and soon the tantalizing aroma of coffee hung in the air.

"What do you think Jimmy will do?" Mia asked once they sat across from one other at the bistro table clutching their mugs.

"Hard to say. He likely thought all he had to do was beat Niko here, snatch you up, and force the diamonds out of your sweet little hands. I doubt he brought a bunch of high-tech gadgets with him. I'm talking night vision goggles or electronic surveillance equipment, so he's not in a position to bust in on us. He may be able to pick up something useful in Walkerton or somewhere else nearby once the stores open, but it'll be consumer grade stuff. No match for our security team and their setup."

"I can't decide if that's a good thing or not. I mean, he'll hardly throw up his hands and simply leave, will he?" Mia said.

"Depends on if his fear outweighs his greed. Since he came all the way here, I'll lay my money on the greed side of the table."

"I guess all we can do is wait and hope for the best," she said, frowning down at her coffee before taking a small sip. "Why does this stuff always smell better than it tastes?"

"I beg to differ. It tastes like heaven to me."

They sat in silence until Roman had finished his coffee and pushed back from the table. "You're not going to drink that, are you?"

"Probably not. I think I'll make some peppermint tea instead."

"I'll put the kettle on for you. Then I'm going out to offer Mitch my services. No point in me sitting around the house all day when I can be of help."

Her eyes fixed on his face. "Promise me you'll stay behind the scenes. If something were to happen to you..." She closed her eyes and shook her head. "I don't think I could stand it."

"Hey. Baby." She opened her eyes again and found he was crouched by her chair. "I'll be fine. Don't worry."

"That's a stupid thing to say," she snapped. "You don't know you'll be fine, and I can't stop worrying if I think you're in danger. Maybe I should go out too. Sweep some of the sectors or whatever it's called. What's good for the goose is good for the gander, right?"

"Except you don't have training, and you're not used to carrying a gun," he pointed out. "And what about the dogs? They'll be upset if you leave them alone in a house full of strangers. How about if I do my best not to volunteer for any suicide missions?"

"Fine." She sniffed and pushed his hand off her knee. "Go play soldier boy, if that'll make you feel better."

He rose to his feet and smiled down at her. "It will. I think I'll go mostly crazy if I have to sit in here waiting."

"You mean like I'll be doing?"

"Yeah. But you're better at it than me. I have my cell, so you know you can reach me. And I'll give you lots of updates. I guarantee you'll be in the loop at all times."

When she said nothing, instead busied herself with making the tea, he sighed and gave Mac a quick stroke along the back before turning away and walking toward the front door. She caught him before he'd managed to open it all the way and threw her arms around him, hugging him from behind.

"Be careful. And make sure you keep those texts coming, okay?" Her words were muffled against his back.

He turned and taking her face in his hands, laid a soft kiss on her lips. "Love you."

"Ditto. Now go already." She stepped back and gave him a playful shove.

He slid out and through the sunroom before stepping down the stairs to the lawn. Behind him, the sky was lightening, and a thin streak of magenta washed across the tops of the trees in the distant field. It was going to be a beautiful day. She couldn't help worrying about all the things that might happen before the sun set again.

As it turned out, for most of the day not a lot happened. She and Molly cooked up a massive breakfast feast and fed everyone in shifts. Nobody was much interested in lunch, so people simply made sandwiches or grabbed leftover stew as hunger spiked throughout the afternoon.

It was a strange interlude of constant gnawing anxiety coupled with acute boredom. And to make matters worse, she was, in essence, a hostess to the small group on her property. She felt it necessary to chat with Lou, who seemed invigorated by all the people and activity and had question after question about the early morning breach. She sat with Frank and Molly playing gin rummy for close to two hours before setting them up with a DVD in the front room to while away the afternoon.

When Roman mentioned there'd been a leak in the water line of the RV's shower, she offered bathroom facilities and toiletry supplies to the Tightline men then felt compelled to roll out coffee and cookies and fruit as they wandered back downstairs for another shift of security duty.

And all she really wanted to do was sit quietly, alone, except for her dogs, and give her nervous system a chance to regulate. She wasn't used to having so many people in her personal space. For someone with her extrasensory abilities, it required a force of effort to block out the barrage of emotions and energy. Being already stressed and low on sleep was, quite frankly, wearing her down.

Please let this be over soon.

Except that was like wishing for the devil, wasn't it? she thought. Because any number of things could bring this situation to a head, and so many of the potential outcomes were beyond awful.

Damn you, Pops. How could you do this to me?

She forced a slow exhale and shook her head. It wasn't a good idea to let her thoughts run wild. Instead, she should just focus on the next thing. And right now, the next thing on the agenda of the hostess with the most-ess was pulling something together for dinner.

It surprised her to find Roman in the kitchen chugging beer straight from the bottle.

"I didn't hear you come in. What's the word?"

He set the empty bottle aside and wiping his mouth with the back of his hand, grinned at her. "All's quiet on the western front. Same goes for the north, south, and east. Mitch has a great team of guys. They're fierce and focused, and I figure it'll take an army to get by them."

She studied his face. "You're enjoying the hell out of this, aren't you?"

His face sobered. "Not the situation. Not us being in danger and dealing with organized crime. But…yeah…it was good to mix in with a group of like-minded guys."

"Sort of similar to being on the force. There you were surrounded by other men, and some women I guess, who were just like you. Plus, you had Kevin as a partner. The two of you out there on the mean streets fighting crime and righting wrongs." She walked up to him and placed her hand on his cheek. "This past year has been hard on you, hasn't it? I'm sorry."

His eyes had gone to molten chocolate when he gazed down at her. "I won't lie, some of it has been hard. But some of it has been great, too, because I've had you."

"Aw, don't you just say the sweetest things." Her smile held all kinds of promise. "That just earned you a whole bunch of brownie points. You can cash them in…later."

He lowered his face, eyes staying locked on hers. "You can bet I'll do just that," he murmured against her mouth before tilting his head and deepening the kiss.

When they eventually broke apart, both a little flushed and Roman's hair tousled, Mia sighed. "I do love a good smooch in the kitchen. And since you're here, let's get you knifed up and started on some chopping. I'm thinking stir fry. Gigantic stir fry."

"Um…" He glanced around in desperation then held up both hands in front of his face. "I'm dirty. Sweaty. I should probably clean up first."

"I'm here." Molly marched into the kitchen. "The afternoon is almost gone. We should prepare dinner."

Roman pointed at his mom, a smug smile on his face. "There. See. Plenty of help for dinner. I'm going to go on then and grab a shower."

"You just lost a whole bunch of those points," Mia called after him.

"Your face is always so happy when you talk to my boy. It's lovely to see," Molly said, her hand fisted against her breast and her eyes misty. "After his sister disappeared, he was different, harder and no longer with an open heart. I worried for so long he'd never be happy. Never find love. Live a full life. Now you've changed him again or maybe reminded him of who he used to be. It's all a mother could ever want for her child."

Mia swallowed over the lump in her throat. "I guess we're both very lucky."

After dinner, Lou and Frank offered to clean the kitchen.

"It's only fair," Lou said. "Everyone needs to pull their weight in a situation like this."

Mia took the dogs out to the run and sat on the deck looking at the stars and listening to the crickets. Everything seemed so blessedly normal out here. Except for the bullet proof panels, of course. And the silhouette of the RV trailer by the garage. But if she blocked that out, she could almost believe it was any other beautiful May night in Tennessee.

Roman poked his head out through the sliding door. "I'm going to head up early and catch some sleep. I promised to take the midnight shift. Don't stay out too long. It's safe enough...but still..."

By the time she'd showered off the remains of the day and gone through her nighttime routine, Roman snored lightly from the pull-out couch. She made sure the dogs had settled in the various beds scattered around the room then slid under the sheet and snuggled against Roman's solid body. Her last thought before sleep was that he hadn't tried to cash in any of his brownie points.

For the second night in a row, they were awakened by the ping of Roman's phone. He sprang up and grabbed it from where it rested on the arm of the couch.

"Shit. The Russians are here."

Chapter Twenty-Four

Mia glanced at the time. Eleven-twenty. They'd only been asleep for a couple of hours. Roman was already pulling on pants, and she scrambled to catch up with him.

"The dogs stay in for now," he said.

"Okay." She glanced down at the four pairs of hopeful eyes. "But I'm coming."

He shoved his phone in his back pocket. "Why don't I go out and get an update first and let you know."

She pulled on a T-shirt and grabbed a scrunchie, quickly twisting her hair up into a messy bun. "Nice try. I'm still coming."

As they were tiptoeing down the stairs, a short barrage of gunshots cracked through the quiet night. They stopped short, listening, barely breathing, and the guns sounded again.

Roman tipped his head. "It's coming from down by the road. Let's go."

At the command center in the trailer, Mitch spoke into a radio issuing orders to stay in position and return fire if necessary. One of the monitors showed an SUV parked directly in front of the barrier by the road and a man occasionally poking his head out from behind the vehicle to fire at the trailer blocking the driveway.

"There're two more cars on the road," Mitch said. "They got here about thirty minutes ago and drove back and forth along the property obviously casing the place. One of the vehicles attempted to drive around the barrier but caught the spike strip and quickly backed out with two flat front tires. The two men abandoned it and climbed into the third SUV. By my estimation, we have two men in the car on the driveway and three to four men in the remaining vehicle on the road."

"Have they attempted to access anywhere else on the property?" Roman asked.

"Not so far. All my men are in position and none of the sensors have been triggered."

"You're sure it's the Russians?" Mia asked.

"Yep. I managed to get a plate and ran it a few minutes ago. It's definitely them. I haven't had a visual of Niko, but I'm guessing he's there."

For several tense minutes, the monitor showed gunfire being traded in short, sharp bursts. From time to time, one of the Russian men attempted to sneak between his SUV and the Tightline trailer but each time, he was forced back.

"Surely they'll run out of ammunition before too much longer," Mia commented.

"Hard to say. They could have cases of it on board their vehicles." Mitch's eyes shifted back and forth along all six monitors while he spoke. "All I know is we have more than enough to withstand days of targeted gunfire."

"Pretty soon someone's going to call the cops," Roman said.

"I'm aware. I just wanted to make sure they understand how serious we are. I'll shut it down now if you want."

"Might be best."

Mitch talked into his com. "Dom, time to toss them some heat."

Mia leaned closer to the monitor. For a moment nothing seemed to happen. Then the back of the Russian SUV was lit up by three quick flashes of light. Rumbling, similar to the sound of fireworks, could be heard and a cloud of smoke drifted around the vehicle. One of the Tightline men stepped out and crouched low, tossing a small object before retreating. Even more smoke bloomed, covering the driveway, and obscuring the camera view on the screen.

Mitch pointed to the top right monitor where two men staggered toward the road. "Looks like we ran them out of there. You guys sit tight, and I'll assess the situation."

Mia sighed and glanced over to Roman. "I know you want in on this, so just go. I'll stay right here. Promise."

Roman's eyes light up. "Yeah? Okay then. I'll come straight back once everything's secure."

"Here." Mitch handed Mia a radio. "I'll leave a man out in the lot so you'll be plenty safe, but you can use this if you need to contact us. And you can watch on the screen."

Mia slid onto the chair Mitch had vacated and waited. Soon enough, the monitor showed Mitch, Dom, and Roman crouched down and approaching the SUV then carefully making their way along the side of it to the back end. There was still a thin veil of smoke drifting around the area, but Mia could see clearly enough. She held her breath until the men stood and Mitch said "all clear" into the radio.

Roman arrived back in the trailer about ten minutes later. "They're gone. At least, the third vehicle has disappeared, and we can't find any sign of them. It tickles me to think of at least six guys, maybe more, all crushed into the one car. I wonder if anyone had to sit on a lap?" He paused to chuckle. "Anyway, we went through the abandoned SUV. Nothing much to see. Some food wrappers. We snagged the receipts, but they paid in cash. No ID anywhere. No insurance slips in the glove box."

"They're obviously coming back though? I mean, they left two cars here." Mia worried her bottom lip with her teeth. "Plus, they still don't have the diamonds."

"Yeah. They'll be back. But we want that, right?" He took her hand in his, squeezing gently. "We need to finish this thing all the way, otherwise we'll always have to be on guard."

"I know. It's just...these last few days have been hard. I wish it was over already. I feel like I'm on a constant roller coaster ride of adrenaline."

He pulled her to her feet and wrapped his arms around her shoulders. "It is hard, baby. I get it. But my sense is something's gonna break really soon. All you have to do is hang in there."

She sighed against his chest before straightening and pushing back. "I know. I can totally hang in there. Sorry. Weak moment. I'm okay now."

"Not a weak moment. A human one." He searched her eyes for several beats then grinned. "One day I'm sure we'll laugh about this."

She felt a smile building. "You think we'll say things like 'remember how fun it was when we were being hunted by two different groups of criminals. At the same time. And one of them tried to shoot their way onto the property. What a great night that was.' Is that what you mean?" she asked.

"See. It's already kind of funny."

"I'm starting to think you and I have a very different sense of humor. Anyway, I'm going back to the house to make sure the dogs and people are all right."

"And since it's after midnight, I'll check in for my Tightline shift." He leaned in and kissed her, light and easy. "I'll see you at dawn."

Five hours later, Mia stirred when Roman slipped into the bed.

"How was it?" she asked, her voice rusty from sleep.

"Interesting." He yawned and rubbed his forehead. "We had a little more action from the Russians."

She bolted straight up, pulling the sheet off him. "What do you mean 'more action'? I didn't hear any shooting."

"Hey. Easy there, tiger. No guns involved this time. Just car stuff." He repositioned the sheet around him and let his head fall back on the pillow. "We called in a tow truck to get rid of their vehicle from the driveway. It was kind of funny actually since they showed up right after the truck pulled onto the road—obviously watching from the bend east of the property. It took them about half an hour to convince the guy to give it back to them. We couldn't hear everything going on, but I'd bet there was some very bad language filling the air. Then they spent a bunch of time changing out the tires on the third SUV. The one that ran afoul of the spike strips."

"I don't suppose they waved goodbye and drove off in the direction of Savannah?"

"Nope. Just moved down the road again and sat watching."

Mia exhaled and flopped down beside him. "Any sign of Jimmy? I'd swear I can still sense him somewhere close by."

"Well, if he's close by, we didn't see him. Anyway, it could be a very interesting day ahead so I'd better get some shut eye. Come here." He shifted over and snuggled in beside her, resting his chin on her shoulder. "You need a couple more hours too."

Within moments, Roman dropped straight into sleep, but Mia was too twitchy to relax. The ball of dread rolled uneasily in her stomach, and she had to actively work to keep her breathing slow and steady. This wasn't like her. She'd been in situations of danger before—too many to count, really—and never had this almost paralyzing reaction in the past. Maybe living on the straight and narrow had turned her soft.

Except she didn't really think so. Something else was off-kilter. Thankfully, it wasn't her relationship with Roman. These past few days had shown them to be back in the groove, working together, and loving one another. Whatever was tripping her senses, it wasn't that. But damned if she knew what it was.

She lay beside Roman, wide awake and brooding, until the dogs insisted it was time for breakfast. Downstairs, she was surprised to find Lou up and bustling around the kitchen. She was wearing full makeup again, and her hair shone like spun gold. Large gold hoops dangled from her ears and a collection of bangles made music every time she moved her arms. Mia was reminded of how stunningly attractive she was.

"Good morning," Lou said flashing a big smile. "I think it's time I took a turn on cooking detail. I'm going to make pancakes. It's one of my favorite breakfasts."

"That's so nice of you. Thanks. Seems like you found everything." Mia opened the sliding door and let the dogs out.

"It's easy in a kitchen as well organized as yours. You look tired. Why don't I make you a coffee?"

Mia frowned and rubbed a hand over her stomach. "No. Thanks. I'd better stick with tea right now. But I'll get it. First though, I should feed the dogs or we might have a riot on our hands."

Neither of them spoke for several minutes while they went about their tasks. Once the dogs were taken care of, Mia slid onto a stool at the counter and carefully set down her mug of steaming tea.

"What happened last night? I heard people shooting, and when I knocked on the bedroom door, you and Roman were gone."

Mia took a sip of tea and sighed. "We had a visit from the Russian Mafia just before midnight. Don't worry. It was over quickly, and we were never in danger. Mitch's men are very good at their jobs."

Lou's fingers fluttered against the base of her throat. "Oh, my goodness. That must have been so scary. No wonder you look tired. They're gone now?"

"Not entirely. It seems they've set up a watching post just down the road a bit."

"Shouldn't we call the police?"

"We could, but it wouldn't make much difference in the end. They'll just come back."

"Lordy, how is this all going to end?" Lou gripped the edge of the counter. "We can't stay locked up here forever."

"No, we really can't. No doubt something will happen soon to bring it to a head."

Lou turned her attention to the pancake ingredients and started measuring out flour. "I was thinking about your father last night. I can't bear—" She paused when her voice hitched then took another breath before continuing. "It's hard thinking of him lying unclaimed in some morgue in Florida. It sort of breaks my heart."

"I know. It is hard. But we can't do anything until we clean up the mess he left for us."

"You're still angry?"

Mia blew out a breath. "Yeah. I am. Aren't you?"

Lou shook her head, and her voice was soft when she spoke. "Not very much. Not anymore. I keep remembering how sweet he was with me. All the little gifts and kisses. Every couple of weeks he'd suddenly say, 'come on, Lou Lou. You deserve to be spoiled, so go put on your best dress because I'm taking you out for a fancy night.' And we'd have dinner in some wonderful restaurant with romantic music or see a play or something. I miss that."

Mia nodded slowly while she tamped down her rage. "Pops could certainly be a lot of fun. I'm glad he treated you so well. And I'm sorry for your loss," she said carefully.

"Did that awful Jimmy Genomi show his face last night?"

"Not that I heard. Maybe he's too afraid now that the Mafia is here."

Lou's expression went hard. "If he disappears, how will we ever make him pay? And what about the other man? Dean Shavers. Will he run away too?"

"It's Dean Chambers," Mia said, fighting back a smile. "And I have no idea where he is. Maybe with Jimmy or maybe gone."

"It's not right they get away with killing a man." Lou cracked an egg with a little more force than necessary, and bits of the shell fell into the bowl. "Now look what I've done. I'm just so mad."

"Hey. It'll be okay. Hopefully we'll figure out a way to get justice for Pops." She stepped over and hugged Lou. "I may be pissed at my father, but he didn't deserve to die like that."

"He surely didn't," Lou said.

Once she was sure Lou was settled again, Mia slipped out onto the back porch and into the dog run and spent a solid half hour throwing balls for the deliriously happy dogs. By the time Molly and Frank came downstairs, Lou had a substantial stack of pancakes warming in the oven and had turned her attention to crisping bacon and arranging bowls of berries.

Molly clapped her hands together. "It's like we're staying at a fancy hotel. I'm going to gain so much weight Frank will have to roll me out of here when it's time to go home."

"Any news from the men outside?" Frank asked.

"Mia said some of the Russian Mafia tried to get on the property," Lou said.

Molly turned to Mia. "Jesus, Mary, and Joseph. Is this true?"

"Yes. They tried but didn't succeed. We're all safe," she said, echoing what she'd told Lou earlier.

Most of the talk over breakfast centered around the activities of the previous night. Molly and Frank were aghast to hear Roman was working with the Tightline men and Mia spent considerable time reassuring them he would be safe even though she had no idea if it was true.

In fact, her anxiety was increasing as the morning progressed. Pinpricks of electricity played across her skin, and she was conscious of her heart beating fast in her chest like a ticking bomb. Somehow, she made it through the meal, and when everyone finally pushed back from the table she jumped to her feet.

"Lou, you made the food, so I'll do clean up. And you wanted to run a load of laundry, right?" she said to Molly as she shooed everyone out of the kitchen.

No sooner was she alone than the dogs came to attention, and Mitch burst into the room.

"We've got a situation. You and Roman need to come."

"Roman's still sleeping. Should I wake him?"

"Yeah. Get him up. I'll meet you outside."

"Is it bad?"

Mitch shook his head. "I don't know yet. Could be good."

The second Mia stepped into the bedroom, Roman became instantly alert. He didn't ask questions, instead pulled on a pair of pants, and followed her downstairs patting his hair into place. Mitch waited in one of the trucks, and they climbed onto the back seats.

Mitch began speaking even as he executed a neat three-point turn and proceeded along the driveway. "As you know, the Russians have been sitting about a quarter of a mile up the road. Approximately ten minutes ago, the three vehicles moved to the front of your property. They idled for over a minute before one of the SUVs approached the barrier on the driveway. It was the same two men who'd attempted to gain access last night. The driver opened his door and leaned out, setting a cell phone on the ground before backing out to the road."

"What do they want?" Roman asked flatly.

"To talk to you and Mia. Face to face on the driveway. They say just Niko. The rest of the men stay on the road."

"But they could shoot us from the road, right?" Mia asked.

"Sure," Mitch agreed. "It's only about two hundred feet, give or take. If they have a rifle scope, it wouldn't be too much of an ask."

"No problem. All we do is bring him up the drive beyond the trailer. That'll block their line of sight. And the trailer is armored so no way to shoot through it," Roman said.

Mitch slowed as they approached the barrier and braked behind one of the Tightline trucks. "Assuming you want to do this face-to-face, that'd be my suggestion."

They congregated inside the trailer where Dom and another man sat at a table set up with monitors and other paraphernalia similar to the one Mitch had back by the house.

"No movement," Dom said. "You still want the drone?"

"Yeah. Let's make sure we're not missing anything," Mitch said.

The other Tightline man picked up a small electronic device from the table and stepped outside. Mitch and Dom shifted to one of the monitors on the right-hand side, and Mia and Roman leaned in. The screen soon filled with live footage from the drone which gave them an overhead view of the trailer and trucks parked by the barricade.

The drone then did a slow pass over the entire property. Mia saw her greenhouse glinting in the morning sun and the path worn in the grass by the dogs racing up and down the fence of their run. The pops of color from the flowerbeds surrounding her house had her longing to spend the afternoon puttering in her garden instead of meeting with a Mafia thug and whatever else that would entail.

Once Mitch was satisfied there were no intruders or any kind of ambush awaiting them, he turned to Roman and Mia.

"If you want to go ahead with the meet, I'll put a man in the woods close to the road and another on the rise by the west property line," Mitch said.

Mia shifted until she faced Roman. "I think we should do it."

"Good. So do I. Mitch, get your men in place."

"A-ok." He turned to Dom. "You take the woods and send Cooper on the rise."

"What kind of hardware do your guys use?" Roman asked.

"Mostly the AI AXSR. Can't beat them for long-range accuracy," Mitch said.

Roman nodded. "Impressive. I've shot one a time or two. Only at the range, but still, it gave me a nice feel."

Mia blocked out the rest of the gun talk and took an internal inventory. She remained anxious, but at least it made sense in this context. They were about to chat with a man who wanted them dead. Anxiety was a normal response.

What wasn't normal was the pit of dread still lodged so firmly in her stomach. If only she knew the cause. It reminded her of those dreams of driving fast and not being able to open your eyes. You keep trying to pry your eyelids apart with your fingers, but it's no use. You still can't see clearly, and you know you're seconds away from a devastating crash.

But what the heck was she about to crash into, and why couldn't she just pump the brakes instead?

Chapter Twenty-Five

Roman touched Mia's shoulder, and she jolted. "Sorry. You okay?"

"Of course. I'm fine. Are we ready?"

"Just about. The snipers are in place. Mitch is texting Niko to come on over."

"Done." Mitch placed the cell phone on the table then leaned down and tapped out something on the keyboard. "Here we go," he said, pointing to one of the monitors.

Mia's breath caught as she watched a man step out from the back of the third SUV. He was tall and wiry and had brown wavy hair swept off his face. A thin but distinct scar was visible below his left ear and continued to his jawline.

"We have a positive ID on Nikolai Davidov. Over," Mitch said into his radio.

Niko walked slowly but deliberately onto the driveway and continued his march until he was about halfway to the trailer at which point he stopped and raised his arms about his head.

"Hold," Mitch said. "Let's see what he's up to. Over."

Using slow and economical movements, Niko stripped off his shirt and held it in his left hand. He stood there bare chested, with a dark bandana around his neck and legs clad in tight black jeans. With his arms held straight out from his shoulders, he turned a small circle giving a good view of his back. Then he continued walking until he reached the trailer.

On the monitor, the man who had piloted the drone stepped into frame and approached Niko. He gave the Russian a pat down before turning to face the camera and flashing a thumbs up.

Mitch stood. "You two stay put. I want to go out and give this joker another look. If everything seems okay, I'll bring him along the side of the trailer. We do the meet 'n' greet out there."

Mia nodded and focused on her breathing. The dread was coming alive inside her. Rising and bubbling and making her feel as though a nest of snakes slithered along her skin. Her mouth had gone to sand, and it was an effort to swallow.

"Hey. Everything'll be fine. You've seen all the precautions we've taken. If you're still worried, I can do the meet by myself. No problem," Roman said.

"No. I should be there. I might get a better sense of what Niko's planning," Mia said.

Roman studied her for several beats noting that all the color had leached out of her lips and her eyes shone like jewels against her deathly pale skin.

"You look almost sick. I don't think I've ever seen you like this. What is it?"

Mia's eyes flicked over to the monitor then she exhaled through pursed lips. "I wish I knew. Come on. Mitch is bringing Niko back. Let's get this over with."

Mitch and the drone pilot positioned Niko at the side of the trailer away from the road. The Russian wore his shirt again and had buttoned it up to where the bandana hung around his neck. The ensemble had a vague cowboy vibe. He stood placidly watching them approach. He wasn't as tall as Mia had first thought when she'd seen him on the monitor. Probably not even six feet but his lean build gave him the illusion of height.

A smile flickered across his face. "I finally get to meet the couple who took my property. You have balls of steel—if you'll pardon the expression—robbing the Russian Bratva."

"I think you need to get your story straight. We didn't steal anything. In fact, without us, you wouldn't have the first clue where your diamonds went. You should be down on your knees kissing our feet," Roman said.

Niko snorted. "And you, Jenny Dawson. Is that your story also? You expect me to believe you had nothing to do with your father and his companions breaking into my shipping container?"

"My name is Mia, as you well know. I haven't been Jenny Dawson for a very long time. And frankly, I don't care what you believe. I assume you want the diamonds back?" She crossed her arms over her chest and arched an eyebrow. "Well, we want something too. Your word that you'll leave us alone. That includes our family and friends."

Roman tipped his head to the side and studied Niko's flat, pale blue eyes. "But how can we trust his word? He's a criminal. A man who kills without blinking. Someone who's methodically planning to ascend the ladder of organized crime."

"Why not call the police then? Tell them to lock me up." Niko paused and looked around as though expecting to hear sirens. "Except you won't because you have no proof of anything."

"Are you saying even if we give you the diamonds, you'll still want revenge?" Mia asked.

"I'm saying—give me the diamonds, and then we'll see."

"We could have you killed right now by this fine gentleman." Roman gestured to Mitch then reached to the small of his back and pulled out a gun. "Or I could kill you."

Niko merely smiled and spread out his hands. "Go ahead, Mister Tough Guy. Kill me. But then you will never be free. It is well known, even by the most uniformed civilian, that the Bratva always pay back their enemies. If you kill me, you might as well kill yourself."

"Why bother talking then? Without some kind of guarantee, we'll never give you the diamonds, so this is a complete waste of time. You may as well go back to your men on the road," Mia said.

"What about the other thieves? Your partners in crime. Are you not scared of them as well? They will happily kill to get the stones. Or maybe you want to give them to Dean Chambers? Maybe old love has been rekindled," Niko said while his gaze wandered up and down Mia before shifting to Roman. "All these beautiful women, they are the same, my friend. Spreading their legs for the highest bidder. I guess millions of dollars' worth of diamonds would make a woman very eager to please in whatever way she could. Miss Reeves has a history of being especially accommodating with men, doesn't she?"

Roman shook his head and tucked the gun back in the waistband of his jeans. "Nice try. But we already have the diamonds, so why would Mia need Dean? Your attempt to bait me was beyond juvenile and mostly just pathetic." He turned to Mia. "I don't think this one's very smart. Forget about becoming a brigadier, he'll be lucky to keep his status as a foot soldier."

"You will not disrespect me," Niko snarled.

Roman stepped forward and into the Russian man's space. "And you will not disrespect my fiancé. Not with your words or your attitude or by so much as a goddamn sneering look. Are we clear?"

They locked eyes for several seconds then Niko shrugged. "So, we've shown one another that neither is afraid. Now I apologize."

He stepped away from Roman and turned to face Mia. "I am sorry to use you in such a way, but I had to take a measure of the man I was dealing with. You will forgive me?"

Mia narrowed her eyes at him. "Don't you want to take my measure? Or is it only men you deem worthy adversaries? I can promise you, I'm just as fierce as Roman."

Niko shook his head and sighed. "Again, I insult you. This time unintentionally. Please accept my deepest apology."

He took her hand and bowed low, grazing his lips across her knuckles. Everything seemed to slow down for a second, and she became aware of a change in the atmosphere around the trailer. Then, as if someone suddenly hit the fast forward button, both Mitch and Roman spun toward her. She saw Roman reach for the gun at his back while the drone pilot lifted both arms straight in front of him, his weapon already trained on Niko.

Quicker than a snake, Niko straightened and pulled a mask from under the bandana and over his mouth. He swung behind her, and his arm wrapped around her waist and forced her against him, so she shielded him from the guns. His hand came across her shoulder, and he shoved something hard against her nose.

"In my hand I have atomized carfentanil. No one moves. No one shoots. Or Miss Reeves will breathe in a massive amount of the opioid. You may not know that carfentanil is about a hundred times stronger than fentanyl. They use it to bring down elephants. Even if you have Naloxone on hand, it won't work for long enough to keep her alive. You are too far from a hospital to save her life."

"We hear you," Mitch said calmly. He lifted his hand, pointed the gun straight up, releasing the trigger and engaging the safety. "You're in charge."

Niko chuckled. "Yes. I am in charge. I've always been in charge. It's only now you understand the situation. Everyone drops their guns."

Mitch and the drone pilot immediately leaned down and set their guns on the ground before stepping back and placing their hands on the top of their heads. Roman, his eyes searing into Mia's, hesitated for several seconds. Niko grabbed a handful of her hair and pulled until her face lifted to the sky.

"Roman, my friend, you don't want me to spray this," Niko said, holding the small dispenser aloft. "I won't even have to put it in her nostril to deliver a killing dose. Additionally, if I do simply spritz it into the air, you three run the risk of inhaling some. I suggest you be smart and put your gun on the ground like the other men."

"Trust me. You need to do what he says," Mitch said in an undertone.

Finally, Roman tossed his gun down and lifted his hands to his head. "If you harm so much as a single hair on her head, you will be very sorry, my friend," he said, spitting out the last two words.

Niko released his grip on Mia's hair and inched backward, dragging her with him until he was flush against the trailer. He held her tight to his chest, and the warmth of his body seeped into her. His cologne had strong citrus notes, and he smelled of cigarettes.

She could feel his heartbeat against her back, strong and fairly slow. Clearly Niko wasn't on any sort of emotional edge. For him, this was probably just another day at the office. Also, he was a psychopath. Or at least someone with strong tendencies in that direction. When she pushed out with her mind, she felt waves of determination and some satisfaction but no madness.

It was a surprise to realize her own heartbeat had slowed and steadied. These past few days, given her state of anxiety, she'd felt like a cardiac arrest was an imminent possibility. Now a sense of calm settled over her. She sighed as the tension went out of her shoulders.

Niko wasn't going to kill her with carfentanil. At least not until after he got his diamonds. She had every faith in Roman and the Tightline men and even the Dalton Police. Plus, she could look after herself and fully believed she would get herself out of trouble.

Now that the worst had happened, she wondered why all the crippling anxiety in the first place. It might not exactly be just another day at the office like it was for Niko, but she wasn't unused to difficult and violent situations. She tiptoed back into Niko's mind and started a little exploration. In her experience, it never hurt to have ammunition against the enemy.

"What's your game here?" Roman called out.

Niko didn't answer. Instead, he half turned his head toward the road and remained in place with one arm gripping Mia tightly around the waist and the other circling her neck. Mia heard engines gunning and the crunch of tires on gravel.

"Don't do anything stupid," Niko warned, his voice muffled behind the mask.

"I won't," Mia said simply.

"You're not putting her in a vehicle," Roman said.

Again, Niko ignored him. The SUVs roared up to the barrier and stopped, skidding slightly, and raising a cloud of dust.

"You will call your men off. The snipers," Niko said.

"I'm not sure I want to do that," Mitch said.

"Okay. Then we all wait here. Like this. Until my patience runs out and I start spraying," Niko said.

A plan was formulating in Mia's mind. She quickly turned it over and examined it from every angle. It should work.

"I think you'd better call in the snipers. Please don't make him mad," Mia said, putting a tremor in her voice.

"Mia, I'm asking you not to talk right now," Mitch said.

Roman leaned over to Mitch, and they held a whispered conversation.

"No talking. Move away from one another," Niko said, his voice like a whip.

Now Mia felt Niko's heart rate increase, but she knew it was from anger not fear. His arms turned to vice grips, and she had trouble breathing against the one at her throat. She fixed her gaze on Roman's face, willing him to see she was on top of the situation. When she pushed her energy—in the form of a sunny wave of optimism—across and into him, he stilled and stared at her. Then he nodded.

"Have your men stand down," Roman said, his eyes still on Mia, so he caught her smile slightly.

Mitch whispered something at Roman then shrugged and spoke into the com on his shirt.

"They're coming in," he told Niko.

It took several minutes for Dom and Cooper to walk in with their rifle cases slung over their shoulders. Dom's eyes went to where Mia was being held by the trailer.

"Where do you want us, boss?" he asked Mitch.

"Put your guns away and stand with the other men," Niko said.

Neither man moved until Mitch nodded, his arms following the motion from where they remained on his head. Doors opened on the SUVs and six men stepped out. They trained their weapons on the area around the trailer. Mia judged the distance to the first vehicle to be around fifty feet. Should be enough time and space.

Niko nudged her forward. "We walk nice and steady and get in the car, okay?"

"Sure. No problem." She paused and gathered herself. It was now or never. "Say, did you ever find out what happened to Ivan. It must be hard not knowing where your big brother is."

He stumbled into her, and she could hear his breath come faster through the mask.

"You don't talk about Ivan," he said. "If you want to stay alive, you don't talk at all."

"Okay. Okay. It's just if I had a brother and he was dragged out of the house in the middle of the night by the Soviet Army, I'd move heaven and Earth to find him. But maybe that's just me."

"Fucking shut your stupid mouth or I kill you right now." He clamped a hand over her mouth and nose.

"But then no diamonds," she managed to say against the hand.

From behind her she heard murmurs and bodies shifting. The hair on her arms jumped straight up and anxiety shot through her core. When the gunfire sounded, she couldn't, at first, figure out where it was coming from. Shaking her head and wheeling her eyes, she caught sight of three dark sedans parked on the road spanning the width of her property.

Men crouched over the sights of the guns they'd laid across the hoods of their cars. They continued shooting and Niko's men spun around and returned the fire. Niko hauled her back to the side of the trailer, and Mia had a glimpse of Roman and the Tightline men grabbing for the guns they'd dropped on the ground.

"Looks like Jimmy Genomi," she heard Dom say. "And he has a posse with him."

"Stay back. No one comes near me or she dies," Niko yelled.

Something rushed by her, dark and low to the ground, and continued around the trailer before thrashing through the tree line. Her eyes saw. She recognized. But her brain simply couldn't make sense of it.

Then, seemingly out of nowhere, Mac sprang at Niko and latched onto his arm.

Chapter Twenty-Six

Niko howled with shock and outrage. He let go of Mia and wrestled to release his arm from the mighty jaws of the Doberman. Mia couldn't tell if he still held the cannister of carfentanil. She frantically searched the ground around her and all but wept when she saw the small container by her feet. Niko kicked and hit Mac then swung toward the trailer knocking Mia off to the side. On hands and knees, she scrambled towards the carfentanil and snatched it up.

"I've got the drugs," she cried. "I've got them."

She lurched to her feet, and Mitch rushed over and took the container from her hand. "Get out of here. Right now," he ordered.

"We need to help Mac," she called over her shoulder before arrowing straight to where Niko was attempting to squash Mac against the trailer.

But Roman beat her there and put his gun against Niko's head. "Stop. Right now. Or you're dead."

"Get this monster off me," Niko wailed.

"Mac, release. Release. It's okay, boy. I'm safe. Release," Mia said.

She grabbed the dog's collar and placed her hand on his furiously wiggling body, sending out a wave of soft energy. Mac quieted though he continued growling low in his throat, and his teeth remained clamped around Niko's wrist.

"Good boy. Good job. You're my hero. Mac, release. Now," she said again.

He rolled his eyes up to meet hers and finally unclamped his jaw and sat back. Blood dripped from his mouth, and she saw it coated his chest and front legs. When she turned her gaze to Niko, she felt her stomach roll. His right forearm was a ragged and bloody mess. Apparently, human flesh was no match for the jaws of a Doberman.

Mitch took the Russian man's shoulders and spun him around before placing a cuff on his left wrist and attaching it to a bar on the outside of the trailer. Niko curled in on himself, cradling his injured arm and moaning continuously as he rocked side-to-side.

"I guess he'll need a doctor," Mia said while she continued to stroke Mac.

"We should wrap that arm so he doesn't bleed to death," Dom said.

Mia blinked at him. The big man held a fierce-looking gun in one hand and Fifi in the other. He tucked the snowflake dog under his arm while he surveyed the area. Fifi gazed up at him adoringly and licked his hand.

Beyond the safety of the trailer, gunfire blasted, and smoke filled the air. Men shouted to one another. When she poked her head out, it appeared every single tire on each of the three Russian SUVs had been shot out. One of Jimmy's men lay prone on the road. Some of the Tightline team were also shooting from the cover of one of the pickups. The whole scene was like something from a nightly news segment on gang violence.

And somehow, somewhere two more of her dogs were running loose in this bloody warzone.

She finally understood all the dread and anxiety of the last few days. She'd never been one to predict the future, but something in her had sensed this would happen.

"Are you okay?" Roman asked, grabbing her shoulders and looking into her eyes. "He didn't hurt you?"

"I'm fine. But we have to get the dogs. We can't let anything happen to them," she said with her heart scrambling in her chest.

"Well, the big guy's right here, and he doesn't look inclined to leave your side. You should maybe grab Fifi from Dom. If this gunfight doesn't wrap up soon, he might want to use that hand."

"Have you seen Layla and Tucker? I think at least one of them ran by me right before Mac attacked." Stepping over to Dom, she pried Fifi away from the tree trunk that was his arm and held on tight in case she tried to jump. "I don't have any leashes or anything to tie them up."

"Put them in one of the trucks," Dom said. "They'll be safe in there. I thought I saw the little brown dog under the trailer a few moments ago."

Mia all but threw Fifi at Roman and crouched down beside the trailer. "Tucker. Are you under there? Oh my gosh, you are. There's my good boy. Come on, buddy. Let's get you out of this mess."

The Dachshund had jammed himself in between two of the back wheels and Mia was forced to crawl partway under the trailer to pull him out. He trembled piteously in her arms and flinched from the gunshots, squeezing his eyes shut and burrowing his head in at her armpit. Meanwhile, Mac pressed himself against her thigh while she continued comforting the little dog.

"Okay, let's put this lot in the truck," Roman said. "Layla's got to be around her somewhere. I'll bet she did the same as Tucker and found a place to hide."

Sirens sounded in the distance, and Roman smiled broadly. "Oh, yeah. A whole bunch of bad guys are going to be in a world of trouble."

They got the three dogs situated on the back seat of the nearest truck. Mia immediately began calling Layla and searching around and under the other vehicles behind the barricade. She branched out to the nearby tree line until Roman pulled her back.

"Are you crazy? You're about twenty feet away from the Russian shooters. It would be nothing for one of them to turn around and pick you off," Roman said as he dragged her toward the trailer.

"But I can't see her anywhere. She must be so scared," Mia said.

"I know. And I'm scared for her, but it won't help if either of us get shot right now."

Mitch strode over, his gun held down by the side of his leg. "How did the dogs get out?"

Mia continued scanning the area hoping to spot Layla. "I have no idea. They were in the house when we left. We've found all of them except the golden lab. Have you seen her?"

"Are you worried there's been a breech?" Roman asked, pulling out his cell.

"The lab crossed the driveway and ran between the SUVs not long ago. She continued east and disappeared into the trees," Mitch said.

Roman held up a finger and pointed to the cell phone clamped against his ear. "Ma. Are you and dad safe?...No. We're okay...Yes. I know. Lots of shooting...The police are on their way. Stay in the house, okay? Do you know how the dogs escaped?" He listened and said 'okay' several times then squeezed the bridge of his nose between his thumb and finger and nodded his head. "That's fabulous. Don't let her out. Thanks, Ma."

He lowered the phone with a smile. "Great news. Ma says Layla came howling to the door about five minutes ago, so they brought her inside. They have no idea how any of them got out. Apparently, they're fine and watching the action from their bedroom window," Roman said after ending the call.

The side door of the trailer opened and Jose, the Tightline man who'd accompanied them to the barn on Shaker's Line, poked his head out. "Sir, we've had a ping from one of the north sensors adjacent to the property line. A woman. Blonde hair. She came through the forested section and continued traveling northwest."

"What? It can't be...do you think it was Lou?" Mia asked, turning to Roman.

"Affirmative. I met Mary Lou the other night. It was either her or her identical twin," Jose said, flashing a grin.

The police sirens were close enough to pierce the air and mostly muffle the remaining gunfire. Mitch gestured Mia and Roman over to the truck with the dogs. "Get in. Jose, you take the other truck. I want to make sure no one makes a getaway before the cops arrive." He tapped his com. "Dom. Jose and I are taking trucks out to the road to run interference for the police. Make sure someone checks on Niko. I don't want him dying on us while cuffed to the trailer."

They drove out into the field, over the spike strips, and past the Russian shooting zone. One man sat slumped against the back tires of the third SUV clutching his shoulder. Another lay unconscious or dead on the grass. Four more remained crouched behind vehicles with guns in hands. A few headlights were smashed and tires flat but otherwise the SUVs were in remarkably good shape.

The same couldn't be said of the three sedans on the road. Unprotected glass and metal were scored with what seemed like a million bullet holes. Windshields and windows had cracked. Many tires were flat. One of the car's engines steamed.

Mia picked Jimmy out from among the men. He appeared unscathed. Not all the others were as lucky. Two lay unmoving where they'd been dragged behind the first vehicle. Another had a blood-soaked handkerchief tied around his head. One more was supporting himself on the front of a car, a bandage covering his upper thigh.

Jose went left out of the driveway. Mitch turned right, and Jimmy immediately spun into position, aimed his gun, and fired several shots. The bullets pinged harmlessly away. When Mitch sped past, Jimmy swiveled his head wildly back and forth and shouted something to the other men before scrambling into one of the cars. The two Tightline trucks angled to a stop across the road about a hundred feet on either side of the property line.

"They're done," Roman said. "Part of me can't believe Jimmy left himself so vulnerable. There was no way he'd have gotten by the Russians, so what was the point?"

Mitch's eyes stayed fixed on Jimmy and his men. "Probably thinking he'd pick off Niko then maybe the rest of them fold like a cheap suit."

"Yeah, because that's typical for the Bratva. What a shmuck. He should've bolted the second he heard the sirens," Roman said.

"I think he's at the point where he can't let go of the diamonds," Mia said.

"Well, he's likely not even going to live long enough to see his trial. The Russians will take care of him lickety-split," Mitch said.

Roman nodded. "And the world will be a better place."

Mia pressed her face against the window and scanned back and forth over Jimmy's men. "I don't see Dean with them. And now Lou's gone."

"You smell a conspiracy?" Roman asked.

"I don't know. Maybe. Or maybe Dean never came here at all, and Lou got spooked by the shooting."

"And decided to run off through the woods? A city girl like her? Where would she go without a car? And if she really was scared, I would think a house protected by an elite security force was the safest place she could imagine," Roman said.

"Uh oh, looks like Jimmy's having car trouble," Mitch said, pointing back along the road.

Roman glanced over his shoulder and smiled. "And right on cue here come Dalton's finest."

A line of four police cars, lights flashing and sirens screaming, drove toward them in single file. Mitch shifted the truck allowing the first cop car to come alongside and Roman lowered his window.

"Lieutenant Schmidt, we have the suspects contained although they're still armed. There are seven Russian Mafia on the driveway and a gang of six on the road although it looks like a couple on each side have been put out of action. Each group has three vehicles. Mostly disabled by now. Weapons are a mix of assault rifles and handguns. The security team are also on the property. Seven in total, including the two men blocking the road," Roman said.

Lieutenant Schmidt remained stone-faced throughout Roman's report. "Any civilians?"

"My parents are in the house. There was another woman, Mary Lou Adler, but she may be offsite at this point. We're just about to investigate her whereabouts."

"And you and Miss Reeves are unharmed?"

"Yes, sir. Couldn't be better. Also, the four canines in residence are alive and well," Roman said, throwing a smile over his shoulder at Mia and the dogs in the back seat.

"We're going to secure the scene for now. I've called over to Walkerton for support and the Feds are on route from Nashville. It'll be a multi-jurisdictional operation. We'll need your full report once we've brought everyone in," Schmidt said.

"Of course, sir."

The police cars proceeded along the road. Mitch held a hand over his earpiece then turned to Roman.

"Dom reports several of the men on each side are attempting to flee across the fields to neighboring properties. He and some of the team are corralling them, and he's sent up the drone to keep watch. We'll hand over all the surveillance footage, including our body cams, to the authorities. That should be more than enough to put these jokers away for a good long time."

"What a sweet, sweet day this is," Roman said. "And once we deliver the diamonds to the police, no one will be interested in us. It was really more of a fight between the Russians and Jimmy's gang in any case. We were basically incidental in the big picture."

"Unless Lou and/or Dean are on their way to snatch up the diamonds. I can't help thinking back to how curious Lou was about exactly where they'd been hidden in the barn. She asked so many questions. When I was clearing the table, I overheard her getting details from Jose on what he'd done to fortify the place. At the time, I didn't think anything of it. But now...it seems suspicious," Mia said.

Mitch put the truck in gear. "What are we waiting for? Let's go snag those two."

The drive to Shaker's Line seemed to take forever. Mia continued to soothe Tucker who gradually stopped trembling and relaxed onto her lap. Fifi seemed undaunted by her near miss with death and curled up in a ball on the seat beside Mia and went to sleep. Mac remained alert, his eyes constantly flicking between Mia and Roman.

"Don't worry, my boy. It's almost over," Mia told him before pausing for a beat. "Now that I think about it, I'll bet Lou let the dogs out. It was a total crap move on her part."

Roman nodded. "Yeah. But a perfect diversion tactic. Mac was so badass. I'll never forget the way he launched himself at Niko. He saved your life. For that, I'll be eternally grateful."

"It was something, all right," Mitch agreed while effortlessly piloting the truck along the back roads at an insane rate of speed.

"How much farther?" Mia asked.

Mitch shifted and pulled out his cell. "Check my messages. A text just came through," he said to Roman.

"It's from Dom. The driveway sensor pinged at the barn," Roman said.

"Shit. We're still three point six miles out. See if you can bring up the cam footage."

Roman swiped and tapped on the screen of the phone. "Got it. So far nothing happening in the barn."

Mitch punched the speed up another notch. If Mia thought they'd been traveling fast before, now they were surely into warp speed territory. She snuggled Tucker closer and looped her fingers through Mac's collar. So much adrenaline was pumping through her body, she felt slightly dizzy.

"Hold on," Mitch called a bare second before careening right onto a dirt road.

The truck bounced and fishtailed, but he didn't take his foot off the accelerator.

"Lookie. Lookie. Who do we have here? Well, if it isn't Lou and our good old friend, Dean Chambers, skulking into the barn," Roman said, his eyes fixed on the screen of the phone.

"Less than a mile," Mitch said.

"They're walking around and shining their flashlights up at all the swallow's nests. Dean has a gun," Roman said.

Mitch slowed marginally and bumped onto the dirt track that led to the barn. Dean's Audi was parked askew on the grass outside the main door. They came to a sudden and dusty stop behind it.

"What's happening in there," Mitch asked Roman.

"They heard the truck, and they're looking out through the southeast opening. Lou's also armed. Both have Glocks. Although Dean doesn't look fully functional on the one arm."

"Good thing we have guns too. First order of business, we need to contain them in the barn," Mitch said, squeezing past the Audi and driving the truck alongside the barn until two of the three doorways were blocked.

"They've got a step ladder, and they're smashing all the bird nests up in the beams. Damn. They found the diamonds," Roman said. He handed the cell phone to Mia and pulled his gun from the small of his back.

"It doesn't really matter 'cause they ain't going anywhere," Mitch said.

"What about the shields and guns stashed in the grain room?" Mia asked.

"Yeah. They could maybe hole up there for a while, but ultimately, this gig is over. I think Dean's smart enough to get the memo, don't you?" Roman said.

"I hope so," Mia said. "They're backing away from the doorway."

Mitch, who was on the side farthest from the barn, lowered his window an inch or so. "Dean Chambers and Mary Lou Adler come out with your hands up. The place is wired with cameras and sensors. We're watching you right now. There's no escape, and the police are on their way."

"They're talking, and Lou's gesturing to the grain room. Dean's shaking his head. Are the police actually coming?" Mia asked, staring down at the cell phone.

"Not yet. I figured they had their hands full back at your property. Let's wait and see if these two yoyos come to their senses. I don't want to shoot them unless I have to," Mitch said.

Mia set the phone on the console between the front seats, and all three huddled to watch the feed. Dean and Lou appeared to argue for a time then she marched over to the grain room and returned a minute or so later carrying one of the assault rifles that had been stashed there by the Tightline team.

Dean shook his head and backed away. He reached into his pocket, took out the pouch of diamonds, and let it fall to the ground. Lou watched Dean walk slowly to the doorway then stared down at the pouch. She stood there for several beats, her head swinging left and right as she glanced around the barn. Finally, she laid down the rifle and followed Dean outside.

Mitch and Roman cautiously opened their doors.

"Throw away your guns, and put your hands on your heads," Roman called out.

Once Lou and Dean had complied, Mitch handed Roman several black zip ties, and they stepped out of the truck and set about securing them. Making sure none of the dogs escaped, Mia slipped out and retrieved the diamonds from the barn. The pouch felt reassuringly heavy in her hand as she marched over to the two captives.

"Did you tell Dean where to find Pops in Fort Lauderdale?" Mia asked Lou. "It never made sense they showed up when they did. Not after all the precautions he took."

Lou met Mia's eyes without hesitation. "So, what if I did?"

"You're the reason Pops died, that's what. How could you do it? Pops loved you. I know he did."

"He didn't love me enough, that's for sure. When he first got sick, I was the one paying all the medical bills and there were a lot of them, let me tell you. Your father never could keep hold of more than a couple of dollars at a time. But why am I telling you something you already know? Anyway, after good old Danny got his hands on all the diamonds, he wouldn't tell me where they were. Like he didn't trust me or something. And he kept talking about giving you half. To hell with that. Far as I could see you didn't deserve them."

"I didn't want them. Looks like you did all this for nothing."

"Except I needed you, didn't I? If anyone could find those stones, it would be you with your special psychic powers. Danny told me all about the things you could do. Dean too. That's how I knew you'd track me down. All I had to do was sit tight and wait for you to come to me with the terrible news," Lou said, putting on a sad face.

"And you pretended to know nothing about any of this including what Danny was really up to," Roman said.

Lou flicked a look at Roman. "Of course. I had to make myself seem like a victim. Otherwise, you wouldn't have brought me home with you. There's no way you'd have trusted me. I needed to stay close and listen. You know, for a cop and a psychic, fooling the two of you was child's play."

"But I never sensed anything from you. How is that possible?" Mia asked.

"Because Dean taught me how to block you. It wasn't easy, let me tell you, but I'm a quick study."

Mia turned to Dean. "And how did you get in on this?"

"Funny story. Lou and I met in Vegas. Danny introduced us at dinner one night. She and I had a little thing going while they were in town for those weeks. Danny was already sick by then and Lou's a smart woman. She could see the writing on the wall. Plus, we were good together."

"Dean soon learned the special allure of a mature woman. I've still got the magic," she said smugly.

"I hate to complain, but could you maybe cuff me in front. This is hell on my bullet wounds," Dean said.

Roman and Mitch exchanged a look. Roman sighed. "Okay. But don't say I never did you any favors."

"If we're talking about favors," Dean said while massaging his arm with his newly freed hand, "let me remind everyone I'm the reason Mia isn't dead or at least shot up. That's gotta be worth something, right? I literally took a bullet for you, Peanut. Two of them, if anyone's counting. I'm scarred for life."

Lou stepped forward. "I want you to know I was desperate when Dean and I came up with this plan. All my money was gone on medical bills, and Danny acted like it was no big deal. Well, it was a big deal to me. I had no idea Danny would get shot in Fort Lauderdale. That was never my intention. But let's not forget he was dying anyway. Don't you think he'd have rather gone out the way he did—thinking he was outwitting the Russian Mafia and his partners in crime while connecting with his long-lost daughter—than in a hospital hooked up to a bunch of machines?"

"We should load these two into the truck and head back to your place. I need to be there with my team for cleanup. Dom says everyone's in custody, and the Feds just rolled up," Mitch said, his gaze on his phone.

Roman studied Mia as she glanced back and forth between Dean and Lou. Frowning, he pulled her off to the side. "It's like I'm right inside your brain and can see exactly what you're thinking. We can't let them go."

"Dean did save me," Mia began. She paused and blew out a breath. "And, big picture, Lou didn't do anything all that wrong. Yeah, she cheated on my dad and tried to get her hands on the diamonds, but I believe her about what happened in Florida. No one knew Karl would go off plan the way he did. And he's dead now anyway, so justice has sort of been served. If we hand them over to the police I have no doubt Dean, at the very least, will be taken out by the Russians. It's a virtual death sentence for him. Maybe Lou too. Hard to say for sure. It seems the price is too high for the crime."

"But they broke the law. Dean stole diamonds and Lou..." Roman trailed off as he looked into Mia's eyes. His sigh was epic. "Is this really what you want?"

She took his hand, threading her fingers through his. "I think so. It feels right. The big question is can you live with it?"

He cocked his head to the side while he considered. Then he shrugged. "Hell. I'm not a cop anymore, so what do I care, right?"

"You're sure. What about your moral compass?"

Now he grinned full out. "Darling Mia, being with you has bent my moral compass to hell and back. But it's not broken. At least not yet. I think I'll be fine with it. Mitch, what about you?"

Mitch straightened his posture to rigid military standards and cleared his throat. "My mission on this security detail was to ensure that both you and Miss Reeves, along with your family and dogs, were not harmed. I was also enlisted to help neutralize any future threat to same. I have satisfactorily completed my mission. And my moral compass is perfectly fine, Sir."

Roman nodded before turning to Dean. "I do have one condition before we release you."

Dean lifted his chin. "Spit it out already."

"You and Lou are going to get in your car and drive away, and we never see you again. Ever. Are we clear?"

"Crystal," Dean said, grinning at Mia.

"What about my stuff?" Lou asked.

"Consider it the price of freedom," Roman said.

"But there was a lot of expensive makeup and all my plants," Lou said.

"Nope. This conversation is over. Get in the car," Roman said.

"I'll take good care of the plants," Mia said. "I promise."

Dean walked up to Mia and took her hand. "It was great catching up after all these years. I wanted to tell you I think Roman's a good guy. Perfect for you."

"Gee thanks. That means so much," Roman said, fisting a hand over his heart.

Mia smiled. "Yeah. He is a great guy. Best I've ever known." She stood on tiptoe and gave Dean a peck on the cheek. "Now get out of here before he changes his mind."

Roman, Mia, and Mitch stood three abreast and watched the Audi bump slowly along the dirt track to the gravel road. Dean turned onto the road, tooted his horn three times, and raised his arm in a wave before sending the car shooting forward. Within seconds, he and Lou had disappeared into a cloud of dust.

"Now that we've said goodbye to my past, I guess we can go home?" Mia said.

Roman slung an arm around her shoulder and pulled her in. "You know I love you, but Holy Hannah, you sure came with a lot of baggage."

"Every family has its issues. Mine just happens to come with connections to organized crime. Anyway, it's all behind us now," Mia said.

Mitch clicked open the locks on the truck. "Sure. But when it comes down to it, can any of us ever really escape our past?"

The End

Afterword

I published ***No Time for Goodbye*** in 2018. It was a delight to write, and my readers embraced Mia and Roman with open arms. I knew this couple had more stories to tell and I was excited to write them. And that's what I've been trying to do for the last five years. Except, for some reason known only to the muse and the collective Writing Gods, I simply could not capture the magic of the original book.

So, I put it aside and wrote a completely different story in another world thinking a palate cleanser was all I needed. And then I wrote three more books. I was at the point of giving up on Mia and Roman when, at long last, everything came together with a bang.

Thank you for being so patient and for keeping Mia and Roman in your hearts. I'm incredibly proud of ***No Escaping the Past*** and hope you enjoyed the story. And now that the Writing Gods are smiling down on me again, I'm already part way into the next book in the series. ***No Place in Heaven*** is currently on preorder on Amazon and will be out sometime next year.

Also By

Marion Myles

No Time for Goodbye
No Escaping the Past
No Place in Heaven
Stars in Our Eyes
Keeping it Real
What the Heart Wants
Drawing from the Heart
Feeding the Heart
Crashing into Liam

About the Author

Hello there. My name is Marion Myles. I haven't always been a writer. I spent the first few decades of my life as a professional equestrian and travelled across North America training horses and competing at horse shows.

Aside from horses, I've had an enduring love affair with the written word. My reading interests run the gamut from mystery to fantasy to general fiction and even young adult. But when it comes right down to it, my heart definitely lies in the romance section.

When not riding or writing, I devote any spare moments to battling a debilitating addiction to Smarties and stalking my favorite authors on the internet. I'm proud to say there are currently no restraining orders filed against me.

I live in Southwestern Ontario with my beloved dachshund and my husband (also very much beloved!)

I'd love to hear from you so please drop me a line by email: marion@marionmyles.com

Printed in Great Britain
by Amazon